Secrets

OF THE

HEART

Secrets
OF THE
HEART

a novel

JoAnn Jolley

Covenant Communications, Inc.

Published by Covenant Communications, Inc.
American Fork, Utah

Printed in the United States of America
First Printing: October 1998

05 04 03 02 01 00 99 98   10 9 8 7 6 5 4 3 2 1

Library of Congress Cataloging-in-Publication Data

Jolley, JoAnn, 1945-
    Secrets of the heart : a novel / JoAnn Jolley.
        p.   cm.
    ISBN 1-57734-331-X
    I. Title
    PS3560.O436S43 1998
    813' .54--dc21   98-37106
                                              CIP

To the memory of my sister, Sharon, who always believed in me.
One day, we'll laugh together again.

CHAPTER 1

Can this day get any longer? I need to be at home—especially tonight,
Paula thought as she focused her attention on the speaker phone in
front of her. Ted was calling from his car; she'd heard all the excuses,
and now he was stalling. She decided to end it.

"I *know* what time it is," she said tersely. "But we're dragging our
feet on the Campbell account, and I need to see some good—no,
some *great* ad copy—by tomorrow morning. Make it *sizzle*, Ted. Your
deadline is nine a.m., and I'll be looking for the scorch marks on my
desk. Are you with me on this?"

"Yeah, boss. Whatever it takes." His voice was tense.

"Okay. I'll see you then."

In a single fluid movement, Paula Donroe switched off the
speaker phone, dimmed her desk lamp, and sank back into the soft
burgundy leather of her chair. She closed her eyes and pressed a
perfectly manicured thumb and forefinger to either side of her nose,
rubbing with a tiny circular motion.

She'd been sharp with Ted, and now she felt a distinct twinge of
regret. Solid, loyal Ted; his life had been a mess lately with the
divorce, and maybe she should ease up on him. On the other hand,
business was business, and even their friendship had to take a backseat when it came to running her successful advertising agency,
Donroe & Associates. It was the story of her days, the mantra of her
nights: Act tough, talk tough, deal tough—then go soak your head in
a martini or two after dinner. All in all, it was not a bad life.

A glance at the small crystal clock on Paula's desk told her it was
late—nearly eight-thirty. It had been a long day; but then, most of

her days began early and ended long after the city lights had come to life beneath her high-rise office in downtown Los Angeles. Why should today be any different?

The answer, of course, was that today *was* different, the way every October tenth was different. This day, for at least a few moments each year, somehow defined the parameters of her life and measured the enormity of her loss. This day was her birthday.

And his.

No one had remembered, and she wasn't surprised. Her entire staff had been working like maniacs on four new advertising campaigns she'd thrown at them a week earlier. The day had passed in a blur of meetings with clients, account executives, creative types, computer tekkies. As usual, everyone had wanted a piece of her; and now, in the stillness of her dimly lit office, she was left with the task of putting herself back together. It was best that no one had made a fuss. She would pack it in and go home to the boys. There would be time later to remember—to dig up the secret and let it sear her soul for as long as she could bear it.

Gripping the edge of her glass-topped mahogany desk and pushing her chair backward, Paula stood. With almost no visible movement except a slight arch of her back and extension of her arms, she stretched for a few seconds and relaxed. The soft wool of her custom-tailored suit fell smoothly into place along the gentle curves of her body. She loved this suit; its graceful lines were perfectly fitted to her slender figure, and its muted charcoal tones set off the vibrant darkness of her hair and eyes. An emerald scarf at her throat lay against her creamy skin like a cluster of jewels. Even at the end of this day, she looked stunning. *Not bad*, she thought, turning to catch her own reflection in the panoramic window stretching across one entire wall of her office. *Not bad for an old lady.*

It was past nine by the time she had gathered up some paperwork, locked the office, and taken the elevator down twenty-three floors. Stepping a few feet into the first-level parking garage, she smiled.

There it was, sitting in solitary splendor, waiting for her as though time had stood still for the past fourteen hours. "Well, now," she murmured, "aren't you something." Instinctively her hand reached out to touch the sleek hood of a new cherry-red Jaguar convertible—

smooth as polished glass, perfect, one of a kind. It was her birthday present to herself, delivered just last week. She had worked hard for this little luxury, paid the price in sweat and sheer determination. And now she was going to enjoy it.

She lowered herself into the soft leather driver's seat, leaned back, and inhaled deeply. The pungent, sensual new-car smell was utterly intoxicating—but even better, she thought, you could never get pulled over for driving under the influence of *eau de Jaguar*. Well, maybe if your foot got a little heavy and the power took over . . .

Freeway traffic was light on the drive home, and Paula decided she was in no hurry. The wind, sharpened by a touch of October freshness, danced in her nostrils and whipped her shoulder-length hair into silken rivulets. There had been other nights like this . . . long-ago, starlit nights with the wind in her hair, but in another time and place. In those days her life was just beginning, her love was new, and the wind would tease her as she rode behind Greg on the Harley, the smell of his leather jacket close to her face, her arms wrapped tightly about his waist. She had been barely seventeen, deliciously happy, with dreams to spare. Their vision of a golden life had eventually come true, but not at all in the way they'd planned. Now she was living the dream alone.

Taking the Woodland Hills exit, Paula knew she would be turning into her driveway in less than ten minutes. The boys would probably be watching TV or playing video games downstairs. Scott, sixteen, and TJ, twelve, were pretty good at keeping themselves entertained. Thank heaven for Millie, their long-time housekeeper, who kept everybody fed and in clean underwear. These past nine years, with Paula buried in her work, would have been disastrous without Millie's kindly and efficient running of their household. Her round, bustling presence and jovial manner had managed to keep them on an even keel. More or less.

From outside, the house was dark; only the porch light gleamed a faint greeting. Turning into the double-wide driveway, Paula pushed a button and the *chunk-chunk-hummm* of the garage door opener split the evening silence. Like a self-satisfied ladybug settling in for the night, the Jaguar glided noiselessly into the spacious garage.

With a parting caress to its leather-bound steering wheel, Paula stepped from her car and walked a few feet to the side door. It opened to a small hallway that led directly into the kitchen—a warm, sweet-smelling place where Millie's culinary arts flourished.

As she passed the breakfast bar, something soft brushed against her leg. "Rudy. Looks like you're the only one who waited up." Reaching down, she absently patted the head of her aging golden retriever. "Think Millie left us anything to eat? Let's go see what we can find . . . but I'd better check the mail first. Maybe there's a card or something."

Kicking off her black pumps, she moved silently across the cool tile of the kitchen floor and into the entryway. Rudy followed close behind, his tail waving gently from side to side. Millie had left the day's mail on a small oak table nestled in one corner; Paula scooped up the pile of envelopes as she headed across the hall and past her small den to the living room. She would relax for a few minutes before raiding the refrigerator.

The room was dark, but her hand moved easily to a switch just inside the arched passageway.

"SURPRI-I-I-ISE!"

"Wha—what *is* this?" Paula swayed on her feet, her face flushed, trying to make sense of this sudden jumble of faces, forms, and voices. A heartbeat later Ted was at her side, smiling brightly, his long arm around her shoulders. He leaned down to whisper in her ear. "It's okay, chief; we're all here to help you celebrate. Now, let's lighten up and look like we're *glad* to be forty, shall we? Good girl . . . you can take it from here." With a quick squeeze of her elbow, he faded back into the cluster of well-wishers.

"Well, uh, this is a *terrific* surprise!" Paula's voice cracked slightly as she collected herself and greeted the half dozen people who had gathered to commemorate her four-decade milestone. "I really thought no one remembered, so I worked late . . . how long have you all been here, anyway?"

"Long enough to be ready to eat *you*, with a little mayo and mustard," a voice boomed from across the room. That would be Dick Southern, her chief account executive, whose greatest loves in life were food, food, and baseball. He was languishing on the couch, feigning starvation.

"Well," Millie said, "I'm afraid Paula's bones would be pretty slim pickings. I've got a better idea." She stepped forward, beaming. Her plump figure was a generous contrast to Paula's slender one, and she took her mother-hen role very seriously. This was her moment to shine, and she embraced it joyfully. "Come on, everybody, follow me." With a flourish, she turned and led the little band downstairs to the game room, where the pool table had been lovingly transformed into an epicurean buffet. As the party descended upon their late-night feast of Paula's favorites—caviar, veal scallopini, three-bean salad, chocolate mousse, and champagne—Millie's face glowed.

"This is unbelievable," Paula sighed, leaning back into an over-stuffed chair while balancing a full plate on her knees. One by one, she surveyed her guests.

Dick had already loaded his plate and was seated at one end of the couch, contentedly inhaling forkfuls of veal. He had been with Donroe for over five years, and was one of the best account executives in the business. His relaxed, congenial manner belied the fact that he was just about the toughest competitor in the advertising game. With the persuasive powers of a politician and the nerves of an air traffic controller, he could bring major clients into the Donroe fold for the long haul. And he loved to demonstrate how it was done; even now, his two junior execs, Linda Travers and Jack Galanti, had gravitated to him and were reviewing the day's business.

Lingering at the buffet table were Ted Barstow and Jennifer McGivens, whose combined creative gifts illuminated the soul of Donroe & Associates. Ted had been a Pulitzer prize-winning jour-nalist when advertising captured his imagination, and his passion for telling a story had easily translated itself into word pictures good enough to win copywriting awards on three continents. Jennifer, at thirty, was the new kid on the block, but a brilliant artist.

Paula's personal assistant, Carmine Brough, looked like her name—wired for action, a streetwise party animal, living with an upwardly mobile garbage collector named Max. She knew computers like Pavarotti knew opera, and she could get through to an elusive corporate executive in less time than it took to peel a banana. At the moment, she was concentrating on sharing her veal with Rudy.

A sip of champagne washed down the lump forming in Paula's throat. These people, in a very real sense, were family; together they had built Donroe into a small advertising dynasty, and together they were reaping the rewards of its enormous success. Tonight they had left behind their separate, private lives to celebrate with their leader and mentor.

Yet none of them really knew what this day, of all days, represented to Paula—and none of them ever would. Her job now was to smile graciously, thank them profusely, and send them on their way before she lost control.

"Happy birthday, Mom. Millie had us helping in the kitchen."

Hearing her older son's deep voice, Paula turned to see the boys standing beside her chair. Scott, tall and muscular, brushed a shock of dark, wavy hair from his eyes as TJ shifted from foot to foot and kept one arm behind his back.

"Hi, guys. I wondered where you were. Come to gloat over your decrepit old mother, have you? Well, plant one on me." Paula pointed to her cheek and grinned. Scott's kiss was the self-conscious peck of a dutiful adolescent, while his younger brother's was accompanied by an awkward one-armed hug. Bringing his other arm from behind him, TJ produced a substantial pile of unopened envelopes, each one addressed to Paula. "We looked through the mail every day this week," he explained, "and kept the stuff that looked like birthday cards. We thought it'd be a good surprise for your party."

"And it is," she declared, quickly shuffling through a dozen or more envelopes to identify the senders. "I really thought no one had . . . well, this is a wonderful surprise, and I'll just save these for a little later. Thanks, guys!"

"Uh, excuse me . . . it's time for a toast—and a little something else—for our guest of honor." Ted, champagne glass in hand, had wedged himself congenially between the two teenagers and was motioning for everyone to gather around Paula's chair. In jeans, sneakers, and a T-shirt, he looked more like one of the boys than a seasoned professional.

"Ladies and gentlemen," he began solemnly, the hint of a grin just curling one side of his mouth, "creative demon that I am, I wanted to compose an eloquent tribute to our dearly beloved leader on the occasion of her passing—uh, make that *passage*—on the occasion of her passage into the glamorous forty-first year of her incredible life. However, as fate would have it, I was held up by a wicked boss lady with

a fixation on the Campbell account. So this little jingle will have to do."
His smiling blue eyes held Paula's for an instant, then he continued:

"There once was a woman named Paula,
Who knew how to value a dollah.
She was good at her work,
But just one little quirk
Made her faithful employees hollah.

Ms. Donroe, you see, was a beauty;
And while no one considered her snooty,
She ate caviar
From a very big jar,
And shared it with no one but Rudy.

Dear, we forgive this obsession;
Your friendship's our proudest possession.
But the dog's a real pain
When he drinks our champagne—
Could you teach him a little discretion?"

Amid clamorous laughter and applause, Ted bowed with a grand flourish. Paula, convulsed with mirth, carried the joke further when she called Rudy to her and extended a nearly empty champagne glass. The big dog sniffed at it and snorted, then dropped to the floor and rolled onto his back, playing dead. "Oh, very funny," Paula growled in mock exasperation.

Rudy barked once, righted himself, and disappeared beneath the pool table.

"Well, now, sports fans," Ted interjected as the laughter subsided, "it's late, and we all have to be at our battle stations tomorrow, so let's get out of here and leave this pretty lady alone. Just one more thing. Carmine?"

Clearing her throat importantly, the chunky redhead stepped forward with a small, gaily wrapped package in one hand. "A little something for the boss lady from all of us," she said brightly. "Because we cared enough to spend the very best." With an exaggerated curtsey, she presented the gift to Paula. It was a pair of ruby and diamond earrings from an exclusive jewelry shop on Hollywood's Rodeo Drive—"to go with the Jag," they explained.

"I love them, and we'll go everywhere together," she assured them with perfect sincerity. "What's more, if anyone wants to get them off me, they'll have to perform a *lobe-otomy*." Paula was a wizard at telling bad jokes.

With good-natured groans, the group decided to call it a night. Ten minutes and as many hugs later, they were filing out the front door. Ted was the last to leave, and when he reached her side he assumed an adorable puppy posture and began to beg. "Hey boss, about that Campbell copy . . ."

"I know, I know," she conceded, both hands in the air. "It would be ruthless of me to insist on seeing anything at nine a.m., what with the party and all."

His face brightened.

"I'll give you until ten."

His face crumbled.

"Just kidding, Snoopy. But show me something before closing time."

He nodded and kissed her lightly on the cheek, savoring the moment and the fragrance of her, then disappeared into the night. If he'd had a tail, he would have wagged it all the way home.

Paula swung the door shut softly and leaned against it, closing her eyes. "That was nice," she sighed.

"And it's not over yet, dear." She recognized Millie's cozy voice and opened her eyes. Standing expectantly before her were Millie, Scott, and TJ, each holding a cupcake with a flickering candle at its center. Off to one side stood Rudy, gingerly clenching the handle of a small wicker basket between his teeth.

"We thought they'd *never* leave!" TJ wailed. "We sorta wanted to have a party of our own . . . no big deal," he grinned self-consciously. His fresh young face, framed by locks of thick sandy hair, would be breaking hearts in a year or so. But for now he was content to shoot endless baskets in the driveway, immerse himself in old Zane Grey western novels, and wreak havoc on any meal set before him. At the moment he was staring intently at his mother, willing her to be happy. For as many years as he could remember, he had seen the faraway sadness in her eyes on this day; and though he couldn't yet define its source, he was determined to soothe it as best he could.

"Can we just *do* this?" Scott's voice had a cool, impatient edge— much like his father's, Paula thought. This kid definitely didn't like waiting around for things to happen, but preferred to lead out and then keep a comfortable distance between himself and whoever was second best. He was a superb athlete, but organized sports bored him. And lately he'd developed an unsettling habit of making his own fun—at night, on the gang-infested streets of the city.

"Well, now," Millie crooned, leading the way across the hall to the kitchen, "I think we can just *do* this." Seating them all at the small oblong oak table, she summoned Rudy, who dutifully padded to Paula's side and proudly deposited the wicker basket in her lap. It contained three colorfully wrapped gifts.

"Gee, this is my lucky day," she said lightly, fingering the packages. She carefully unwrapped and opened each one. Millie's was a glistening silver brooch; Scott's an elegant leather key case; TJ's one of those nondescript wooden creations that pass for jewelry boxes in seventh-grade shop class.

"Just right for your new earrings, huh, Mom?" TJ said eagerly. "I made it myself!"

"They're perfect, all of them. This really *is* my lucky day," she said warmly. "And German chocolate cupcakes . . . what more could I ask for?"

"Maybe a self-cleaning kitchen," Millie murmured, surveying the remains of her day. "So little time . . . so much devastation."

Paula chuckled, then glanced at the wall clock above the sink. "And speaking of time, my loving children," she said, "you'd better wrap your tonsils around those goodies within the next thirty seconds, or they'll spoil your breakfast."

In two bites, the cupcakes had been devoured.

"And," she added, "although the day after a party should really be a holiday, I believe you'll both be expected to show up at school in the morning. So let's call it a night, shall we? Thanks again for the great presents, guys."

Groaning, the two boys rose and shuffled toward the stairs and their separate bedrooms. A moment later, TJ's voice floated back into the room. "G'night, Mom. Hope I look as good as you when *I'm* really old."

"Thank you for sharing that, dear," Paula muttered, shaking her head. "You'll make a fine politician some day."

Millie sat across from her, looking weary but content. A few rays of light from the overhead lamp danced in her short, graying hair. She leaned back, resting her arms across an ample midsection. "Was it good?" she asked, smiling shyly.

"Good? Millie, you are *incredible.*" Paula stood and moved quickly to the older woman's side, spreading her arms to encircle her friend and planting a kiss on her soft cheek. "It was wonderful, and so are you." Millie's eyes glistened at these words of praise.

"Now," Paula continued, "it's been a crazy day for all of us, and we'll be nodding in our oatmeal tomorrow if we don't get some rest. Just leave all of this," she said with a sweeping gesture toward the party remnants, "and get yourself to bed. I'll lock up."

"Well, all right. I'll get to it first thing in the morning. Glad you had a good time—and happy birthday again." Millie pulled herself to her feet with a small grunt, then moved slowly out of the kitchen and down the hall. A few seconds later, the door to her room opened and closed softly.

Paula sank heavily into a chair, raised her elbows to the table, and cradled her face in her hands. Midnight. This day—her day, his day—had come and gone, and the party had undone some of her pain. But the mementos were still there, waiting upstairs in that little drawer, bound together in satin and tears. She owed it to both of them . . . she would not, could not leave this day until their silent, sacred observance was complete. And she could not face another year without the hope that he had forgiven her.

Climbing the thickly carpeted stairs in darkness, Paula slipped into her room and closed the door behind her. A bedside lamp bathed the walls in a subtle glow as she paused to open a dresser drawer and retrieve its contents—a nondescript rectangular box. Then she lowered herself into the small wooden rocker a few steps from her bed. It was time to remember.

CHAPTER 2

The box might once have held a pound of candy, but for more than two decades now it had been the place where Paula's soul had settled each October tenth. She carefully lifted the lid and laid it aside, her eyes coming to rest on a small, flat bundle secured by a single band of blue satin ribbon. Her gentle tug untied the simple bow, and the ribbon fell away from a worn, two-page document folded into thirds. The yellowed papers rustled slightly as she picked them up with one hand, revealing two black-and-white photographs lying underneath. These items, along with a tiny pair of infant's booties, were the box's only contents.

Paula studied the photos minutely, first one and then the other, for several minutes. A sensitive, handsome young man smiled at her from one. Greg—the gifted artist, the maddening idealist, the irrepressible comic who had loved both life and Paula with unrelenting passion. Greg, dead at nineteen, but still very much alive in the heart he'd left behind. Paula held his photo tenderly against her cheek for a long moment, then replaced it in the box and picked up the second picture.

Twenty-two years earlier, this photo had documented the beginning of a new life. Tonight, it was the faded reminder of a past from which Paula could never wholly escape. Or wanted to. It was the scrunched-up little face of an hours-old infant boy, one eye tightly closed against the encroaching world, the other opened just far enough to see what it might be all about. A tiny fist had burrowed into one of those newborn cheeks, giving the baby a lopsided, quizzical expression. As had happened each year, Paula couldn't help smiling a little at his elf-like appearance. She brushed her lips lightly over the surface of the photo, then carefully placed it back in the box beside Greg's picture.

Finally, Paula reached over to the nightstand where she had laid the folded papers. They felt light in her hand, yet her fingers trembled as she unfolded the copy of a handwritten letter dated within a day after the baby's birth—written by her to him, so that one day he might understand. But honestly, how could she ever expect him to understand, when *she* could never understand? She guessed that it probably made no difference to him now, anyway . . . it had happened so long ago. And maybe he didn't even know; he might never have received the letter. But at least she'd tried.

This part of the ritual was the most painful—reading the letter. It filled all her hollow places with despair, with grief for the loss of a past and a future, with regret and a senseless fantasy about how it might have been if only . . . if only. Yet at the same time, she couldn't deny a certain feeling of satisfaction at having done the right thing— if there was anything right about a mother giving up her child. Some years, she had almost felt as if he was standing beside her, telling her it was all right. But she could never be sure.

The years fell away as she read.

> *My darling son,*
>
> *I hardly know how to begin a letter like this—I don't know when or if you'll ever read it. But I want so much for you to know the real circumstances of your birth, that you were conceived and brought into this world surrounded by the greatest love imaginable, and that because of this love—and not for any other reason—I have made the decision to allow you to be adopted by a family who can give you the good life you deserve. As I try to explain, you may wonder how I could do this— and I'm sure I'll ask myself the same painful question every day of my life. But it's done, I've signed the papers, and now I can only hope it will work out for the best.*
>
> *According to the adoption agency's rules, I can't tell you my name, your father's name, or anything that would help you find me, even if you wanted to. Your new*

parents will be the ones to decide if you ever receive this letter. The best I can do now is to let you know that you've come from good people, and if things had happened differently, I think you would have enjoyed growing up in our family.

All of this has happened because your father died a few months ago. We'd been married less than a year, and were deeply in love, though we were very young. He was a wonderful man, a talented artist who could make me laugh or cry just by the way he looked at me. We had great dreams for the future; he would draw and paint, I would write, and we would grow old together. I had never been so happy.

Then there was a terrible motorcycle accident, and he was gone—just gone. I can't begin to describe the shock and sadness of it, like having a big chunk of my heart ripped away. At seventeen, I was a widow. My parents had fought our marriage and were very bitter after we eloped, so I couldn't go home. I was utterly alone. I kept our tiny apartment and went through the daily motions of going to work at a little café in town, but nothing seemed to matter.

It wasn't long before I found I was pregnant—with you! At first this made me very happy, knowing that a part of your father would be with me always. But as I thought about it (it was the only *thing I thought about), I realized it wouldn't be fair to either one of us if I tried to raise you on my own. I couldn't make a decent living; I hadn't even finished high school, and I had so many plans for the future. And what about this tiny life growing inside me? Nothing, it seemed, would be more unfair than to selfishly hold to the belief that I could do a good job of taking care of a child when I was so young myself. Somewhere, I knew there was a better home—a better life—for this baby.*

It seems almost unbelievable, doesn't it? I didn't think any mother could give up her own flesh and blood. But something deep inside—a feeling, maybe, I don't really know—told me it was best.

Finally, I got up my courage and made a few calls. It wasn't hard to find a good agency, and the arrangements were made almost before I knew it.

Which brings us to today—this special and terrible day. Less than twenty-four hours ago, just after you were born, I held you in my arms and silently begged your forgiveness. Later, I asked if I could have you to myself for an hour or two, and permission was given. Knowing these would be our final moments together, I tried to memorize every detail of your little body as I bathed it with my tears. I kissed the top of your head, your eyes, nose, cheeks, then each tiny finger, and even that small purple birthmark on the inside of your arm—it looks exactly like a bumble bee in flight! Your father would have been so proud to have such a fine, healthy son.

When it was time, I held you close for one last moment, closing my eyes and inhaling the sweet scent of you until I thought my lungs would burst. The nurse came, and through my tears I watched her disappear down the hallway, carrying my baby. I haven't stopped crying since.

This all sounds pretty corny, doesn't it? Well, I hope when (or if) you read it, you'll understand just a little bit of what I'm feeling at this moment. There are no words to describe my loss, and right now I don't see it getting any better in the next ten or twenty or fifty years. But at least there is the hope that one day you will know why I did what I did—for you.

My precious child . . . if there is a God, I hope he will give you a happy life. You deserve much better than this poor beginning, and I'll try to trust your new parents, whoever they are, to make it right. I'm not very old or wise right now, but always, always, I will be thinking good thoughts for you. And loving you—forever. That's a promise.

Your Mother

Paula folded the letter carefully in her lap. She closed her eyes, leaned her head back against the chair, and rocked slowly, letting the tears flow down her cheeks. *It doesn't get any easier. Thank God for the boys and my work. He's a grown man now. I hope he's all right.*

Like a fast-forward movie, thoughts and memories flooded her consciousness. These twenty-two years had been a mixed bag, but no one could say she hadn't been successful. After Greg's death she had worked until the baby came, finished high school, then moved west, and worked her way through college, earning advanced degrees in communications and advertising.

Along the way, Richard Donroe had come and gone. He was a poor excuse for a husband, an indifferent father, a womanizer whose penchant for risk-taking had cost them their fledgling advertising business. The divorce was bitter, but at least she had come out of it with her two sons, their modest home, and a few loyal clients who believed in her. Thousands of sixteen-hour days later, her ad agency had become one of the most prominent in the Los Angeles metropolitan area. And she was more than comfortable—the new Jaguar in her garage was proof of that.

I've worked hard . . . made a place . . . made a difference . . . raised great kids. I have every reason to be satisfied—and I really am, usually. Is it this fortieth birthday, my son's twenty-second, that leaves me so hollow? Well, get over it, Donroe. Tomorrow it starts all over again.

The trace of a smile crossed Paula's lips as she drifted into sleep, still cradling the small box in her lap, rocking slowly to the rhythm of her dreams.

The morning sun hit her full in the face and woke her. A panicked glance at the crystal clock on her nightstand illuminated the awful truth. "Good grief! I'm *way* late! The sales meeting is in half an hour! Should have been at the office two hours ago . . . Dick will be gloating . . . *get the lead out!*" As she bolted from the rocking chair, the small box tumbled to the floor, spilling its contents. Quickly kneeling to gather the tender mementos, she murmured, "Sorry about that . . . until next year, then." She slipped the box into a dresser drawer, closed it soundly, and raced for the shower.

Minutes later, her hair still damp and buttoning her suit jacket on the run, Paula bounded down the stairs and into the kitchen. Millie was just finishing her party cleanup; she smiled brightly, paying little heed to the exasperated look on the younger woman's face. "Morning, dear," she beamed. "Did you sleep well?"

"Too well, I guess. I'm *really* late. Call my office and tell them I'll be there in a few minutes, will you?" Paula grabbed her attaché from the hall and was halfway out the kitchen door by the time she heard Millie pick up the phone.

Her low heels clicked on the cool cement of the garage floor as she punched the garage opener button and moved quickly to the side of her car. "Look out, freeway. I'm making time," she announced, sliding behind the wheel. A graceful snap of her wrist brought the Jaguar's engine roaring to life. Shifting into reverse, she backed rapidly down the gently sloping driveway toward the street.

She didn't see the bicycle until it was too late.

CHAPTER 3

Oboy. Please don't let it be serious. Paula's heart was beating wildly as she sat frozen in the car, stunned, for a few excruciating moments. Finally, inhaling deeply, she glanced over her shoulder. A mangled blue bicycle lay in the street, thrown clear of the vehicle by the impact. Its rider was nowhere in view. *Oh, no! I've killed a child. He must be under the car.*

Releasing her white-knuckled grip on the steering wheel, Paula cautiously opened the door and swung her legs outward, keeping her eyes on the ground for any signs of the victim. She stood on rubbery legs, leaning against the door for support. *Life is so fragile . . . how could I have done this? It's all over. Everything's over.*

Suddenly, from the other side of the car, she heard voices.

"You okay?"

"Yeah, sure. Just give me a hand."

Instantly alert, Paula lost no time getting around the car. There, seated in the driveway and leaning against the Jag's rear tire, was a young woman. Bending over her and extending a hand was another young woman. Both seemed embarrassed and were tittering nervously. A second bicycle lay on the lawn a few feet to the side of them.

"What in the—are you all right?" Paula's breathless question was directed to the woman on the ground, but the other one answered it.

"She's fine. I saw the whole thing; she was riding a little bit in front of me. Her skirt got caught in the chain, so she stopped in your driveway to untangle it. She was barely done when you came barrel— uh, backing out and hit the front end of her bike. Knocked her to the ground and the bike into the street. I guess it's pretty much a loss."

She glanced toward the sorry little heap of metal. "On the other hand, it could have been worse—a lot worse."

"So, are you really okay?" Paula spoke directly to the victim, a waif-like young thing who by this time had gotten to her feet and was brushing herself off. *Am I dreaming?* Paula thought as her eyes took in the scene. *Are they crazy? What twentieth-century women in their right minds would ride bicycles and wear skirts?*

Then she noticed their small black-and-white name tags with the word "Sister" on each. *Terrific. Two crazy NUNS, wearing skirts and riding bicycles, and I've just run one of them down. Can this day get any better?*

"Uh-oh," one of them said. "Your car is very pretty. Sorry about the—"

Dents and scratches! Paula felt her jaw tighten as she swung around to survey the damage: a streak of blue above the wheel, a slightly hammered rear bumper, a cracked tail light. She inhaled deeply and chewed her lip. *Careful, Donroe . . . don't say anything you wouldn't want God to hear. These are, after all, nun-people. They probably have a direct pipeline to heaven. Or at least a beeper.*

She spoke politely. "Well, gosh, these things happen." *Steady now . . . don't lose it. A smile would be appropriate here.* She smiled. "As you said, it could have been worse." *I could have hit a priest.*

Paula's train of thought was interrupted by Millie's alarmed voice. The older woman was rushing from the house, where she had watched from the kitchen window as this little drama unfolded. "Oh, dear! What's happened? Is anyone hurt? Do we need an ambulance? Oh, dear!" Rudy followed gravely a few steps behind her, his feathered tail waving slowly in the sultry morning air.

"Everything's all right, Millie. I wasn't looking, and this, uh, *sister* and I just had a little run-in. She's okay, but I'm afraid her bike has seen better days." They watched as the two young women, moving quickly and efficiently, dragged the disabled cycle onto the grass. By the time the task was finished, they had regained their composure and were smiling broadly.

As they approached her, Paula thought the pair seemed curiously mismatched. The one whose name tag read "Sister Kent" was tall, large-boned, athletic, and darkly intense. *Probably a beach volleyball player in some past life,* Paula mused. The other, "Sister Tibbetts," who had been riding the ill-fated bicycle, was small and fragile-looking but had a smile that could stop an eighteen-wheeler in its tracks. *Bet she used her daddy's inheritance on some fancy dental work just before entering the convent. What a waste.*

Millie had dashed out to the sidewalk and was trying to make the young women feel welcome as they walked toward the house. "It's getting pretty warm out here," she said. "Can I get you girls some iced tea?"

"No thanks, ma'am," said the taller one. "But we really do need to do something about getting another bike. If we could just use your phone to call the president—"

"The *president?* My, you two must really have some connections!" Millie was awestruck.

"Oh, not *that* president. You see, we're—"

"Listen, I can take care of this." Paula had slipped into her executive mode. "Just tell me how much the bike was worth, and I'll cover it. You probably don't take Visa, but I can certainly write a check."

The Tibbetts sister shot a dubious look toward her partner. "Gee, I don't know."

"Well, when *will* you know?" Paula felt irritation rising in her throat as she glanced at her watch. "If you need to check with your Mother Serene or Superior or someone for permission—"

"Mother Superior?"

"Yes, isn't that what you nuns do when you need to get something done?"

"Nuns?"

Paula stared pointedly at their name tags. "That's what I said, *Sister* Kent and *Sister* Tibbetts."

For a few seconds, the two women stared at each other. Then their faces split into grins.

"Um, I think we can explain," the Tibbetts woman said, stifling a giggle.

Paula shook her head and raised her hand, dismissing any further comment. "No explanation necessary. You probably have rounds to make, or whatever. I'll just get my checkbook." She turned toward her car.

"No, wait. Please."

The sudden decisiveness in this young woman's voice stopped

Paula in mid-stride. She swung around to face the pair. "So . . . what's
to explain?" She glanced again at her watch.

"Well, I guess we got off on the wrong foot—er, pedal, actually.
The least we can do is introduce ourselves."

"I really don't see any reason—"

"I'm Sister Tibbetts, and this is my companion, Sister Kent. We're
not nuns; we're missionaries."

"Oh, I see." *So why aren't you at the airport, handing out flowers with
the rest of them?* "It's nice to meet you, but I really have to get to my—"

"We represent The Church of Jesus Christ of Latter-day Saints."

Paula stared at them blankly. *Should this mean something to me?*

The tall one spoke. "Maybe you've heard of us by another name . . .
the Mormons."

The crease between Paula's eyebrows deepened as she concentrated on the word. *Mormons.*

"Sure! I know something about the Mormons." Millie, who had
been inspecting the ruined bicycle, now bustled up to the trio. "Don't
you folks have a big church or something in L.A., and a new one
down in San Diego? I see the one downtown every time I go shopping
in the city, and it seems like I read about the new one in the paper a
few months back. They even had a picture . . . it's *so* beautiful."

"That's exactly right," Sister Tibbetts beamed. "We call them
temples. They're very special buildings, and we'd be happy to explain—"

"Well, this is just *lovely*," Paula interrupted, "but I have a business
to run, and this"—she waved an arm in the direction of the fallen
bicycle—"is costing me time and money. Millie, could you help me
out here? Take these young ladies inside, find out what they need, and
see that they get it. I'll pay for everything. Now, if you'll excuse me,
I'll just be on my way." She felt a small piece of gravel dig into her
shoe sole as she spun around and moved quickly toward her car.

"B-but we have an important message we'd like to . . . share with
you," Sister Tibbetts called out. Her voice faded as the Jaguar's engine
came to life. Moments later, the sporty car had cleared the driveway
and was rapidly disappearing into the late morning smog.

"Oh, never mind, girls," Millie chirped, seeing their crestfallen
looks. "Come on inside, and we'll get everything straightened out.
Now, tell me, who is this *president* you were going to call?"

CHAPTER 4

Paula hated to be late. Worse, she hated to be late and rattled. Now she was both, thanks to the morning's events. "Not a pretty way to begin my forty-first year," she muttered as the sleek Jag hummed softly beneath her. She mentally replayed the accident again and again, her thumbs beating a staccato rhythm on the steering wheel. "Why don't people like that get a life and stop pestering the rest of us?" The important thing now was to get her day back on track. There were meetings to attend, ad strategies to plan, sales figures to digest. And a car with ugly Mormon scratches to get fixed.

By the time she pushed through the glass doors to her office suite, it was nearly noon. Carmine was frantic. "Are you okay?" she asked, planting herself firmly in front of her employer. "Millie called and said you were on your way, but that was over two hours ago, and we thought maybe there'd been an accident or something."

"Or something." Paula's tone was brusque, but softened when she saw genuine concern in her assistant's eyes. "Nothing to worry about, really. I, uh, ran into something, scratched my car, had to leave it at the shop and walk a few blocks. It'll be ready tonight. No harm done, except that now I'm in major deadline trouble on the Campbell account. I hope Ted's up to speed; give me a few minutes and then ask him to come see me, will you?" Pushing aside the chaos of her morning, Paula once again took control.

She had barely flipped on her computer and settled behind the desk when a few light taps on her door told her that someone wanted to see her. If it was Ted, he'd wait for a few seconds and walk in without further invitation; anyone else would wait until her verbal

"Yes?" gave them permission. Ted had never been one to stand on formalities, and she knew better than to insist on such things from a man who had seen more of life—from its darkest underbelly to its shining moments of glory—than she could even imagine. When the heavy brass knob turned and the door swung silently inward, she sighed and leaned back in her chair.

"Hey, chief. Carmine said I was first in line. Checking up on me, are you?" Ted was grinning breezily as he sat on one of the leather chairs across from her desk, but Paula could see tension in the firm set of his jaw. She was the boss, but he didn't like to be pushed.

"Not really checking up, Ted. I just need to know where we are with the writing for this Campbell account. It's a very big deal, and after the morning I've had, I don't want to have this whole thing falling apart around me." Paula's voice had a hard edge, and Ted shot her a questioning glance.

"Whoa, Paula, this is *Ted* you're talking to. I told you I'd have something terrific by the end of the day, and a promise is a promise. A few more hours, and I'll have those Campbell kids dancing in the streets, okay? Now, what's this about your morning that has totally unperked you?"

Paula smiled through her edginess and relaxed a little. "Oh, nothing much . . . you know, just your everyday stuff—got up late, rushed like a maniac to beat the clock, got a rip in my pantyhose, ran over this crazy lady on a bicycle—"

"Excuse me? You *ran over* someone?" Ted straightened in his chair and stared at her, his eyes wide.

"Well, not exactly. I mean, I demolished her bike, but she jumped clear and was just a little shaken up. Of course—and here's where the crazy part comes in—if she hadn't been wearing a skirt, it never would've happened. Must be some kind of religious thing, or maybe they're just trying to get to heaven early. They put some nasty scratches on my new car, too. I must say, if I were God, that alone would keep them away from the pearly gates for at least a millennium or two."

"Religious? They? Heaven? Am I missing something here?" Ted's eyebrows were drawn together in a quizzical expression.

"Oh, nothing," Paula replied with an impatient shake of her head. "The whole thing is insane, really. These two girls—they're recruiters or something for their church. The Mormons. I didn't see them as I was backing out of my driveway—"

"The Mormons?"

"That's what they called themselves. Anyway, I had Millie take care of it, and my car should be good as new by later today." Paula began rifling through a stack of papers on her desk. "Let's see now, where were we? Oh yes, the Campbell account. We need to create an image—"

"The Mormons." Ted's hollow, repetitive statement stopped Paula in mid-sentence. She looked up to see a shadow flicker across his face as he slumped back in his chair, his eyes fixed on some point in the vague distance outside her office window. She waited for a few moments before reaching out to wave her hand in front of him in a delicate figure-eight motion. She'd seen a similar expression on his face from time to time, and she was one of the few people who could bring him back to the present.

"Hey, Ted, where are you?" Her voice was gentle but insistent. "Is there something you'd like to say before we get back to business? Ted? Was it something I said—something about the Mormons?"

He shook his head as if to clear away a mental cobweb. "Oh, um, I was just thinking . . ."

"That's pretty obvious," Paula noted, putting one elbow on the desk and resting her chin in the palm of her hand. "Would you care to elaborate?"

"Well," he responded, "there's not much to tell. I once—I was once—that is, I belonged to—uh, I grew up as one."

"One *what?*"

"One of *them*—the Mormons."

"Oh, I see." Paula leaned back in her chair and folded her arms, a bemused grin playing across her lips. "And is this a good thing, or simply a part of your unsavory past that I don't want to know about?"

"Gosh, it's been a long time—years since I've even thought about it. As a kid, I pretty much went along with all the stuff they taught me. But then my parents split up, and I never really went to church after that. A couple of my friends went on missions to try and convert people; I thought it was a pretty stupid thing to do, wasting two years like that when they could've been having a good time or getting an education, or both. I did my own thing, and I never regretted it. Who knows? Things might have been different if I'd stuck with the Church. My marriage—one of them, anyway—might have survived, and I could've settled into a comfortable little rut in West Jordan, Utah. The place sounds prettier than it is; the whole valley basically resembles one giant piece of burlap. Anyway, that's ancient history . . . sorry we got sidetracked." Ted moved decisively forward to the edge of his chair, signaling his readiness to get down to business.

"Well, this is all very interesting," Paula observed, leaning back in her chair. "I haven't heard you talk so much at one time since we were trapped together in that elevator a few years ago."

"Yeah, well, you know I'd rather be skiing or writing than sitting around socializing. It's just that when the Mormons came up, a few old memories started rattling around in my brain. Funny how something like that can come back to haunt you without warning; I certainly didn't see it coming. But it's over now, okay? That part of my life was over for me a long time ago, and there's no reason to revisit past grievances. So—why am I here, anyway?"

Now it was Paula's turn to pull herself back to reality. She'd been intrigued by the curious animation in Ted's face and eyes as he talked about things that had once meant something to him, and she was tempted to pursue the conversation further. A brief glance at the clock, however, told her that too much of the day had already been consumed by trivia. After all, she had a business to run, and time was money. She decided to put personal things aside and get on with it. "Ted, you know as well as I do that we *have* to get going on the Campbell account. It can't wait; there's a lot of money resting on this promotion."

"Ah, yes . . . you're wondering where my brilliant advertising copy is. What can I say? It's right in here"—he tapped his right temple—"and I fully intend to liberate it, if you'll just cut me a little slack. You need it by the end of the day; I'll have it to you by the end of the day. All right?" His deep blue eyes were flashing, and Paula knew he was on the defensive.

"Fine, I'll trust you for it," she said quickly, raising her hands as if to ward off a verbal blow. "Just so we're on the same track here." His jaw relaxed slightly and she continued, "I'll be leaving the office a little early. The auto shop is open until six, and they've promised to have the Jag ready by then. If I can have your copy by five-thirty, I'll look it over tonight."

"Deal. I'd better get going on it." Ted stood abruptly, flashed her a tense, lopsided grin, and was out the door in a few easy strides.

Four hours later, after a day of hurried meetings and phone calls, a small sheaf of papers had magically appeared on Paula's desk when she returned to her office from a quick trip to the rest room. She knew it was Ted's copy, and she knew it would be good. Whatever their personal or creative differences, she could always count on him to come up with an ingenious ad campaign when she needed it. These Campbell people, with their "21st century lawn mowers," didn't know how lucky they were to have Ted Barstow on their team. Still, the irony of a prize-winning journalist writing about lawn mowers didn't escape her.

Slipping the Campbell folder and other papers into her slim burgundy attaché, Paula stepped lightly into the elevator. She smiled, realizing that she was only minutes away from sliding behind the wheel of her new Jag. *This has been a truly bizarre day,* she mused as she pushed through the front doors of her office building and became one with the undulating wave of humanity clogging the sidewalk at rush hour. *A quiet evening at home is just what I need—a long bath, maybe a video with the boys, and there'll still be time to get a little work done.* Suddenly, she realized how exhausted she was after the night's and morning's events as she mentally replayed the party, the wrenching memories, the accident. *Maybe I'll just hit the sack before midnight, for once, and forget about all the rest.*

The idea was beginning to grow on her by the time she found herself ringing the bell at the service desk of Lieberman's Auto Works. It was the best paint and body shop in the city, and to have it within walking distance of her office was unqualified luck, in her opinion. If one must be at the mercy of weird women on bicycles, it paid to keep Jerry Lieberman's number in one's Rolodex. She'd never had occasion to use the shop, but it came highly recommended by several of her business associates.

"Hi. I've come for my car—the red Jaguar," she said to the young woman behind the desk, who looked up politely from her game of computer solitaire. "I brought it in this morning with a couple of little scratches."

"Oh, you don't have to remind me—not about a gorgeous car like that," the girl replied with a toothy grin. "Hold on a sec . . . I've got your keys right here." She rummaged briefly through a desk drawer. "Wanna check it out?"

"Sure." Paula followed her into the back shop, where the Jag sat regally among a varied assortment of lesser vehicles. *Just as pretty as I remembered*, she thought as she leaned forward to caress the car's side where the impact had occurred. Its now-flawless steel was cool to her touch. "Perfect," she murmured. "No one would ever know."

"Well, thankya," said a gruff voice behind her. "We aim to get it right the first time."

"And you certainly did," Paula replied, turning to smile warmly as Jerry Lieberman, a short, round, middle-aged man in rumpled overalls, handed her a small white slip of paper. As her gaze rested on the paper, her smile faded.

"*Eighteen hundred dollars?* What in the—"

"Perfection doesn't come cheap, ma'am. Special paint, expert labor, the best polish, a rush job. It adds up."

"Obviously," Paula growled under her breath as she fumbled with her billfold to locate a credit card and hide her growing sense of helplessness and irritation. *Eighteen hundred dollars for a couple of hours of pounding and buffing. I think I'm in the wrong line of work.*

Minutes later, creeping down a traffic-clogged avenue leading to the interstate, she thought she saw two young women in skirts pushing bicycles along the sidewalk. *Don't get me started*, she seethed, grinding her teeth. *It's all their fault . . . those crazy Mormons. Heaven help us.*

Chapter 5

Millie was clearing up the dinner dishes when Rudy's head shot up from its comfortable place on top of his paws. On his feet in an instant, the dog sprinted toward the garage door, skidding to a stop with his nose just inches away from the brass knob. He waited expectantly, open-mouthed, his feathered tail waving gracefully behind him.

Chuckling, Millie knew exactly what to expect. She had seen this little drama replayed hundreds of times over the years. Rudy always knew when Paula was home; he could sense it almost before his keen hearing picked up the sound of a car in the driveway. As Paula approached the door, a shiver of elation would begin at the end of his nose, climb up over his shaggy brows and wrinkle his forehead, undulate down his honey-blond back, puffing out his tail like a sturdy summer breeze, and finally radiate to his legs and feet until he danced in place, hardly able to contain his excitement. All the while, his intense gaze would be riveted on the door, his brown eyes bright with anticipation. As Paula's footsteps drew near and paused just beyond the door, Rudy would assume his "greeting" position, sitting grandly back on his haunches and raising one front paw an inch or two above the floor. There he remained, frozen with joy, until the door swung silently open and Paula appeared. Then, and only then, the air would be split with a single deep, triumphant bark—the signal that all was well, that the queen of the house had returned. On late nights, when Paula arrived after the rest of the household had retired, there was no welcoming bark—only a soft swish of the tail and a companionable nuzzle in the darkness.

Paula trudged wearily through the door, her face and body showing the strain of an anxious day. Rudy was at her side in an instant, pressing his massive body against her leg just firmly enough to get her attention. His golden head came almost to her waist as he raised his eyes in greeting.

Slipping her keys into her jacket pocket, Paula reached down to scratch the short, soft fur between Rudy's eyes. Her face relaxed slightly, and a tiny smile played at the corners of her mouth. "Hi, bud. How's my favorite four-legged friend?" The dog's tail wagged more rapidly. "Well, it's nice to be home. Missed me, did you?" As if he understood every word, Rudy's head nodded in perfect rhythm to the soft cadence of her voice.

Millie's voice floated down the short hallway. "You're early. I didn't really expect you until the wee hours, what with all the commotion this morning. The boys and I have already eaten; they're down in the TV room. Shall I fix you a plate? It'll heat up quick in the microwave."

"Thanks, Millie, I think I'll relax a little bit first." *A very dry, very full martini should do the trick.* Paula deftly kicked off her black suede pumps; they fell together back to back like two weary, one-legged scarecrows, finally coming to rest against the wall. Feeling the cool Spanish tile beneath her feet, she padded quickly through the kitchen to the entryway and picked up her mail from the small oak table near the door. Rudy followed her a few steps into the den, where all six of their feet sank deep, deep into the ivory carpet.

While the dog settled himself amiably between the spindly legs of a quaint Victorian writing desk, Paula deposited her mail on the desk and made silent tracks to the glass-faced liquor cabinet. Moments later, with a contented sigh, she leaned back into the depths of a large, deep blue overstuffed chair. Closing her eyes, she carefully raised a brimming long-stemmed glass to her lips. Almost shyly, she flicked the shimmering liquid with her tongue, then slowly opened her mouth. The silvery mixture slid down her throat with a slow, delectable burn—a sensation she relished, sometimes even dreamed about. This first swallow felt almost as good as the relaxed, dreamy feeling that would soon overtake her and smooth out all the rough edges of her day. After a few minutes and perhaps another martini, even old Jerry what's-his-name, with his fancy little auto shop and his deep pockets, would no longer be able to intrude on her simple pleasures.

"Ah, Rudy," she sighed after a few more sips, "you really should take up drinking, at least on the weekends. It could make you into one fine, mellow fellow." The dog, hearing his name, opened one eye and thumped his tail on the carpet, then sank back into his peaceful canine oblivion. Paula, too, soon nodded off, her head nestled cozily against the chair's velvet upholstery, a half-empty glass on the table beside her.

"Mom?"

"Hmmm?" Hearing the word from a distance, Paula screwed up one eyelid and peered at her youngest son, who was standing in the doorway, silhouetted by the light behind him. Pulling herself sluggishly to the edge of the chair, she motioned for him to come closer. "Hi ya, TJ, what's up?"

"Oh, nuthin'." He was dressed in his usual attire—baggy jeans, a faded sports tee, Air Jordan sneakers.

"How was school?" she asked.

"Okay." He shrugged.

"Now, there's a bit of sparkling conversation. Come over here and tell me about your day." Paula patted a leather ottoman next to her chair, and he eased himself down to it. "Guess I dozed off for a minute—well, an hour," she corrected, glancing at her watch. "So . . . have you guys done your homework?"

"Yeah, I have," TJ reported. "But you know Scotty—he doesn't care. He'd rather be out with the Crawlers."

The Crawlers. I wish he wouldn't spend so much time with that gang. They can't be up to any good.

"He's gone? I thought Millie said you were both downstairs watching TV. This is a school night, and he's not supposed to—"

"It's cool, Mom. He's here, downstairs, like Millie said."

Paula leaned back and sighed with obvious relief. "I don't know what he sees in the Crawlers, anyway. They look bad, they smell bad, they're always getting into fights with that other gang—the, uh, the—"

"The Scabs," TJ prompted.

"Oh, yes, the Scabs. And what a charming mental picture *that* calls up. What in the world does he see in these people?"

"I dunno . . . someone to hang with, I guess."

There was a long pause as TJ dug one of his sneakers into the carpet and rocked his foot from side to side. Finally, he spoke again.

"Uh, Mom, can I ask you something?"

"Sure. What's on your mind?" *He's probably having trouble with his math again—as if I, who hire an accountant for those sorts of things, could ever help him.*

"Well, nuthin' exactly. I just wanted to know . . ." Leaning to one side, he plunged a fist into his jeans pocket and retrieved a small item. Opening his hand and holding it out toward his mother, he asked quietly, "What's this?"

Paula's eyes widened as she stared at the tiny blue cotton bootie nestled in her son's palm. It was *his*—her lost baby's hospital slipper, somehow escaped from the upstairs drawer as if it had a life of its own.

"TJ, where did you get this?" she asked sharply, snatching it from his hand and curling her fingers around its softness. *I never thought he'd go through my things. Now he's seen it all.* Her heart sank. She had never told her sons they had a brother.

"Gee, I didn't think you'd be mad . . . I just found it. After school, Millie asked me to take some fresh flowers up to your room—her hip's been bothering her, an' she didn't wanna go up all those stairs, so I told her I'd do it. Anyway, as I was leaving the room I saw it lying on the floor, right by your rocker. Looks like a little shoe or something. I just wanted to know." He stared gloomily at his empty hand and shifted his weight on the ottoman.

Paula felt a steel band tighten around her head as she struggled to remain calm. *Get a grip, Donroe. He doesn't know, and he doesn't have to know. Not now—not like this. Tell him what he wants to hear. The truth can wait.*

She cleared her throat and smiled warmly into the puzzled eyes of this innocent child. "Oh, honey," she said softly, reaching out with her empty hand to smooth a wayward lock of sandy hair above his ear. "I'm sorry I jumped on you. It's just that I didn't expect to see— that is, I've always kept this special little tradition to myself."

"Special little tradition?" TJ studied her face intently.

"Yes. You see"—she uncurled her fingers, exposing the bootie to a soft beam of lamplight—"this *is* a little shoe. *Your* little shoe, kiddo. It's one of a pair that I brought you home from the hospital in. Can you believe how *small* your feet were?"

"Yeah," he said, grinning self-consciously. "They're a little bigger now."

"You'd better believe it," she chuckled. "Anyway, every year on my birthday I do this special thing . . . I take out your little booties and remember that wonderful day you were born. Then I cry a little—happy tears, of course—and I think what a terrific kid I have, and how glad I am to be your mom. And Scotty's mom."

"Do you have his booties, too?"

"You bet, right there in my drawer. I must have dropped yours last night . . . so now I'll just run up and put it away. Is your mom a crazy lady, or what?" She went cross-eyed and made a silly face. *Has my nose started growing yet?*

"Does it make you sad?" TJ's eyes bored into hers.

"Does what make me sad, sweetie?"

"Well, there's always something about your birthday—something that makes you sad. We have parties and stuff, but every year there's something not quite right—not quite happy. I haven't figured it out . . . maybe the baby shoes have something to do with it. But I still don't get it—why something like that would upset you."

He knows something, senses something. Turn it around. Don't let him follow it.

She sighed, making up the lie as she went along.

"Listen, kiddo, it's only because the older I get, the older *you* get—and I just can't help thinking how it won't be very many more years before you and your brother sprout wings of your own and leave the nest. And that, my dear, handsome boy"—she brushed the back of her hand dramatically across her forehead and lowered her voice to a pouty whisper—"is worth a little weeping and wailing."

He relaxed, grinning at her. "Boy, Mom, you're a real softie," he laughed, leaning over to give her a peck on the cheek. "But I like it. And you know what?" He stood and lifted one shoe off the floor.

"What?" She was breathing a little easier now.

"I bet my feet smelled better then than they do now." Roaring at his own joke, he turned and sauntered through the door, his shoulders shaking with mirth.

Long after TJ left, Paula gazed after him at the empty doorway, contemplating her willful deception. The thought came and lingered. *I have never, ever lied to my children.* She shivered, bit her lip, and closed her eyes tightly to block out the memory of TJ's trusting stare. *Until now.*

Even when things had been so bad with Richard, she'd been straight with the boys, helped them understand that when the marriage ended, they could still count on her for the important things—love, trust, honesty, a sense of family. During those first years alone, the three of them had built memories from scratch: a trip to the beach here, a ski weekend there, Saturday mornings laughing and talking over cozy waffle breakfasts. Paula had always come away from such times feeling cleansed and refreshed, as if their innocence could somehow rescue her from the crush of a cankered world that expected too much and gave too little. Their shining young faces had reminded her that there was something essentially good and noble about life, and in her heart she'd hoped, even trusted, that it would always be so. In the little time she had outside of business, she had taught them about trusting her and each other, about always telling the truth, about looking for the best in every situation. She'd spent countless hours wondering if she could have done better, fretting over the demanding career that so often robbed her of precious time with her sons. But as the years passed and they grew to be strong and appealing boys, she was satisfied—almost—that she had done the best she could.

And yet, there had always been that dark little corner of deception, hidden carefully away in an upstairs drawer—until tonight, when one stray baby bootie had made the lie necessary. But why? Why couldn't she have just laid it all out—told her son that he was one of three, that he had a twenty-two-year-old brother somewhere on the planet, that she had given him away when he was less than a day old? That she had *given him away.* Why couldn't she just say it?

Not a chance. Not tonight, not next week. Maybe not ever.

CHAPTER 6

As she reached for the half-full martini glass on the table beside her, Paula fought the emotion brimming in her eyes. She couldn't help it; she felt betrayed by the wayward little bundle of cotton clasped tightly in her free hand. Betrayed by the son who had found it and forced her to lie, and lie again. Even betrayed by the luminous young man who had selfishly died so many years ago, leaving her without a future. She had, of course, made her own future without Greg or their son. But at what price? A solitary tear slid silently down her cheek as she lifted the glass to her lips. *A swallow or two, and the pain will fade.*

The glass stopped in mid-air as the front doorbell chimed. Moments later, a few hesitant taps sounded against the den's open door. "Excuse me," Millie said softly. "You have some visitors."

"Who in the world—?" Paula set the glass down and hurriedly wiped at her face. She glanced at her watch, noticing that it wasn't as late as it seemed.

"The sisters . . . you know, those missionaries. The *Mormons.*" Millie's tone was indulgent. Or was it hopeful? Either way, Paula wasn't interested.

"What's the matter? Didn't you get everything straightened out earlier today?"

"Yes, and they were very grateful. But—"

"Well, what do they want now?" *Another crack at my car?*

"I'm not sure, exactly; they just asked for you. I told them I'd—"

"Oh, Millie, I'm really not in the mood to deal with this tonight." *Or any night.* She rubbed a finger up and down between her eyebrows. "Just take care of it, will you please?"

Millie knew better than to argue. She was old enough to be Paula's mother, but she didn't feel right about interfering. "I understand," she said, turning to leave. "Shall I close the door?"

"Yes, thanks. I'll be out in a little while to get something to eat, but I need to get some work done first." The older woman closed the door as Paula settled herself at the small desk. Tucking the bootie into her jacket pocket, she began to rummage through her attaché for Ted's advertising copy

Rudy, having been routed from his peaceful resting place, snorted impatiently. He padded around the overstuffed chair in a slow circle, then moved stiffly toward the door, coming to a standstill with his nose only inches from its gleaming brass knob. A low rumble escaped his throat.

Paula sighed and looked up from her papers. She chuckled softly as she eyed her aging pet. "Oh, I know that tone of voice," she murmured. "You want to go out, don't you?" The dog inclined his head as if in assent, arched his furry eyebrows, and briefly waved his tail in the air. "Well, I guess at your age you're entitled to a bathroom break every couple of hours. C'mon, I'll do the honors; I didn't really want to work, anyway. Besides, a little turn around the block will do us both good. I'll just run upstairs and put on something comfortable, okay?"

Rudy waited stoically by the front door while Paula changed into a lightweight jogging suit and her Nike walking shoes. She bent beside him a few minutes later and secured a leash to his collar. "Back in a few minutes," she called to Millie as she pushed open the door.

The sun had barely settled itself behind a cluster of distant foothills when they stepped outside and began a leisurely stroll down the sidewalk. Streaked a dusty red by particles of dying sunlight, the air glowed around them, dancing lightly on Paula's dark hair as they walked. It was a mild evening; the heavy smog that usually settled close to the ground had been scattered by a light breeze late in the afternoon, and a fragile crispness had taken its place. If there had been real seasons in southern California, this would have been her favorite. At odd moments and with a certain nostalgia, she caught herself replaying in her mind the stark seasonal contrasts of her childhood in New England; but it was purely a visual memory, and was never allowed to filter down into her heart. Now she breathed in deeply, satisfied with the moment.

While Rudy made use of a tall, neatly trimmed bush at the corner of a sloping driveway, Paula's gaze wandered from house to house. One by one, windows lit up as the sky yielded to dusk. Some of the people behind these walls would be enjoying a late dinner, having a good conversation, making love. Others would be rushing off to school board meetings or catching up on a little work at home. Still others would be squinting through the peephole in their front door, wondering why there were two young women—

Two young women! Paula froze as her eyes pinpointed the silhouettes—one tall and lanky, the other short and, well . . . perky-looking—waiting expectantly beneath the porch light of a home just down and across the street from where she was standing. She moved quickly, silently into the shadow of the bush and considered her options. *I could run, but they'd hear me. I could stay here in the shadows, but they might come this way. I could turn Rudy loose as a diversion, but he'd probably lick them to death. I could—*

Suddenly the door of the house opened, and Paula saw her moment of opportunity. If they were distracted for even a few seconds, she could sneak by them and make it home without being detected. "Come on, boy, we're finished here. Let's go!" she whispered hoarsely, yanking the leash to make her point. Startled, Rudy planted his feet firmly and resisted. When she jerked the leash harder and pulled with both hands, he began to move slowly, trotting reluctantly a leash-length behind her. In less than two minutes she was leaning heavily against the inside of her front door, sighing with mingled relief and irritation. Rudy had shuffled off to find a place where he could snooze, uninterrupted, until bedtime.

Millie hurried into the entryway, a puzzled expression clouding her face. "My goodness, what's the matter? You look like you've just seen some alien from another world."

"Well," Paula replied between ragged breaths, "in a manner of speaking, I guess you could say that—except there were *two* of them."

"Really?" The older woman's eyes grew dark with curiosity. "What did you see, exactly?"

"Oh, all right, maybe they weren't aliens—but they certainly come from a different world, as far as I can tell. You know, those two

Mormon people—the girls who were here a while ago." Millie closed her eyes and nodded.

"What are they doing in the neighborhood, anyway?" Paula continued. "It looked like they were going house to house—peddling their religion, I suppose."

"They're really very nice girls," Millie said. "They just stopped by to thank you for your kindness and generosity this morning."

Ah, yes, the bike. The checkbook. "And just how much, uh, *generosity* did I extend this morning, Millie?"

"Oh, they were quite frugal. After they called their friends to come pick them up—a couple of nice-looking boys in a little white car—they went directly to a bicycle shop downtown. They called me and said they'd found a good deal on a used bike for about two hundred dollars, so I wrote them out a check. They were awfully nice about it."

"Two hundred. Well, I guess it could have been worse," Paula observed, grinding her teeth. *Car repairs and a new bike—a perfect $2,000 day. If I ever got religion, it could bankrupt me in a month.*

"You're right about that," Millie smiled. "Now, come into the kitchen, dear, and have some dinner. I'll heat up some of the leftovers from last night; my veal is even better the second time around."

"I'm sure it is," Paula agreed, suddenly realizing how hungry she was. A good meal, in quiet company, would help her relax. "Can I have some champagne, too?" Her voice was almost childlike in its pleading quality.

"Sorry, we're fresh out. Your friends have a real taste for the bubbly," Millie observed

"It figures. At least water is cheaper." Paula shuffled into the kitchen and settled herself on a padded stool at the breakfast bar. She drummed her fingertips on the beige and turquoise tiled counter while Millie filled a plate and fussed with the microwave timer. Minutes later, a tantalizing replay of last night's feast was steaming beneath Paula's appreciative nose. Closing her eyes and inhaling deeply, she felt contentment seep into her bones.

She ate slowly, deliberately, welcoming the warm, fragrant food into her mouth like an old friend. There was no need to hurry; after a day like this, she wanted nothing more than to settle peaceably into this quiet corner of her world and shift her brain into one of its lower gears. *Even Ted's stuff can wait,* she thought, nudging a remnant of three-bean salad across her plate with a fork. She would spend the next hour or two being a normal person. *Normal—I like the sound of that. But first, the chocolate mousse . . .*

Millie had already put in a load of laundry, checked on the boys, and tidied up the kitchen by the time Paula licked the last molecule of chocolate from her spoon. "Mmmm . . . superb," she sighed. "I don't suppose there's any more where that came from."

"You suppose correctly," Millie confirmed. "Your sons have definitely inherited their mother's sweet tooth. It was all I could do to save that little dish for you."

"And I do thank you for that. Where are the little chocoholics, anyway? I saw TJ earlier, but the house has been pretty quiet since I got back from walking Rudy."

"They're both downstairs. Scotty's got some papers spread out on the pool table, and TJ's watching one of those *Star Trek* videos. They've got school tomorrow, and they were up late last night with the party and all, so they should probably be getting to bed before long." Millie glanced at her watch. "I think I'll turn in pretty soon myself, if that's all right," she said.

"Oh, of course. I'll lock up for the night," Paula promised, trying to remember how many times in the last month she'd been home before her children were in bed. Counting last night—two. Maybe three. She headed for the stairs, intent on spending a few quality hours—well, minutes—with her sons.

"Oh, I nearly forgot," Millie called out, stopping just outside her bedroom door and turning toward Paula.

"Yes?"

"The sisters—they brought you a little something to thank you for your trouble this morning. They said to tell you it's really special, and they wanted you to have it. I put it on your nightstand."

"Okay. I'll get it when I go up to bed." *What could those two give me that I could possibly want—besides a restraining order?* "Thanks, Millie, and good night." The older woman shuffled into her room and closed the door softly behind her. Paula made her way slowly down the stairs, a puzzled expression lining her brow.

She promptly dismissed the matter from her mind when the boys came into view. "Hi, guys, what's up?" she said casually. TJ dutifully lifted a hand in greeting, but his eyes never left the large-screen TV in one corner of the room. *At least he's done his homework,* she mused.

Turning toward Scott, her eyes grew round with curiosity, then alarm. He was bending over the pool table, his lean, muscular frame casting a shadow across several large sheets of heavy construction paper scattered on the green surface in front of him. Most of the sheets were covered with crude drawings of grotesquely positioned snakes, worms, spiders, scorpions, and other disgusting creatures. Scott was studying them intently.

Paula decided to ease into this one. Had her son suddenly developed a consuming passion for entomology, and would this challenging science project launch him into a lifetime of bug-related scholarly pursuits? She smiled at the mental picture. *It wouldn't exactly be my first choice for his career—but hey, who's complaining? This could mean he'll actually finish high school.*

Moving close to the table, she reached out tentatively to touch one of the sheets. "Scotty, honey," she said softly, her voice a silken thread of endearment, "this is so . . . so . . . *interesting*. I didn't know you had such a gift for science. Which class are you doing this project for? I bet you'll get a really good grade, and—"

"Aw, *Mom!*" The irritation in his voice cut her off abruptly.

"What? I was just complimenting you on your project. It's wonderful to see you getting interested in school."

"School? Who said anything about *school?*" His tone was mocking.

"Well, why else would you be looking at all of these crawly—"

The realization hit her like a blow to the midsection. *Oh. The Crawlers. Oh.* She put a hand to her forehead and backed away a few paces. "It's that gang, isn't it?"

"It's a *club*, Mom, and yeah, it's the Crawlers." His voice was tight and defensive. "We found this cool place to hang out, and the guys wanted some stuff for the walls. I told them I thought I could come up with something."

"I see . . . and so you have," Paula observed, glancing with fresh dismay at the sketches. *Keep it cool, Donroe. This may be your only chance to talk him out of this nonsense.* "And just what is your gang—uh, your *club's*—purpose?"

"Geez, Mom, does everything have to have a reason? I mean, we like to hang, and there's stuff to do. What's the big deal?"

"The big deal," Paula said in a measured tone, but feeling anger beginning to throb at her temples, "is that these 'clubs' can get completely out of control. You're playing ball or video games one minute, shooting each other the next. And don't tell me it doesn't happen, Scotty, because I know different. Just please, *please* tell me you'd never get involved with something like that." Her tone had now changed to something between pleading and whining, and he responded belligerently.

"Right, Mom. I can tell you really *trust* me." He glared at her with disgust, then began snatching the drawings from the table. "These guys are my friends, okay? What do you care what we do, as long as it doesn't get *you* into deep soup?"

"That's not fair, Scotty. You *know* I care, and I just want to help you—"

"Leave it alone, will ya? I've got work to do. 'Night, Mom." Clutching the sheaf of drawings tightly in one hand, he gave her a final icy look and disappeared up the stairs.

"Scotty, come back here! We still have some talking to do."

Silence—then the slamming of a door upstairs.

Paula slumped into the nearest chair, shaking her head in disbelief. Whatever happened to the gangly, fun-loving young comic who had inhabited her son's body only a few months earlier? *Whoever snatched him, I hope they're treating him well.* A tiny smile flickered across her face at the thought.

"So, what was that all about?" TJ's voice came from across the room, where he had just switched off the TV. He was standing, yawning, stretching his arms to the front and sides. Clad in a rumpled blue T-shirt and baggy jeans, his twelve-year-old body had not yet developed a lean, hard-muscled form like his older brother's.

"Oh, I don't know," she sighed. "I guess your brother's just going through one of those phases where he knows everything, I know nothing. All he can think of are his buddies in that gang."

"Yeah, he's really into that stuff. They hang together all the time."

"Do you know anything about these boys?"

"Naw, Scotty doesn't talk to me much about it. A couple of 'em have cars, that's all I know. They cruise a street in downtown L.A. sometimes. He asked if I wanted to see their place a couple of weeks ago, but I haven't yet. I'd rather read or shoot baskets. Besides, he thinks I'm a pest—says little brothers oughta mind their own business. He's not as much fun as he used to be . . . he's darker now."

Paula's eyebrows knit together in a frown. "Darker? What do you mean, TJ?"

"Well, it's kinda hard to explain. Like he thinks he's *so cool*, but he's all empty inside, you know? He gets mad all the time, too, for nuthin'. The other day I asked him where my basketball was, and he 'bout bit my head off. I've learned to give him space . . . lotsa space."

Paula pressed for more information. "TJ, think about this very carefully. It's important. Do you think Scotty could be doing drugs?" She bit her lip, waiting for his response. It came without hesitation.

"I really don't think so, Mom. In school they teach us all the signs of drug use, and he just doesn't fit with 'em. I know—I've been watching him."

"Well, then, what do you think's going on?"

TJ shrugged and stuffed his hands into his pockets. "Heck, I don't know." Suddenly a thought glimmered in his eye. "Wait a minute, this might be something. See, there's this girl . . ."

"A girl?"

"Yeah, Vicky something. Scotty really has it bad for her, but she's a year ahead of him in school and it's goin' nowhere. She won't even look at him."

"Uh-huh. That would do it." Paula's head was swimming with relief. *The kid's hormones are playing hopscotch, and he's out to punish the world.* "My dear second son," she said, grinning at TJ, "it appears that what we have here is nothing more than a lovesick teenager."

"Huh?"

"Never mind, big guy. It's past your bedtime. Come over here and say good night." She opened her arms, and he covered the distance to her chair in seconds. Reaching up to curl her arms around his neck, she kissed him warmly on the cheek. "No doubt about it," she whispered close to his ear, "you're my favorite pest in the whole world. And don't you forget it."

"I won't, Mom," TJ laughed. "See you tomorrow, okay? I'll take Rudy out." She nodded as he bounded up the stairs.

Now alone in the quiet, dimly lit room, Paula sank back into the chair and drew her legs up close to her body, encircling them with her arms. Resting her head on her knees, she closed her eyes and listened to the sound of her own soft, measured breathing. In that moment of time, she was not Ms. Donroe, the successful, high-rolling business executive. She was not Mom, the single parent of two impossibly active sons, one of whom could be slipping away from her. And she was certainly not young Mrs. Gregory Morrison, the grieving teenaged widow and mother of so long ago, whose dreams had vanished almost before they'd begun.

Tonight, for these few peaceful moments torn from a pressure-cooker day, she was just Paula. Paula—the pretty, dark-haired child who danced and weaved and twirled in the early morning mist across a wide expanse of dewy grass on her father's Connecticut estate. The agile, energetic youngster who, running home from school, leaped above the brown, dusty path and fancied she was flying. The high school cheerleader whose irrepressible humor and warmth bonded her to classmates and endeared her to teachers.

Those were the golden days. *That* was the Paula she wanted to remember—not the Paula whose early love affair had ended in disaster and opened a chasm in her family that had never been bridged. Not the Paula whose single-minded rise to success had left a trail of unfulfilled promises and broken friendships, whose marriage had ended badly, whose quality of life was now measured by the speed of rush-hour traffic and the cruel braying of her cellular phone. Which was the real Paula, and how had it all come to this?

That's enough, Donroe. You should have stopped at the "humor and warmth" part. Paula blinked her eyes and shook her head sharply, as if clearing away the cobwebs of memory, then planted her feet on the floor. *Besides, it's not all bad. You've got two great kids, a wonderful home, and Millie to fill in the gaps—not to mention that spiffy new set of wheels in the garage. It's just the turning-forty thing, the double birthday. But this is no time for a pity party. You're okay.* Gripping the arms of the chair, she resolutely pulled herself to a standing position. *And tonight could have been worse.* She grimaced. *Scotty could have been drawing pictures for the Scabs.*

The house was dark and still as she made her way up the two short flights of stairs to her room. Switching on the light, she saw her gray Armani suit sprawled on the floor like a sleeping puppy. Earlier, she had quickly changed into her jogging outfit and tossed the skirt, blouse, and jacket toward the bed as she rushed out the door to take Rudy for a walk. Obviously, she had missed. Now she stooped to retrieve each piece, depositing the soft white blouse in an oak laundry basket inside her closet.

When she reached for a suit hanger, the jacket slipped off her arm and fell to the floor. She secured the skirt to the hanger, then bent over to pick up the jacket. As she grasped a sleeve, something shook loose and tumbled from the pocket. In an instant, the soft blue color told her what it was

The baby bootie. His bootie.

She stared at the speck of blue huddled on the beige carpet. Her eyes widened, then narrowed as she remembered the feel of the tiny shoe in her palm while she lied to TJ and stuffed it in her pocket. *This isn't fair. I should only have to deal with it once a year, but this time it won't leave me alone.* Moaning faintly, she smoothed the suit jacket onto its hanger, then bent down to scoop the bootie into her hand. Instinctively she lifted it to her face, pressing her lips against it for a few seconds before gently placing it next to its tiny mate inside the small box. "Now it's finally over," she said softly as she pushed the drawer closed. "Until next year."

As she changed into an oversized cotton T-shirt and slipped between the cool sheets of her bed, Paula didn't notice the small blue book lying on her nightstand.

CHAPTER 7

"More coffee, dear?" Millie was holding the pot, poised to pour.

"No, thanks," Paula replied, using her fork to swirl a few soggy crumbs around in the syrup on her plate. "More than two cups and I'm a mass of nerves. Have to put on my 'cool cap' for an important meeting with some clients this morning. I could use a second helping of that wonderful French toast, though. Maybe another shot of juice, too."

"You bet." Millie bustled into the kitchen, and Paula glanced at her watch. She'd need to be on the road in a few minutes if she expected to be at the office by seven. Picking up the *Business Week* magazine beside her plate, she flipped through a few pages. It never hurt to see what the competition was up to, even if her own company was small potatoes compared to the national advertising conglomerates.

"So, did you find it?"

Paula had quickly buried herself in the magazine's pages, and she started at Millie's voice close to her ear. "Uh, excuse me, what did you say?"

"I said, did you find it?"

Paula chuckled dryly. "Millie, I don't have a clue what you're talking about. Was I supposed to find something?"

"Oh, just that book," Millie replied cheerfully as she lowered a steaming piece of French toast onto Paula's plate. "I thought maybe you saw it last night."

Reaching for a small glass pitcher of syrup, Paula shook her head. "I'm afraid you're still losing me. *What* book?"

"The little blue one . . . I left it on your nightstand, like I said."

Paula stared at her blankly.

"Those girls—the missionaries—said it was special. They gave me one, too."

"Oh, I see." *Like I have time to read their Mormon propaganda.* "Well, I had a little run-in with Scotty last night, and by the time I got upstairs I wasn't exactly in the mood for any bedtime reading. Besides, I'm not really interested in—"

"What about Scotty?" Millie's voice was suddenly filled with concern. She had watched over the boy since he was a mischievous first-grader, and she wasn't about to stop mothering him now. Seating herself at the table, she studied Paula's face intently.

"Nothing, really. He's just acting like—well, like a teenager, I suppose. Won't listen to anything I say."

"I know what you mean. When my Molly was his age . . ." Millie stopped in mid-sentence as her eyes clouded over. She didn't have to remind Paula that her only child, now dead for a dozen years, had caused her enough grief for several lifetimes. A beautiful and promising young model, Molly had ravaged her body with amphetamines to keep her weight down and her energy up. In the end, her heart stopped before Millie even recognized the signs, and she blamed herself for the girl's death. She and her husband, Joe, had tried to rebuild their lives, but the toll of their daughter's tragic end had settled upon him like a dense, impenetrable fog. A year after Molly's death, Joe had followed her at the end of a rope hung from a rafter in their garage.

"Don't," Paula said softly, reaching out to touch Millie's hand. "It's all right; nothing happened. Scotty and I just had a little misunderstanding, that's all. Everything's—*cool,*" she grinned, trying to lighten the mood. "Now, what were we talking about?"

The older woman smiled tightly, relieved to be changing the subject. "The book—the little blue book?"

"Ah, yes, the book. What is it, anyway?"

"The sisters said it's scripture—like the Bible, I guess, only different somehow. The Book of Mormon, that's what they call it. Anyway, I left it upstairs for you; I told them I'd be sure you got it."

"Thanks, Millie. I'll take a look at it when I get home tonight," Paula lied, pushing back her chair. "But I've got to get going now—you know how busy it gets in the middle of the week."

"That I do. But I just wanted to say . . ." Millie's voice faltered, and emotion welled in her kind eyes. "I just want you to know how much it means to me to be here . . . with you. The three of you are my family now—my own. And I couldn't ask for a better one. Ever." She smiled gratefully.

Paula returned her gaze. "And you never get tired of . . . this?" she quizzed gently, motioning with one hand toward the kitchen and dining area.

"Never," Millie answered firmly. "I've always been a homebody, loved to care for folks. I couldn't ask for a better way to spend my days."

"Well, my dear Millie," Paula said warmly, "there's no doubt that you're the best thing to ever happen to this family. It's a fact, and we love you for it." She moved to Millie's side and bent to put her arm snugly around the older woman's shoulders. "We couldn't ask for a better friend. Ever." Millie's contented sigh told Paula that she was returning to the present, pushing her heartaches to the back of her mind where they belonged. "Now, will you be okay?"

Millie stood and busily smoothed her apron with gnarled, work-worn hands. "Sure I will," she said brightly. "You just go and enjoy your day."

"It's a deal. I haven't the foggiest idea when I'll be home; but what else is new? As always, I trust you to hold down the fort." Millie grinned and turned to clear away Paula's breakfast dishes and set out clean ones for the boys. By the time she had done so, Paula had disappeared into the garage. It could be a dozen hours or more until her sassy little red car pulled into the driveway for the evening.

There was a certain solemn anticipation with the beginning of each new day at Donroe & Associates, and Paula liked to be the first to feel it. Sitting behind her desk, she would gaze out the window toward the east and watch the early morning sun scatter its brilliance over the still-sleeping city. It was like witnessing a visual symphony of color, and she never tired of the performance. The show began with shy, muted tones of pinks and oranges, intensifying to transform the clouds into vibrant, red-rimmed puffs of cotton, finally climaxing half an hour later with white-gold flames reflected in the shimmering panes of hundreds of glass-faced buildings. Even the smog, which later in the morning would clog the air with debris and the sinuses with impurities, seemed to cast a benevolent glow over the city at this early hour.

Paula savored the moment this morning as she sat quietly contemplating her day. It had begun, she thought, in a satisfying way as she and Millie had shared some peaceable moments, a bond of concern, a few tender words. For many years now, Paula and her own mother had rarely been in touch, except for an occasional Christmas card. Her parents had shut her out when she'd eloped with Greg, and she'd never really tried to get back into their lives. Even her children's births and her father's death had brought them no closer. Perhaps Connecticut was just too far away, and their hearts couldn't— wouldn't—bridge the distance. Which made Paula all the more grateful for Millie, who watched over the three of them as if they were her own. In a sense, they *were* her own—as she had gently reminded Paula that very morning. They were the family Millie had lost, and Millie replaced the mother and grandmother that Paula and the boys had never really known. It was a comfortable fit.

A door opened and closed somewhere in the outer office. Moments later, Carmine's long, crimson-tipped fingers snaked around the edge of Paula's office door, followed by her broad, amiable face. "Morning, boss," she grinned. "I see you're up with the pigeons . . . makin' up for yesterday, eh?"

"I guess," Paula responded idly, reaching for her appointment book. "Is there anything I should know about before we get started on this day?"

"Well, let's see." Carmine had settled herself into a chair across from Paula's desk, and she now began ticking off a list from some-where in her computer-like memory. "The big Northridge Electronics meeting is at eleven; lunch with your banker at one-thirty; that studly Morris dude from Hill Publishing at three; and my personal favorite"—her green eyes rolled up and back in their sockets—"Mr. 21st Century Lawn Mower himself, Melvin Campbell, at four. Other than that, you've got the day to yourself."

Paula gulped. *Uh-oh. Campbell is coming, and I haven't done my homework. I could tell him my dog ate it . . .* She remembered that she'd once tried using that excuse in high school. Her teacher, who clearly had no sense of humor, reminded her that she didn't *have* a dog. *Turtle-lips Campbell probably wouldn't even crack a smile. I guess I'd better get my act together on this one.* "Nothing before eleven?" she asked.

"Nada," Carmine replied. "I pretty much have the Northridge stuff ready for the meeting, so you're in the clear until then."

"That's good news. Hold my calls for a couple of hours, will you? I need to go over Ted's copy for the Campbell account. I'll let you know when I'm finished, then I'll probably want to see Ted."

"I'll tell him as soon as he gets here."

"Thanks. See you later." That was Carmine's signal to leave; she whisked out the door without further comment, closing it behind her. Her employer was all business when she was up against a deadline.

Paula gazed into the mirror-like finish of her glass-topped desk. *Now, where did I put that file? Oh, right—the one I was going to look at last night.* She felt a tug of guilt as she rummaged in her attaché and came up with the manila folder, slightly dog-eared, with Ted's one-word identification—"Campbell"—scrawled across the front in large block printing. *At least I know I can count on him to do a good job. If anyone can make a lawn mower into man's best friend, Ted can.*

Absently smoothing one curled corner of the folder, she opened it and picked up the sheaf of papers inside. As she began to read, her eyes hovered for a moment over the bolded headline. She blinked once, twice in astonishment. Then she started to smile. "I don't believe this," she murmured aloud, studying the words before her. "It's not like Ted to do something like this . . . but why not take advantage of it? The joke is on him, and this is gonna be *fun*."

She leaned far back in her chair and studied the ceiling for several minutes as a jumbled cadence of wickedly clever remarks assaulted her brain. She began to giggle, then laughed until her eyes filled with tears. Finally, she willed her voice into a normal range and buzzed Carmine. "I'm, uh (cough), ready to see Ted now. Would you (sniff) ask him to come in, please?"

"Sure thing, boss." Carmine paused, then cautiously inquired, "Is everything okay in there? You sound a little . . . *watery*."

Paula held her breath and bit her lip for a split second before answering. "Oh, I'm fine," she insisted, grinning into the speaker phone. "Is Ted here yet?"

"Yeah, he's been in his office for about half an hour. I'll send him in."

"Good. I'll be waiting." Grabbing a few peach-colored tissues from her drawer, Paula hurriedly wiped at the damp mascara on her eyelashes, and had just blown her nose when she heard Ted's familiar triple knock. She carefully placed both hands on the desk top and looked up solemnly as he swung open the door and walked toward her with elaborate nonchalance. Her intense expression stopped him in his tracks.

"I guess this is about the Campbell copy." His voice was casual but alert as he sat down.

"You guess right. I've been reading it," Paula said in a flat tone, "and there is a major concern."

"A concern," he parroted tersely. "And what might that be?" She could feel his defenses rising like a periscope, and she fought back the smile pushing against her teeth.

"Well," she said in a measured tone, planting her elbows on the desk and pressing her fingertips together to form a tent, "I do have a rather important question."

"Shoot. I'll answer it as well as I can." A muscle twitched along his jaw.

"I certainly hope so. Now, let's see if I can put my finger on it." Her eyes moved slowly, painstakingly up and down, up and down the typed page in front of her, as if searching for a particular word. "Ah, yes, here it is—the thing I needed to know. The important thing. The *really* important thing."

"What *really important* thing would that be?"

Seeing the frustration in his eyes, Paula decided to get to the point so they could both have a good laugh. "Well, Ted," she replied earnestly, subduing a sudden impulse to giggle, "what I really want to know is—" She cleared her throat as he stifled an epithet. "What I *must know* is . . . Ted, what in the world is a 'Lawn Mormon'?"

"A *what?*" He stared at her blankly.

"See? It's right here—in the headline." She pointed at the page, turning it so he could read the words as she repeated them. "'*The Lawn Mormon Built to Take You into the 21st Century.*'" No longer able to control her mirth, she grinned broadly and waited for his roar of laughter. What came out was more like a gurgle near the bottom of his throat, but he smiled gamely.

"Gee, I guess I really did it this time, didn't I?" he snorted, slapping his palm against his forehead with an exaggerated motion. "Talk about a Freudian slip . . . those Mormons get into your brain for a second, and they're likely to pop up again anywhere—even on the lawn. Anyway, I'll just go and fix this." He chuckled sheepishly and reached for the paper.

"Hey, wait a minute—not so fast, buddy. Stay right where you are." Paula's voice was insistent as her thoughts raced. *I've got to have a little more fun with this. It isn't often that one catches Ted with his pants—uh, with his guard—down. This is just too rich.* "We may be on to something here," she continued. "I'd like to know a little more about these lawn Mormons."

He shot her a sharp, questioning glance and remained poised on the edge of his chair.

"I mean," Paula persisted, "a lawn Mormon . . . is that anything like a lawn *jockey*—you know, one of those little cement people standing out in the front yard with a lantern in his hand and nowhere to go?" A mental picture of the two energetic lady missionaries flashed through her mind. "No, I guess not; from what I've seen of the Mormons, they *always* have somewhere to go."

Ted sat motionless, a thin smile holding up the corners of his mouth. His blue eyes were riveted on Paula's face.

She was just warming up. "Let's see now. I've heard of lawn chairs, lawn bowling, lawn tennis, even the Lawn Ranger"—her eyes sparkled with mirth as she continued with an exaggerated western drawl—"but ah cain't say as ah've ever heerd of them thar lawn *Mormons.*"

He grinned tightly and bit his lower lip, then shifted his gaze to the window.

"C'mon, Ted, give me a hand here," she pressed, drumming her nails on the desk. "Lawn Mormons . . . is that Mormons who live on their lawns? Are there lawn Mormons as opposed to non-lawn Mormons, or patio Mormons, or driveway Mormons?" *Oh, I'm good.* "Mormons given to patience and lawn-suffering? But maybe the ones you know are lawn-*gone* Mormons, Ted. Here's a good one: How many lawn Mormons does it take to—"

"*Stop it!*" Ted hissed as his open hand crashed down on her desk. His jaw was working uncontrollably, and for long seconds he stared at her with unspeakable rage boiling in his eyes. When he spoke, his voice was controlled but vibrating with resentment. "It was a stupid mistake, okay? I'll change the headline."

Startled, Paula lapsed into an awkward silence, waiting for him to explain this odd outburst. Instead, he stood abruptly, marched to the door, and jerked it open. A few seconds after he strode from the room, she heard the slam of his office door. She stared after him incredulously, her mouth hanging open slightly, her face a study in disbelief.

"Hello? Is anybody alive in here?" Carmine's voice preceded her tousled head into the office. Seeing Paula's glazed eyes and blank expression, she began by stating the obvious. "Good grief, girl, you look like you've just been to lunch with the Stepford wives, and I've *never* seen Ted so riled. What in the world happened?"

Paula continued to gape mutely at the open door for several seconds, then slowly shook her head. "Beats me," she mumbled. "I thought I knew the guy."

"And what's that supposed to mean?" Carmine prodded.

"Oh, I don't know . . . I thought I was just being clever, but he seems to have developed a mighty short fuse all of a sudden."

"Yeah? What set him off?"

"Well, we were talking about his work on the Campbell promotion . . . I said a few things about the 'lawn Mormons,' and he—"

"The *what?*"

"The lawn Mormons. Ted used to be one of them, you know."

"Ted used to be a lawn Mormon?" Carmine was clearly puzzled.

Paula laughed, releasing the knot of tension in her throat. *I was funny, darn it. What's his problem?* "Yes—no—yes, he was a Mormon, but no, the lawn thing was just a mistake." Seeing Carmine's confused expression, she added, "Forget it. You had to be there."

"Right," the younger woman replied in a perplexed tone. "Is there anything I can do?"

"Not a thing. I'll talk to him later. Meanwhile, I still have an hour or so before the Northridge meeting at eleven, and I really need to get this Campbell thing tied down. Later, okay?" Taking her cue, Carmine nodded and ambled out of the office.

Paula turned her attention back to Ted's copy. Forcing herself to skip over the headline, she concentrated on the body of the promotional piece. As she'd expected, it was very good—better than anything she could have written herself. Ted could paint word pictures so vivid and convincing that customers would invariably line up to buy the product whether they needed it or not. The lawn mower copy was no exception, and Paula was not really surprised when she actually began conjuring up mental images of herself on a placid summer morning, at the helm of a Campbell machine, mowing the heck out of her back lawn.

Her eyes narrowed as they scanned the next-to-last paragraph, which suggested that even in one's underwear, trimming the turf would be more fun with a Campbell mower. Again an image came to Paula's mind—this time of Ted in his shorts and socks, padding glee-fully behind one of the machines, clicking his heels in time with its pulsating motor. She smiled. *Only in California.*

Without warning, the image dissolved into another. Paula closed her eyes and let a slow grin spread across her face as she considered the picture. It wasn't so very far-fetched, she thought; with a little imagina-tion, one could see it clearly. A slow chuckle erupted deep in her throat, and her teeth vibrated with laughter as she made the mental connection. Ted might be even madder if he knew what she was thinking at this moment. But it didn't matter; she would straighten it out with him later. For now, she just needed one more hoot.

"Of course," she giggled, leaning back in her chair. "A lawn-john Mormon."

CHAPTER 8

It was hours past closing time when Paula turned the key in her office door and headed down the short, carpeted hallway toward the elevator. It had been a long, intense day, and her shoulders sagged under the weight of a dozen projects needing her personal attention. *Was I ever young and carefree?* She grimaced at the thought, straining to remember the last time she'd tossed a tennis ball, tossed a horse-shoe, even tossed a salad. *It's all in the wrist and elbow,* she mused, considering each of the three in turn. *And with my lifestyle, carpal tunnel syndrome is a lot more likely than tennis elbow.*

Shuffling past Ted's office, she noticed a faint light beneath the door. It was odd, she thought, to find him here at this hour; he was usually at the gym by this time, working out the kinks of his day. It occurred to her that she hadn't seen him since their encounter earlier in the day, and this might be a good chance to put the incident to rest. Or at least to put a lighter spin on it. She stopped and tapped softly on his door—but not before swallowing a tiny, wicked smile as she thought of the "lawn Mormons" and their peculiar effect on Ted.

"Come in." His voice sounded flat, preoccupied. She turned the knob gingerly and pushed.

The paneled oak door eased open to reveal the command center of a man who had once lived on the outer edge of excitement. Photographs lined the walls—Ted with presidents, kings, prime ministers, sports legends. Ted with movie stars, military heroes, business moguls. Ted with the pope, Ted with Mother Teresa, Ted with his arms wrapped around a cluster of starving, swollen-bellied urchins in Zimbabwe. Ted with Princess Diana. Ted waving an American flag on the summit of

Mt. Kilimanjaro. Paula said nothing for long moments as her eyes raced from picture to picture, finally coming to rest on the framed Pulitzer prize certificate above his computer. She'd been in this office many times, but the breadth of Ted's experience never failed to amaze and impress her. Why had he let it all go, she wondered, for the infinitely quieter life of an advertising writer? He never talked much about his past—never talked much at all, in fact. Perhaps someday she would ask.

"Take a load off." Ted's voice startled her back to the present, and she sank into a deep leather chair across from his desk. He stared at her intently, much like a youngster trying to read a parent's mind. "What's up?" His tone was suddenly expectant, almost eager—not at all the mood of the man who had filled himself up with anger and willfully poured it out on her several hours earlier. He looked at her almost shyly, and she thought she saw a trace of embarrassment in his eyes. She would be careful.

"I, um, saw your light on my way out," Paula began, "and thought I'd stop by and bring you up to date on the meeting I had with Mel Campbell this afternoon."

A slow blush snaked along Ted's jawline as he considered how to respond. Finally he asked, "And how did it go?" His eyes held hers for an instant.

"Pretty well, I think. He loved your copy—which, of course, didn't come as any great surprise to me. I loved it, too."

Ted swallowed audibly as a small, self-effacing grin flickered at one side of his mouth, making his lips appear slightly lopsided. "And how," he inquired, "did Mr. Campbell like the headline?" He was staring directly into her eyes.

Now it was Paula's turn to smile discreetly. "Well, after I made one minor revision," she reported, "it was fine. Just fine."

Ted slumped back into his chair, clasped his hands behind his head, closed his eyes, and sighed deeply. "Whew," he breathed. Then, opening his eyes, he added, "I guess I pretty much blew it this morning, didn't I?"

"Well, you certainly blew something," Paula said, her eyes showing a trace of humor. "Just offhand, I'd say it was a major gasket. I've never seen you like that before, Ted." Studying his expression carefully, she waited for his response.

"No excuses—at least none that I'm proud of." He shrugged. "It was one of those freaky gut reactions, and I just didn't handle it very well. I've spent the day trying to figure out a couple of things—why I made that stupid typo in the first place, and why I went ballistic when you started playing games with it."

"And have you come to any conclusions?"

Ted paused and chewed on his bottom lip, as if considering his next words. Finally, he shook his head. "No. Except to say that I haven't given a second's thought to the Mormons for a lot of years, and I'm not about to start now. They're pushy, self-righteous hypocrites, and they never did me any good. They were just lurking in my mind as I was writing, that's all. I figure that's all those Mormons are good for—lurking. I'd just as soon forget the whole thing, okay?" Ted was smiling now, an artificial brightness fluttering in his eyes.

Paula decided to take him at his word. "Deal," she agreed. "We'll send the lawn Mormons back to where they came from—back to where the, uh, grass is greener," she laughed.

This time, Ted joined in. "Yes, indeed," he chuckled. "Back to all their lawn-lost relatives."

"Oh, you're good," she said, taking hold of the arms of her chair and pulling herself to a standing position. "And on that cheery note, I'll be on my way." She moved gracefully toward the door, hesitating briefly as her skirt brushed against Ted's desk. Without warning, he reached out and grasped her hand. Pressing it gently between both of his, he looked up at her, a sudden veil of melancholy darkening his blue eyes.

"Paula," he said earnestly, "I . . . I just want you to know how sorry—how *really sorry* I am about this morning. I shouldn't have let myself get so worked up, and there's no excuse—"

"Hey, we all have our moments . . ." Paula was transfixed by the pleading in his eyes, and she felt herself drawn to him by some unfathomable yearning. It seemed as natural a thing to do as breathing when she bent toward his upturned face and pressed her lips lightly against his cheek. He closed his eyes and exhaled slowly, squeezing her hand again.

With the feel of his day's growth of blond stubble tingling on her lips, Paula pulled back meekly and smiled. Ted opened his eyes and leaned forward in his chair.

"Does that mean I'm forgiven?" His voice was warm, even playful, and he didn't release his hold on her hand.

"I suppose so," she said, "if by 'forgiven' you mean 'reprieved.' But let's not make this a habit, shall we?"

"What—the tantrum or the kiss?" he teased.

"Both," she replied, gently disengaging her hand from his. "Although—" she slowly ran the length of her index finger across her lips—"if I had to choose between the two, it wouldn't be all that hard." Then, feeling a warm blush creep up her neck, she quickly cleared her throat and continued. "So, now that this is all settled, I'd like you to work with Mel Campbell directly on the lawn Morm— lawn *mower* account, okay?"

Ted grinned broadly at her near-miss, and she noticed a tiny chip in one of his gleaming front teeth. "Right, boss," he assured her. "I'm on top of it."

"Terrific. I'll see you tomorrow, then." Paula raised a hand in farewell and moved toward the door. "Don't work too late."

"Not a chance; I'm just about ready to head for the gym. It's good for working off all sorts of . . . energy. Maybe you should try it some- time," Ted suggested as he switched off his computer and collected his briefcase and jacket from a nearby chair.

"I probably should, but sweating just isn't my forte," Paula joked as she made her way into the hall. "Besides, Rudy gives me a pretty good workout when we go for our nightly strolls. And it's no secret that precision driving—especially in a new Jag—is intensely aerobic. So you go pump iron, and I'll go pump gas."

"Yeah, right," Ted groaned as he rolled his eyes and followed her into the elevator.

A few minutes later, Paula was fighting the freeway traffic on her way home. But her mind was traveling a very different road as it replayed the unsettling events of her day, finally coming to rest on the cozy interlude in Ted's office. Recalling every detail of her behavior, she began to scold herself roundly. *Donroe, what in the world possessed you? Whatever it was, it had nothing to do with professionalism, or decorum, or employer-employee etiquette. A kiss, for heaven's sake! The man's divorce isn't even final, and you kissed him! Okay, it was on the cheek . . . but you've been friends for years, and such a thing has never even occurred to you before. Well, maybe once or twice. He is drop-dead gorgeous, after all. But you do have a few years on him, you know . . . and besides, you're his* boss! *This can't do anything but damage your working relationship, can it? Can it?*

Paula frowned at the memory of her indiscretion. But by the time she pulled into her wide driveway, she was smiling.

CHAPTER 9

"Plum sauce," Millie explained. "That's what does it." She was clearing away the dishes as Paula separated the last bit of moist, plump chicken meat from its bone and rolled it around appreciatively on her tongue for a few seconds before swallowing. Enjoying a late meal long after the usual dinner hour, Paula had asked what made the meat so juicy and succulent; she couldn't quite identify the source of its delicate flavoring. But now, hearing the words, she nodded.

"Ummm," she acknowledged, licking the last of the thick, piquant sauce from her fingertips. "I should have known. Any chicken worth its stuffing would be proud to share a pot with your plum sauce."

"Well, I don't know how glad the chicken was," Millie chuckled, "but everyone seemed to enjoy my new recipe at dinner. You know," she continued as she filled the dishwasher, "my mother, the Lord rest her soul, grew up on a farm in Iowa. They raised cows, pigs, chickens, vegetables—everything they needed to feed the family and make a decent living. I doubt if Mama even saw the inside of a grocery store until after she was grown and married. No sir, none of this skinless, boneless, bloodless, plastic-wrapped meat in her family's refrigerator. If they wanted chicken for supper one night, it meant a trip to the coop out back, a lot of chasing and squawking, and finally a swift stroke or two with the business end of an axe. It was over in a second, but I guess it was pretty messy. The blood just kept spurting—"

"Uh, thanks, Millie, for sharing that," Paula interjected, wiping her mouth on a cream-colored paper napkin, "but I'd just as soon pass on hearing the vivid details. I'll take my chicken wrapped, cooked, and served without knowing its blood type and family history, thank you very much. But it was delicious." She reached for her water glass.

"Sorry about that," Millie said with a sheepish smile. "I guess I just got a little carried away. It's been on my mind ever since the girls told us about some of their ancestors. It was just so interesting, and it reminded me of some of my own people . . ."

Paula lowered her glass to the table and stared at Millie. "The girls?"

"Why, yes . . . I thought I'd mentioned it, but maybe not. They just dropped by to say hello."

"The *girls?*" Paula was drawing a blank. "Am I missing something here?"

"The girls. You know, the sisters—the missionaries."

Sudden understanding flooded Paula's mind, followed by sudden irritation. *Of course. The Mormons. They've haunted my day and muddied up my relationship with Ted, so why not make it a night to remember?* Her voice was cool as she asked, "So they were just . . . in the neighborhood?"

"That's right. They wanted to show us the new bicycle. It's very pretty, a nice maroon color. We visited a little, then before I knew it the boys were asking about dinner and the oven timer went off. I invited them to stay and eat with us, and we had a lovely time. I hope you don't mind; they didn't eat very much, and there was still plenty left when you got home."

"Don't worry about it," Paula muttered, thoroughly annoyed. She determined to put it out of her mind as she pushed her chair away from the table and glanced at the wall clock. It was nearly ten. "I think I'll go upstairs now. Are the boys in bed yet?"

"I think so. Scotty went right to his room after dinner, and TJ did his homework and watched TV for a while. I took Rudy out just before you got home, so I think he's okay for the night." At the mention of his name, the big dog lifted his head slightly and peered out from beneath the kitchen table, where he had been snoozing. Satisfied that he was not being summoned or offered something to eat, he settled his golden muzzle on his front paws and dozed off again.

"They asked if you'd started the book." Millie's words reached Paula's ear just as she bent over the small table in the entryway to collect her mail.

"And what did you tell them?" she called tersely over her shoulder as she sorted through a handful of envelopes.

Millie followed her into the hall. "Well, I didn't want to seem ungrateful, so I told them I was sure you found it very interesting, and you appreciated their gift."

"That's nice." *You're a good liar, Millie Hampton.*

"It is, you know."

Paula stopped short at the bottom of the stairs, her back to Millie. "It's what?"

"Very interesting. The book—the Book of Mormon." Millie's voice was subdued, but it held a quiet intensity.

Paula turned to face her. "What are you saying, Millie?"

"Nothing . . . just that I've been reading a little today—the girls gave me a copy, too, you know—and the story seems to make sense. I'll probably finish it eventually."

"So, now you're into religious novels?" Paula teased. "I thought romances were more your style."

"Oh, no, dear," Millie responded lightly, letting the comment slide. "This isn't a novel. The sisters told me it's really a history—a record of the people who lived on this continent hundreds of years ago. They said the people knew about Christ before, during, and after his life, and he even visited them here."

Gee, that *little trip must have used up a good chunk of his frequent-flyer miles.* "And you believe this?" Paula stared at her housekeeper incredulously.

"Well, the story they were telling didn't seem too far-fetched, so I thought I'd do a little more reading—"

"That's fine, you go right ahead," Paula interjected. "But that's between you and these girls; I'm really not interested, okay? Now I need to do some things upstairs, so I'll say good night." She turned abruptly and started up the stairs.

"Good night, dear." Millie shook her head as she padded back toward the kitchen.

At the top of the stairs, Paula glanced at the closed doors of the boys' rooms. She tapped lightly at TJ's door, then quietly turned the knob and pushed inward. Peering into the darkness and hearing no sound, she moved silently into the room, leaving the door slightly ajar so a narrow shaft of light illuminated her path. Kneeling next to the bed, she saw TJ's still form beneath the covers. He was lying on his side, snoring softly, one arm tucked beneath his head, the other dangling over the side of the bed. Sticking out from beneath his pillow was the blue edge of a book—undoubtedly one of his Zane Grey westerns.

He's been reading in bed again, she mused with a tender smile, recalling her own childhood adventures with books. *Somehow, Nancy Drew was always better late at night, under the covers, with a flashlight.* She reached out to retrieve the small volume and put it back on the bookshelf, then caught herself. *I always hated it when Mom did that.* Instead, she let the book alone and bent to brush her lips lightly across her youngest son's forehead. He stirred briefly, then settled deeper into his pillow.

"Sweet dreams," Paula whispered. She tiptoed from the room and closed the door softly behind her.

Taking a deep breath, she moved down the hall toward Scott's room, setting her teeth against the raucous sounds that grew louder with each step she took. She pressed her open hand against his door; it pulsated with the deep bass vibrations of Kurt Cobain and his grunge band. In a final burst of rage against life, the rock star had finally killed himself. *I'd probably do the same,* Paula thought, *if I had to listen to this heavy metal stuff day and night.* She made a fist and pounded on the door. Hearing a faint "Yeah?" from the other side, she pushed it open.

Assaulted head-on by the nerve-deadening screech of retching steel guitars, Paula faltered momentarily before mentally commanding her feet to move forward into the room. The place wasn't really so bad—although Dante's *Inferno* did come to mind, suggested by wall-to-wall Stephen King horror posters and blood-red bulbs in the light fixtures. *It's just a phase,* she reminded herself grimly. *He'll get over it. At least he keeps his dirty underwear off the floor.* Pasting a smile on her face, she shouted, "Hi, Scotty, how's it going?" Her vocal cords throbbed with the effort to be heard.

Scott, standing with his back toward her, was leaning over his desk, concentrating intently on the paper before him. Sidling up to look over his shoulder, it didn't take Paula long to figure out that he was deeply engrossed in a continuation of the previous night's project. He was putting the finishing touches on an elaborate and intricately designed pen-and-ink drawing of a spider's web. She grimaced. *Ugh. The Crawlers.* Her skin itched to make a quick exit, but she thought better of it. Instead she tapped him on the shoulder, made a pleading gesture toward the CD player, and sighed with relief when he reached over to switch it off.

"So," she repeated, her voice echoing in the suddenly silent room, "how's it going?"

"It's goin'." He had returned to the drawing, and now his nose almost touched the paper as he worked.

Peering over his shoulder, Paula decided to make the best of her son's newfound fascination with household pests. "That's very good," she observed, reaching across the desk to point out a particularly intricate system of webs and channels. *This is not a lie. Weird as it is, the stuff shows artistic merit. Keep that thought.*

"You're in my light." Scott's voice had an irritated edge.

"Oh, sorry." Paula backed away. *At least he's talking. You can take it from here.* "I'll let you get back to your work, but I just wanted to say I'm sorry about last night. I shouldn't have jumped all over you; I know you have your friends and they're important to you. It's just that I worry about all the things that could happen—"

"Well, you worry too much." Scott's voice was flat, and his eyes didn't leave the drawing.

"Maybe," Paula replied. "But I'm a mom; that's my job."

"One of 'em," Scott chuckled humorlessly as he penned a thin line beneath one of the more athletic-looking spiders.

His implication sliced her heart, but she willed herself to respond cheerfully. "Yep," she said earnestly, "but it's the most important one. And it's my favorite." A tight lump rose in her throat when he shook his head silently, still concentrating on the paper in front of him. "Anyway," she continued, "I do care; really I do. I know it seems to you like I'm running interference, but it's only because I know from my own experience—"

"Then why don't you let me learn from *my* own experience?"

"Don't you understand? You can save yourself a world of grief if you'd only—" Suddenly Paula's tongue seemed to freeze against her teeth as her own words echoed in her brain. *No, those are not my words . . . they're my* mother's! How many times had Marjorie Enfield spit them at her daughter across an anger-filled room, and how many times had Paula thrown them back in her mother's face? *You never learned the lessons, did you, Donroe? She made it hurt too much. Don't re-open the wounds now—not with your own child.* For long moments, she stared silently into the space above Scott's head.

"Uh, Mom? You were saying—?" After several seconds, Scott had shifted his attention from the drawing to his mother and was regarding her quizzically. Seeing her face drained of color, he asked, "Are you okay?"

Paula started at his deep voice and quickly pushed her memories away. "Yeah . . . sure. I'm fine," she insisted. "I was just thinking about some things that happened a long time ago." *Be careful. Preaching and reminiscing never worked on you; no reason to think they will on him.* "Nothing important. We can talk about it another time," she smiled. Scott seemed satisfied and turned back to his sketching.

Not willing to release her hold on this slim thread of communication, Paula decided to continue on a more benign note. "So," she said, casually leaning against one of the Stephen King posters, "when I got home a little while ago, Millie had saved me some of her chicken with plum sauce from dinner. Pretty spectacular, huh? I thought I'd died and gone to heaven."

"Yeah, it was great," Scott agreed, wiping an ink-splotched finger on his jeans. "I didn't mind the company, either." He glanced up at her, arching his eyebrows while a small grin pushed his lips upward, deepening the dimple in his right cheek.

"Oh, yes. Millie said she invited a couple of lady missionaries to eat with you. I met them a few days ago when we had a little accident in front of the house."

"Uh-huh, they told us all about it—came to show Millie their new bike, then stayed for dinner. They were kinda weird, always talkin' about their church. But I got over it, and managed to look past all the religion to the really important stuff."

"Important stuff?"

"Yeah, man . . . those two women are *foxes*." His eyes were glistening, and his hands moved to form a rough hourglass shape.

"*Scotty!*" Paula didn't know whether to laugh or to scold him. She opted for a middle course. "They're *missionaries*, for goodness sake!" *And considerably older than you are, I might add. What is this fascination with older women?*

"Aw, I know," he sighed. "I guess they don't date much, what with all the preaching they have to do, and their clothes—well, some of the girls I know could show them the way around Nordstrom's. But I see real . . . *potential* there, you know? What a waste." He leaned heavily against the desk and folded his arms, a forlorn look playing across his face. "All I can say is, I'd like to be there when they turn in their name tags."

Paula gulped. This was a side of her son she'd never seen first-hand, and her thoughts raced. *It's true . . . TJ was right . . . Scotty's discovered the opposite sex. Of course, I knew it would happen sooner or later—but he's only sixteen! I'd hoped this wouldn't start until he was just a little older—say, thirty. But it's too late now . . . he's probably even started shaving. What a choice—the Crawlers or girls. Or both. Fasten your seat belts and remain calm.*

Outwardly, Paula showed little emotion beyond a forced smile. "Well," she observed, "I suppose these young ladies are off limits for the present *(and forever)*, but I'm sure you'll find plenty of other things to keep you busy. *(Have you considered taking up bowling?)* There's always your schoolwork . . ."

"Terrific," Scott grunted.

"And the Crawlers."

"Yeah, I guess you're right." He glanced toward the drawings on his desk. "And I've gotta get these done; we're moving into our new place tomorrow."

"That's nice, dear." *(What? No engraved invitations to the open house?)* "I'll say good night, then." She reached out to pat his cheek. "Don't stay up too late."

"See ya," he murmured, turning back to his drawings as she stepped from the room and closed the door with a soft click.

She had taken exactly three steps when the walls again came to life with the throbbing rhythms of a dead rock king. Shaking her head as she shuffled down the hall toward her own room, she wondered how TJ could sleep through the noise. "The slumber of the innocent," she mused aloud. "Or, in my case, the exhausted."

The air in her room was cool; Millie had left the window open and the drapes pulled back. A light breeze ruffled the ivory sheers, casting delicate shadows on the wall in the soft light of the table lamp. The sheets on Paula's queen-size bed had been freshly changed; the floral comforter was turned back, and several decorative pillows had been piled neatly in a chair near the walk-in closet. Glancing at the two plump sleeping pillows lying side by side beneath the gleaming brass headboard, Paula remembered how she'd fallen into bed the night before, too tired to even think of washing her face. Somewhere, there was a pillowcase smeared with her blush and mascara . . . *but hey, that's what washing machines are for. Bless you, Whirlpool. And you too, Millie.*

Tonight, she carefully removed all traces of makeup and smoothed a thin layer of rich moisture cream over her face before pulling on a royal blue satin nightshirt and slipping between the cool, clean sheets. Lying on her back, she closed her eyes and felt her body melting into the fibers and textures around her, their softness urging her gently into the peaceable twilight of relaxation. She could feel every cell of her body growing heavy, easing into unconsciousness. Moment by moment, she sank deeper into the welcoming valley.

Darn. The light. It was a rude thought at this final edge of wakefulness, but it had to be dealt with. *If I don't turn the silly thing off, it'll wake me in the middle of the night.* Keeping her eyes closed, she laboriously raised an arm that now seemed weighted by several sandbags, reaching sluggishly from beneath the comforter toward the light switch at the base of the lamp. *Almost there . . . almost out . . . almost . . .*

Paula grunted as her hand hit against an unfamiliar object next to the lamp. Her eyes opened reflexively, and she turned her head just far enough to glance toward the light. A small blue object, displaced by her groping hand, now teetered on the edge of the nightstand. Again her reflexes took over, and she reached out to grab the object before it fell. The rapid and unexpected movement set her heart pounding. Clutching the unfamiliar item to her chest, she leaned back against the pillows to catch her breath, her eyes closed but no longer heavy with sleep. Finally, after several seconds of deep breathing, she opened one eye and looked down to see what she had rescued.

"Oh, good grief," she muttered aloud, her lips forming a grim line of frustration. "It's that book those missionaries left." Taking careless aim at an oak waste basket across the room, Paula lifted her arm and let the book fly. When it fell into the basket with a soft whooshing sound, her mouth twisted into a smirk. "And that," she gloated, "is what I think of you Mormons. Foxes or not."

She snapped off the light and once again burrowed into the smooth sheets and soft pillows. Down the hall, she could hear the faint pounding of heavy metal.

CHAPTER 10

A dull thud beneath her open bedroom window wrenched Paula from sleep. "It must be Saturday," she mumbled, recognizing the sound of a basketball landing on the front lawn. The bedside clock confirmed her suspicion that it was still early, so she pulled the comforter over her head and drifted back to sleep.

These weekend morning hours, usually between seven and ten a.m., were sacred islands of time for TJ—hours when he could pour himself wholeheartedly into the pursuit of perfection in dribbling, slam-dunking, and free throwing. There was a regulation hoop mounted over the garage, and the driveway's smooth cement surface, with a well-manicured expanse of lawn on either side, extended nearly a third-court length outward from the house before beginning its gradual slope to the street. It was a perfect practice arena.

Though he had not yet hit his adolescent growth spurt, TJ already stood a respectable five-foot eight, and he had painstakingly developed a long jump shot that could rival those of much taller boys on the high school varsity team. His determination was unflinching; over the next two years, while he was waiting to be old enough and tall enough to make the team, he would do whatever it took to make sure his skills on the court were as nearly perfect as thousands of hours of jumping, shooting, and dribbling could make them.

On rare occasions when Scott joined him on the court, TJ's grin lit up the smoky morning landscape. His older brother was a natural at sports; TJ studied his easy movements and tried to imitate them, practicing smooth turns, lightning dodges, and fluid trajectories long after Scott tired of the game and went looking for excitement with the Crawlers. TJ hoped that one day he would move beyond being a pest and actually make his big brother proud of him.

This morning, TJ had been shooting baskets alone for nearly two hours when the front door swung open and Scott emerged, moving awkwardly down the brick path to the driveway. Each of his long arms pinned two or three large pieces of cardboard to his body, and he was clutching several poster-size papers in each hand. His front teeth were clamped solidly over his bottom lip as he concentrated on pinning, clutching, and walking at the same time. A moderate breeze wasn't making his task any easier.

"Hey, Scotty, need some help?" TJ had already tossed his basketball sideways, where it thudded and rolled to a stop on the lawn. "I can hold some of those if you want," he offered, still catching his breath after having brilliantly executed an imaginary full-court press against the entire Chicago Bulls team.

"Naw, I'm okay," Scott responded, making his way gingerly down the gentle incline of the driveway toward the street. "Ben and the guys are picking me up in a couple of minutes." A sudden puff of wind threatened to dislodge one of the papers; he tightened his grip and turned his back to the gust.

"Oh yeah, it's moving-in day for the Crawlers," TJ grinned. He followed a few paces behind his brother, his baggy white T-shirt billowing in the unsettled morning air. "Didja get all your posters done?"

"What does it look like? You got eyes," Scott growled. Behind him, TJ's steps slowed and stopped as the younger boy shoved his hands into the pockets of his cut-off jeans.

Without warning, a sudden burst of wind curled itself around Scott's midsection, snatched two of the papers, and sent them flying. The teenager could only clench his fists tighter and watch, cursing under his breath, as the drawings twirled lightly on the air currents and fluttered in different directions.

Almost before Scott's epithets cleared his lips, TJ sprang into action and surprised even himself with his speed and agility. Yelling "I've got 'em!" over his shoulder as he lunged for one paper and then the other, he ended up face down, spread-eagled on the far side of the lawn, a dark, damp swath of green staining the front of his shirt from top to bottom. "I've *got* 'em!" he repeated breathlessly and rolled onto his back, holding up both papers for his brother to see. "Both of 'em . . . the spider and—" he glanced up at one of the drawings, "—the snake. I got 'em!" His smile was triumphant as he lurched awkwardly to his feet, one sheet of paper grasped carefully in each hand. Out of the corner of his eye he saw Ben Salter's ancient Chevy pull up to the curb. "Just in time," he panted, running up to Scott and carefully securing the papers under his brother's arm. "The guys are here." He backed off a few paces as Scott shuffled toward the car, then watched as two boys helped load the drawings into the trunk.

Relieved of his burden, Scott quickly opened the car door to join his friends. He had one leg inside the Chevy when he stopped and turned back toward TJ. Raising his hand partway into the air, he shouted, "Thanks, little brother. I owe you one." Then he disappeared inside the car and slammed the door.

TJ lifted his arm in a half wave as the Chevy lumbered around the corner and out of sight, then he walked slowly up the driveway and across the lawn to retrieve his basketball. "I got 'em," he repeated aloud as he wiped his hands on his jeans and eased back into the slow, sure rhythm of a comfortable dribble. "I got 'em."

Paula stretched lazily beneath her comforter, then poked her head out, sat up in bed, and inhaled deeply as the fragrance of freshly brewed coffee made her smile. "Good grief," she mumbled, brushing a few locks of dark hair away from her face, "I've become a TV commercial. 'The best part of waking up . . .' All we need now is the symphony." She lay back against the pillows and closed her eyes, imagining what Millie might be doing in the kitchen. *Mmmm . . . could be a waffle morning. Or I certainly wouldn't turn up my nose at one of her famous Southwestern omelettes.* The thought made her stomach rumble as she tossed back her covers and headed for the shower. A few minutes later, her hair still damp and her lithe body clad in a lavender sweat suit and beige terry cloth slippers, she ambled into the breakfast nook.

"Morning, Rudy," she said, stifling a yawn as the big dog pressed his soft muzzle against her knee in greeting. Reaching down to scratch the top of his head, she asked, "Have you been out yet this morning, pal? I could take you for a quick run."

"Oh, he's fine," Millie's cheerful voice called from near the stove. "TJ was up early, and they went for a walk before he started shooting baskets. That boy is sure determined when it comes to playing ball," she added, a bemused smile playing across her face.

"I know," Paula agreed, "but I have to admit I'm glad to see it. TJ isn't a very social kid, not really sure of himself yet, but he's willing to work hard and do whatever it takes to be a winner. Especially in sports."

"I've noticed," Millie said as she flipped a blueberry pancake on the stove-top griddle. She looked up at Paula. "Scotty used to be like that, didn't he?"

"I'm afraid so," Paula answered. "He's always had a lot of natural ability, but now he seems to feel like the world should do his work for him, just let him coast through life. The most interest he's shown in anything the past few months is this weird preoccupation with the Crawlers. He's terminally grumpy, too; and if that's not enough, he seems to be developing an eye for women lately. It all terrifies me—and I'll tell you, if this is what's ahead for TJ, I hope he *never* grows up."

"Well, I guess there's no way we can stop it—the growing up, I mean," Millie observed. "Probably the best we can do is hope he'll be so involved in sports and other things that the gangs won't have a hold on him. The girls—that will be harder." She shook her head gravely and flipped a few more pancakes.

"Amen," Paula agreed, slipping into one of the oak chairs at the table near the bay window. Rudy had already curled up under the table and was snoring lightly. Millie was just setting out a plate of steaming pancakes when, as if on cue, the front door opened and slammed shut. TJ sauntered in from the entryway, his basketball under one arm, beads of sweat streaming down his forehead. Spying a large laundry basket in the hall near the garage door, he casually aimed and launched the ball. It fell just to one side of the basket, bounced a few times on the floor, and came to rest against the wall. "First basket I've missed all day," he grinned. "I must be hungry . . . what's for breakfast?"

"Nothing until you've made a quick trip to the showers, sports guy," Paula said, eyeing the muddy green stripe down the front of his shirt. "Looks like you've been playing football, not basketball."

"Oh, that," TJ laughed, glancing down at the stain. "I just took a flying leap to catch something. It was *great!*"

"Well, go get cleaned up," Paula ordered. "We'll save some scraps for you."

"Aw, Mom . . ." Seeing the determined look in his mother's eyes, he gazed longingly at the plate of pancakes, then shrugged and bounded from the room.

"Now that," Paula smiled, "will be the fastest shower in the history of civilization. Except, perhaps, for those who bathe with piranhas."

The two women sat for a few minutes in companionable silence, enjoying the sun's warmth streaming through the window, alternating bites of syrupy blueberry pancake with sips of rich coffee and fresh-squeezed orange juice. Earlier, Millie had cut flowers from the garden and arranged them in a small ceramic vase on the table. Their delicate blossoms and subtle fragrance created a mood of familiar intimacy. *Like Norman Rockwell*, Paula mused with quiet satisfaction.

The mood was altered somewhat when TJ strode into the room. His wet hair was slicked back against his head, his cheeks tinged with color from the hot shower. He wore the baggy brown corduroy trousers and blue sweatshirt that had become his regular weekend fashion statement. And he was hungry. "Got any strawberry jam?" was his greeting as he sank expectantly into the nearest chair and grabbed a fork with one hand, a knife with the other. Seeing the orange juice, he laid the knife across his plate and poured himself a tall glass of the golden liquid. His eyes closed as he leaned back in the chair and took several large gulps, then smacked his lips as he set the half-empty glass back on the table. He speared four pancakes with his fork, plunked them on his plate, and slathered them with butter.

While Millie rummaged in the refrigerator, Paula pursued the obvious. "Where's your brother?" she asked. "His bedroom door is closed, and I haven't seen him this morning."

"The guys from the Crawlers picked him up early—around eight. They're moving into their new place today." TJ glanced up at Millie appreciatively as she set an economy-size jar of strawberry preserves next to his plate. "They took a lot of Scotty's pictures . . . guess they're gonna use 'em to decorate or something."

"I think that was the general idea," Paula said as she watched her youngest son pile several large spoonfuls of preserves on his pancakes and spread them with the knife. As he balanced a substantial wedge on his fork and guided it toward his mouth, she asked, "Where is this hangout of theirs, anyway?" She was too late.

"Sumblbm im . . ." TJ shook his head, chewing vigorously, and held up his hand as if directing traffic. Paula waited as he washed down the lump of pancakes with a few swallows of juice. "Give a guy a chance to get a little fuel, will ya?" he sputtered.

"Of course, dear," Paula smiled. She leaned back in her chair. "Take your time."

Several mouthfuls later, TJ came up for air. "Man, that really hit the spot," he sighed after draining his juice glass. "Now, what were you saying, Mom?"

"Oh, I just wondered where the Crawlers might be setting up their new headquarters. Did Scotty tell you?"

"Not exactly, but he said I could go there with him sometime. I think it's a few minutes from downtown—one of the side streets on the north side of the boulevard."

Paula was not pleased to hear this bit of news. She knew the boulevard was home to several of L.A.'s most vicious gangs. "Dare I ask how they found this place?"

The boy's eyes met hers. "You can ask—but you might not like the answer."

"Why's that?" Paula tried to keep her tone casual, but she felt her throat tighten. The morning was beginning to lose its Norman Rockwell feel.

"Uh, it's like this . . . a few years ago it was a crack house—"

Paula groaned and cradled her head in her hands.

"—but the cops cleaned it up real good, and there aren't that many drugs in the neighborhood anymore. The house was a mess, nobody livin' in it, so Scotty said they talked the cops into letting 'em hang out there—promised they'd clean the place up and keep drugs out. That's all he told me . . . doesn't sound too bad, does it?"

"Not exactly the Hardy boys," Paula mumbled through her fingers. "Huh?"

"Nothing. Hey, TJ . . . would you do something for me?"

"Sure—as long as it doesn't have anything to do with girls."

"No problem," she smiled. "Here's the deal: I need you to keep me up to date on what's going on with Scotty and the Crawlers, okay? I'm not asking you to spy, but I want to make sure he's safe and not getting into trouble. Just ask a few questions now and then—know what I mean?"

"Right, Mom, I hear ya. I wasn't born yesterday, y'know." His gaze held hers for a moment, and she caught a trace of humor in his deep brown eyes.

"Yeah, pal, I know." She patted his arm. I just want you to be—"

"I *know* what you want me to be, Mom. You want me to be a *spy.*" He grinned.

"Well, okay," she admitted. "But I want you to be a *careful* spy. Understand?"

"He'll never know I'm watching out for him," TJ promised. His eyes glowed as he moved his hand in a circular motion in front of him. "Smooth as glass."

"That's my boy," Paula said warmly. "I knew I could count on you."

"So what am I, an abacus?" TJ laughed, rising from the table. "I think I'll go shoot a few more hoops, then Jeff Tunney invited me over to play video games. Okay, Mom?"

"I guess so. I have to go to the office for a while, anyway. Have a good one."

"You too. See ya later." The doorbell rang just as TJ bent to scoop up his basketball from the floor. "I'll get it on my way out," he offered, heading toward the entryway.

"Thanks," Paula said, pouring a final cup of coffee. "Breakfast was great," she called to Millie, who had started loading the dishwasher. "Too bad Scotty wasn't here to enjoy it—blueberry pancakes are his all-time favorites."

"Maybe next time," Millie said cheerfully. "You know what they say . . . if you build a breakfast, they will come." She chuckled, then glanced toward the entryway, where she heard voices.

"Sure, they're here," TJ was saying to some unknown visitor. "Yeah, I was just gonna play a little ball. C'mon in."

A few seconds later TJ walked back into the kitchen, the basketball still under his arm. Paula looked up from stirring her coffee just in time to see two young women following close behind her son. They wore nondescript dresses, practical shoes, and black name tags.

Paula's fingers tightened around the edge of the table as she manufactured a frosty smile. *The Mormons again. This can't be happening.*

"Well, good morning, girls!" Millie beamed, bustling over to greet them. "We didn't expect to see you again so soon."

Paula nodded crisply. *We didn't expect to see you again* at all.

The little one—Sister Tibbetts—laughed daintily. "Oh," she explained, "we just wanted to stop by and bring you these." She held out a paper plate of brownies, secured by a double thickness of plastic wrap. "It's to say thanks for a great supper last night. I can still taste that *yummy* plum sauce." She closed her eyes and smacked her lips.

"One of the best meals I've had since I've been in the mission field," Sister Kent added. "And the company was great, too."

Paula grimaced. *My sons. My babies. There ought to be a law against cradle-robbing.*

"And how are you today?" The Tibbetts woman was looking directly at Paula, a wide smile framing her perfect white teeth. "We missed you last night."

"Me? I, uh, had to work late," she stammered.

"Yes, Millie told us you work long hours. We were hoping we might catch you at home today." She set the plate on the oak table.

"Oh?" Paula looked at them sharply. *What do they want now?* "I was just leaving for the office . . ."

"That's all right," Sister Kent interjected. "We know you're busy, and we won't take much of your time. We just wondered if you'd had a chance to read any of the book."

Paula stared at her blankly.

"The Book of Mormon we left for you," Sister Tibbetts prompted. "You did get it, didn't you?" She smiled expectantly.

"Oh . . . yes, of course," Paula replied. A mental image of the book's perfect dive into the waste basket flitted across her memory, causing a small grin to appear at the corner of her mouth. "And you can be sure it's . . . in a safe place."

The two missionaries exchanged glances. "So," Sister Kent inquired, "what do you think of it so far?"

"Well, I haven't actually *read* much of it," Paula admitted tersely. "It seems so . . . so *religious.*"

TJ, who had been leaning against the wall with his basketball still tucked under one arm, walked over to examine the plate of brownies. He lifted a corner of the plastic wrap, then replaced it and turned toward Paula. "Well, Mom, maybe you ought to give it a try," he said.

"Excuse me?" Paula croaked. She stared at him, her eyes wide.

"The Book of Mormon. I was kind of interested in what the sisters said about the angel Moroni and all last night, so I read a few pages. There's this cool guy named Neffi—"

"That would be *Nee-fie*," Sister Tibbetts corrected gently, her eyes sparkling.

"Okay, *Nee-fie*. Anyway, he's just a kid, and he has these two delinquent brothers he's always fighting with. Their dad isn't the most popular guy in town—he's always telling everybody to repent—so the whole family skips town and goes to live in the desert. Then the guys have to go back to town to get some gold plates, and they get into a bunch of trouble trying to talk this guy, Laban, into handing 'em over. So they go back to their old house to get some ransom money, and—"

"Okay, okay," Paula interrupted, holding up her hand. "Sounds like quite an adventure. But I really don't see what it has to do with me."

"The only way you can know that," Sister Kent explained, "is by reading it yourself. The Book of Mormon, like the Bible, is a record of God's dealings with his people in—"

"That's nice, but I really have to get to work." Paula pushed her chair back and stood up. "If you'll excuse me, I'll be going now." She nodded curtly and turned toward the garage door.

"In those?" Sister Tibbetts asked, glancing at Paula's feet.

Terrific. I'm going out the door in my fuzzy slippers. "Uh, well, I guess I'll just go upstairs and change. Nice of you to drop by," she mumbled, moving toward the entryway. Her exit was blocked when a tall, angular frame moved deftly into the doorway and Paula found herself at eye level with the "Sister Kent" name tag.

"Would you do one thing before you go?" Sister Kent spoke softly, but with a certain tone of authority.

"What did you have in mind?" Paula asked as sweetly as her clenched teeth would allow.

"Will you promise to read a little in the Book of Mormon over the next few days? We marked some passages that might interest you, and we'd like to come back and—"

"Whatever . . . if I get around to it." *If pigs fly.* Paula's throat was tight with irritation.

"*O-kay!*" Sister Tibbetts exclaimed, perkier than she had a right to be. "We'll be in touch."

"Right," Paula murmured, swallowing a caustic reply. "Now, I *really* have to go." She elbowed past the taller woman, crossed the tiled entryway in three steps, and disappeared up the stairs. A few minutes later she crept silently downstairs to the TV room, out the basement entrance to the backyard, and into the garage through the back door.

Backing out, she was brought to a sudden stop by the missionaries' bicycles, which were parked squarely in the middle of the driveway. *Uh-oh. Caught in mid-escape.* She felt her face redden with a hot flush of embarrassment, but it was quickly replaced by a flash of anger. She responded by shifting into park and leaning heavily on the horn.

Within seconds the front door opened, and the sisters darted out to move the offending wheels. Their task accomplished, they hurried to the driver's side of the Jaguar. "We're *really* sorry," Sister Tibbetts wheezed apologetically. "If we'd known you were leaving—"

"Never mind," Paula said in a measured voice. "I'll just be on my way."

"Well, it was nice seeing you again. And by the way," she said, her eyes ranging over the Donroe home's meticulously groomed yard, "you have a lovely place here. My dad's in the landscaping business, and I notice these things. You've got a terrific lawn."

"Why, thank you," Paula said, smiling in spite of herself as her irritation subsided and she eased the gearshift into reverse. *Spoken like a true lawn Mormon.*

Late that night, she retrieved the small blue book from her waste basket. "I know I promised. But I never said *when* I'd get around to it. Rest in peace," she whispered as she dropped the book into her dresser drawer.

CHAPTER 11

"Mom . . . Mom? Mom! Telephone!" TJ's insistent voice pierced the mid-morning silence and catapulted Paula into another day. Sunday . . . Millie's day off, a day for cold cereal breakfasts, sandwich lunches, fast-food dinners. Paula drew in a deep breath, yawned, and stretched the full length of her bed.

TJ rattled the doorknob, his voice more urgent now. "Hey, Mom, whoever it is *really* wants to talk to you. Are you gonna get it?"

"Yeah, okay," she mumbled, her throat still raspy with sleep. Then, realizing that he likely couldn't hear her throaty response through the door, she called out, "Got it, TJ . . . thanks."

"Okay, I'm gone," he bellowed back. "I'll hang up the phone downstairs."

Paula threw back the covers, swung her legs over the side of the bed, and reached for the phone on her nightstand. She'd kept the ringer permanently turned off since Scott had begun cultivating the art of day-and-night telephone communication. Besides, Millie was usually around to answer any calls.

She cleared her throat twice and picked up the receiver. "Hello?" To her dismay, her voice was still gravelly.

"So, just waking up, are we? Must've been a great party last night."

The amused female voice on the line had a vaguely familiar sound, but Paula couldn't place it. "Excuse me?" she asked. "Who's calling, please?"

"Well, you can't be hung over—you're way too polite. After one of those all-nighters in college, you were in a foul mood the whole weekend." The voice chuckled amiably. "I remember when we were in grad school . . . that night we snuck over the fence and went skinny-dipping in the dean's swimming pool, then drank champagne until four in the morning to celebrate not getting caught. It was such *fun*, even though you were a total witch when the haze lifted."

A wide grin spread across Paula's face as she listened. "Lauren . . . *Lauren Banks!* That's you, isn't it?"

"The one and only—a voice from your frivolous past. How are you, Paula?"

"Lauren! How many years has it been—ten? Fifteen? We were both just getting started in our careers when we lost touch, and then life got so hectic . . . I'm fine. How did you find me? I mean, I got married, moved a few times, got unmarried—"

"But you never stopped climbing the ladder, and I never stopped watching," Lauren interrupted. "I've kept track of the steady rise of Donroe & Associates over the years, and I knew you were behind every bit of its phenomenal success. You were a rising star at UCLA; no reason to think you'd be anything less than spectacular in the business world."

"And I'd be willing to bet you haven't done so badly yourself, Lauren. In fact, didn't I read about you in the paper a couple of years ago—something about a merger you engineered with Teletronics?"

"Oh, that. It was a cakewalk, but it made headlines because I was a woman. I've had some fun, though, playing with the big boys, and the game has been pretty good to me. Now, if only I could say the same about my marriage . . . but then, I suppose you know all about, shall we say, the 'cost of doing business'?"

"Amen," Paula concurred. "But that seems like a hundred lifetimes ago. Where are you, by the way?"

"I've been in the Midwest for about a year—Chicago. It's okay, but I miss the sunny climate and California beaches. I'll move back as soon as I can sell the little business I've built here. And speaking of business, that's kind of why I'm calling . . . I know it's out of the blue, but I could sure use your help if you're available over the next few days."

"*Moi*, a lowly advertising executive? What's up?" Paula was intrigued.

"Well, there's this thing happening next week at a university back east—a huge women's conference. Women come from all over the country to be there for three days every year. They have all kinds of speakers, workshops, displays—a woman can get information on just about whatever she wants. A lot of them come looking for career opportunities."

"Sounds pretty interesting—like something I wish we'd had back in the seventies at UCLA," Paula reflected. "I assume there's a reason you're sharing this information with me."

"You always were one to get right to the point," Lauren laughed. "Here's the skinny. A few months ago, one of the conference organizers—a professor in the economics department—asked me to participate. She said I'd be making a couple of hour-long presentations on my work in corporate sales and marketing, then I'd sit on a panel with some business and professional types. We'd talk about our own careers and answer questions."

Paula mentally pictured her friend's blazing green eyes, ash-blonde hair, flawless complexion and tall, regal bearing. "The perfect woman for the job," she observed.

"Yeah, well, I don't know about that," Lauren replied, "but I was thrilled to be asked, and of course I said yes. But then last week . . ." Her voice faltered, and the line went silent for several seconds.

"Lauren, are you still there?"

"Yes, I . . ." Lauren coughed and continued in a soft voice. "A couple of days ago my father had a stroke. He's hanging on, but it doesn't look good."

"Oh, I'm so sorry."

"Thanks. He was always incredibly healthy, so this has come as quite a shock to the whole family. You never really expect it, you know?"

Lauren's voice was quavering, so Paula gently moved the conversation toward where she felt sure it was headed. "I know. And you need to be there, don't you?"

"I really do. Mom asked us all to come, so I'm catching a plane to Phoenix this afternoon. We probably won't know for a few days whether or not he'll make it." She cleared her throat and continued in a stronger voice. "Which means I've had to make a choice, and I won't be attending the women's conference. I was calling to see if you might consider taking my place."

"Under the circumstances," Paula said, "I'd say it was the only choice you could make. When exactly is the conference?"

"Wednesday through Friday. Your sessions would be on Thursday morning and afternoon, then the panel is Friday morning. You'd need to be there on Wednesday for some orientation meetings."

"Whoa, that pretty much means the whole week away from my office, doesn't it? I'd have to leave on Tuesday, and the earliest I could get back would be late Friday." Paula's tone was suddenly cool. She'd hoped it could all be done in a day or two.

"I know it's a huge chunk of time," Lauren agreed. "But you'd have a lot of free hours to go to other sessions, catch up on some reading, maybe get in touch with some of your clients in New York. Besides, I seem to recall that you grew up somewhere around there, and thought there might still be some people you know—"

"Where did you say this university was?" Paula asked with renewed interest as she slipped her feet into the terry slippers beside her bed.

"Sorry, I guess I didn't really say. It's in New Haven, Connecticut. Yale University."

Paula sucked in a ragged breath. *Yale—my father's alma mater, where he became a professor after retiring from business. Yale—where he wanted me to study. Yale—the school I turned my back on when I fell in love and out of my family. Yale—a twenty-minute country drive from the home where I grew up. Where my mother still lives. Yale.*

"Paula?"

"Oh, uh, I was just thinking . . . I did grow up in Connecticut. Haven't been back in over twenty years, though, except for a one-day trip to my father's funeral." Paula's throat felt as dry as sand. "I just don't know if I want to . . ."

"Well, look at it this way," Lauren said, her voice taking on a plaintive quality. "Everything's taken care of—air fare, car rental, hotel, meals, even a daily stipend for incidentals. And except for your parts on the program, you wouldn't even have to leave your room if you didn't want to. I've already talked to Dr. Salisbury—the one who asked me—and she's absolutely thrilled that you might come. You've developed quite a reputation for advertising savvy, you know. *Everyone* has heard of you."

Paula smiled through her uneasiness. "Oh? And who is *everyone*?"

"Anyone who knows anything about women—or men, for that matter—in the high-stakes business of advertising," Lauren explained.

"You're one of the best and the brightest, and you'd definitely put a prestigious spin on this conference if you could arrange to be there."

"Oh, come on," Paula protested. "You know I'm a sucker for flattery. *Everyone?*"

"Hey, I call it like I see it," Lauren insisted. "Remember when we hired on in the UCLA student union kitchen, then wrote an exposé for the newspaper about food that was making students sick? We called it 'Botulism Is Beautiful,' as I recall."

"Yeah, you always had an antenna for the outrageous," Paula laughed. "But back to Connecticut . . . I don't know—"

"I'd owe you—forever." There was a hopeful lilt to Lauren's voice. "Or until I treat you to dinner at Planet Hollywood—whichever comes first."

Paula sighed. "You're really serious about this, aren't you?"

"Well, to tell you the truth, I desperately wish it *weren't* happening—you know, my father and all. But as long as it has to be this way, I can't think of anyone I'd rather see representing successful women in business than Paula Donroe."

"Uh-huh . . . setting the hook now, are we?"

"Something like that." Lauren sounded suddenly weary.

"Okay."

"I guess you can have a couple of hours to think about it, but I really need to know before—"

"I said okay. I'll do it."

"You'll do it? You *will?*" Lauren seemed momentarily stunned. "No kidding?"

"No kidding. Now, tell me what I need to do before I change my mind." *Before I lose my nerve and decide that a twenty-minute country drive isn't nearly far enough. Before I utterly fail at being a nice person.*

"This is spectacular! You've just saved the day, you know that?" Lauren was jubilant. "I have everything you need. I'll fax you all the instructions, guidelines, time schedules, and all my notes right away. If you have any questions, either call me in Phoenix or talk to someone at the conference on Wednesday. That should give you plenty of time to pull it together; you could probably do it blindfolded and without thinking, anyway. All you need to do, really, is talk about your business and how you made it so successful. I think these women will be hungry for ideas about how they can make their lives mean something."

"So you think my life *means* something, do you?" A small tide of melancholy rose in Paula's chest.

"Don't you?"

"Oh, I suppose. I guess I don't think about it very much—the meaning of life, stuff like that." *Except on October tenth.* "I just get along the best I can."

"And that, I'd say, is pretty darn good. Something to be proud of. Anyway, you're a major hero in my book, and I won't forget this."

Paula spoke quietly, her thoughts far removed from the moment. "Just give your family my best. I hope everything works out."

A long shower and three cups of coffee didn't help the gloom settling over Paula's day. She slumped in her chair and shook her head, glumly watching the fax machine in the den spit out a stream of Lauren's notes and conference information. *I'm a pushover*, she grumbled to herself. *Here I am, up to my eyeballs in work, and now I'm tooling off to Yale like a debutante on a summer picnic. What was I thinking? Maybe I wasn't thinking at all.*

But Paula knew it wasn't the work. Donroe & Associates would survive her brief absence without skipping a beat; she'd trained her employees to be team players, and they'd simply close ranks for a few days to pick up any slack. The real problem was with her heart. There were far too many searing memories, too many undiluted grievances lying back there in Connecticut to permit a simple drive up the canyon (*the fall colors are spectacular this time of year*), or even a casual knock at her mother's door (*what a surprise—the prodigal daughter returns*). No, she wasn't ready for such complications. This would be a business trip, pure and simple. Her mother would never know she'd been there. That decision made, she closed her eyes and leaned her head back against the soft upholstery of the overstuffed chair. *I could use a monster martini*, she reflected. *Where's a good bartender when I need one?* Her body felt too heavy to move, too tired to obey any mental command.

As Paula's hand rested on the arm of the chair, something cold and wet touched it. Keeping her eyes closed, she smiled and raised her hand slightly—just enough for the cold spot to burrow beneath it and make a soft, whimpering sound. "Rudy," she said, walking her fingers up the dog's soft muzzle and patting the top of his wide head, "you might not make a great martini, but you're awfully good medicine, anyway." He stood patiently beside the chair for several minutes as she stroked his long body, finally relaxing, grateful for the amiable connection they shared.

"Why can't people be more like dogs?" she asked absently, gazing into the retriever's soulful eyes, where she saw nothing but unqualified adoration. "It'd sure change the face of politics." Rudy woofed softly. "You would? You'd consider running for *president*? Well, I don't know if the country could deal with that much of an improvement," Paula chuckled. "But you'd certainly be the best man—uh, dog—for the job." She scratched behind his ears, and his half-closed eyes glazed over with pleasure. "I bet you'd even settle for a reasonable salary—say, a couple of great dog biscuits and a giant bone every day—wouldn't you, pal?" Rudy's tail waved slowly in the still air.

Their pleasant exchange was interrupted by a light knock at the den's open door. TJ dropped his basketball in the entryway, leaned against the door frame, and folded his arms across his chest. "Talking to yourself again, Mom?" he smiled.

"Not a chance," Paula laughed. "I'd bore myself to tears. Rudy, here, on the other hand, is a great conversationalist; he has wisdom beyond his years. Besides, he always agrees with me."

"You're right about that. I've known this big guy most of my life, and he's never talked back to me yet." TJ bent at the waist, making several soft, clucking sounds. The dog ambled over, sat back on his haunches, and pressed himself affectionately against the boy's leg. "Catching up on some work?" TJ looked at the fax machine. Its green "receive" light was blinking, the pages of Lauren's transmission still coming through.

"Not exactly—more like getting ready for an unexpected adventure," Paula replied. "A friend asked me to help her out at a conference back east, so I'll be away for a few days this week."

"When?" TJ was accustomed to her frequent business trips, but always liked to know the particulars.

"I'll leave Tuesday, probably be back on Saturday. Millie has a number where I can be reached. Will you be okay?" It was a question she always asked, even though she had his answer memorized.

"Why wouldn't I be? I'm not a kid anymore. I can take care of myself."

"I know, kiddo," she assured him. "I just want to be sure—"

"Besides," TJ broke in, "I'll be pretty busy. There's a lot going on."

"Oh?" Paula questioned. "New projects at school, or what?"

"You know very well *what*," he insisted. "I've gotta look out for Scotty. You said so yourself—remember the spy stuff we talked about yesterday?" His eyes sparkled.

"Of course . . . how could I forget?" she grinned. "I knew you'd stay on top of it. Any news yet?"

"Naw. He was at the C-house—that's what they call their hangout—all day yesterday, and the guys picked him up again real early this morning. I heard their car out front. It's a noisy old Chevy clunker. Scotty says as soon as he gets his license, he's gonna get a job and get his own car."

Paula's mind reeled. *Oh, joy. The only thing standing between Scotty and his license is driver's training at school, and he's next in line for the course. I can see it all coming—and it ain't gonna be pretty.* "Well, we'll see about that," she said. "In the meantime, just keep your eyes and ears open, will you?"

"You bet, Mom. I'm pretty sure I'll get to see their place in the next couple weeks, soon as they get it fixed up so it's cool. Maybe I'll even take pictures so you can see Scotty's drawings on the walls, and all their other stuff, too."

Paula shuddered at the thought of wall-to-wall crawling things captured on film. "That's nice," she said. "Now, don't forget to keep up with your homework this week."

"Yes, Mutha," TJ replied, stuffing his hands into his back pockets and rolling his eyes with good-natured sarcasm. "I'll be a g-o-o-d boy."

"I know you will, TJ," Paula said, smiling warmly at her son. "You've never let me down yet. Now, I guess I'd better start going over these notes. I've got a lot of reading to do before this conference." She pulled herself forward in the chair and extended an arm toward the fax machine, its tray now bulging with the pages of Lauren's transmission.

"Sure." TJ patted Rudy's head and turned to go. Halfway to the door, he made a U-turn and paused. "Uh, Mom . . . I almost forgot . . . can I ask you about one little thing?" His voice was hesitant.

"Shoot," Paula mumbled, her eyes never leaving the sheaf of papers in front of her.

"Well, I wondered if . . . it's just that . . . I thought it might be all right if—"

"I'm listening," Paula interrupted, still leafing through the pages.

"Yeah, sorry. I just thought I might like to go to . . ." He swallowed self-consciously. "To church. Not today," he added quickly. "Maybe just . . . someday." He shrugged. "No big deal."

The papers stopped rattling, and dead silence hung in the air for long seconds. Finally, Paula's eyes rose to meet the uncertain gaze of her son. "Excuse me?" she asked, her eyebrows forming two high, perfect arches above her wide eyes.

Drawing in a quick breath, TJ continued. "Well, yesterday after you went to work, the missionaries—the sisters—hung out here for a while. They just talked to me and Millie, you know? I asked 'em some stuff about Nephi in the Book of Mormon, then they told us more about their church and invited us to go with them. Millie said she might, an' I said I'd have to ask you. They're gonna check with us later. I'd kinda like to go sometime, you know? They said there's lots of kids my age. They even have a basketball team, and—"

"Whoa, can we slow down here?" Paula raised her hand in a staccato motion. "Tell me, kiddo, what makes the Mormons so all-fired special that now you want to go to church with them? Besides the basketball team, that is." She suppressed a smirk.

"I dunno . . . just a feeling, I s'pose. Nephi seems like a pretty cool kid, the way he's always figuring out the right way to do things, like God tells him to. The sisters said the whole Book of Mormon teaches about God and Jesus and how they love regular people like us, but guys who don't do what they say can get into big trouble. Sister Kent says their church teaches people how to keep the rules and stay out of hot water. I s'pose a guy could do worse than go to church and learn stuff like that."

Paula sighed and leaned back in her chair. "You're probably right about that," she murmured, shaking her head as she pressed her full lips together petulantly.

"Then it's okay?" TJ pressed. "I can go?"

"I didn't say that," she responded tersely. "I said we'll see."

"So . . . when will we see?"

"I really don't know, TJ. Let's talk about it when I get back, all right?" *Give him some time to cool down. No kid thinks about religion for longer than thirty seconds at a stretch, anyway.* "Now, don't you have some baskets to shoot?" Her clipped tone dismissed him as she turned again to the sheaf of papers in her hand.

"Sure, Mom—when you get back," TJ echoed. "And don't worry . . . I'll take care of things here. C'mon, Rudy, wanna go for a walk?" At the sound of his name the dog was in motion, trotting happily after TJ as the boy stooped to retrieve his basketball and disappeared into the entryway. A moment later, the front door opened and closed.

Paula's eyelids felt weighted as she inhaled and released a long, slow breath. *So . . . Scotty's got the Crawlers, and now TJ's got the Mormons. I think I'll have that martini, after all.*

CHAPTER 12

With the possible exception of Paula's office, the boardroom at Donroe & Associates was the firm's most appealing space. It was not a large room, but it had ten-foot windows and was situated in a corner of the building where, on a rare smog-free day, one could look out and see the gray-blue-green Pacific Ocean. The room was papered with narrow stripes in subtle tones of muted burgundy and green on white, and oak-framed pieces of original art hung on the two windowless walls. A cluster of robust green plants nestled in the corner between the windows, where a wide swath of light nourished them for several hours each day. Six forest-green leather chairs circled the oval conference table, and two or three smaller chairs lined the walls behind them. A small oak credenza, used for paperwork, coffee, and refreshments during meetings, sat just inside the door.

Paula had summoned her staff to this room early Monday morning and explained that most of her week would be spent in Connecticut. As she'd expected, it took the group no more than a few minutes to rearrange their schedules to accommodate her absence. Dick would postpone his trip to Dallas and pinch-hit for her with three or four new clients. Ted would meet with the Northridge Electronics group on Wednesday to begin developing an Asian marketing strategy. Then he'd spend a chunk of time in the art department, working with Jennifer to create spectacular visuals reminding the consumer that life would simply not be worth living without a brand-new Campbell lawn mower in the shed. And Carmine? Well, Carmine the Terrible would smile and cajole and water the plants, holding it all together like Super Glue, and Paula would have her to thank when she got back and found things in better shape than ever.

"Thanks, people. I appreciate your help," Paula said as she pushed her chair back and stood. "Anybody want anything from Connecticut?"

"Syrup—maple syrup would be nice," Dick said after a brief silence. "The real thing from New England . . . you can't beat it on hot cakes." His eyelids fluttered briefly as he licked his fleshy lips and patted his broad belly.

"I'll see what I can do," Paula smiled. "In the meantime, I'm putting a little something extra in the kitty—for donuts and such. Make it a sweet week, okay?" The troops nodded appreciatively and began to file toward the door. "Ted, can I see you for a minute?" she asked as he brushed past her.

"Sure." He pivoted to face her. "What's up?"

"I just need to ask a little favor . . . for tomorrow."

"Ask away," he said, his intense blue eyes focusing momentarily on the tiny half-moon shaped scar above the left corner of her mouth.

"Would you mind terribly running me out to LAX? Millie can bring me to work in the morning and pick me up at the airport this weekend, but she has a doctor's appointment the same time as my flight tomorrow. Besides, I'd feel a whole lot better about leaving my new car at home instead of here in the parking garage or at the airport."

"Not a problem," Ted smiled. "What time's your flight?"

"Twelve-thirty. I'll even give you the rest of the day off to sweeten the deal."

"And donuts, too? Boy, it doesn't get any better than that," he grinned.

"You don't get out much, do you?" Paula smirked. "Seriously, I really appreciate this, and everything else you do for me—for Donroe. I know the place'll be in good hands while I'm gone."

"Yeah, well, Carmine will see to that. We're all scared to death of her, you know."

"I know. So am I," Paula laughed.

Darkness had long since settled on the quiet Woodland Hills neighborhood by the time Paula pulled the Jag into her driveway. Her nerves were frayed after a day of unrelenting pressure to tie up as many loose ends as she could before taking off for Connecticut, and now the task of packing loomed before her like a bad weather forecast. It had been so long—what kind of a wardrobe did one haul to New England in October?

Floodlights glared from above the basketball standard and at the sides of the driveway—a sure sign that someone had been playing ball. Gazing toward the perimeter of the yard as she waited for the garage door to rise, Paula could just make out the silhouettes of three individuals—one quite tall, two of medium height—standing on the sidewalk near a small car parked on the street. While she watched, two of them got into the vehicle and drove away. The third person turned and began jogging across Paula's front lawn, then across her driveway as the Jag crept into the garage. She finally recognized the figure as it poised for a few more shots at the basket: TJ. She wondered briefly who his friends were. *Hope he's found some nice kids to play with.* She'd ask him later; but for now, she had at least a couple of hours of packing ahead of her. Nursing that cheerful thought, she pushed open the door leading into the kitchen.

Except for Rudy, the house seemed quiet and empty. Paula kicked off her shoes, glanced at her watch, and shuffled silently into the entryway, where she reached for a small pile of mail on the corner table near the door.

"You're home!"

Startled, Paula whirled around to see Millie standing at the foot of the stairs. "Good grief," she huffed, "do you usually go around scaring people like that, or are you practicing for Halloween?"

"I'm sorry, dear," Millie said mildly. "I was upstairs and didn't hear you come in. Dinner's in the fridge. We had enchiladas; they'll heat up real fast in the microwave. And there's salad—"

"That's nice, but I think I'll pass," Paula said absently as she shuffled through the mail. "I've got to pack for the trip I told you about this morning . . . don't have a clue what to take, but I'll have to figure something out. If all else fails, I guess I could just go shopping when I get there. On second thought, forget that—too much of a hassle." Glancing up, she saw an impish grin spreading across the older woman's face. "What?" Paula questioned.

"Well, I kind of thought you'd be in a dither, what with this trip coming up so quick and all," Millie explained. "I hope you don't mind . . . I called that university where you're going and asked about the weather and such, and what kinds of things the ladies usually wear to this conference. They were so nice—told me everything I needed to know. I packed a few things for you . . . the suitcase is on your bed, so you can add whatever I've missed. Is that okay?"

"Is that *okay*? Millie, you're the absolute best!" Paula dropped her handful of envelopes on the table and gave her housekeeper a quick hug. "You know how I hate to pack, and I've been grouchy all day just thinking about it. This is a *huge* load off whatever mind I have left," she laughed. "How can I ever thank you?"

"No bother. Just go and have a good time. Now, how about some of those enchiladas?"

"You know, I do believe I'm feeling a little hungrier than I did about ten seconds ago," Paula said easily. "Shall we?" Linking arms, the two women walked companionably toward the kitchen.

A dull throb of pain in Paula's lower back woke her from a light sleep just after midnight. She had nodded off in her bedside rocker while reviewing Lauren's notes to the sound of TJ's basketball pummeling the backboard. Opening her eyes, she saw that the sheaf of pages had slipped from her lap and now lay strewn around her bare feet. "Guess I need a softer cushion for this chair," she muttered, bending over to retrieve the scattered papers. "And better sleeping habits."

As she stood to stretch the kinks out of her back, another throbbing caught her attention. It was faint but insistent, and it was coming from down the hall. She groaned inwardly. *Heavy metal. Doesn't that kid want to have eardrums when he grows up?* Pulling a loose robe over her green silk pajamas, she padded down the hall and knocked on Scott's bedroom door. There was no response, so she knocked again, louder. "Scotty?" she called. "Can I come in?"

"It's open," her son's deep voice boomed through the door.

She turned the handle and pushed until the door was about half open and she could see into the dimly lit room. Scott was sitting cross-legged on his bed, clad in gray sweat pants and a yellow T-shirt, hunched over a sketch pad balanced on his knees. His thatch of thick, dark hair hung in his eyes and almost down to his shoulders. Paula was taken aback by his shaggy appearance. *Where have I been while this mane was growing? Time for a trip to the barber . . . I'll tell Millie to see to it while I'm gone. No use ruffling his feathers tonight.* As she moved closer to the bed, he switched off the radio on his nightstand and moved his arm to cover the sketch pad.

"Hi, guy . . . haven't seen you for a couple of days," she said lightly. "I'll be leaving for a few days, so—"

"Yeah, Millie told me. Connecticut, right?"

"Right. I'm flying out this afternoon," Paula confirmed with a quick glance at her watch. "Anyway, I heard your, uh, music, and thought I'd see how you're doing before I take off. I heard your club moved into its new place. Are you liking it?"

"Yeah. It's cool." His tone was distant, distracted, his eyes hooded. The pencil in his right hand tapped the sketch pad restlessly.

Paula sighed. *So much for meaningful conversation.* She leaned against the wall near his bed and nodded toward the sketch pad. "Still working on your clubhouse decor?"

"Not really," he said, flipping the pad face-down. "I was just . . . doodling."

"Ah, doodling. A noble pastime," Paula reflected. "A man I once knew had a promising future as a doodler. He was an artist, actually." Without warning, her eyes glazed over in a fixed stare as the decades fell away.

It was her sixteenth summer and she was with Greg, perched close beside him on an outer ledge of the old covered bridge spanning a serpentine brook on her father's estate. She was curling her fingers in the dark hair at the nape of his neck while he tried to concentrate on sketching a cluster of ducks at the water's edge. Finally, he abandoned the project and did the only sensible thing—he kissed her. She could feel the shy, tentative pressure of his lips on hers, the insistent fluttering of her heart, the late afternoon sun's warmth on their faces, the wiry strength of his arms as he . . .

In the distance, someone cleared his throat. "Uh, earth to Mom, do you read me?"

Wrenched back to the present, Paula felt her face burn. She laughed self-consciously, suddenly grateful for the room's dusky lighting. "Whew, I guess I just drifted off for a minute . . . when you get to be as old as I am, you know, these things happen," she joked, buying time as she breathed deeply to regain her composure. "Anyway, he was a friend of mine and an artist—a good one."

"Whatever happened to the dude, anyway?" Scott's tone was mildly curious.

"He . . . died."

"Oh." A silence. "Did you save any of his stuff?"

"I don't think so . . . well, maybe a couple of sketches, but I don't know where they are. It was a long time ago. What are you working on, anyway?" She reached out a tentative hand toward the sketch pad.

"Nuthin," he said sharply, jerking the pad out of her reach. "Just stuff. I got school tomorrow; guess I'll turn in. See you in a few days . . . could you shut the door on your way out?" Stuffing the sketch pad roughly under his bed, he tunneled beneath the covers and pulled a sheet over his head, bringing their conversation to an abrupt end.

"Sure thing, Scotty. Have a nice week." Paula rolled her eyes as she closed her son's bedroom door behind her and scuffed down the hall. *Love these intimate mother-son chats.*

Millie yawned as she backed her ten-year-old Buick out of the driveway just after dawn. Paula had offered to take the Jag, but Millie preferred the solid, comfortable feel of her Buick to the unfamiliar power of the sleek sports car. As Millie drove, Paula studied her reflection in the visor mirror and applied a few finishing touches of makeup. By the time they eased onto the freeway, she was well into a litany of instructions for the coming week. Millie listened, nodded, and smiled serenely as she made mental notes to check TJ's homework, shuttle Scott to the barber, and call the gardener about a patch of brown grass in the front yard. She'd been doing it all for the past nine years, anyway; what made Paula think this week would be any different?

"Oh, I know you've got everything under control," Paula's voice broke into her thoughts, "but it just seems a little different when I'm three thousand miles away instead of thirty."

"That's what telephones are for, dear," Millie said with a genial clucking sound. "Besides, I don't think you'll have to worry about the boys. Scott's taking the test for his driving learner's permit on Friday; he's determined to pass the first time, so I suppose he'll put in at least a few minutes of study time—"

"If that gang of his will leave him alone long enough," Paula interjected sarcastically.

"Not to worry," Millie soothed. "Scott *really* wants his permit, and I don't think even the Crawlers can make him forget it. And TJ—well, between his schoolwork, his reading, his *Star Wars* videos, and his new basketball buddies, I doubt he'll have much time to get into trouble." She smiled at the thought. TJ in trouble? Only if his older brother put him up to it.

"Hey, that reminds me," Paula said. "Just as I got home last night, I thought I saw TJ with a couple of kids out front. It was dark, so I couldn't really see them, but I think they'd been playing ball—"

"Those are the ones," Millie affirmed. "They played for a long time. Seemed to get along real well. I liked them, too."

"Oh? You've met these kids?" Paula's eyebrows arched as she glanced at Millie, who was concentrating on maintaining a safe distance between her Buick and the large truck in front of them.

"Sure have," Millie replied, keeping her eyes on the road. "One of them was even an all-American on his college team before he—"

"College? TJ's playing ball with *college* kids?" Paula sank back in her seat as an amazed expression filtered across her face.

"Well, not exactly." Millie sighed with relief as the truck lumbered off the freeway. They're the elders."

"The elders?" Fleeting images of shrunken, white-haired men in togas assaulted her brain waves. "What are they, some kind of senior citizens group?"

"Oh, my, no!" Millie laughed. "They're just like the sisters— they're missionaries. Only they're young men."

"You mean—Mormons?" *Terrific . . . just when I thought I'd seen the last of them.*

"That's right," Millie confirmed. "'Elder' is a title they use— instead of their first names, I guess. Anyway, when the sisters were at our place on Saturday, they got talking to TJ and found out he's a basketball player. They said they knew someone who could help him with his game, and naturally his ears perked right up. It turns out their day off is Monday, so they brought these two fellows over after school and introduced them. One of them is real tall—he's the one who was all-American in college. They played and talked, played and talked for hours, until just before you got home. I think TJ had a real good time, and they seem to be awfully nice boys.

They ate with us, and I swear the big one has an appetite the size of Wisconsin."

Paula grunted in displeasure, and her next words had a sharp edge. "Millie, you seem to be pretty generous all of a sudden with our food and facilities. What are these missionaries up to, anyway?"

Millie's hands tightened on the wheel, and her lower lip quivered slightly. "I—I didn't think you'd mind," she said. "They were having such a good time, and TJ invited them to dinner. I couldn't very well shoo them away."

"I suppose not." *Back off, Donroe. Millie was just being her motherly self; you can't blame her for that. It's not like you're too poor to spring for an enchilada every once in a while.* Paula shifted her voice into casual. "You say they play basketball?"

"They certainly do," Millie said, relaxing. "The tall one never stopped talking about his college team . . . BYU, whatever that stands for."

Paula stifled a snicker. *All the Mormons probably go there. I wonder if he majored in lawns.*

"They were real good with TJ," Millie continued. "I think he got more pointers in a few hours than he would've picked up on his own in a whole year. They wanted to play with Scotty, too, but after dinner he just went to his room. Maybe next week . . ."

Paula shot her a sidelong glance. "What about next week?"

"Oh, the elders talked about playing some more on their next day off; I believe they have Mondays to themselves. TJ seemed pretty excited about it—promised them he'd practice hard all week. He kept at it, even after they left."

"I know," Paula observed, recalling the rhythmic dribbling that had put her to sleep the night before. "But this whole thing seems a little strange to me. If TJ really has his heart set on playing with these guys, I just hope they don't flake out on him."

"I don't think they will," Millie said with calm certainty. "If you'd seen them playing . . . they were having every bit as much fun as TJ was. Besides, they told him they were going to check up on his reading."

Paula grimaced. "They're helping him with his schoolwork now, too?"

"Oh, no. The thing is, he's taken a shine to the Book of Mormon, and he—we've been reading it. It's a lot like the Bible."

"So now he's reading the Mormon Bible? That's a pretty far cry from Zane Grey and Louis L'Amour, don't you think?"

"I guess so, but I don't see any harm in it. The book teaches about God and Jesus, and about people who risked their lives to do what God told them—"

"Wait a minute," Paula interrupted. "Isn't this the same book you told me about a few days ago—the one some angel hid in a mountain or something?"

"Something like that," Millie chuckled. "You told the sisters you were reading it, remember?"

"Oh, that," Paula sputtered. *Well, I looked at the cover.* "I'm not really into one-size-fits-all books about religion."

"Even the Bible?"

"I read some of that, but it was when I was a kid. You know, the interesting parts—Daniel in the lions' den, Moses parting the Red Sea on his way out of town, those three fellows with strange names getting tossed into a furnace, things like that. Great stories—I think I even read a few of them to the boys when they were little. But they were just stories; we've all outgrown them by now."

"Don't you believe in God? We've never really talked about it, but I thought you did." Millie sounded slightly confused.

"Oh, I suppose I do, in a general sort of way," Paula said. "I mean, everybody likes to think there's a higher power out there, looking out for the human race in some sense, or at least watching while we muddle through our lives. If that's believing in God, I guess I do. But I wouldn't exactly say we have a meaningful relationship." She smiled at her own cleverness.

Millie nodded. "I think a lot of people feel the same way. I've always liked to think of God as someone who cares about me—cares *for* me, you know? Like a father who keeps an eye out for his children. In fact, that's what the missionaries call him—Heavenly Father. They say he really is our father, that we knew him before we were born, and we'll go back to him when we die. It makes sense to me."

"Uh-huh," Paula said grimly. "Well, if he's anything like my own father was, he's too busy at the office to care much one way or the other." She shook off the memory with a toss of her dark hair. "We're almost downtown. Is there anything else we need to talk about?"

"I don't think so," Millie said as she turned carefully into the light stream of early morning traffic a few blocks from Paula's office building. "We have your number at the hotel in case anything comes up. When should we expect you home?"

"Probably Saturday, no later than Sunday. It'll depend on how things go (*or don't go*). I have a couple of old acquaintances (*like my mother*) that I might get in touch with (*but probably won't*), so everything's up in the air at this point. I'll take a taxi from the airport when I get back. Don't worry about meeting me."

"Whew!" Millie exclaimed as she pulled up in front of Paula's building. "LAX is a nightmare on the weekends, so that's a relief. Have a nice trip, dear. We'll be just fine."

"I know you will. And thanks bunches for everything—especially the packing," Paula said. She retrieved a suitcase and a small carry-on from the backseat. "If it weren't for you, I'd still be trying to figure out what to take—and I'd probably get it all wrong."

"Oh, pooh," Millie grinned. "Go, have a good time. Show all those ladies what *real* class is. We'll expect a full report."

"Count on it," Paula said as she slammed the car door. She waved at Millie, picked up her luggage, and disappeared through the glass doors.

"I really appreciate this, Ted," Paula said as she sank back into the supple green leather upholstery of his Jeep Cherokee. "It's been a wild day, and facing this freeway traffic would've been the frosting on the cake." She stretched her arms and legs in front of her, taking a moment to admire the rich burgundy color of her form-fitting silk pantsuit.

"No problem. It isn't every day a guy gets to chauffeur the boss and take the rest of the day off." Ted smiled as he pulled into the freeway traffic. "I might just take a run along the beach on my way home. To celebrate."

"To celebrate what—my leaving?" Paula questioned absently. Her brain was beginning to wind down, her body starting to relax as the road hummed beneath them.

"Well, there's a thought," he laughed. "Actually, I had more of a life-liberty-pursuit-of-happiness type of celebration in mind, with 'liberty' being the operative word. Something along the lines of 'Free at last! Free at last! Thank God almighty, I'm free at last!'"

"Mmmm? Since when did you become a Martin Luther King, Jr., fan?" Paula was starting to feel drowsy in the warmth of the sun streaking through the windshield.

"Since his words came to sum up my life," Ted grinned. Making a grandiose gesture with one arm, he said in a formal tone, "I am pleased to present to you, Madame Donroe, the newly single, newly emancipated, newly divorced Mr. Ted Barstow. As of this day, the infamous Janice Barstow, a.k.a. Jezebel, jerk, and juvenile, is history. We are, as they say, *kaput*." He sighed contentedly and gunned the Cherokee's motor.

"No love lost between the two of you, I gather," Paula murmured.

Ted grunted. "You know, sometimes this seems like a full-length feature nightmare. Janice was always so pretty, so smart, so pleasant. Kind of like a wolverine in Meg Ryan's clothing. I really wanted to make it work, made myself believe I could, even forgave her the first time she stepped out on me—and the second. After that, it was pretty much all downhill." He snickered grimly. "Funny thing . . . she always insisted that I call her *Janice*—got her nose out of joint when I called her Jan." His grip tightened on the steering wheel. "She called me on it for the umpteenth time during one of our worst fights, and I nailed her. 'Fine,' I said. 'I'll be happy to put the *ice* back in your name. It seems to be everywhere else in our relationship, doesn't it, Jan-*ice*?' She was hopping mad—hopped right off to bed with another man, in fact. Needless to say, we separated soon after."

"You always did have a way with words," Paula chuckled.

"Yeah, I know. Sometimes I'm not sure if that's a blessing or a curse, though."

"It won you a Pulitzer," Paula reminded him.

"Hey, I guess it did, didn't it?" When Ted glanced over at her and grinned, she noticed the crinkled laugh lines around his eyes and mouth.

They rode in comfortable silence for several minutes, until it occurred to Paula that this was the perfect opportunity to pursue a question that had gnawed at her for months. She decided to jump in with both feet.

"Uh, Ted, as long as we're on the subject of your creative gifts . . ."

"Ah, yes . . . a subject I never tire of," he said easily.

"I've been wondering about something lately. I hope you don't mind if I ask . . ."

"Shoot," he said breezily. "My life's an open book, boss lady." He pursed his lips and looked as though he was about ready to start whistling a Broadway tune.

"Well," she began, "I'm always a little bit awestruck when I come to your office—"

"Sheesh, is this gonna be a lecture about neatness?" he said, knitting his brows into a solid line and assuming a pained expression. "I never was very good at—"

"I said *awe*struck, not *dumb*struck," Paula broke in. "Give me a little space here, will you?"

"Sorry."

"So, where was I? Oh, your office . . . I was referring to your wall-to-wall collection of pictures and mementos. Seems like you've been on a first-name basis with pretty much every major world figure of the past two decades."

"Yeah, it's quite the rogue's gallery, I'll admit."

"We've never really talked about it," Paula continued, "but you must be awfully proud of your accomplishments. I mean, you've traveled the world and written stories about people and places that most of us can only fantasize about."

"Right again. It was great while it lasted." His suddenly detached tone sent a tiny shiver of warning down Paula's spine, but she persisted.

"While it lasted? Ted, you were at the top of your business, a world-class journalist who had the eyes and ears of everybody who was anybody. But somewhere along the line, you made a choice to do advertising work instead. So now you're writing about lawn mowers instead of space launches, consumer daydreams instead of consumer fraud, ice cream instead of—"

"And I do a pretty good job of it, too," Ted snapped. "Unless, of course, you have any complaints . . ."

"Are you kidding? You're the best thing that ever happened to Donroe. I'd say journalism's loss was definitely the advertising world's gain. It's just that—well, I can't help wondering what made you change your focus."

A muscle along Ted's jaw knotted into a tight spasm. After a long silence, he spoke in cold, carefully modulated tones. "I don't see why in the world that would interest you."

Paula knew she'd hit a nerve, but she had to know. *Keep it light, Donroe.* "Why wouldn't it interest me? *Everything* interests me—especially when it means good business. And you're *very* good business, Ted." She put a hand on his shoulder and squeezed gently.

His tense muscles relaxed, but his guard was still up. "Gee, boss, I didn't know you cared," he said lightly.

"What am I, another Jan-*ice?* Of course I care. So, what's the scoop?" She stared at him intently.

"The 'scoop'," he glanced at his watch, "is that you'd better hurry if you want to catch your flight. No time to hunt for a parking place." She looked up just as the Cherokee reached the check-in curb. *Rats.*

Ted let out a long breath as he opened the door and swung his feet to the pavement. "I'll get your luggage."

"Okay, okay," Paula grumbled. "But promise me we'll continue this conversation when I get back."

"You're the boss." His smile was cheerful, but not quite carefree as he delivered Paula's bags to the skycap and turned to face her. "Now, you go out there and wow 'em with all your business savvy. We'll do our best to keep the wheels grinding for the next few days without you."

"Gee, thanks," she said glibly, then more seriously, "You know, I've been so busy getting ready that I haven't really had much time to be nervous. But now that I think about it," she gulped, "I'm not all that sure I can—"

"You'll be great." In a sudden rush of movement, Ted wrapped his arms around her and brushed his lips across her cheek. A second later, he stepped back awkwardly and cleared his throat. Raising his hand to his forehead in a mock salute, he said gruffly, "Catch ya later, chief." Then he disappeared into the Cherokee.

"Ma'am?" The skycap's gravelly voice finally penetrated her consciousness as she stared after the Jeep. "Here's your ticket. The gate's to your right."

"Oh, uh, thanks," Paula said absently, tipping him with a crisp bill. She moved slowly toward the building's double doors as her eyes remained locked on Ted's vehicle. "I'll just be . . . on my way." Moments later, she turned and disappeared into the airport.

CHAPTER 13

The university had made good—and then some—on its promises. A luxury rental car was waiting for Paula at the Hartford airport, along with directions to the Westbury Inn, a charming Victorian bed-and-breakfast only a few blocks from campus. With the time difference, it was late evening by the time a tall, courteous young man ushered her into a cozy second-floor room. "Have a pleasant stay," he said as he deposited her bags near the queen-size bed. By the time he closed the door softly behind him, she had already kicked off her shoes and folded herself into one of two overstuffed chairs near the window.

"Now, this is hospitality," she murmured. Everything about her surroundings suggested a comfortable intimacy—antique crystal light fixtures, wallpaper etched with delicate floral patterns, the intricately carved French armoire set against one wall, a thick down comforter and pillows on the bed, scents of floral potpourri and bayberry candles. The room seemed to invite her back into an easier century, where time wasn't measured by the eerie glow of a digital box in the night, but by the slow, measured cadence emanating from the steadfast heart of a benevolent grandfather clock in the hallway. There was, in fact, just such an elegant timepiece standing at attention in one corner of this room, its gentle ticks and mellow tocks soothing Paula into a relaxed, meditative mood. "Thank goodness," she sighed, "there's more to life than the Marriott."

It was a full hour before she reluctantly stirred from her chair, and then only because the clock bonged a gentle reminder that it was past midnight. Her Wednesday would begin with an early-morning meeting, so she rummaged in her suitcase until she found the small travel alarm Millie had packed. As she adjusted the time and positioned the angular, plastic-cased clock on a walnut table beside the bed, it seemed out of place in this winsome nineteenth-century alcove of subtle shapes and shadows. But it would have to do.

Now to get comfortable. In three or four deft motions Paula had shed her suit and blouse, and was pawing through her suitcase looking for something to sleep in. She knew she'd found it when her hand brushed across the smooth cotton fabric of her favorite nightshirt, and she tugged on one sleeve to pull it from beneath a small cluster of brightly colored silk scarves. Slipping it over her head, she stretched her arms into its sleeves and sighed languidly.

Within minutes, she had burrowed deep beneath the thick down comforter, filed her brain in some shadowy mental library for safekeeping, and was adrift on a soothing swell of unconsciousness. For the moment, Paula Donroe was in a safe harbor where nothing and no one could disturb the pieces of her broken past or call up visions of her strangely unsettled future. Tomorrow was another day, and she would take it on its own terms . . . but tonight, comfortably secreted away in this pristine Victorian hideaway, she was at peace.

A curious sense of well-being accompanied Paula through the next day's activities. Perhaps it was the clean, bracing autumn air— such an invigorating contrast to the heavy, almost palpable smog that settled in for months at a time to obscure the southern California skyline. Or it might have been the campus itself, so animated yet at the same time comfortably staid and unaltered, even after 300-odd years of accommodating the best and the brightest. She had last walked these Ivy League corridors nearly a quarter of a century earlier as a sixteen-year-old high school junior, taking AP journalism classes twice a week. In those days, she had approached the campus with a sense of reverence, even awe. Today, she felt right at home.

It might also have had something to do with the red-carpet treatment she received—a sumptuous breakfast in the private faculty dining room (cloth napkins and no greasy student fare, thank you very much), personal welcomes from the university president and a handful of deans, cordial orientation meetings with student leaders, faculty, and other participants, and even a tour of the large lecture hall—an auditorium, really—where she would make her presentations. *This is a big deal,* she thought to herself as she lifted a crystal goblet of iced mineral water to her lips during a luncheon with the president's wife. *Imagine that. I'm a big deal.*

Late in the afternoon, the sun was beginning to lose its hold on the sky, slipping reluctantly behind one of the massive stone buildings on the west edge of campus. Paula's official obligations had ended a few hours earlier, so she'd spent some time in the library and bookstore. She smiled as she purchased several volumes to add to her business library at the office. *They'll never come up with a computer that smells like a good book.*

Now, as she walked alone in semidarkness toward the Westbury Inn, a brisk wind snapped at her dark hair and chased a few gold-crimson leaves across her path. She was glad for the sweater coat Millie had packed, and she buttoned it to the top for her quarter-mile journey. By the time she reached the Westbury's quaint, dimly lit lobby, her nose and hands were tingling. She liked the feeling . . . there was a certain *aliveness* to it.

Knowing she'd be spending the evening in seclusion to prepare for her lecture the next morning, Paula had stopped at a small deli near the hotel and picked up a chicken salad, a few cinnamon-raisin bagels, some cream cheese, a large cluster of red seedless grapes, and a bottle of Chianti wine. It had been several hours since lunch, and her stomach was rumbling as she pushed open the door to her room. It was neater than she'd left it in the early morning hours, and there was fresh coffee brewing on a small table near the armoire.

Her bed linens had been expertly changed, and a glistening foil-wrapped chocolate mint rested self-importantly on one of the blue and white striped pillowcases. *Okay, it's your call,* she thought with a rush of self-indulgence as she kicked off her shoes and tossed her parcels and attaché into the nearest chair. She unwrapped the mint and popped it into her mouth as she sprawled on the bed. Tilting her head back, she closed her eyes and felt the smooth candy melt and drizzle slowly, seductively down her throat. *Dessert first. And then maybe just a little . . .*

"Good *grief!*" Paula was suddenly wide awake, her heart thumping and her throat tightening in panic as the grandfather clock told her how long she'd been asleep. "What in the world do they put in those mints, anyway? So much for a long, leisurely evening of collecting my thoughts and planning a dynamite presentation," she lamented. "At this point, it'll be more like a *firecracker* presentation. Or a popgun, if I don't get busy."

As her adrenalin kicked in, she changed into her nightshirt, poured herself a cup of coffee, and began to munch on a bagel. Then, sitting cross-legged on the bed with a yellow legal pad balanced on her knees, she started to make notes. It was three in the morning by the time her plan was laid out, but she was satisfied with the sense and feel of it. She sighed deeply, laid her notes on the unused side of the bed, and switched off the lamp beside her. Then, easing her tired body beneath the comforter, she lowered her head to the cool pillow and closed her eyes. Lying still and relaxed, aware that she had only three hours before the alarm was set to go off, she expected sleep to overtake her in a matter of seconds. It didn't. Thoughts, images, memories, regrets swirled in her mind like fireflies. *Must've been the coffee,* she thought.

Half an hour later, she switched on the lamp and grunted irritably. *Gotta put my best face forward in a few hours . . . these girls need a cheerleader, not a zombie. Just relax, Donroe. Count sheep or something. Read a magazine, a travel brochure, a room service menu—anything to slow down the brain waves.* She pulled open the nightstand drawer and reached in to rummage through its contents.

Her hand brushed against something small and firm. Curling her fingers around the edge of it, she lifted the object into view. It was a small paperback book with an intense blue cover, highlighted by the striking golden figure of a robed man pressing his lips to something that looked like a long bugle or trumpet. Oddly, the way the book was positioned in her hand, the burnished figure seemed to be aiming his instrument directly between Paula's eyes, so lifelike that she felt a momentary impulse to duck. "What in the world—?" she wondered in a half-whisper.

Then her gaze fell on the title of the book, and her eyes narrowed. "Humpf," she grunted. "The Book of Mormon. This one looks different—certainly more imaginative than the plain blue cover Millie has. I wonder if it's really the same book. Strange that someone left it here." She idly turned back the cover, revealing a small, pasted-on Polaroid snapshot of a young family—father, mother, and three children, all smiling out at her like long-lost relatives. Beneath the picture was a brief handwritten note "to whoever might find this book," assuring the reader of its truthfulness and divine origins. It was signed, *Your friends, the Hillman family. February, 1982.*

A bemused smile flitted across Paula's face as she studied the volume more carefully. "This book is in perfect condition," she observed. "No one would ever guess it's nearly twenty years old. Not an overwhelmingly popular choice for bedtime reading at the Westbury, I guess. On the other hand . . ." She grinned wickedly as a thought occurred to her. "This could be just what I was looking for— a sure-fire cure for insomnia!" Leaning back against her pillows, she began leafing through the book's front pages. "Let's see now, where does the story start?" she muttered. "TJ said something about a kid and his brothers . . . oh, here it is." Stifling a tiny yawn, she began: "'I, Nephi, having been born of goodly parents . . .'" Her thoughts began to wander. *Goodly? What an odd word. But then, these were pretty odd people, from what TJ said. They probably didn't even exist; somebody just made up a good story—or is that a* goodly *story? Ho hum. They're putting me to sleep already.*

As her eyes moved from verse to verse, Paula's expression quickly changed from bored to annoyed. "This isn't a book," she finally scoffed aloud, "this is a tedious exercise in meaningless repetition. 'And it came to pass,' 'And it came to pass,' 'And it came to pass' . . . couldn't this Nephi think of anything better to start his sentences with? He'd never have made it in the advertising business." She slammed the book shut, and with a final glance at the golden figure on its cover, shoved it under her pillow. "Rest in peace, Nephi, honey," she cooed with more than a little sarcasm. "Too bad you couldn't have found yourself a *goodly* editor."

As she reached over to turn off the lamp, the brown paper bag from the deli caught Paula's eye; it was leaning crookedly against the arm of a chair near the window. Her bottle of Chianti extended a few inches above the notched top of the bag, glowing a soft rose color in the room's dim light. "Well, looky there," she murmured, throwing back the comforter. "I believe I've just found the answer to my sleep-deprivation dilemma." She moved quickly across the room, opened the bottle, and found a crystal tumbler in the bathroom. Moments later, a small measure of the rosy liquid was swishing down her throat with a sultry promise of deep relaxation.

"Now, that's more like it," she sighed after a few more swallows. "And it came to pass," she said in a deep voice, lowering her head once again to the pillow, "that I, Paula Donroe, having been comforted by *goodly* spirits, did lie down to a peaceful night's sleep. So there."

"A brilliant presentation, Paula—one of the best I've heard." Carla Transtrum, associate dean of the business school, was pumping Paula's hand. She was a tall, spindly woman who looked like a woodpecker but had kind, intelligent eyes. "We hope you'll join us again next year. Can we count on you?"

TJ's abacus joke sprang to Paula's lips, but she stifled the impulse and smiled sweetly instead. "Why, I'll certainly think about it. But first things first—can you tell me where I can get a good cup of coffee?" It was late morning, and her energy was flagging in the wake of too little sleep followed by her high-octane performance in front of two hundred bright-eyed, aggressive young women. *I was them, twenty years ago,* she mused. *I'm still them—but tireder. Lonelier.* She smiled ruefully.

"There's a little espresso place over in the Student Union. They have the best coffee in New Haven," Dean Transtrum said proudly. "You can get there by—"

"I think I saw it yesterday on my way out of the bookstore," Paula broke in. "I'll just run over there for a few minutes, then maybe I'll sit in on a couple of the other sessions before my next one this afternoon. Would that be all right?"

"Oh, of course," the dean said brightly. "You just feel free to go anywhere, do anything that suits you. We'll see you later, then?"

Paula nodded. "Three o'clock sharp, at Smythe Hall." Her afternoon presentation would be a repeat of this morning's, but she hoped to add a slightly different perspective by talking about husband-wife partnerships. She grimaced as it occurred to her that she and Richard had, in a sense, been casualties of the advertising wars. There were far too many beautiful women in this business, and he wanted them all—darn near had them all, too. *How to Fail in Business without Really Trying*. Well, maybe she wouldn't go into the partnership thing after all. She'd think about it over a few cups of coffee.

Leaving behind the throngs of women crowding the large lecture halls in the business and communications building, Paula hurried down one of its long marble corridors toward a glass door marked "Exit." From there, it was only a short stroll to the Student Union. As she strode down the hall, her peripheral vision registered banks of glass display cases mounted on either side of her. Without slowing her pace, she took in two hundred years' worth of memorabilia—plaques, trophies, citations, turn-of-the-century office machines, a monstrous paperweight with the initials "FDR" emblazoned on its brass trim. And there were photographs—Einstein, the Pope, Albert Schweitzer, Amelia Earhart, JFK (a Harvard man, but what the heck?), Bill and Hillary, Paula's father . . .

"*Daddy?*" Her gait collapsed in midstride, and she stood stock still as the intense gray-brown eyes of Howard Enfield gazed out at her from one of the smaller glass cases. There was simply no mistaking the high, broad forehead haloed by distinguished gray-flecked hair; the dark, bushy eyebrows that knit together in a solid, unbroken line when he was perplexed or displeased; the full lower lip and tight upper one, giving him a perpetually brooding appearance; the two-inch scar at his temple, a wartime testament to some young Japanese soldier's faulty aim.

Long moments passed as she stared, transfixed, at the photo. Then her eyes moved to a small brass plaque at his right: "With deep appreciation for substantial gifts and perpetual scholarship endowments, and for distinguished faculty service."

Seeing him there on the wall shouldn't have surprised her, really; he'd given a lot of money to his alma mater over the years—maybe more than anyone else, certainly enough to finance several new buildings. It was simply *seeing* him that momentarily sucked the breath out of her. When had she last seen him? That was easy—at his funeral, seven (or was it eight?) years ago. He hadn't looked his best then (what did she expect? he was *dead*, for goodness' sake—taken quickly by a heart attack), but at least she'd been able to look down at him and mentally put some closure on the scattered remains of their kinship. Now Marjorie, her mother, was the only one left . . . and this photograph was a stark reminder that the woman from whom she'd been estranged for more than two decades was, at this moment, a twenty-minute drive away. The thought unnerved her. *I should go . . . I can't . . . but I should . . . it was her fault, all those years ago . . . but I should . . . but I—*

"Oh, shut up," she chided herself aloud as she spun away from the display case and strode toward the exit sign. *What are you afraid of?* she continued silently. *A confrontation? Get real; you've spent your life dealing with confrontation. Maybe what you're most afraid of is—* She couldn't say the words, even to herself, until they came from nowhere and stuck in her throat. *Maybe what you're most afraid of is reconciliation.*

"Yeah, right," she muttered, pushing through the exit door to leave her disquieting thought behind. "I'm just tired. I'll think about it again when I've had a good night's sleep. Now, where's that little espresso place?"

Paula's afternoon presentation drew a large crowd, and their questions cut right to the heart of the advertising business. Sensing their interest and ambition, she couldn't help remembering why she'd chosen this career in the first place. She'd wanted to make the world brighter, happier, more fun—for herself, for her friends, for her children. Looking back, she thought she'd done it for all the right reasons. *Just one catch,* she observed wryly as she looked out over a crowd of firm-fleshed young women half her age. *At this point in time, I'm too tired to have fun, my only friends are an old dog and a new car, and my children don't care. Who would've guessed?*

Sheer exhaustion propelled Paula back to the Westbury after an early dinner. All she could think of was kicking off her suede pumps, peeling off her Armani suit, and slipping into a comfortable terry robe. She would take a long nap, then simmer in the tub for an hour or so before bedtime. The only conference item on her agenda for the next day was a two-hour panel in the morning, where she and four other successful businesswomen would each make a few remarks and then field questions from the audience. The best thing she could do to prepare, she told herself, was to get a good night's sleep.

The phone was ringing as she pushed open the door to her room. It was Carmine, calling to report that things were going smoothly at the office. Paula was relieved at the news; her eyeballs ached with weariness, and she wasn't in the mood to put out any fires just now. "You're terrific, Carmine," she said appreciatively as she shrugged off her sweater coat and sank into an overstuffed chair. "I knew you'd keep the Donroe team on target."

"Oh, target shmarget," the younger woman laughed. "You underestimate the power of the almighty donut to keep us on our best behavior. But I'm guessing the sugar high can't last forever, y'know what I mean? So, inquiring minds want to know . . . when will we see you again?"

"Gee, I thought you'd never ask," Paula replied. "Tell all those 'inquiring minds' that I'll expect to see them—preferably with bodies attached—at staff meeting first thing Monday morning. I have one more conference session tomorrow, then I might do a little shopping, or" —a fleeting image of her father's photo flashed through her mind— ". . . see a few people, maybe some old friends. I'll be back in L.A. over the weekend. Until then, I'm sure you've got everything under control."

"Yeah, but you know this group. We'll all be glad when our leader is back."

"Oh, Carmine, you flatter me. Please don't stop," Paula grinned.

"Okay, but it'll cost you. Aren't I up for a raise next month?"

"Oooh, I should've seen that one coming," Paula joked. Her voice took on a more serious note when she added, "I haven't forgotten about it, you know . . . of all people, you certainly deserve something special. We'll talk next week, all right?"

"All *right!*" Carmine sang out, obviously pleased with this turn of the conversation.

"All right, then," Paula echoed. "In the meantime, keep an eye on things for me out there, will you?"

"Don't even ask. I've got it covered. And thanks."

Paula hung up the phone and turned her attention to the matter of getting comfortable. The shoes and clothes were off, the robe was on in less than two minutes, and her tired mind was just steering her tired body toward the bed when an unexpected thought occurred. *Maybe I should call home.*

"So what am I now, E.T.?" she grumped aloud as she fluffed a pillow. "Millie would call if anyone needed me." *Still,* she argued silently, *it'd be nice to hear the kids' voices—if they're even home. My nap has waited all day; I guess it can wait a few more minutes.* She punched in the numbers.

Scott answered after the second ring. "Well, this is a surprise," she said. "I mean, it's nice to find you at home for a change, but I thought you'd be out with the Crawlers. Did your friend's car break down or something?" She couldn't hide the trace of sarcasm in her voice.

"Hi, Mom," Scott replied dully. "Sorry to disappoint you, but it's nuthin' like that. I guess you didn't remember . . . I have the exam for my learner's permit tomorrow. Gotta hit the rule book big-time tonight if I'm gonna ice the test. A bunch of the driver's ed kids are takin' it at eight in the morning."

"Oh, gosh . . . it's been so wild back here, I guess it just slipped my mind," Paula lied. *Yeah, like a root canal would slip my mind.* "When do your driving classes start, anyway?"

"Monday, for whoever passes the test."

"That's . . . that's great, dear. I'm sure you'll be one of the lucky ones." Her voice warmed as she added, "You've got a good head, Scotty, and you can do whatever you set your mind to. I just hope . . ."

"You just hope *what?*" the teenager snarled. "That I'll set my mind to whatever *you* want? That my 'good head' will make you look good in front of your friends?"

He thinks I have friends. Does that mean he also thinks I'm human? Don't get your hopes up, Donroe. "No, Scotty, I just meant . . . you're a smart kid, that's all. I hope you'll find what makes you happy and do it." *Soon. Before your life goes down the toilet with the rest of the gang.*

"Right, well, I'm workin' on it," he said sullenly. "I gotta get back to the rule book now. Millie went to the store. You wanna talk to TJ? I think he's around." Scott set the phone down before she could respond.

You have a pleasant evening, too, dear.

Moments later, TJ picked up the receiver. "Is that you, Mom?" His buoyant young voice warmed her through. "Howzit going?" He sounded slightly out of breath—probably just came in from shooting baskets.

"Pretty good," she reported. "I've been going to a lot of meetings, talking to a lot of people; they're keeping me awfully busy, but it's fun. How about you, kiddo?" She lowered her voice conspiratorially. "Any, you know, *news* along the creepy-crawly front?"

"What, you mean the Crawlers?" TJ laughed. "'Fraid not, Mom. It's been pretty quiet around here. A couple of the guys came by last night, wantin' to cruise the boulevard, but Scotty just kicked 'em out. He's been studyin' like crazy. He isn't gonna let *anything* get in the way of his passing that test tomorrow."

"I know," Paula said. "He told me about it. I'm sure he'll do just fine."

"Well, he'd better, because if he doesn't, we may all have to leave home for a few days. You know his temper."

Paula shook her head. "Don't remind me. Is everything else under control?"

"Yeah, sure. I banged up my knee a little playing ball yesterday, but it's fine. Are ya gonna be gone much longer?"

"Only as long as I have to," she promised. "I miss you guys, and I'll be home in a couple of days—Saturday or Sunday, I guess."

"Cool," TJ said. "Maybe you can go with us to—" His voice broke off suddenly, and there was a long silence followed by a low-pitched "Uh-oh."

"What? Go with you where? I didn't think your team had a game until next—"

"It's not basketball, Mom."

"Well, what then? I can't guarantee I'll be back in time, but I can try to—"

"It's church."

"Oh. I see." A deep silence. *He's on his own to explain this one.*

"See, uh . . . ," her son began haltingly, "the sisters came over to see Millie last night. They were talking, so I sat in and listened. It was pretty interesting."

"I'm sure it was," Paula muttered. *That's probably what the Heaven's Gate recruits said, too—and look where it got them. Caught somewhere between Hail Mary and Hale-Bopp.*

"Anyway, they invited Millie and me to church on Sunday. She sort of said maybe she'd go, and she didn't think you'd mind if I went along. Honest, we didn't exactly promise to go . . . but I'd *really* like to, Mom. I've already read a lot of the book, and—"

"You mean the Book of Mormon?"

"Yeah . . . *Wait* a minute," TJ said, his voice suddenly expectant. "They gave you a copy, too, didn't they? Have you read it yet, Mom?"

"Only a little bit. I couldn't really get into it," Paula said defensively. *Or out of it fast enough.*

"Don't worry, you will," her son said with such certainty that she was momentarily speechless.

"Are we talking about the same book?" she finally asked incredulously. "The little blue one?"

"Yeah, that's it," TJ replied cheerfully. "You know, where Nephi and his family leave Jerusalem. I'm way past that now, and there's this cool guy—a prophet named Abinadi—who gets burned at the stake, and—"

Terrific. A witch hunt in Mormonville. "Don't tell me . . . 'And it came to pass,' right?"

"Hey, right! You *have* been reading it, haven't you?" He sounded positively gleeful. "So you see why I—why me and Millie want to go to church and learn more."

"Well, I wouldn't exactly say—"

"So," TJ broke in, more sure of himself now, "if you're gonna be home Sunday, you probably wanna check it out, too, huh? I'm sure the sisters wouldn't mind, and I've already told the elders all about you. What do you say, Mom?"

"Whoa, kiddo," she said sharply. "Let's just slow down a little, shall we?"

"Sorry." His tone was subdued. "I just thought since you'd been reading . . ."

"Well, I *haven't* been reading," she snapped. "I said I couldn't get into it, remember?"

"Yeah, I guess. But they'd still let you come." He sounded mildly hopeful.

"Listen, TJ," Paula said wearily, "we talked about this a few days ago, and I haven't given it much thought since then. But I can tell you right now that I'm really not interested in these Mormons, and I'm not thrilled that you are, either. So don't push me on this, okay? It's giving me a headache."

"Sorry. Okay."

"That's better."

"But can I go on Sunday?"

Paula sighed deeply and pressed her fingers over her eyes. *Try using a little strategy here, Donroe. Let him go. He'll be bored out of his skull, and you won't have to worry about it again.* "Well," she said slowly, "I suppose one time wouldn't hurt."

"All right! Thanks, Mom!" She could picture him doing a playful little jig around the kitchen.

"Just be careful. Did you say Millie's going, too?"

"Yep, she said she would. She'll keep an eye on me. And you're still invited too, if—"

"Not a chance, TJ. You're pretty pushy for a kid, you know that?" she added lightly.

"I know," he answered sheepishly. "But like you always say, you gotta go for what you want."

"True," Paula conceded. "But let's face it, dear—what you want right now and what I want are not exactly the same thing. Let's just leave it at that, shall we? It's not a matter of life and death, after all."

"Sure, Mom," he agreed readily. "But thanks for letting me go."

"No problem. Now, I've got some things to do, so I'll say good night. I'll see you this weekend. Give Rudy a squeeze for me, will you?"

"You know I will," TJ said. "He always mopes around when you're gone, so I try to spend extra time with him. I'll go take him for a walk right now."

"Good boy," Paula smiled. "You take care now, and I'll see you soon."

"Bye, Mom."

"Whew," Paula breathed as she hung up the phone. "That kid's got a career in sales ahead of him—if he doesn't become a professional Mormon." As though the thought made her head spin, she closed her eyes and sank back on the bed. "But I'll worry about that later. Now it's time for my little nap," she sighed, lowering herself toward a horizontal position.

Her eyes flew open as the back of her head made contact with a hard object lying on the pillow. "This is no chocolate mint," she quickly surmised as she turned over. "It feels more like a—" Her jaw tightened as she saw the blue book lying where her head had been a few seconds earlier. Once again, the gleaming trumpeter on its cover seemed to be aiming his horn directly at her. "Oh, joy," she muttered as her hand closed around the book. "The housekeeper must've found it under the pillow and left it for me. How thoughtful." Seeing no waste basket handy, Paula strode across the room and chucked the book unceremoniously into a bottom drawer of the armoire.

This annoyance, together with the residual sting of her conversations with Scott and TJ, convinced Paula that a long, hot, lavender-scented bubble bath would be more welcome sooner than later. She settled indulgently into the deep porcelain tub and let the steaming water rise around her. Soon the fragrant, swirling liquid was working its soothing magic on her tense muscles, weary joints, and unsettled thoughts. "Mmmm," she murmured from behind heavy eyelids, allowing her body and mind to be carried far away from the moment. Not that the moment was so terrible, but if she could only leave it for a little while . . .

She was seated on a broad, warm patch of earth in a sea of iridescent wildflowers, inhaling their perfume. Greg waved to her from across the meadow; he was busy sketching, and she dared not disturb him. Then, without warning, he was beside her, trailing his finger across her forehead, down her cheek, over her lips. She closed her eyes and he kissed them. They had been married only a few months; this was their first springtime as husband and wife. They would share countless hours making memories here among the flowers, beneath the sun and the moon, their firm young bodies baked by sultry heat or drenched by sudden summer storms. It was heaven . . . fire and ice . . . time in a bottle . . . time before time.

Suddenly his touch changed. Paula opened her eyes and found herself staring into the pale, brooding face of her father. He had crushed all the wildflowers in sight, and was silently mouthing the words she knew all too well: "You gave him away . . . you gave away my grandson . . . my grandson. No forgiveness . . . never!" She shuddered and recoiled from his icy stare.

From nowhere, a massive hand grasped her father's shoulder from behind with a firm but gentle grip. It was like no hand she had ever seen—flesh of a rich, bronze-gold color, its strong muscles and sinews clearly defined. As her father's image seemed to freeze, Paula's line of vision angled upward, following a chiseled golden arm, ascending to a Herculean shoulder draped in glowing amber fabric. From there, her eyes moved quickly up a tawny, trunk-like neck to the gilded face of a man who towered above them but appeared to pose no threat. His eyes, blazing with blue fire, seemed to pierce her soul, even as the hint of a smile flickered around his golden lips. She sensed a solemn comfort in his presence, but she had to know more. "Wh—who are you?" she asked the golden giant.

"I am called Moroni," he boomed. "I hail from another time and place, but I know you, as I know your father. And I come with a simple but important message."

"And what might that be?" she asked with growing curiosity.

At this question the giant smiled broadly, revealing a perfectly chiseled set of massive, glowing white teeth. "Well, my friends," he said, "I have learned that to avoid error and misunderstanding, one must speak concisely. And when the engraver's tool is set in motion, such brevity also saves valued space on the plates."

"Plates? Those wouldn't by any chance be golden *plates, would they?" Paula questioned, a faint memory surfacing in the back of her mind. Something about an angel.*

"Ah, then you know my work," he said eagerly. "From the book. At one time, there was a fine likeness of myself on its cover. But that is beside the point."

"And your point is?" Paula pressed, her voice threatening impatience.

"My point," replied the magnificent stranger, "is that you must remember to NEVER SAY NEVER." He nodded curtly and stepped back a pace, seemingly satisfied with his three words of wisdom.

She stared at him in disbelief. "That's it?"

"Verily," he answered. "It seems a simple bit of wisdom, but its meaning will become clear soon enough. In the meantime, I must be on my way. Adieu." He bowed slightly from the waist, turned around, and began to march briskly away, each thundering footfall causing the earth to shudder a little.

Suddenly he halted in midstride, executed a clipped about-face, and approached Paula and her father once again. This time, there was a slightly sheepish expression etched on his lustrous features. "If you will pardon me," he said with a subdued bellow, "I seem to have forgotten something." Pointing toward the ground, he directed her gaze to a long, slender, trumpet-like horn lying half submerged in a large pool of crystalline water. "Ah, this could be a great tragedy," he lamented, "for this is my best trump. I must hope that my instrument still has its voice. The Second Coming is not far off, you see, and I will most certainly be expected to perform."

He knelt beside the horn and tenderly retrieved it from the water. "Wish me good fortune, my friends," he implored. "You will not mind if I test it, will you?" Without waiting for permission, he lifted the horn to his lips and blew from the depths of his massive lungs. Instantly, hundreds of gallons of icy water cascaded over Paula's head, sucking her breath away and chilling her to the bone. Clamping her hand over her mouth and squeezing her eyes shut, she waited for the deluge to pass. But it just kept coming, splashing all around her and threatening to freeze her like a woolly mammoth for posterity. She tried to swim but kept bumping her head. Finally, she opened her eyes to get her bearings . . .

Paula woke abruptly as her head slipped beneath the water, which by now was running cold from the tap, overflowing the huge, claw-footed antique tub. Her body shook with chills as she reached to turn off the water, then clutched the tub's smooth porcelain edge and pulled herself to a standing position. A sharp nudge of her toe unplugged the drain as she reached for a heavy towel from the nearby rack. The water whirled swiftly downward to her shins, ankles, toes, and finally disappeared altogether with a resounding gurgle.

"Nice job, Donroe," Paula moaned as she surveyed the bathroom floor. Its square black and white tiles shimmered beneath a thin covering of slightly murky water, now lapping lazily at the room's white baseboards. She stood, trancelike, in the tub for several minutes, finally becoming aware that small floor drains in each corner of the room had solved the problem. By the time she had almost stopped shivering and towel-dried her hair, the tiles were virtually dry and none the worse for wear.

Stepping gingerly out of the tub, she hurried across the tiled room and into the thickly carpeted living area. There she bundled herself in her terry robe, turned up the thermostat, and dived into bed. "So much for escaping the moment," she mumbled as warmth slowly returned to her extremities. "I've had tax audits that were more fun than that dream."

Paula's heart gradually slowed and her mind relaxed, allowing her to give in to complete exhaustion. She could wait until morning to finish her notes for the panel. As she sank into a deep sleep, her last thought focused on the unique personage of her dream, with his pithy message and water-logged trumpet. *Never say never,* she repeated silently. *Simple enough for you to say, golden boy, but what does it mean for me? That's easy . . . nothing. Absolutely nothing. Catch you later, Mr. Moroni. Maybe at the Second Coming.*

Chapter 14

Overnight, the biting autumn air had turned warm and mellow—a fact that brightened Paula's mood as she strolled toward campus and her final part in the women's conference. *A sunny morning makes a big difference*, she reflected as her feet displaced small piles of gold and crimson leaves along the sidewalk. Ahead of her stretched a day that was all hers; after the panel, she was free to do whatever she wished. She nibbled her lower lip as she walked, weighing the possibilities. Maybe she'd sit in on a few workshops; take in a matinee at the cineplex downtown; do a little shopping; call a client or two in New York; spend some more time in the bookstore.

Or . . . there was the matter of that little twenty-minute drive into the country.

Paula snorted at the idea. *Don't be ridiculous, Donroe. She wouldn't even want to see you. She gave up on being your mother a long time ago, and you haven't exactly been a model daughter, either. She's old and tired and bitter, just like Daddy was before he died. Why try to pick up the pieces now? It's too late—for everyone. Don't bother.*

She paused inside the entrance of the business and communications building. Her brow furrowed, and her lips pressed themselves together in a determined line. "Focus, Donroe," she said to herself. "You've got a presentation to make in ten minutes. Let the rest take care of itself." She quickly pasted a cheerleader's smile on her face and headed down the marble hall to the auditorium. As she strode past the glass display cases, the image of her father scowled out at her. She didn't stop.

Just over two hours later, Paula was on her own. The panel had gone well, and she'd received Dean Transtrum's effusive thanks and an invitation to attend next year's conference. "I'll do my best," she'd promised. And she'd meant it. The week had been fun and exhilarating, a welcome respite from the daily grind of her office.

The sun was warm on her face as she left the building. Before she'd taken many steps, a gentle gnawing in the pit of her stomach reminded her that she'd had no breakfast, and it was now past noon. *Okay,* she told herself, *I can plan my afternoon over lunch.* As she sauntered toward the student union, she wondered idly if Scott had passed the test for his learner's permit. *Of course he passed; he's a smart kid. And he lives to make his mother suffer.* Paula smiled humorlessly, feeling a sudden chill as she conjured up images of her son's celebration with the Crawlers.

She settled cozily behind a small table at the espresso café and ordered a club sandwich and cappuccino. Then she considered her options. Half an hour later, she had mentally explored a dozen different uses for this golden afternoon, and had reluctantly put each of them aside. She had argued, reasoned, even bargained with her better judgment, utterly confused at the stubborn urging of some driving force within her. But finally, the day came down to one destination: 102 Mapleton Crossing, at the end of a twenty-minute country drive. The Enfield estate.

I'll only stay a minute. Really, it would be downright indecent of me to come all the way across the country, then go back home again without even trying. "Hello, Mother. I was in the neighborhood, just thought I'd stop by. The weather seems nice." How hard could it be? Don't answer that.

Paula gulped. She didn't want to do this—*really* didn't want to do this. Her mother's icy demeanor at the funeral haunted her to this day; they hadn't exchanged more than a dozen words on that occasion, and they weren't warm ones. *I was—am—their only child, for heaven's sake. My only sins were falling in love too young and wanting a good life for my son, but they could never forgive me for either. So we drifted apart—and we're still drifting, even after all these years. Why go crawling back to her now?*

She shook her head as if to clear out the fuzz, then pushed aside her half-eaten sandwich and rested her arms on the table. Glancing around the small café, its intimate round tables for two or four spaced haphazardly across the worn wooden floor, she saw that she was the only one alone. Everyone else was talking, laughing, arguing—*being* with someone—while she passed the time of day with a wilting piece of lettuce on her plate. At this moment, an unexpected loneliness crept into her heart. *All right, I'll do it. But only because my guilt—or whatever it is—will never let me rest if I don't. Like it or not, Mother, here I come.* She rose from the table and collected her purse and attaché, paid her bill, then marched purposefully out into the spicy autumn afternoon. A moderate breeze had come up, and now it fluttered at her back, urging her forward faster than she wanted to go. *Just what I need,* she grimaced. *A tailwind.*

Back at the Westbury, Paula shed her navy business suit, showered, and slipped into a pair of dark green wool slacks, brown suede loafers, and a cream-colored silk blouse. The outfit, one of her favorites, showcased her trim figure and put her at ease in virtually any company.

"Thanks again, Millie," she breathed, pausing to admire her youthful profile in an oval full-length mirror beside the armoire. "On this visit, I'll need all the help I can get." She tossed a light jacket over her arm, picked up her keys from the nightstand, and locked the room behind her. Then she took the stairs one at a time, slowly, down to the lobby, where she stopped to chat with the receptionist for a few minutes.

Once outside, she quickly found her rented luxury sedan tucked safely into a parking space at one side of the inn. *Maybe I should wash the car . . .* She smiled in spite of her growing uneasiness. *Really, Donroe. She's your mother, not Cruella De Vil. Get a grip . . . it'll all be over in an hour or so—tops.*

Paula had forgotten what a charming drive it was to her parents' home. The gleaming silver Lexus seemed to float effortlessly over twenty miles of two-way country road flanked by grassy meadows and stands of birch along a convergence of icy, bubbling streams. She and Greg had traveled this road hundreds of times on the Harley, sometimes stopping at dusk to hold hands and watch in respectful silence as a small herd of deer stole timorously down from the foothills to feed and drink along the banks of Crystal Creek. The trees were taller now, vivid in their autumn colors, and the brooks seemed wider and deeper. If anything it was more beautiful, more peaceful than before. The narrow, meandering road had been carefully maintained, and Paula was relieved to see that it hadn't become a freeway. There were enough of those in California.

Her thoughts were still years and miles away when a sudden curve of the road warned her to slow the Lexus in order to navigate a sharp bend just ahead of Mapleton Crossing. Stepping lightly on the brake, she decreased the speed of the big car as it rounded a corner and her mother's home came into view.

Paula gasped suddenly—not so much in fear or anticipation as in awe at the beauty and enormity of the Enfield estate itself, now spread before her like a panoramic photo in a travel brochure. From the road, acres of carefully manicured lawn, bordered by meticulously trimmed shrubs and lush flower gardens, sloped gently up toward the house, which sat imperially on a low rise flanked by centuries-old evergreens. It was a two-story Colonial mansion, its front pillars and second-story porticoes gleaming white in the mid-afternoon sun. "Wow," she breathed, as if seeing it for the first time.

Her eyes traveled to the upper right-hand window—her room. What was it used for now? She hadn't seen it since the night she'd thrown a few things into a suitcase while Greg waited patiently on the shiny seat of his Harley. They'd been married three days later by a Mississippi justice of the peace.

I'll just take a minute to collect my thoughts. Pulling to the side of the road near the estate's wide circular driveway, Paula turned off the car's motor and leaned back against the headrest, inhaling its faint aroma of leather and lemon-scented air freshener. She exhaled slowly, and her eyes closed as a rush of memories flooded her senses.

Out behind the house there was a canopied gazebo where, as a child, she often went to read or dream of being a dancer. In the still, early-morning hours of summer, she would glide barefoot in silent, joyful circles around this small building, her arms extended to catch the slightest breeze, as though she could fly. She would dip and twirl, bending over until her fingertips just brushed the moist grass, then she'd run and leap like a spring lamb over the narrow neck of one of her mother's prize-winning flower beds. Finally, exhausted, she would sprawl on her back and stare up at the sky, where she could see forms and faces in the clouds. Later in the morning, as the sun grew warmer and the humidity more oppressive, she would move to the gazebo. There she would retrieve one of a dozen books from a built-in cupboard below one of the cushioned window seats. Curling her slim legs beneath her, she would quickly lose herself in the pages of some exotic fantasy or adventure novel. Sometimes she would read through lunch, and it was dusk before her mother called her in. As she grew older, she spent less and less time there, except for an occasional afternoon of reading or daydreaming. But then she met Greg, and the gazebo quickly became their special romantic hideaway.

Greg. Paula could almost feel him next to her in the car, and she dared not open her eyes for fear of losing the sensation. So much of this place, this house, this green countryside was yet filled with the sight, sound, scent, and spirit of him. Why, after all these years—even after a successful career, another marriage, and two more children—why couldn't she just let him go? *God only knows,* she reflected with the flicker of a smile. *And he's not telling. Besides, nothing lasts forever—not even Greg.*

In her mind's center, a sudden shaft of sunlight seemed to strike a long, golden object and explode into millions of glowing embers. At the same instant, she felt the words burn into her brain: *Never say never.*

Paula's eyes flew open. "What in the—" Her heart was racing, and she felt beads of perspiration on her forehead. She inhaled deeply and willed herself to be calm, but it was several minutes before she felt in control. Finally, she set her jaw in a determined line and gave herself a good talking to. "Donroe," she said aloud with as much conviction as she could muster, "you're being stupid and silly. You didn't drive all the way out here just to sit and stare at the old homestead, wallowing in the past. You came here to, uh . . . to . . . to salvage what you can of the present." She smiled inwardly, glad and relieved to have hit upon a reason. "Yes, that's it . . . you came to salvage the present. Maybe even the future." *Don't push your luck, Donroe.*

She turned the key and the Lexus hummed to life, responding instantly to her light touch on the wheel. As the car moved noiselessly up the smooth, quarter-mile-long cement driveway, she checked her makeup in the rearview mirror, practiced flashing a breezy smile, and repeatedly swallowed the Texas-size lump in her throat. By the time she pulled up in front of the house, she felt marginally confident. *What's the worst that could happen? I'm too old to be grounded, too smart to be intimidated, too successful to be mocked. And too scared to think past the next thirty seconds.*

Paula got out of the car, closed the door carefully, and leaned heavily against it for several tense minutes, her arms folded across her chest. *Now, what was that reason for coming? Oh, yes—to salvage something or other; I'm sure it'll come back to me. In the meantime . . .* She straightened her back, squared her slim shoulders, and marched doggedly up four wide cement steps to the porch.

With one perfectly manicured nail poised a fraction of an inch from the doorbell, Paula hesitated for about a second, then resolutely pressed her finger against the small white button. Instantly the silence of the still, warm afternoon was splintered by a sixteen-note cadence of bell sounds, round and loud and ostentatious. *Hell's bells, that's what I used to call them.* She held her breath, waiting, while the echoes played themselves out. *Any second now, that big door will swing open and I'll be face to face with my past. Will Mother answer it herself, or will she send the maid? And if it's old Gretchen, will I have to introduce myself after all these years? No, Gretchen's long gone by now; she was several years older than Daddy. Mother's undoubtedly hired someone new—a perky little thing who specializes in dusting and answering the door. And she probably doesn't even know I exist . . . what's taking her so long, anyway?*

When a minute or two passed without a response, Paula nervously punched the white button again, setting off a second round of chimes. She waited, tapping her foot on the cool cement porch. *Come on, Mother . . . you never go anywhere, except to an occasional concert or evening bridge game. Are you having an affair or something?* Her mouth twisted into a smirk at the thought. But no one came to the door.

All right . . . once more, then I'm gone. She set her lips in a thin line and leaned hard with her thumb against the bell—an action that made no difference in the loudness of the chimes, but gave her a certain feeling of satisfaction. Then she took a few steps to the side, leaned against one of the massive white pillars, and stared intently at the solid mahogany door, her hands in her pockets. *I've come home, Mother . . .*

come home to see you. I don't expect much—just one of your famous socialite smiles, maybe an invitation to tea, possibly a couple of disinterested questions about my life. A handshake would do at the end . . . Don't you see? This could be something like a new beginning for us—two grown-up women who've both learned a lot over the past twenty years. Maybe we could even be friends . . . if you like.

Paula felt hot tears on her cheeks. She tossed her head back and reached up to brush them away, but more kept coming. *This isn't the way it was supposed to be,* she thought, dabbing at her eyes with a crumpled tissue retrieved from her pocket. *I never thought I'd actually be sorry if I didn't see her—just relieved. Has your forty-year-old heart suddenly gone soft, Donroe?* "This could be serious," she mumbled, chuckling ruefully. "I'm too young to have heart trouble." *Or too old.* She sighed.

"No one's coming." She spoke the words softly, sadly, as she turned away from the door and slowly descended the few steps to her car. Pausing, she turned and looked back at the door. *Maybe next year . . . but I can't come again this time. I just can't.* Her legs felt like two rubber bands, and her whole body trembled as she lowered herself into the Lexus. Slumping down in the leather seat, she cradled her head in her hands for a few long moments, then wiped at her eyes again and rummaged in her purse for the keys. With a quick sideways glance at the house of her childhood, she started the motor, shifted into drive, and allowed the car to carry her silently down the sloping hill and out to the country road.

As Paula disappeared down the driveway, there was movement at an upstairs window of the mansion. A pale hand released the layered lace curtain back to where it had been ten minutes earlier, hanging heavy and flat against the pane. By the time the silver sedan was out of sight, the thin shadow at the window had evaporated into the bowels of the Enfield estate.

CHAPTER 15

"Triple-decker peanut butter and tuna . . . my favorite!" TJ grinned and smacked his lips as he pressed the final slice of Wonder bread down firmly on top of his sandwich. "Don't let anyone touch that, Rudy," he warned as the big dog yawned and settled himself under the kitchen table. "I'll be right back." Rudy was snoring softly by the time TJ had jogged over to the refrigerator for a Coke and rifled the cupboard for a bag of chips. "Big help you are," he muttered as he returned to the table, pulled out a chair, and sat down to his usual after-school snack. He grasped the huge sandwich resolutely with both hands, then closed his eyes and unlatched his jaw to fit it around the three-tiered work of art that would soon be only a delectable memory. As his mouth closed on the first morsels of fish and nuts, he heaved a sigh of perfect satisfaction. Now he could survive until dinner.

The front door opened and slammed shut just as he stuffed the last third of his sandwich into his mouth and followed it with a fistful of Doritos. He looked up, his cheeks bulging, as Scott swaggered into the kitchen and tossed his books on the floor beside the table. Rudy started at the sudden thump near his face, but was soon breathing evenly again.

"Hey, little brother," Scott boomed in a deep voice, his face split by one of the widest grins TJ had ever seen. "How's tricks?" He turned one of the chairs around and straddled it with his long, wiry legs.

"Mufm wmbn tmdbm," TJ replied, straining to chew, swallow, and talk at the same time.

"Is that so?" Scott said with an amused expression. "Well, then, I don't s'pose you wanna hear what I've been up to . . ."

"Nm, pmbm bubmin—"

"Gee, I thought you'd *never* ask." Scott leaned forward and folded his arms across the back of the chair while his brother reached for a Coke chaser. "But seein' as how you're my baby brother, an' you *lean* on me for, you know, *stuff,* I guess you oughta be the first one in the family to know."

TJ gulped loudly and wiped his hand across his mouth. "Know *what,* Scotty?" Then he caught the gleam in his brother's eyes, and understanding dawned. "You did it, didn't you? You passed the test. You *passed!*"

"Well, let's put it this way," Scott drawled, reaching into his back pocket and pulling out a small blue slip of paper. "Your big brother is now one *hard-drivin' man.*" He tossed the paper onto the table with a flourish.

TJ snatched it up and studied it for several seconds, then looked at his brother, his eyes shining. "Wow, this is *so cool!*" He high-fived Scott and whooped his approval, then leaned over and shouted under the table. "Hey, Rudy, didja hear that? Scotty's got his learner's permit! He *did it!*" The dog opened his eyes halfway and thumped his tail a time or two on the floor before nodding off again.

TJ leaned back in his chair and shook his head. "Geez, I can't believe it . . . I mean, I know you're real smart and all, and I knew you'd pass—"

"One . . . hundred . . . percent," Scott said, punctuating each word. "I was the *only one* who totally iced it. Most of the guys missed three or four, and one of the chicks bombed." His hazel eyes were doing a victory dance. "Here's what's really cool: I'll have my license in two or three months, and then . . . *vrrrooomm!*" He mimicked a race car driver finishing first in the Indy 500.

"Awesome!" TJ grinned. "When does your class start?"

"Monday, seven a.m. sharp, before school in the parking lot. They divided us up—three kids to a car, with one instructor . . . mine is old man Swope, the chemistry teacher. The guys say he's a geek, but he's a really good driving coach. I'm ready to *fly,* man!" Scott stretched his lean, muscular arms over his head, interlaced his fingers, and cracked all of his knuckles at once. Then he reached across the table to rumple TJ's hair. "Just think, little man . . . before you know it, I'll have my own license, my own car, and I'll be able take to you anywhere you wanna to go. Is that an offer you can't refuse, or what?"

"Deal," TJ agreed eagerly, his deep brown eyes glowing. "So, what're you doin' to celebrate?"

"Party with the Crawlers, what else? Ben and the guys are comin' for me at five. We put in a rippin' sound system at the C-House last week, and they've got some awesome new CDs—not to mention a bunch of food and stuff from Bart's dad. He runs a grocery store, ya know? Wanna tag along?"

For a moment TJ hesitated. "Naw," he finally said, "I better stick around home tonight. The sisters are coming, and I told 'em I'd be here—"

"Whoa, you mean those Mormon foxes are paying you a *visit* this evening?" Scott's eyebrows rose and fell rapidly as he cast a lecherous sidelong glance at his brother. "Little man, are you makin' some moves I don't know about? Or, more to the point, are *they* makin' some moves I don't know about?" He grinned snidely.

"Geez, cut it out, Scotty," TJ laughed, his cheeks burning. "You know they're just teaching Millie and me about their church—"

"Uh-huh," Scott snickered. "A likely story."

TJ shook his head. "Well, whatever you think, I promised. And I'm sure you've got better things to do than hang out with your kid brother. Besides, I gotta practice some of my jump shots." He lifted the can of Coke to his lips and dribbled the last few drops into his mouth.

"Suit yourself, then." Scott retrieved his learner's permit from the table and stuffed it back into his pocket. He ambled around the table and bent over until his face was almost touching TJ's. "Just remember to watch your manners tonight, kid," he whispered. "And be sure," he added, reaching out to quickly pinch his brother's cheek, "to give my *very* best to those bodacious Bible-toting beauties."

"Get outa here!" TJ giggled, brushing Scott's hand away. "I don't know what you're talkin' about."

"Oh, yeah? Well, just give it a year or two, and you'll know *exactly* what I'm talkin' about. A man knows these things. See ya later, little bro." He clapped TJ on the shoulder, then turned and sauntered from the room. A few seconds later, TJ heard Scott's bedroom door close, and within moments the muffled beat of heavy metal was drifting down the stairs.

A glance at the kitchen clock told TJ that he had a couple of hours before dinner, so he grabbed his basketball from the entryway closet and headed out the front door. He was still practicing when the old Chevy lurched up to the sidewalk and Scott bounded out to greet his friends. Tucking himself into the wide front seat with two or three other Crawlers, he waved out the window as the car jerked into gear and moved slowly down the street. TJ watched the massive vehicle shudder as it rounded the corner and rumbled out of sight, and he knew it wouldn't be long before Scott would be driving his own car.

"Man, are we gonna *fly!*" he grinned. "Just like Scotty said!" Energized with anticipation, he tossed the ball toward the basket. It swooshed in without touching the rim.

"TJ, time for dinner," Millie called from the front porch. "And you need to wash up for our visitors," she reminded as he continued to shoot and dribble.

"How long before it's ready?" TJ panted, landing a three-pointer from the lawn's edge.

"Nice basket! About ten minutes," Millie said.

"Okay, I'll hit the showers." He vaulted up the front steps and into the house almost before Millie could move out of the way. "What's for dinner, anyhow? I'm starving," he called from halfway up the stairs.

"Stuffed zucchini and spinach salad," she answered with a deadpan expression.

He stopped in mid-stride. "Aw, geez, rabbit food?" He leaned over the bannister and gave her a pained look. "A guy can't live on that stuff. I bet Michael Jordan never ate a zucchini in his life, and he isn't exactly a runt." Now TJ was whining. "Shoot, Millie, Mom's not even home. Why do we hafta—"

"*Gotcha!*" Millie chirped gleefully, her hands on her plump hips. "How does burgers and a homemade milkshake sound?"

"Whew!" TJ grinned, the relief on his face obvious. "Now we're talkin'. Chocolate or pineapple?"

"Both, if you'd like."

"Well, then I guess I forgive you. Thanks, Mill . . . I'm practically there!" He bounded up the stairs, and a few moments later Millie heard the water pipes roar to life, accompanied by a grating, high-pitched wailing sound.

"He's singing in the shower again," she chuckled. "The school choir doesn't know what it's missing . . . and I'll never tell." Humming softly, she bustled into the kitchen to put the finishing touches on their meal and to prepare a light refreshment for the missionaries.

TJ was gulping down his last mouthful of a creamy pineapple shake when the doorbell rang. "That must be the sisters," Millie said from across the kitchen, where she was loading the dishwasher. She quickly began to untie her apron.

"I'll get it." TJ hurriedly wiped a napkin across his mouth and pushed back his chair, then loped easily into the entryway. Smiling broadly, he pulled open the door with a flourish. "Hey, sis—" He swallowed the word as his gaze took in the two young men in dark suits standing on the porch. "Uh, we were expecting . . ."

"I know; you were expecting the sisters. How ya doing, TJ?" The taller of the two men stuck out his hand.

"Uh, fine, thanks, sir." Then, as recognition set in, he blurted out, "Oh, yeah . . . you're the guys I played ball with the other night." He glanced at the missionary's name tag: Elder Richland. "Sorry 'bout that . . . I didn't recognize you with your clothes on. I mean—well, you know what I mean," he said shyly.

"No problem," the other missionary said as he, too, shook TJ's hand. He tugged on the lapel of his suit jacket with its black and white tag identifying him as Elder Stucki. "These are our everyday uniforms," he grinned, "but it's sure nice to get into something more comfortable once in a while."

"TJ?" Millie's voice came from the entryway. "Aren't you going to invite the sisters in?"

"Sure thing—but it's not them," TJ called over his shoulder.

"What do you mean, it's not—oh, my," Millie said as she peered around TJ.

"You didn't recognize them either, did you, Millie?" he laughed. "They're the elders—you know, the ones who came over to play ball on Monday night. You fed 'em, remember?"

Millie stared silently at the two young men for a few moments, then her face crinkled into a smile. "Why, yes, of course—the elders.

You just looked so . . . *different*. Certainly very handsome tonight," she said in a motherly tone. "Please come in." She stepped back, ushering them across the entryway and into the living room.

When the four were settled comfortably, Elder Richland began to speak. "I know you were expecting the sisters," he said, "but Sister Tibbetts had a little accident this morning—"

"Oh, dear," Millie said, her eyes filling with concern. "Sister Tibbetts does seem to be just a bit accident prone, doesn't she? I hope it's not serious."

"Well, it could've been a lot worse," the elder continued. "She took a pretty bad spill when her bike hit a monster pothole—went right over the handlebars and landed on her shoulder. Her companion called us, and we got her to the hospital. The shoulder was dislocated, and she had some pretty deep scrapes and bruises. They released her after a couple of hours, but she won't be up to going anywhere for a few days, and Sister Kent is taking care of her. So . . . it looks like you're stuck with us for a while. Hope that won't be too much of a pain." He smiled apologetically at Millie and winked at TJ.

"No, of course not," Millie said. "But I'd certainly like to do something to help—you know, take the girls some food or something. Would that be all right?"

"I don't see why not. That's awfully nice of you," Elder Richland said, flashing her a dimpled smile. "Remind me before we go, and I'll give you their address and phone number."

"Thank you," Millie smiled. "Now, where shall we start? Last time we saw the sisters—they dropped by late one afternoon, you know, and we visited over dinner—we mostly just asked them questions about the Book of Mormon, and they told us about Joseph Smith and the angel Moroni . . ." She paused expectantly.

"That's great," Elder Richland said, "and we'll be talking more about that in a minute. But first, could we have a prayer to invite the Spirit of the Lord to be with us?"

"Oh, I'd like that," Millie beamed.

"Sure, I guess so," TJ shrugged.

"Terrific. TJ, would you like to offer it?"

"M—me?" TJ gulped and his back stiffened. "What makes you think *I* know how to say a prayer?"

Elder Richland slid forward to the edge of the couch, rested his forearms on his thighs, and looked TJ in the eye. "It's easy, really—just like talking to someone you trust and love very much, someone who cares about you more than you could ever imagine . . . a kind Heavenly Father who has power to make wonderful things happen in your life because he loves you so much. Just thank him for the good things in your life, ask him for anything you feel you might need, then close in the name of Jesus Christ. Do you think you could do that?" The elder's voice was gentle and reassuring.

"I . . . I dunno." TJ stared at the floor. "Do you think God could really hear me?"

"I'm sure of it. He'll hear you, and he'll answer your prayers—just like he answered mine when I was about your age and wanted to know the truth for myself. Will you try?"

"Well, I guess so," TJ agreed reluctantly. "But it won't be anything great."

"Doesn't have to be," Elder Richland said quietly. "Just let it come from in here." He tapped his chest.

The elders folded their arms and bowed their heads; Millie and TJ did the same. After long moments of tense silence, TJ cautiously began to speak.

"Uh . . . Hello, God? This is TJ . . . TJ Donroe. I live at 10410 Valley View Drive in Woodland Hills, California—just in case you ever need to find me. Hey, I have a nice life, and I want to thank you for a great mom, a cool big brother, Millie (she's our housekeeper, but I kinda think of her as my grandma), and Rudy, the best dog ever. I've got lots of stuff, too, and I thank you for that.

"Anyway, there's not much I need—I mean, I have friends and a cool bike and everything. I'd like to learn how to play better basketball, if that's okay with you. Please help Scotty learn to drive real soon so we can go out together when he gets his car. An' please help my mom to be happy and not have to work so hard.

"I guess that's about it. Oh, and thank you for the sisters and the elders, an' for the Book of Mormon—I've been readin' it, ya know. I wanna be a good kid, and I hope you believe me. Please help us all to be good . . . and thanks again. I'd like to say this in the name of Jesus . . . so, uh . . . goodbye."

TJ opened his eyes. He sank back in his chair, heaved an enormous sigh, and grinned self-consciously. His gaze met Elder Richland's, whose dark eyes were moist. Millie's eyes, too, were shining. "Was that okay?" TJ asked uncertainly.

"Better than okay," the missionary smiled. "How do you feel right now, TJ?"

"Better than okay," the boy echoed after a moment. "Almost like . . . somebody was listening. Really listening."

"You can bet on that," Elder Richland said with conviction. "Thank you, TJ, for getting us off to a *very* good start tonight. And I hope you'll keep praying to Heavenly Father every day. He really does listen, and he answers prayers."

"Yeah, I guess I could do that," TJ nodded. "It felt . . . okay. It felt good."

"*Okay*," Elder Stucki broke in. "Now, let's talk about the plan of salvation."

For the next hour, these two earnest young men taught and testified, expertly using their leather-bound scriptures to support their convictions and answer any questions. The two seemed to work together like a well-oiled machine, seamlessly shifting from one point of doctrine to another, calmly explaining the finer points of gaining a "testimony," eagerly declaring the truth of their message.

They were wholesome and appealing young men, though not at all alike. Elder Stucki was a sandy-haired, ruddy-complexioned boy of medium height with a stocky build that made his thick neck bulge slightly over the collar of his white shirt. His zeal for missionary work was apparent; one could see it in his intense blue eyes, hear it in his rapid-fire conversation. He smiled often, and made small jokes that were actually funny in a tasteful, ingenuous sort of way. His current idol in life was his senior companion.

Elder Richland was older—maybe by a couple of years, Millie surmised—and much taller, with wavy, dark brown hair and eyes the color of chocolate. His build was lean but muscular and athletic, the skin on his face and hands evenly tanned by spending countless hours walking the neighborhoods of Los Angeles. And he had the worn (but carefully polished) shoes to prove it. His voice was deep and resonant, his manner relaxed and polite but clearly focused. When he smiled, with deep dimples at the corners of his mouth and disarmingly white teeth that were ever so slightly crooked, the temperature of the room seemed to rise a few degrees.

Not long after the elders began their presentation of the "families can be together forever" concept, Millie gasped a little and reached into her pocket for a handkerchief. As tears began to trickle down her cheeks, TJ knelt beside her chair. "What's the matter, Millie? Did they"—he glanced sharply at the elders—"did they say something to upset you?" He put his hand on the chair's arm and looked at her protectively.

She patted his hand. "Oh, no, dear," she sniffed, wiping at her eyes. "It's just that"—her eyes moved from one elder to the other—"I . . . lost my husband and daughter some years ago . . . they're both dead . . . and I didn't think I'd ever . . . see them again. Ever. Now you're telling me that I *will* see them—that we can really be together again?"

Elder Richland nodded soberly, a kind light flowing from his dark eyes. "You can not only be together again—you can be together as a *family*. Heavenly Father wants that for you, Millie. I know it."

"Even if things weren't . . . weren't so good at the end? I mean, I loved them more than anything, but my Joe took his own life . . . he missed our girl too much. I always thought God wouldn't forgive him for that."

"There are lots of things we don't understand, Millie." Elder Richland's voice was low and soothing. "But I do know God loves us, and he'll make things right if we do our part. Your part, right now, is learning about the gospel; the Lord will take care of the rest. You can trust him."

"Oh, I hope so," Millie sobbed, pressing the wet handkerchief to her eyes. "Please, God, I hope so."

A small sound—something between a cough and a chuckle—came from TJ, who was still kneeling beside Millie's chair. Three pairs of curious eyes darted to his face, and his cheeks reddened. "'Scuse me," he mumbled, clearing his throat. "I was just thinkin' . . . I don't see how this togetherness stuff would work out very well for me, on accounta the fact that our family was never really together in the first place."

"How's that, TJ?" Elder Stucki asked, his blue eyes studying the boy closely.

TJ sat cross-legged on the floor. "Well," he explained, "my mom and dad split up when I was just a baby. Scotty—that's my brother—was about five, but he doesn't remember much. My mom doesn't talk about it, and we've never even seen our dad; he took off with some babe before Mom and him even got divorced. It seems like my mom would wanna be with us guys forever, even though it seems like a pretty long time—and Rudy, too—but that's all the real family we've got. I guess I just wonder . . . is that enough? I mean, do you need *everybody* to make it work? And if you do, does that mean all of us are on our own—forever?"

Elder Richland riveted his warm, brown eyes on TJ's face. "In Heavenly Father's plan, *nobody* has to be alone, TJ. I'm not quite sure how it'll all work out, but I can tell you that for everyone who tries to do the right thing, for everyone who follows the commandments of God, there'll be a way to have an eternal family. As you learn more about the gospel and pray to Heavenly Father for a testimony, he'll help you understand how it can happen. It's different for everybody, because his plan for you is different from anyone else's. Except that all the paths lead back to him—home to his presence. Home to his love. Does that make any sense?"

TJ chewed on his bottom lip and stared at the floor for a few seconds. "Yeah, I guess so. I mean, I don't understand it all that well, but it sounds okay—not stupid or anything."

"That's good enough for now," the elder smiled. "You just keep reading the Book of Mormon and praying. Heavenly Father won't let you down, TJ. I promise."

"Okay. Thanks." TJ sighed and leaned against Millie's chair.

Millie gently squeezed his shoulder. "It'll be all right," she whispered, her eyes now dry but still glistening. "I can *feel* it."

"I know," he whispered back. "I can feel it, too."

The discussion wound down after a few Book of Mormon questions and answers, the fervent bearing of testimonies by both elders, and a brief closing prayer by Elder Stucki. Following the "amen," TJ grinned shyly at the missionaries and ran his fingers through his thick sandy hair. "I guess I could use some more practice at that prayer stuff, huh? Especially the beginning and end. You guys are pretty smooth."

"You did just fine, TJ," Elder Richland said warmly. "You know what they say . . . practice makes perfect. And speaking of practice, I hear they've started a junior basketball team over at the ward. They get together on Saturday mornings and one or two nights a week, and the word is that there's a tournament with some of the other wards starting next month. Those guys could sure use a shooter like you . . . are you interested?"

"You hafta ask?" TJ laughed. As Millie served mountainous helpings of strawberry shortcake, he scribbled dates, times, and places on the back of an old envelope retrieved from his pocket. "What time tomorrow? Nine a.m.? Cool . . . I'll be there. Are you guys comin' over here to play again on Monday? Great!" His mind raced with anticipation at the prospect of a thoroughly athletic week.

At the door, Elder Stucki cheerfully extended his hand—and the invitation that both Millie and TJ knew was coming. "So, can we pick you up for church on Sunday? Meetings start at ten a.m., and we'll have you home before dark," he explained. "Just kidding," he quickly added as their eyes grew wide. "You'll be home in time for lunch—almost." He winked at Millie. "You get used to it. So, is it a done deal?"

TJ's eyes met Millie's as each seemed to recall the satisfying feelings of the past hour. "Deal," TJ said, reminding himself that his mother had given her grudging permission the evening before. Millie nodded, and it was agreed.

"Terrific," Elder Richland said. "We'll be here around nine-thirty. Until then"—he shook both their hands firmly—"think about what we've discussed tonight, and pray about it. If it's true, you'll know. Maybe not right away, but soon. Okay?"

"Yeah, okay," TJ said.

Millie thanked the elders for coming and closed the door softly behind them. "Well," she said, "that was nice. Now I think I'll just finish cleaning up in the kitchen. Would you like some more strawberry shortcake, dear? I made quite a bit, and I believe there's some left."

"Naw, I'm pretty full; save it for Scotty. I guess I'll shoot a few more baskets, then read a little before I turn in. I'm almost finished with the Book of Mormon."

"So am I," Millie said. "I don't think your mother's read much of it, though, from what I've seen."

"Who, *Mom?*" TJ rolled his eyes. "I wouldn't exactly call her the religious type, would you?" He snickered at a mental image of his mother reposing on a heavenly cloud, delicately strumming the strings of a golden harp as her wings flapped in the breeze.

"I guess religion comes in all kinds of packages," Millie replied. "And no, I don't suppose Paula is 'religious' in the traditional sense. But she's always been a good person—honest, hardworking, taking care of you kids the best she knew how, loving you to pieces. If God is keeping track, I expect he'll give her pretty high marks . . . she's done a lot with her life, you know."

"Yeah, I know," TJ agreed. His brow furrowed. "But if there's really only one true church, like the elders said, and she can't see it, I could be in *big* trouble when it comes to that forever family stuff they were talking about. I just don't see how—"

"Let it rest, my sweet boy," Millie soothed, putting her arm around his shoulders. "We both have families that—well, that need a little help at the moment. I'm just going to try to remember what the elders said . . . it'll all work out. And if—somehow, someday—I'm ever able to see my precious Joe and Molly again . . ." Her voice faltered and she took a deep, ragged breath. "If that ever happens, I'll have a lot to be thankful for."

"I know you will," TJ said softly as he curled an arm around her waist. "And so will they. You're the best, Mill." He bent forward slightly and brushed a light kiss across her cheek. "Hey, I have an awesome idea," he added abruptly. "The dishes and basketball can wait a little, and Scotty's probably eating himself into next week at the Crawlers' blowout . . . so how 'bout if we took the rest of that yumbolicious shortcake over to the sisters? I can't think of a better way to take care of poor Sister Tibbetts' pain, can you? An' I bet Sister Kent wouldn't complain any, either." He stepped back to flash her an eager smile.

"Why, I'd say that was a definite stroke of genius, young man," Millie beamed. "Whoever sings the praises of chicken soup has obviously never tasted Millie Hampton's strawberry shortcake. Let's *do* it!"

CHAPTER 16

Paula didn't understand. As the Lexus glided through mile after mile of pristine Connecticut countryside, her thoughts returned to Mapleton Crossing and the silent reproach of her mother's empty house. *So what were you expecting, Donroe?* she chided herself. *It wasn't like you called and made an appointment to have tea with her. She could've been shopping, napping, chatting on the phone, digging in her flower beds out back—anything. Next year, you'll let her know you're coming, spend the afternoon, maybe take care of some unfinished business. Yes, next year things will be different . . . better.*

"Right," she jeered at her reflection in the rearview mirror. "And Elvis, back from the dead, will put on his blue suede shoes and father a child with Madonna." The thought triggered a faint smile in spite of her dour mood. "Oh, well," she sighed, "I guess anything's possible." She giggled. *Well, maybe not for Elvis . . . but perhaps for Mother and me.*

The thing now, she decided, was to get on with her well-organized, highly productive life. She'd go back to L.A. where she belonged, settle into the normal routine, and forget about all of this for eleven months and twenty-nine days or so. Then she might be ready to try again. Or not.

Paula's frame of mind had improved somewhat by the time she pulled the Lexus into her parking space at the Westbury. Dusk was just falling on the horizon; she'd taken the long way back to New Haven, turning off the main road to leisurely navigate Quaker Canyon Loop and drink in its stunning display of fall colors. Nothing on the West Coast could compare to this exuberant blast of kaleidoscopic hues, ranging from deep emerald through gold and rust to vermillion. It was a visual symphony of light and shadow, and its music seemed to calm her inner storms.

"First things first," she declared as her room key turned in the lock and she pushed the door open. "The sooner I'm home in L.A., the better." Tossing her purse and jacket on the overstuffed chair, she kicked off her shoes, sat down heavily on the bed, and retrieved a telephone book from the nightstand. Dialing the airline was easy; being put on hold for five minutes set her teeth on edge. The familiar pillow-top chocolate mint eased her aggravation; she popped it into her mouth and folded its green foil wrapper into a tiny, perfect square, which she lobbed expertly into the waste basket a dozen feet across the room. *I guess Scotty and TJ come by their athletic gifts naturally.* She lay back against the pillows and smiled as the melting chocolate drizzled down her throat. By the time a fresh-voiced young airline representative came on the line, she was feeling almost civil.

The first available flight to LAX was mid-afternoon the next day, with a couple of long layovers. It wasn't the most direct route, but she'd be home before midnight. That would give her Sunday to unwind and regroup for the week ahead. She made the reservation, hung up the phone, and glanced at the tall grandfather clock in the corner. When its chimes gently bonged the eight o'clock hour, Paula's stomach rumbled. It had been many hours since her forlorn little lunch at the espresso café, and now she reached into the nightstand drawer for a room service menu. Most bed-and-breakfasts (at least the ones she knew in California) lived up to their names and served only the first meal of the day. But fortunately, while an elegant morning buffet was still the meal of choice at the Westbury, a modest selection of light entrees was available around the clock. *No use going out; a cozy meal and "must-see TV" will be good enough tonight.*

She called the kitchen and ordered chicken teriyaki, a small caesar salad, chocolate-cherry cheesecake, and a decanter of white wine. While she waited she changed into a comfortable royal blue sweat suit and terry slippers, then opened the top half of the antique armoire to reveal a large-screen TV. She fingered the remote and studied a list of classic and late-run movies showing through the night. *Not bad,* she mused as she punched a button and the screen came to life in vivid color. *The solitary life has its pleasures.*

Given Paula's melancholy afternoon, it was bound to be a Kleenex evening. Wrapped snugly in the thick floral comforter, she sat cross-legged on the bed, munching her dinner, sipping wine, and dabbing at her eyes as the tragic melodrama and haunting music of *Beaches* unfolded on the screen. Later, the classic black-and-white version of Dauphne DuMaurier's *Rebecca,* a hopelessly romantic story of mystery and passion, wrung her heart and sent tears coursing down her finely sculpted cheeks. *It isn't fair,* she thought as she drained the last ounce of wine from a small glass. *Everything reminds me of . . . everything.* Finally, exhausted and grieving for her own losses, she sank into a barren, dreamless sleep.

Thin sunlight streaming through half-drawn Levelor blinds brought her to sodden wakefulness the next morning. She stretched languidly; the room was so quiet that she could almost hear her muscles contract and expand. A glance at the clock told her she'd slept for more than ten hours, and she smiled at the notion that a good cry worked even better than a bad book when it came to getting a decent night's rest. The wine had done its part, too.

Paula showered and slipped into a pair of loose-fitting jeans and a pink cotton T-shirt, then joined a few late-rising guests downstairs at the tail end of a scrumptious breakfast buffet. As she swirled a final morsel of Belgian waffle in the glistening pool of thick maple syrup on her plate, she remembered Dick Southern's request and made a mental note to pick up several small bottles of the syrup on her way out of town. They'd be great souvenirs of New England for her family and office staff.

Back in her room, she decided not to waste any energy on careful packing. Instead, she began to quickly empty the nightstand and armoire of all her possessions, tossing books, lecture notes, and clothing haphazardly together in her suitcase. *Okay, so I'm no Millie when it comes to getting my act together on the road,* she reflected as she bent to open the armoire's bottom drawer and gather a handful of magazines she'd bought at the campus bookstore. *At least everything will get home in one—*

Paula's gaze froze as she lifted the last magazine and saw the Book of Mormon snuggled in one corner. "Shoot," she grumbled, recalling her strange, soggy dream of two nights earlier and the brief flash of brilliance as she sat outside her mother's house. "Don't you have anything better to do than taunt me, Mr. Moroni?" She smiled grimly. "Yeah, I know . . . 'Never say never.' What's that supposed to mean, anyway?" She paused for a moment, almost as if she expected an answer to leap at her from the book. "Oh, I don't know . . . who cares? You might as well come along for the ride—if they'll let you." A quick call to the front desk assured her that she was free to take the book. Scooping it up along with her magazines, she pitched them all into the suitcase.

Less than an hour later, she had checked out of the Westbury and made her souvenir purchases at a small gift shop near campus. Now the Lexus was speeding down the interstate toward Hartford and the airport. As she watched the diminishing New Haven skyline in her rearview mirror, Paula's thoughts freewheeled over the New England countryside and settled just outside the perimeters of the Enfield estate. *That's where I've always been—just outside,* she brooded. *Growing up wasn't all that bad—everything so beautiful and proper, and I had a place. Greg came along and gave me a new place, a wonderful place, shining with love and promise. Then he died, and I gave our baby away, and Mother and Daddy could never forgive me. They took my place away, and they never gave it back.*

"Not that I wanted it back, or even asked for it," she murmured. "I guess it's true . . . you can't go home again. So I made my own place." She sighed and wiped a stray tear from her cheek. *But maybe I'll try one more time . . . next year. For the boys. They should know their grandmother. Maybe. Old grudges die hard, don't they, Donroe?*

It was well past midnight when a cheese-colored taxi crawled slowly to the curb on Valley View Drive and deposited Paula at the corner of her driveway. "I can get it from here," she insisted, pressing two twenty-dollar bills into the driver's hand and jumping out to retrieve her luggage from the backseat. "Thanks." She easily navigated the terraced walk to the front porch and let herself in the front door.

Rudy met her in the entryway, his sturdy golden body rippling with excitement as he woofed softly in greeting. She reached out to pat his head, and he nuzzled her downturned palm with his cold nose. "Hi, buddy," she grinned. "I don't suppose you've missed me, have you?" At the sound of her voice, his tail wagged briskly and a small whimper of joy erupted from his throat. "That's what I thought," she whispered. "Me, too. We'll go for a nice long walk in the morning." She rubbed the top of his forehead, and he grunted in satisfaction.

The house was dark except for a dim overhead light in the entryway, and Paula was glad to steal silently upstairs to her room. She was exhausted, and a good night's sleep was her first priority. Millie had turned down the bedcovers and left the window open; a light, cool breeze gently lifted the curtains and made the room fresh and inviting. It took Paula about two seconds to drop her luggage and kick off her shoes, and a few more to shed everything else. She found a comfortable cotton nightshirt in her drawer and shrugged it easily over her head and shoulders as she lay back on the bed. Closing her eyes, she inhaled deeply and breathed out a long, slow stream of air that seemed to settle comfortably on her chest like an infant's receiving blanket. "Home," she sighed tranquilly. "My own place. Nice." Moments later, she slept.

The closing of a door followed by deep male voices outside awakened her. "We'll be right on time," one of them said in a cheerful tone.

Even half awake and with her eyes closed, Paula instantly recognized the next voice. "That was a cool practice yesterday," TJ said. "The guys invited me to come again—even play in the tournament next month. It's gonna be fun."

"They're a great bunch of kids," the other voice said. "Most of them will be at church today."

"Cool," TJ replied.

Paula's eyes flew open. *Church?* She remembered her recent phone conversation with TJ, during which she'd given her reluctant permission. *He actually took me up on it. Unbelievable.* Shaking her head, she threw back the covers and swung her legs over the side of the bed, then stepped quickly to the window and pulled back the curtain just far enough to see what was going on.

Looking down on the driveway, she saw two young men in dark suits, one very tall and the other about TJ's height, shepherding Millie and TJ toward a small white vehicle parked at the curb.

Millie's brightly colored floral print dress billowed slightly in the morning breeze, and she carried a small black handbag. TJ was neatly dressed in tan Dockers, brown suede loafers, a pale blue shirt, and a red-and-navy striped tie. His sandy hair, still damp from the shower, was carefully combed back from his forehead. *Hmmm*, Paula reflected, a bemused smile playing across her lips. *I didn't even know he owned a tie.*

She watched until the little car was out of sight, then crawled back into bed and closed her eyes; it was still much too early to consider facing the day. But sleep would not come again, and her thoughts kept returning to her youngest son. *I know this kid . . . for the past three years, he's never missed a Sunday morning shooting baskets. Now, even on this perfect basketball morning, he's all dressed up and traipsing off to church. What's wrong with this picture?* She sighed. *Maybe nothing . . . maybe everything. Just give him a little time; he'll get over it. In the meantime, you've got another kid to worry about—he's a Crawler, and he's just about ready to get his driver's license.*

"Oboy." Paula groaned aloud and pressed her palms against her eyelids. "I can hardly wait to hear how the learner's permit test went." Her mind flashed to another field of battle. "And I can bet I'll have a dozen fires to put out at the office tomorrow morning."

Suddenly, like an obscure dream, New Haven and Marjorie Enfield faded into the distant past as Paula butted up against the challenges of the present. *Goodbye, Mother. Hello, real world. Welcome home, Donroe,* she thought tersely as she tossed back the covers and headed for the shower.

Scott was sitting at the table, sipping orange juice and thumbing through a *Car and Driver* magazine when Paula walked into the kitchen. He looked up, and, in a rare departure from his behavior of recent months, flashed her a wide smile. *He ought to do that more often,* she thought, grinning back at him. *He's really a good-looking kid.*

"Hiya, Mom," he said, rising from his chair. "I heard the water running, so I figured you were home." To her amazement, he bent to kiss her lightly on the cheek. "How was your trip?"

"Uh, fine, thanks," she stammered, studying his face intently. *Okay, what have you done with my son, and how much can I pay you to keep him?* "What's up?"

"Oh, nuthin," he replied, reaching casually into the back pocket of his jeans. "Except . . . this." He slowly, meticulously unfolded the slip of paper in his hands and held it close to her face. His eyes sparkled as she read "Department of Motor Vehicles" and understanding dawned.

I knew it. He passed the test. We're doomed. No, don't do this . . . take it easy. Look at him—so utterly happy and proud. Play along . . . you can worry later.

"Hey, Scotty, way to go!" she gushed, throwing her arms around him and genuinely relishing the hug he gave her in return. "I *knew* you could do it! Congratulations, honey!"

Scott was beaming as he pulled away from her. "Thanks, Mom," he said. "I got a hundred percent."

"Doesn't surprise me a bit," she grinned, gently pummeling his shoulder with her fist. "Any kid with a brain like yours is bound to come out on top." *And hopefully has the sense to stay there.* "So, what's next with this driving thing?"

For once, Scott was in no hurry to brush her off. "Well," he began, settling into a chair, "tomorrow's my first driving lesson at school—seven a.m. sharp. Three of us and the instructor in one car. We practice in the parking lot for a few days, then we hit the road. Cool, huh?"

Paula smiled gamely. "You bet." *As long as the road is the only thing you hit.* "And how long is this, uh, class?" she asked, moving to the sink to pour herself a steaming cup of coffee.

"Around two months, I think," Scott answered. "It'd take the whole semester if we only practiced three times a week, but there are so many kids waiting for the course, they scrunched up the time. Now we practice every day, so we can do it faster. Which is fine with me."

"I'm sure it is," Paula mumbled bleakly, then caught herself and added brightly, "So, my number one son, what shall we do to celebrate this happy occasion?"

"Aw, Mom," Scott protested, shifting awkwardly in his chair. "It's no big deal. Really. Besides, I've already—"

"Of *course* it's a big deal," Paula insisted. *This is going well. He loves the attention. Keep it up.* "We could have cake, or go out for a special family dinner, or—"

"Mom." The hard edge had returned to his voice, and it stopped her cold. "It's already been taken care of."

"What do you mean, it's already—"

"I mean," he said coolly, "there's already been a party. With the Crawlers. We celebrated on Friday night. It was awesome."

"Oh. I see. The Crawlers." A lump of lead settled in her chest, and she stared at him for a long moment.

"What?" he finally said with a defensive sneer. "It was a cool party, okay?"

"Uh-huh." Her voice was distant. *So much for the warm fuzzies.* "I just hope this gang"—he shot her a withering glance—"all right, this *club,* isn't going to get you into any trouble. You know I worry."

"Unbelievable," Scott growled, rolling his eyes. "Is that all you can think about—the trouble we're getting into? Have you seen any trouble yet, Mom? *Have you?*" The decibel level of his voice was rising.

"Well, no," she said, setting her coffee mug on the table. "It's just that I don't trust—"

"It's just that you don't trust *me,* isn't it?" He stood and glared at her.

"That's not it, Scotty, and you know it." She struggled to keep her voice even. "I only meant—"

"Thanks a lot, Mom. I knew you'd understand. That's what moms are for, right?" He gave the table leg a solid kick and stalked from the room. The front door slammed, and she looked out the window as he jogged across the lawn.

Shaking her head in disbelief, Paula sank into the chair Scott had just vacated. She thumbed idly through the *Car and Driver* magazine he'd left behind, noticing pictures of several sports cars he'd circled in red ink. "Here we go again," she sighed. *And again. And again.*

She felt a heavy warmth settle on her stockinged feet. "Hi, Rudy," she said absently, wiggling her toes against the soft underside of the dog's broad chin. "I thought that went well, didn't you?" She grimaced, noticing that Scott's kick had moved the table a few inches to the left. "At least he didn't break anything." Rudy snorted empathetically and nuzzled her ankle with his nose.

She closed the magazine and pushed aside her coffee mug. "Tell you what, big guy," she said resolutely, leaning over the table's edge to talk to him. "It won't do me any good to mope around here all morning . . . wanna go for a little walk?" Rudy's tail thumped the floor several times, then he got to his feet and ambled toward the entryway. "I guess that answers my question. Just hold on a minute; this sweat suit is fine for outside, but I'll need to go get some shoes on." Hurrying upstairs, she rummaged in her closet for a pair of sneakers, quickly put them on, and closed her bedroom door behind her.

As she strode briskly down the hall, she noticed that Scott's door was ajar. A faint buzzing sound was coming from inside the room. She stopped and pushed the door open, looking for the source of the noise. It was his clock radio. *He must've gotten up before his alarm went off. I'd better turn it off.* She moved across the room to his nightstand, shut off the alarm, and swung around to leave. As she did so, her shoe caught on an object extending a few inches from underneath the bed. Glancing down, she thought it looked familiar. *It's that sketch pad he was working on earlier this week. I'll just put it on his bed so it won't get torn or anything.* She bent over, grasped the pad, and pulled it up to eye level. What she saw drained the color from her face. "Oboy," she whistled. "We're in big trouble."

CHAPTER 17

Paula gaped open-mouthed at the sketch pad for several seconds before her thought patterns stabilized. "This is very good," she breathed. "And very bad."

Staring up at her was an intricate pen-and-ink drawing of one of the lady missionaries, Sister Kent. Scott had expertly captured the essence of her fresh beauty—the high, thin cheekbones; wide, almond-shaped eyes; a perfectly straight and symmetrical nose; wisps of dark hair framing her face in halo fashion and resting casually on her shoulders; full, petulant lips parted in a half-smile. Her face was perfect.

And so was her body. Perfectly naked.

Paula gulped as her eyes scanned the voluptuous figure. "What was he *thinking?*" she wheezed. *You have to* ask *what he was thinking, Donroe?* She put three fingers of one hand to her temple. "This is . . . this is blasphemy or something. She's a *missionary*, for goodness' sake." *And he's a hot-blooded adolescent with more on his mind than fast cars.*

"Whew," she said, exhaling a long stream of air as she carefully flipped the pad to a blank page. "I think my son and I are going to have to have a little talk. He's definitely not grown-up enough to draw something so . . . so . . . anatomically correct." She shuddered.

A short, insistent bark from downstairs reminded her that Rudy was waiting. "Coming, pal," she called out, then slipped the sketch pad back under—far, far under—Scott's bed. "We'll have that little talk, my boy," she vowed as she firmly closed her son's door and headed down the hall. "Soon."

The sun was straight overhead, winking through the smog as Paula and Rudy jogged easily along the sidewalk. She gradually cleared her mind of the morning's calamities, replacing them with more pleasant images: Millie's home cooking, TJ's contagious grin, a spin down the freeway in her new convertible . . . Ted's kiss at the airport. *Whoa, where did that come from?* She suppressed a light giggle. By the time they had jogged two or three miles, her mental gloom had lifted and she felt refreshed.

Half a mile later, a gurgling in the pit of her stomach reminded her that she hadn't eaten since her flight home the evening before. *I could use a monster sandwich right about now . . . I wonder what Millie's got stashed in the fridge.* "C'mon, buddy," she called to Rudy, who was getting acquainted with a lilac bush at the end of someone's driveway. "It's past lunchtime, and I'm jogged out." She changed direction abruptly, and the dog was at her side in an instant, his loping gait matching hers in a relaxed rhythm. Within a few minutes they had circled around to Valley View Drive and slowed to a brisk walk, then to a casual stroll as the house came into view. Their run had worked its magic, and now Paula was ready to refuel.

Stopping only long enough to kick her shoes off just inside the front door, she headed for the refrigerator. She assembled cold roast turkey and all the other ingredients for a perfect high-rise sandwich, then stood at the breakfast bar and began to build it with the skill and patience of an architect, pausing occasionally to flick a small morsel of meat in Rudy's direction. "If they ask, I'll tell 'em you ate it all," she joked.

Finally satisfied with her triple-decker offering to the gods of hunger, Paula carefully balanced her plate on one hand, clutched a Coke and a napkin in the other, and padded over to the table. Closing her eyes, she took in an expectant breath as she lifted the bulky sandwich to her mouth, savoring the anticipation of at least two million thunderous howls of approval from the army of tastebuds standing at attention on her tongue. She smiled indulgently. *You little guys will be talking about this for weeks.*

Just as Paula's front teeth sank into the top slice of Millie's thick, nut-flavored wheat bread, the sounds of voices on the front porch reached her ears, followed by the door swinging open. *Perfect timing,* she grumbled silently, licking a small glob of mayonnaise off a protruding tomato slice as she returned the barely dented sandwich to its plate. She wiped her lips with a napkin and looked up to see Millie, TJ, and the two elders rounding the corner into the kitchen.

"Mom! You're home!" TJ whooped, narrowly missing Rudy's tail as he dashed to her side to plant a noisy kiss on her cheek. His eyes were shining as he pulled back and grinned at her. "How's it going?"

"Just great, kiddo," she replied, squeezing his arm affectionately as she looked him up and down. "My, aren't we handsome today, all dressed up. I take it you, uh, went to . . . church." Her tone was less than enthusiastic, but he didn't seem to notice.

"Yeah, it was cool. And next week . . . I mean, can I go again next week?" His voice had an uncertain edge as he glanced from his mother to the elders and back again. "Can I?"

"We'll see," Paula said coolly, rising from the table. "In the meantime, I don't believe I've had the pleasure of meeting your . . . friends."

"Oh, sorry," TJ said, straightening his back into a slightly formal posture. "Mom, this is Elder Stucki." He paused while the elder, beaming with enthusiasm, shook her hand vigorously. "And this," TJ added, gesturing toward the taller missionary, "is Elder Richland. He was a BYU basketball star before he went on his mission."

"I see," Paula responded as though her vocal cords had been bathed in ice water. *These must be the guys he was playing ball with the other night.* "BYU?"

"Yes, ma'am . . . Brigham Young University," Elder Richland explained as he extended his hand. Paula looked up into his chocolate-brown eyes and felt them studying her with friendly interest. "It's very nice to meet you," he said in a deep, resonant voice. His handshake was firm and gracious, unlike Elder Stucki's frenetic pumping. "You seem to have quite a rising basketball star yourself here," he added, nodding toward TJ, who grinned self-consciously. "The ward is awfully excited about having him play on their team."

"That's nice," Paula murmured. "It's . . . good of you to show an interest." *I don't suppose it'll last very long once you find out he's not going to join your church.*

"Hey, there's nothing we like better than a good game on P-Day," Elder Stucki broke in.

"P-Day?" Paula's brows knit in puzzlement.

"Sorry," Elder Richland clarified with a dimpled smile, "that's 'Preparation Day.' It's every Monday—the one day a week when we can get some exercise, write letters, do our laundry, things like that.

Even people on the Lord's errand need a break once in a while, and
we love it when there's someone to play ball with. TJ was great last
week . . . he really gave us a workout." The elder's eyes sparkled; it
was obvious that basketball was one of his favorite topics of conversation. Paula noticed that he was tan and fit-looking.

"This guy's a terror on the courts, all right," she agreed, putting an
arm around her young son's shoulders. "He practices day and night."

"It shows," Elder Richland observed.

"All *right* already," TJ laughed. "This is gettin' embarrassing. But
I'll beat ya both cold tomorrow night," he vowed with a playful
punch to Elder Stucki's arm. Then he tugged at the edge of his shirt
collar. "That is, if I can get rid of this tie before it chokes me to
death. How do you guys stand it all day, every day?" The elders
smiled at each other as TJ wrestled briefly with the Windsor knot
holding his throat captive, then yanked his tie off and undid the top
button of his shirt.

"It's a learned skill," the taller missionary said. "You get used to it."

Millie had been listening to their conversation, and now she put
an arm around Paula's waist and smiled at the elders. "Well, here's
another learned skill for you to practice today," she said. "Eating.
How does a nice pot roast with potatoes and gravy sound?"

"Like manna to a couple of hungry wanderers," Elder Stucki
sighed, patting his sturdy midsection.

"Good. I set the automatic oven timer before we left for church,
so we won't have long to wait. Just have a seat in the living room, and
dinner will be ready in no time. You'll join us, won't you, dear?" She
gave Paula a little squeeze.

A searing flash of irritation swept up Paula's spine. She screwed
the corners of her mouth into a tight smile as she shrugged off Millie's
embrace. "Gee," she said, "I'd love to, but I've got a ton of work to do
upstairs . . . and, as you can see," she motioned toward the table, "I've
already made my own lunch. So I think I'll just take it and get out of
your way." Reaching to pick up her plate, she caused the oversized
sandwich to sway precariously. She steadied it with her free hand.

"Are you sure?" Elder Richland asked. "We'd really like to talk
with you about some of the things TJ's been learning. Maybe answer
some of your questions and—"

"That's easy," she snapped. "I don't *have* any questions. I'm not the one who's interested in your church, remember."

"Oh?" Elder Richland said, his brow furrowing slightly. "We just thought, since you've been reading the Book of Mormon, you might want to—"

"Me? Reading the Book of Mormon?" She chuckled snidely, then caught herself. *Keep it friendly, Donroe. They seem nice enough.* "Well," she continued, willing her voice to remain calm, "I did, uh, read a few pages. But it wasn't exactly my kind of book."

"Could I ask what you mean when you say it's not 'your kind of book'?" The tall elder spoke quietly and looked down at her expectantly, but with no trace of judgment in his dark eyes.

She returned the sandwich plate to the table and rested her hands on her hips. "Well, for starters," she began, "I couldn't get past the language. I mean, my entire career depends on my ability to convince people to buy what I'm trying to sell. My staff and I build short, tantalizing word pictures to attract customers for our clients, and we do a darn good job of it. Whoever wrote your book should've had some serious lessons in grammar and usage. C'mon," her voice grew more edgy, "'It must needs be' . . . 'In the own due time of the Lord' . . . what kind of sentence structure is that?" She shook her head in exasperation.

The muscles along Elder Richland's jaw tensed and quickly relaxed. "I see what you're saying," he responded evenly. "All of that must be quite distracting to someone of your capabilities. On the other hand," he continued, a glint of humor rising in his eyes, "I suppose if I were etching a book on gold plates, taking days or weeks to pound out one little page, even if I knew I'd made a dumb mistake, I'm not sure I'd be willing to melt the whole thing down and start over, just to get the punctuation right. As long as there wasn't any doctrinal problem, I'd probably just forge ahead. Does that make sense?"

Paula was not persuaded. "I might suggest that if your scribe had been all that concerned about getting it done in a hurry, all he'd have to do was cut out the 'And it came to pass' at the beginning of every verse. He'd have saved himself a lot of time and precious metal, not to mention sparing his readers a load of tedious repetition. In fact, the whole 'golden plates' thing sounds just a little far-fetched, don't you think?" She eyed the elders accusingly.

"We don't think so," both men answered in unison. Paula was briefly taken aback by the fervency in their voices. "In fact," Elder Richland continued, his index finger jabbing the air for emphasis, "if we didn't know the Book of Mormon was a true record, as well as being an important testament of Jesus Christ and the word of God, there's no way we'd take two years of our lives to tell other people about it." His intense gaze bore deeply into her eyes as Elder Stucki nodded his agreement.

Paula backed off. "Two years . . . that's a long time," she said in a more subdued tone. "Don't you boys have college, jobs, girlfriends, basketball—a *life* to get back to?"

"All of the above," Elder Stucki grinned. "But this . . . this is *important;* we know it can make a difference in other people's lives. Like Millie's and TJ's . . . and yours."

The next few moments seemed suspended in silence. Paula stared at the floor until TJ whispered, "They really mean it, Mom. Church was awesome. If you'd just read the book . . ."

Paula's mind snapped back to reality. "Maybe someday, but not now. Definitely not now," she replied more softly, then turned toward the elders. "Like I said, I have work to do, so I'll leave you all to your dinner. See you later, honey." She kissed TJ's cheek, gathered up her sandwich and Coke, and disappeared into the entryway. Seconds later, the door to her room opened and closed.

Elder Richland rubbed the back of his neck and let out a long sigh as they walked to the living room. "Your mom's a very interesting lady," he observed with a tight chuckle.

Elder Stucki laughed feebly. "You can say that again," he moaned, reaching into his pocket for a handkerchief to wipe at the tiny beads of perspiration on his upper lip.

"Relax, Elder, you did great," the taller man said, resting one huge hand on his companion's shoulder. "For a greenie, you held up remarkably well; and as your senior companion, I commend you for a job well done."

Elder Stucki gulped and turned toward TJ. "Is she always like . . . this?" The expression on his face was desolate.

"Naw . . . sometimes she's worse," TJ joked, sinking into a chair. The missionaries seated themselves on the couch. "Seriously, you gotta understand . . . my mom's the best, y'know? But when she gets her mind set for or against somethin', there's no way you can stop her without a sledgehammer. She's not all that religious, if ya wanna know—probably just needs some time and space to figure it all out."

"Yeah, like ten years and ten thousand miles," Elder Stucki muttered.

"At least," TJ laughed. "What's a greenie, anyway?"

"That's what we call a missionary who's new in the field," Elder Richland explained. "Elder Stucki here has only been out for three months, but he's catching on real fast." A distant expression glazed his eyes for a moment. "Seems like I was a greenie myself just a few months ago, but it's been almost two years. I'll be home in Idaho for Christmas."

"Wow, I bet you're getting pretty excited," TJ said. "Two years is a long time to be away from home."

"Yeah, I'm getting a little trunky," the elder admitted. "But these two years have been—well, they've helped me see what's really important in life . . . helped me grow up and learn how to serve the Lord. Moving his work along, making a difference—it's even better than . . . even better than basketball." He grinned at TJ. "'Course, I can hardly wait to get into that BYU uniform again. I hope the coach'll let me play a little next year."

"He'd be pretty dumb not to," TJ said. "But as long as you're here in L.A., you'll still come over and shoot baskets with me on your days off, won't ya? I need all the pointers I can get—you know, for high school." He eyed both elders expectantly.

"We'll be there; you can bet on it," Elder Stucki assured him with a warm smile, and his companion nodded in agreement. "The more the merrier."

"Terrific," the boy beamed.

"I'll tell you what's terrific," Millie called from the entryway. "My famous pot roast. Come and get it, gentlemen—and bring your appetites."

"Yes, *ma'am,*" Elder Richland said eagerly, unfolding his long body and rising from the sofa in one easy movement. "C'mon, brethren," he directed, motioning to the other two. "Let's go see what damage we can do."

Just over an hour later, Paula glanced up from the book she was reading when she heard the front door open and close. Through her open window she caught snatches of conversation as TJ walked the elders to their car. "Tomorrow? Great!" her son was saying. "I'll come right home after school." They laughed about something, then two car doors slammed and the small compact pulled away from the curb.

She lay back against her pillow and rested the book on her chest as she let out a long, slow breath through pursed lips. *It's about time they left . . . now the day can get back to normal.* She closed her eyes, expecting momentarily to hear the rhythmic thumping of TJ's basketball on the driveway, followed by a gentle *swoosh* as it slipped through the net. Sunday was, after all, his favorite practice day.

Instead, she heard only the front door opening, closing. Then the door to TJ's room opening, closing. Then silence.

He's probably changing into his sweats and sneakers . . . can't very well play basketball in his church clothes. Paula returned to her book, at the same time listening for sounds of activity in the driveway. Several minutes passed without TJ's reappearance, and her curiosity mounted. She stretched leisurely on the bed, then pulled herself to a sitting position. *I suppose I could use another Coke—or maybe something a little stronger. Guess I'll head downstairs and see what I can find. On the way, I might as well look in on him . . .*

She slid her feet into a pair of terry slippers and shuffled into the hall. TJ's door was closed, so she knocked softly. "TJ, honey?"

"Yeah, Mom?" His voice was muffled through the door. "C'mon in."

Paula found TJ sitting at his desk, his shoulders hunched over, writing in a small book. "Hi, guy," she said brightly. "We didn't get much of a chance to visit earlier, so I just thought I'd check in with you. Whatcha doing?" She squeezed his shoulder affectionately.

"Oh, just writin'. I got this book in Sunday School today . . . cool, huh? The teacher gave 'em to all the kids in class. It has Jesus on the front." He held the book up so she could see its rich, leather-like binding and the portrait of a gentle-looking man on its cover. Beneath the picture, the word "Journal" was embossed in gold.

"A journal, huh?" Paula was mildly interested.

"Yeah. Sister Sperry—that's our teacher—was talkin' about good things to do on Sunday, an' she said we should write down our thoughts and feelings about stuff. I told her I wasn't a member, but she gave me one anyway. She says it's good for everyone to keep a record of what they think and do. So I thought I'd give it a shot. It's hard, though."

Paula glanced over his shoulder and saw that he'd written about three lines. "Well, I'm sure you'll get the hang of it," she said. "Maybe someday you'll be a famous writer, and people will pay millions of dollars for a copy of your first journal." She smiled down at her son.

"Naw," he scoffed good-naturedly. "Too hard—I couldn't sit still long enough. Besides, I'd rather be playing ball."

"I knew that," she said with a little laugh. "In fact, it's such a gorgeous day, I couldn't help wondering why you're not out there right now, sinking those three-pointers. You haven't missed a Sunday for as long as I can remember . . . are you feeling okay?" She rumpled his sandy hair.

"Sure, I'm doin' great. It's just that, well, uh . . . ," he stuttered, hesitating.

"What, kiddo? I'm listening." She plopped herself on his unmade bed.

"Well, okay," TJ said resolutely, propping one arm on the back of his chair. "Remember when I said Sister Sperry talked about good things to do on Sunday?"

"Yes, I remember."

"Well . . . the thing is . . . doing sports isn't one of them." He looked at her sheepishly. "So I thought . . . leastwise for today . . . I'd try some other things. Reading, doing the journal—quiet stuff, y'know?"

"I see," Paula said in a measured voice. *You can take the boy out of basketball . . . how does that go? Oh, yeah . . . but you can't take basketball out of the boy.* "And did this 'Sister Sperry' explain exactly *why* playing sports is not appropriate?" She was seething. *Now they're telling my boy how to spend his free time.*

"Not every day, just on Sundays. She said it's the Lord's day, and people should do things to learn more about him and help each other. Stuff like that." His dark eyes met hers. "It sounded . . . all right, Mom. Sounded good."

Paula sighed loudly. *Stay calm, Donroe. After one day of this "quiet stuff" he'll be climbing the walls, and you'll never hear the word "Mormon" again.* She swallowed a biting remark and smiled indulgently. "That's nice, dear." *Change the subject before your eyeballs explode.* "By the way, I saw Scotty this morning; he was heading out to spend some time with his friends—the Crawlers, I guess." *Let's play Jeopardy . . . this is the only thing worse than a Mormon. What is a Crawler?* "He told me he passed the test for his learner's permit."

TJ's eyes glowed. "Yeah, I know . . . he was totally excited. It's awesome."

"It sure is," she agreed. "And speaking of Scotty, is there anything—you know, with the club and all—I should know about?" She had lowered her voice to a conspiratorial whisper.

"Oh, yeah, the *spy* deal," TJ grinned. "Hmm, let's see," he said, scratching the top of his head with the blunt end of his pen. "I think the clubhouse is almost finished. Scotty said something about christening the toilet next weekend." Paula winced at her young son's giggle. "He promised to show me around real soon. I'll have more to report after that, okay?"

"Deal," she said, shaking off an involuntary shiver that tightened the muscles in her shoulders. "In the meantime, I'll leave you to your writing." She stood and moved to give him a quick kiss on the cheek. "It's good to be home, kiddo. I missed you."

He crossed his eyes and made a comical face. "Yeah, I know. What's not to miss?"

"My son, the joker," she laughed, pausing in the doorway. Her expression suddenly became sober as she looked into his eyes. "Don't ever change, TJ."

"What's that supposed to mean?" he asked, his brows knitting together.

"Oh . . . nothing." She stared at a place above and behind him on the wall. "I just hope you'll always be happy, that's all."

"I'm planning to," he said without hesitation. "A guy's gotta have fun, ya know."

"I know, son," Paula replied. "I know. Just be careful." She turned toward the door. "I'll see you later, okay?"

"You got it, Mom." She was halfway out the door when he spoke again. "And Mom?"

She turned to face him. "Yes, dear?"

"I missed you, too."

Ignoring the small lump in her throat, Paula crossed her eyes and scrunched her face to imitate TJ's earlier expression. "Yeah, I know," she said. "What's not to miss?" She blew him a kiss and sauntered from the room. In the hall, she closed her eyes and took a deep breath. *Please, God or Zeus or somebody, let him fast-forward through puberty. I can't bear to watch him disappear into adolescence like his older brother. Once is enough. Once is too much.*

Downstairs, Rudy followed her into the study, where Paula rested her hand absently on his broad head. "Hey, pal. What say I get myself a little liquid refreshment, then we go hang out on the patio for a while? This place is like a tomb." The dog grunted his approval, and she made a beeline for the liquor cabinet. "One double martini, coming up."

Paula rarely spent time in her backyard; it was always too early in the morning or too late at night, too cold or too hot, too windy or too still to suit her. But this afternoon a blue-green expanse of sweet, close-cropped grass, the fragrant scent of late-blooming roses by the hundreds, and a comfortable chaise lounge beneath the patio canopy beckoned her without mercy. The air was comfortably warm as she stepped out onto the smooth, cool cement and closed the sliding door behind her. Setting her brimming martini on a small glass table beside the chaise, she lowered herself into the deep chintz cushions, stretched out her legs, and closed her eyes as the tension began to drain from her body. *Just the peaceful interlude I need before tomorrow's onslaught at the office.* She smiled lightly as Rudy's furry chin came to rest on her leg just above the knee. *I could get used to this.* Minutes passed, and her mind flickered on the edge of consciousness as she slipped deeper into relaxation.

A persistent low droning near her head pulled her partway back to the moment. She listened passively, mentally studying the sound, her eyelids too heavy to raise themselves more than a fraction of an inch. The humming circled closer to her head at eyebrow level, its intensity rising and falling in wavelike undulations. Then a rapid fluttering motion caught the edge of her eyelash, and she was startled into full wakefulness. Opening her eyes, she was momentarily transfixed by a small black and yellow body hovering in the air, just to one side of her nose. Her heart raced, but not in fear.

Faster than thought, an indelible image pressed itself into Paula's mind as she stared at the round-bodied bumble bee flitting curiously about her face.

It's just like I remembered.

She drew in a ragged breath and startled the small creature, who bobbed in the air a few times before resuming its benign inspection of her forehead.

Her eyes locked onto the bee, but her mind had already leapfrogged back over two decades and settled in a quiet, sunwashed hospital room just outside New Haven. She was cradling her newborn son in her arms, softly humming a lullaby as she committed the infant's every feature and movement to memory, securing each one silently in the chambers of her heart. He yawned and stretched one tiny arm toward her face, revealing an unusual and distinctive birthmark on the inside of his elbow. She gently grasped his arm and studied it for long minutes. The mark was small but perfectly defined, deep purple in color, and its likeness was unmistakable.

Exactly like a bumble bee in flight. Round body, short wings extended, spindly legs dangling below.

She kissed the mark tenderly and caressed her son's tiny cheek as the social worker gently lifted him from her arms and quickly disappeared down the hall. *Goodbye, my darling boy.*

The image faded as quickly as it had come, leaving Paula breathless and distracted. Her hand trembled as she brushed at the insect, and it calmly flew off toward the rose garden. *Why now? I can always bear the pain for a few minutes on my—our—birthday; then the memories fade and leave me mercifully alone for another year. But this time it's different . . . this time they won't let go. I've never been one to wallow in the past, but somehow the past is wallowing in me. Why . . . now?* Tears burned at the corners of her eyes, and she wiped at them fiercely with the back of her hand. "Get a grip, Donroe," she scolded as her gaze moved to the small table beside her. "Better yet, get a drink."

She reached quickly for the long-stemmed martini glass and cradled it with both hands before taking a long sip. "That's more like it," she sighed, resting her head back against the lounge cushions. *I'm just overreacting. It's probably the stress of the trip, the way it stirred up all those memories. I should have expected this . . . maybe an annual visit to Connecticut wouldn't be such a good idea, after all. Especially in October.*

Paula's glass was long empty, the sun settling at the horizon when she slid open the patio door and made her way slowly upstairs to her room. The house was silent except for the faint whirring of an overhead fan in the kitchen.

CHAPTER 18

It was never actually chilly in Los Angeles, but once in a while a cool breeze from the ocean would snake inland and take the temperature down a few degrees. Paula was hoping for such an effect as she pulled her new red convertible onto the freeway, and she wasn't disappointed. At six a.m. traffic was light, the wind whipping through her hair was fresh and almost smogless, and she could feel the car's powerful motor pulsing rapidly, rhythmically beneath her. Connecticut's bundle of sorrows seemed to recede into the distant past as she sped toward a new and invigorating set of challenges at the helm of her small but influential advertising dynasty. This day would be endless, but she was ready for it.

At the office, she carefully placed a miniature jug of New England maple syrup on each employee's swivel chair, then began her assault on the prodigious accumulation of paperwork concealing her own desk. In the two hours before her staff began to arrive, she managed to sort most of it into piles according to urgency and fill her waste basket with the rest. She was on the phone, listening to the first of dozens of voice messages, when the office came to life.

Carmine was the first to appear in Paula's doorway. "Welcome back," she mouthed with a toothy grin and flashing green eyes as Paula continued to hold the phone to her ear, acknowledging her assistant with a slightly raised hand and a crisp nod of her head. Carmine silently deposited a steaming mug of coffee and an apple Danish on a napkin beside Paula's desk, then returned to her own office and started up her computer.

As the morning progressed, each of her employees stopped by to thank her for the syrup and report on current projects. The work was generally under control—not a big surprise, since her staff members were the best in the business and she'd trained them to work independently. What surprised her was that Ted Barstow was nowhere to be found.

She stepped out of her office to question Carmine, whose explanation was vaguely disconcerting. "I dunno . . . I think he had an early meeting with Mel Campbell, the lawn mower guy, but he didn't really say. You know, I can't figure it," she added with a puzzled frown. "Something's been eating at him the past few days. He didn't say a dozen words to anyone around here last week, except when he had to work with the art people on that Northridge proposal. His office door was closed most of the time, too—like he didn't want to be bothered. So we kept our distance. He'll probably be in later." She shook her head in bewilderment, her tousled red hair bobbing from side to side, then returned to her computer screen.

Odd . . . Ted spends almost as much time here as I do—and he's a heck of a lot more social with the staff than I am. What's going on? Paula made a mental note to talk to him before the end of the day.

Morning became afternoon, then faded into early evening as she answered phone messages, met with a few clients, put out a dozen small fires, and chipped doggedly away at the piles of paperwork on her desk. The skyline outside her window was crimson with the lowering sun, the office long since silent and deserted when she finally leaned back against the soft leather of her chair and closed her eyes. *Not a bad day,* she mused as a small, satisfied smile appeared on her lips.

Paula decided to leave the rest of it until morning. She switched off her computer, retrieved her small handbag from the desk drawer, and moved silently across the thick carpet to her office door. As she pulled it open, a muffled sound reached her ears from down the hall, and she cocked her head to one side to listen. It was music . . . Mozart. And she had no doubt where it was coming from. *Ted does his best work to Mozart.*

She mentally slugged herself in the arm. *You were going to talk to him today, remember?* She sighed wearily, recalling Carmine's puzzled expression as she described Ted's unusual behavior. *I should at least say hi . . . but I'm way too tired for much of a conversation,* she thought as she shuffled down the hall. *Anything major will have to wait until tomorrow . . . he should've checked in with me earlier, anyway.* She knocked lightly at his office door, which was a few inches ajar. When there was no response, she pushed the door further open and stepped partway into the room.

Ted, dressed in faded jeans and a rumpled blue T-shirt, was hunched in his high-backed swivel chair, his elbows resting on its arms, his fingers forming a tent to support his chin. His eyes stared straight ahead, unseeing, at some invisible object in space, while one Nike-clad foot tapped almost in time with the cadence of Mozart's *Marriage of Figaro* overture. Paula's gaze was drawn to his face; she couldn't miss the unusual pallor of his skin, the dusky shadows under his eyes, the deeply etched furrows between his brows. Her eyes widened in alarm. *He's aged ten years in the last week. Is that a touch of gray at his temple?*

She took a few hesitant steps into the room, but he gave no acknowledgment of her presence.

"Ahem." She cleared her throat and waited in silence while his eyes moved slowly, gravely to meet hers. They seemed overly bright, almost as if he was feverish, yet at the same time lacking animation. She decided to take a casual approach. "Hi, Ted. I was on my way out and heard your music . . . thought I'd stop by. You're still into Mozart, I see."

Ted blinked rapidly several times before a gleam of recognition flickered across his face. "Oh, hi, Paula," he croaked, straightening himself in his chair as he squeezed out a minuscule smile. "I thought you'd be home with your kids by now." He ran the fingers of one hand through his short blond hair, pausing to tug at a cowlick near the crown of his head. "Sorry I didn't check in earlier. I've been . . . busy. I met with Campbell this morning, and a lot of other stuff . . ." His voice trailed off, and silence hung in the air like an unanswered question.

"I see," Paula said. She was ready to say something flippant about Melvin Campbell and the lawn Mormons, but caught herself when she gazed into his desolate eyes. Something was wrong. Moving closer to his chair, she leaned toward him and spoke intently. "Ted, are you all right? You look terrible."

"That good, huh?" he responded grimly. "Well, you know what Abe Lincoln said: You can fool all the people some of the time, some of the people all the time—"

She put her hand on his arm and felt his muscles tighten. "Ted, this is Paula—not your boss Paula, your *friend* Paula." She remembered his light kiss at the airport, could almost feel his lips on her cheek now. "Your *good* friend Paula. So, between friends, what's going on?" She lowered herself resolutely into the overstuffed chair beside his desk and fixed her eyes on his face, expecting an answer.

He sank back into his chair and closed his eyes, the muscles in his jaw twitching rapidly. "Nothing . . . you just caught me at a bad time, that's all."

She folded her arms across her chest and stared at him. "Ted Barstow, I know you better than that. You've been with Donroe for over six years, and I've never once seen you like this. You get excited, you get mad, you get frustrated, you get over it. But from what I've heard about last week, and from what I'm seeing now, I'd say you're being eaten up from the inside out. So I'll ask again . . . what's going on?"

His eyes were still closed. "Nothing you'd want to hear about," he mumbled.

"Why don't you let *me* be the judge of that? You know I'm on your side, Ted. Now, if something's going on here at the office, if any of the others are giving you a hard time, if you need a vacation, if I've done something, or if there's anything—"

"Friendly fire."

"—I can do to help in some . . ." She stopped abruptly. "What did you say?"

"Friendly fire." He opened his eyes and looked directly into hers. "I said friendly fire."

Paula shook her head in confusion. "Good grief, Ted, that sounds like something out of a war story. I don't see what it has to do with—"

"It *is* a war story, Paula." His eyes were burning. "The Gulf War. And it has *everything* to do with this conversation."

She regarded him curiously. "I don't understand."

Ted let out the longest, deepest sigh she had ever heard in her life, like the ebbing of a tide out to sea. When he closed his eyes and didn't breathe again for many seconds, she became alarmed. "Ted, are you still with me?"

He took in a ragged, shallow breath. "Oh, yeah," he murmured. His eyes opened, and he looked at her wearily. "Got a few minutes?"

"Sure." She scooted forward to the edge of her chair. "I'm here for as long as it takes."

"That's what I was afraid of," he said with the hint of a smile. "It's all your fault, y'know."

Paula's eyes widened. "Excuse me?" This was not what she'd expected.

"Well, not really," Ted began, "but I can't help giving you some of the credit."

She shook her head. "I'm clueless here, Ted."

"Okay, I know. Just stay with me," he said, leaning forward in his chair and resting his forearms on his thighs. "Remember last week, when I took you to the airport?"

"Yes, of course." *Is he feeling guilty about that little kiss? Not my fault!*

"And remember our conversation about my office—the photos on my walls, the Pulitzer, all the mementos?"

"Yes, I remember that." *Okay, so maybe it wasn't the kiss. Just like a man to not notice.*

"And you asked me why I'd abandoned the journalistic life while I was at the top of my game—why I'm now settling for writing about lawn mowers instead of space launches?"

"Oh, yeah," Paula nodded. "I wanted an answer—and you conveniently brushed me off." She poked a finger at him good-naturedly.

"Well, there's your answer," he said in a deliberate tone. "Friendly fire."

She groaned. "Now we're back to war games. Would you mind elaborating on this, my friend? I'm still in the dark here."

"I'm getting to it." Ted seemed to relax a little as he leaned back in his chair and rested his right ankle on his left knee. "I was there, Paula—right in the middle of the Gulf War. On assignment for the Associated Press." He pointed to a framed picture on the wall in which he was wearing battle fatigues, a camera slung over his shoulder, standing in front of a fighter jet. He was shaking hands with General Schwartzkopf.

"Wow," Paula breathed. "That must've been some assignment."

"Yeah—and it was my last," Ted responded, his voice barely a whisper.

She had to ask. "How come?"

"Because," he said, meeting her intense gaze, "I was in the wrong place at the wrong time." He held up a hand as she began to question him further, then continued. "I was one of the front-line reporters who got to go along on the bombing missions. I went on about a dozen."

"Sounds scary," Paula said.

"Could've been, but I found it exhilarating. Anyway, on our last run we were supposed to come in low on a cluster of enemy barracks and blow them away, and we did exactly as we were told. 'Boy,' I thought as the bombs exploded, 'those middle-eastern hotheads are smithereens. God bless America!' I shouted to myself. I was almost singing the *Star-Spangled Banner* as those poor fools bought the farm. And then . . . then . . ."

His voice cracked, and it was many seconds before he gulped hard and resumed the narrative. "And then the pilot had a radio transmission. 'Dear God in heaven,' he said. 'Dear God. They sent us to kill our own people.' All those barracks . . . all those bodies . . . they were Americans, Paula. They were *us*." His sentence ended in a strangled sob.

Paula shook her head but couldn't find words; she was transfixed by the horror of his revelation. When he spoke again, his voice was weary.

"Friendly fire. Killing your own soldiers. Not on purpose, of course, but as a result of some horrendous misinformation and errors in calculation. But I guess it doesn't really matter whose bombs they are, does it? Either way, the people are just as dead. It happened all the time in Vietnam, and at least a couple of times in the Gulf." Ted's shoulders slumped, and he stared at the floor. "I just wish I hadn't been a part of it."

Paula chose her words carefully. "That had to be one of the worst times of your life," she said softly.

He looked up at her with pain-filled eyes. "It gets worse. I wanted to write about it, tell the story, if only to get some of it off my chest before it consumed me. But there were hard-line briefing sessions, total gag orders, and nasty threats from higher-ups in the military. Did I say 'higher-ups'? I mean *the* higher-up . . . the Commander-in-Chief himself. No one wanted the American public to know that its sons and daughters had been sacrificed for no reason. That its children lay dead in the desert because some idiot made a stupid mistake and gave the wrong orders."

"What did you do?" Paula's voice was hoarse with emotion.

Ted began to rub his thighs with the palms of his hands. "What *could* I do? I kept my mouth shut, even though I was plagued with nightmares and a fire in my gut. To go up against all that power would have cost me—well, it could've cost me my life." He shook his head sadly. "But I felt like a prostitute . . . like I'd never be able to write a decent or truthful story again. That was the beginning of the end for me, and I quit a couple of months later. I bummed around on the L.A. beaches for a while, then took some freelance advertising jobs. The money was good, and I seemed to have a knack for the writing, so I put the high-profile life behind me and . . ."

"Came to Donroe?" Paula prompted.

He nodded. "And came to Donroe. I haven't regretted the change, you know, and I don't usually allow myself to look back. It's just that . . ." He paused for a long moment, until the warmth in Paula's dark eyes told him that he could safely continue. "It's just that every so often, something happens to remind me of . . . of that night . . . in the Gulf . . . and the nightmares start again. I haven't slept more than a few hours in the past week." His red-rimmed eyes bore silent testimony to his words.

"I know about looking back," Paula said, recalling the events of her own week. "But what happened this time to bring it all to the surface?"

Ted smiled ruefully. "Just a simple question, Paula . . . *your* question on the way to the airport."

Her eyes expanded in horror as understanding dawned. She raised her fingers to her lips and the color drained from her face. "You mean . . . when I asked you about all the pictures and things, and why you weren't still—"

"That's exactly what I mean." Ted's voice was not accusing, but instead held a depth of sadness that matched the anguish in his eyes.

"Oh, Ted," she groaned. "I'm so sorry. *So sorry.*" She stared at him forlornly. "I had no idea."

"I know," he said. "To be honest, my reaction surprised me a little, too. I guess I just sort of flipped out—maybe because it happened so soon after that lawn Mormon thing, which brought up another part of my past I'd just as soon forget. Memories can do that, I suppose." He leaned back in his chair and sighed mournfully.

Paula chuckled without mirth. "Well, I'm certainly not winning any awards for being Miss Sensitivity these days, am I? First the Mormons, and now the war . . . talk about 'friendly fire.' I just hope your wounds aren't mortal." She looked at him, her eyes brimming with unspoken apologies.

"Life goes on," he said simply. "Even if it doesn't seem to be very convenient."

"You can say that again," she agreed, curling an errant strand of dark hair around her finger.

"Life goes on. Even if it doesn't seem to be very convenient."

She glanced at him quickly, and for an instant saw the sparkle in his eye. *Thank goodness. He's back.* "Okay, okay," she said with a little laugh. "But tell me something . . . was my lawn Mormon teasing really *that* bad?"

Ted's irrepressible grin was once again surfacing as he rose from his chair. "Oh, no you don't," he said easily. "One pesky ghost is enough for this evening. Let's save that one for another time, shall we?" His tired but determined eyes told her that arguing was useless.

"All right," she conceded, coming to her feet with an easy grace. "What say we call it a night?"

"I'm with you on that one." He switched off his computer and desk lamp, then motioned toward the door. "Can I walk you to your car?"

"I'd like that," she said. He smiled, and she thought he looked better now. More relaxed.

They walked down the hall and rode the elevator in companionable silence. When the door opened, he grasped her elbow lightly as they entered the dusky interior of the garage. "I guess you won't have any trouble finding your new car," he joked. "That baby glows in the dark." They rounded a corner and saw the Jag nestled cozily between two enormous concrete pillars, its polished steel gleaming in the semidarkness. "See?" he whispered. "I told you."

"Yeah . . . don't you love it?" Paula giggled.

A few steps more took them to the side of the car, where she unlocked the door and swung it open. Then she turned to look up into Ted's face, and a fresh wave of remorse washed over her. She wanted, needed to tell him again how sorry she was for opening old wounds, for stirring up new pain. "Ted," she began, resting her hand lightly on the smooth, cool metal of the door frame, "there's no way I can express how sorry I am, how thoughtless it was of me to—"

"Don't, Paula." His hand found hers and squeezed it firmly, while his vivid blue eyes ranged over the delicate features of her face and finally locked themselves into her gaze. "It's over . . . forgotten. In fact," he grinned, "now I actually owe you one." Seeing her puzzled expression, he continued. "These flashbacks are never easy to get through, and I don't mind telling you I've been to hell and back this past week."

She nodded soberly. "I know. That's why I feel so—"

He held up a hand to quiet her. "As I was saying, it hasn't been any fun. More than anything, it's been . . . well, it's been lonely, trying to deal with it on my own. If you hadn't come to my office tonight, I don't know what would have happened. I'd just about hit rock bottom and was brooding myself into a major depression. I never thought simply talking about it could help so much, but it seems to have lightened the load. For the first time in a lot of rugged days and sleepless nights, I actually feel better. And I have you to thank for that."

Paula grimaced. "You also have me to thank for pushing you toward the edge of the cliff in the first place."

"You couldn't have known. If you had, you wouldn't have done it. I can tell that by the heartsick expression on your face."

"You're right, I guess," she replied. "Thanks for understanding."

"No, thank *you*," he said. "And without belaboring the point, I'll just say . . ." He decided not to say it, but instead gathered her into his arms. She returned his embrace, and he pressed his lips to the side of her forehead, feeling a rapid heartbeat fluttering at her temple. Long moments later, she pulled away and he smiled down at her. "I guess that pretty well sums it up."

"You're crazy, you know that?" she laughed. "I like that in a man." She lowered herself into the car. "Meanwhile, don't you usually head to the gym about this time of night?"

"Yeah . . . that's another thing I've missed this week. A good workout is just what I need right now. Then a long, hot shower. Then a double pepperoni pizza. Then—"

"A good night's sleep, I hope," Paula added.

"You can bet on it," he said resolutely. "It's been too long coming, but there's gotta be a pleasant dream with my name on it tonight."

"Terrific . . . then we'll see you tomorrow?" She pulled the car door closed and rested her elbow on the open window frame.

"Bright and early, boss." He saluted smartly and stepped away from the car as she started the motor. As the Jag moved noiselessly up the parking ramp, she glanced in her rearview mirror just in time to see Ted mouth the words "thank you" before he turned and headed for the elevator.

It was late evening by the time Paula turned into her wide cement driveway and punched the garage door opener button. By now it was too late to watch the Mormon elders playing a lively game of basketball with her youngest son. Too late to see Scott swagger through the front door, announcing importantly that he'd "iced" his first driving lesson. Too late to properly enjoy a slice of Millie's incredible banana cream pie. Even too late for a stroll around the block with Rudy. Still, she felt good about the day; she'd catch up with things at home once her work at the office was under control. Now that Ted's problem was resolved, he'd be able to move forward rapidly on several projects, and . . .

Ted. She switched the motor off and sat in the silent Jag for several minutes, her fingers toying with the stray locks at her hairline where his lips had so recently pressed against her skin. *He could be playing with fire here,* she smiled to herself. *Friendly fire.*

CHAPTER 19

Wake up, Donroe. Your stomach's trying to tell you something. Paula turned over in bed and squinted at the clock as the rumbling in her midsection intensified. *Five a.m., and I feel like I could devour the whole kitchen, refrigerator first. But I'd settle for half a dozen Twinkies and a couple of chocolate eclairs. And milk . . . gotta have milk.*

She yawned and stretched, pondering the reason for this early-morning food fantasy. *That's it . . . I haven't eaten since noon yesterday. I was so intent on getting my work caught up last night, then there was that heavy discussion with Ted, and I just toppled into bed when I got home. No wonder those little critters are gnawing on nails in my stomach.*

Her solution was simple. *This is not a day to leave home without one of Millie's soul-satisfying breakfasts. It'll be on the table by seven, and I can still be at the office by eight. Which gives me time for a long, leisurely soak in the tub and a bit of time to myself. I'll need it to gear up for this day.* She stretched again and threw aside the covers.

Paula felt enormously relaxed and energetic as she ambled into the kitchen almost two hours later, dressed in a classic beige suit with a vibrant green scarf at her throat. Millie was clearing some dishes from the table, and the spicy aroma of fresh-baked cinnamon rolls quickly reminded Paula of how famished she was. "Mmm, smells marvelous," she said, inhaling deeply.

"I heard you come in late last night and go straight upstairs," Millie smiled, "so I figured you'd be ready for a good breakfast this morning."

"You have no idea," Paula replied, lowering herself into a chair. "I'm actually faint with starvation." She eyed a bowl of fresh fruit in the center of the table, and reached toward a particularly juicy-looking apricot.

"Uh, I wouldn't do that if I were you, dear," Millie chortled. "I'm afraid plastic is sadly lacking in flavor and nutritional value."

"Wow," Paula laughed, studying the fruit more closely. "I must *really* be hungry!"

"Not to worry. I think I have just the ticket." Millie bustled over to the stove and was back in less than a minute, balancing two plates laden with cinnamon rolls and a fluffy cheese omelet. "Your favorites," she beamed as she carefully lowered the steaming plates to the table.

Paula's face crinkled into a wide smile. "Millie, you're fabulous."

"Oh, go on," the older woman sputtered. "I'm just feeding the folks I care about. My family." Her eyes shone as she looked down at Paula.

"Well, this family is mighty lucky to have you," Paula said as she lifted a roll to her lips. "Won't you join me?"

Millie sat down on the other side of the table. "Thanks, but I've already eaten. Scotty left early for his driving lesson, so the two of us had breakfast together."

Paula nodded, her mouth too full to speak. She washed a forkful of omelet down with several swallows of orange juice and asked, "What about TJ?"

"He's sleeping in, I guess. Up late studying . . . seems to me he has a test today. He'll likely gallop down here two seconds before the bus pulls up, and it'll be all I can do to stuff a cinnamon roll in his backpack. I made him a good lunch, though." Millie nodded toward a bulging brown paper sack on the counter.

Paula lowered her fork after a few more bites. "You know," she said, staring out the kitchen window to the green expanse of backyard, "this week is shaping up to be pretty horrific for me, what with all the catching up I have to do."

"I know," Millie said quietly. "Yesterday was a long one."

"Yes, and it's likely to get worse before it gets better. Which means it'll be a few days before I'll see the boys again, much less catch up on their lives. Especially Scotty—and you know how I worry about him. So . . . I was wondering . . ." Paula's gaze moved to Millie's face.

"Uh-huh?" Millie said expectantly.

"Well, if it wouldn't be too much trouble . . . I wondered if maybe you could plan something for the weekend—you know, an extra-special breakfast with the boys' favorites. That way we could enjoy one of your spectacular meals"—Paula patted her slightly bulging stomach—"and bring each other up to date at the same time. What do you think?"

"I think," Millie said, rising from the table, "that's one of the best ideas I've heard in a long time. How does Saturday sound? I'll make those young men an offer they simply can't refuse." Her eyes sparkled with anticipation.

"Perfect. Just perfect," Paula smiled. "I'll need to go to work on Saturday, and I'm sure they'll have plans. But if we make a date—say, 8:30 in the morning—to just eat and visit for half an hour or so, I think it could work. Scotty and I had a little misunderstanding on Sunday, and maybe we could mend a few fences—"

"Then let's do it!" Millie's voice bubbled with enthusiasm. "You just leave everything to me, and we'll have a breakfast to remember."

"No doubt about it. Thanks, Millie—I can always depend on you," Paula said as she laid her napkin beside her plate. "Now, I'm afraid I've got to run; I have a staff meeting in less than an hour. Have a wonderful day, Millie . . . you've certainly gotten mine off to a terrific start." She pushed her chair back from the table and reached for her attaché.

"Drive safely, dear," Millie chirped as Paula disappeared into the garage. "I'll leave your dinner in the fridge."

Paula's assessment of the week proved itself in her pre-dawn arrivals at the office, hurried lunches wolfed down with Coke chasers, and late-night homecomings when only Rudy would greet her in the still, solemn silence of a household at rest. Her days were consumed by interminable meetings where she served as referee between clients and her creative team. She hated the moments when she and Ted faced off across a cluttered conference table, arguing heatedly over the direction of an ad campaign. She loved the rare occasions when they agreed, sailing forward together on a wave of creative energy. And she frankly forgave him for the occasional lapses in decorum that caused him to laugh a little too loudly at her jokes, pull his chair a little too close to hers in staff meetings, visit her office a few too many times in a day. *He's been through a lot,* she told herself. *He needs a friend.*

She found Millie's note late Friday evening: "Breakfast at 8:00 a.m. tomorrow. TJ has a practice at nine, Scott's going for another driving lesson. Don't forget—and come hungry! M." Despite her exhaustion, she looked forward to this time with her boys. *We should do this more often,* she thought. *They're growing up and away from me.* She vowed to do better.

Paula awoke early in the morning, the spicy aroma of cinnamon-nutmeg coffee cake swirling delicately in her nostrils. She inhaled deeply and sat up in bed. *Millie knows exactly how to start things off in style,* she reflected. *This will be a good day . . . a very good day. The boys and I will catch up and patch up, I'll get a ton of work done at the office, and who knows? Maybe we'll even find something fun to do together tomorrow. It could happen.* The thought buoyed her; a pleasant expectancy danced in her eyes and animated her body as she headed for the bathroom and a quick shower. Minutes later, clad in a dusky blue sweat suit and her favorite pair of Adidas, she ambled downstairs to join Scott and TJ at the breakfast table.

"Hi, guys," she said cheerfully, lowering herself into a chair across from her sons. "How's it going?" As if on cue, both boys glanced up at her in concert, nodded amiably, then continued foraging among the scrambled eggs, waffles, sausage, coffee cake, and fresh fruit on their plates. "That's great," she smiled, noticing their obvious relish for this morning's feast. "I see Millie has outdone herself—as usual." The comment brought another emphatic nod from the boys, who were now gulping down staggering volumes of milk and fresh-squeezed orange juice. Paula smiled indulgently. *They're so cute, with their hollow legs and overactive metabolisms. If I ate like that, the Fat Police would have me on their most-wanted list.*

"Good morning, dear," Millie called cheerfully from the kitchen. "One waffle or two?"

"Just one, please." *Oh, what the heck?* "Make that one of *everything,* please," Paula grinned. While Millie filled her plate, Paula unfolded her white cloth napkin, took a sip of orange juice, and decided to get down to business. "So," she said in a casual tone, setting her long-stemmed juice glass down on the blue-and-white checked linen tablecloth, "it seems like forever since we've had a meal together. I thought it might make sense today, since I've been away and you've been so . . . busy." The boys nodded again, their mouths full.

"Anyway," she continued as Millie set a steaming plate before her, "I just wanted to catch up on what's been going on the past week or so—you know, so your old mom can keep up with you guys." She winked at them and lifted a bite of syrup-soaked waffle on her fork. "How are the driving lessons coming, Scotty?" She urged the waffle between her lips and used her tongue to press it against the roof of her mouth. A million tiny bursts of sweetness flooded her senses with contentment.

"Good," Scott mumbled between bites of sausage. "Old man—uh, Mr. Swope says I've got the best feel for the road he's seen in a while." He worked at keeping his expression casual, but his eyes shone and his lips parted in a self-satisfied grin that couldn't be controlled. Paula noticed a shred of sausage meat caught between his front teeth.

"That's terrific . . . awesome!" Paula smiled warmly at her son, consciously swallowing a sudden tightness in her throat. *Be glad for him this day, this moment, Donroe. He's not in any trouble yet . . . give him the benefit of the doubt. Teenagers drive and survive every day . . . you were once one of them yourself, remember?* She relaxed and draped one arm over the back of her chair. "So, what have you learned?"

"Just 'bout everything," he said, pride bubbling in his voice. "We've been trying stuff in the school parking lot—y'know, signaling, shifting, backing up, things like that. But we've been out on the road a lot, too . . . well, a couple of times. It felt awesome." He leaned back in his chair and folded his arms smugly across his chest. "What can I say? I'm a natural." A deep rumbling came from his throat as he smartly turned an imaginary steering wheel with his large hands.

"I can see that," Paula said a little too brightly. "And you have another lesson today?"

"Yeah, in about half an hour," Scott replied. "The quicker we learn, the faster we'll be able to get our licenses. Mr. Swope said he'd help. This driving thing is really *cool*, Mom." His voice vibrated with adolescent energy.

"*Totally* cool," TJ added, using the back of his hand to wipe a glob of syrup from his bottom lip. "I can hardly wait till I get *my* permit."

"Whoa, young man," Paula laughed, shifting her gaze to her younger son. "Your day will come . . . but let's not rush it, okay? There's plenty of time."

"Yeah, I know," TJ grinned. "Besides, I got more important things to do right now." He continued to smile, but his voice was suddenly intense, his eyes focused directly on hers.

"And don't I know it," Paula agreed, eagerly changing the subject. "How many baskets do you think you can shoot in the next three and a half years, kiddo? You'll be so good by then that colleges will already be recruiting you. Come to think of it, you won't even *need* a license; your coach-to-be will chauffeur you around in some big limousine, and—"

"Mom." TJ's quiet, serious tone stopped her in mid-sentence. Seeing that he had her attention, he continued. "Mom, that's not what I was talking about."

"Oh?" She speared a piece of sausage with her fork and nonchalantly swirled it in a small puddle of syrup on her plate. "Well, I always thought basketball came first, but . . . oh, now I get it." She winked and smiled slyly at him. "TJ has a *girlfriend*," she teased.

He didn't blush or stutter as she'd expected, but returned her gaze with perfect sobriety. When several seconds passed in silence, she shrugged and resumed her casual monologue. "Okay . . . what, then?" Listening half-heartedly, she raised the sausage-laden fork toward her mouth.

"I want to be baptized."

Time and motion evaporated as Paula's hand froze halfway to her lips. "Excuse me?" she croaked.

"I want to join the Mormon church. Be baptized. Get the priesthood."

Scott cleared his throat nervously and mouthed *uh-oh* as his mother slowly lowered her fork to the plate. Then she calmly, deliberately pushed the plate aside and placed both hands, palms down, on the table and focused her eyes intently on the large brown freckle between TJ's eyebrows. "Come again?"

TJ glanced quickly at Millie, who was leaning against the breakfast bar, then back to his mother. "I want to join the Church, Mom . . . The Church of Jesus Christ of Latter-day Saints."

"I thought you said the Mormon church." Paula was grasping at words while she tried to steady her reeling mind.

"Yeah, it's the same thing. 'Mormon' is sort of a nickname, because of the Book of Mormon. I've read it . . . twice. It's true, Mom."

Paula snorted. "True? How can a book be *true*? A book can be interesting, or stupid, or enlightening, or boring—but true? I don't think so."

TJ's eyes never left her face. "But the stories are true, and the things it teaches are true, and God—Heavenly Father—told me it's true."

"Oh, and he dropped by and told you that himself, did he?" Paula smirked.

"Well," TJ said, ignoring her sarcasm, "the elders taught me and Millie about the gospel, and they taught us how to pray, and—"

"I see," Paula said tersely, shooting a dark glance in her house-keeper's direction. "Did God speak to you, too, Millie?"

The older woman nodded and smiled slightly. "I have a testi-mony," she said quietly.

"Uh-huh." Paula rested her chin in her hand. *What's going on here—have I suddenly been zapped into a rerun of* Saturday Night Live? *One, two three, I'm the Church Lady . . . isn't that* special?

"A testimony is when you know the Church is true," TJ explained. "When you pray and get one, the next thing is to get baptized. Millie already told them she would, but they said I needed to ask you first—to get permission, 'cause I'm a kid and all. 'No problem,' I told 'em. 'My mom wants me to be happy—and this will make me happy.'" He grinned at her, his eyes brimming with eager expectancy. "So when can I do it, Mom? Next Saturday would be good."

His words penetrated her skull like a migraine, but she willed herself to remain calm. "Now, just hold on a minute, TJ," she said evenly, reaching across the table to pat his arm. "It's one thing to shoot a few baskets with these missionaries and the kids at church, and even to talk religion with them. But this baptism thing is a pretty big step, don't you think? Millie's been around a few years longer than you have, and she can make up her own mind; but I think you still have a little growing up to do before you jump into Mormonism—or anything else, for that matter. Let's give it a while, and if you still feel like it's something you want to do, we'll talk about it later." *Well put,*

Donroe. He'll be over his little religion phase in a few weeks, then we can get on with our lives. She flashed him an indulgent smile.

"So, how long do you think 'a while' might be?" TJ asked fervently.

Paula leaned back in her chair. "Oh, a year or two." *Or twenty.* "Then we'll see."

The boy's face crumbled. "Aw, Mom," he pleaded, "I *can't* wait that long. I have a real strong testimony, y'know?" His dark eyes grew large and imploring.

"I'm sure you do, honey," she said absently, snatching a small slice of cantaloupe from her plate. "And if you're really serious about this, I'd be willing to bet that the Mormons—and your testimony—will still be around when you go looking for them again." She popped the fruit into her mouth and quickly crushed it with her teeth.

"But Mom—"

"No buts, young man," she interrupted. "We'll talk about this again later." *Much later.* "But right now, I just can't see it."

TJ stared at her as his eyes filled with tears and he struggled to control the trembling of his lower lip. "But Mom, it's *true.*"

"Later, okay?" Paula said sharply. This discussion was getting tiresome, and she had to get to the office.

A single tear fell to the tablecloth as TJ rose abruptly. Without saying a word, he turned and hurried from the room. Rudy, who had been dozing in a corner of the kitchen, shook himself briskly and followed after his young friend. Seconds later, a door closed upstairs.

Scott drained the remaining orange juice from his glass, then clasped his hands behind his head and tipped his chair back until its front legs were two inches off the floor. "Geez, Mom," he said, rolling his eyes, "give the kid a break, will ya? It's just a dumb church, anyway. So a couple of missionaries talk him into taking a dive . . . what's the big deal?"

Paula had been wiping at her mouth with a napkin, and now she glared at him sharply, her eyes flashing with indignation. "Oh, so now you're the judge and jury?" Her eyes were hard as she focused on his face. "And I suppose you'd let the missionaries talk *you* into taking a dive, wouldn't you? Especially—" her eyes blazed—"if those missionaries just happened to be foxy young women—*chicks,* I believe you'd call them."

He opened his mouth to speak, but she raised her hand. "Don't," she hissed. "I know *exactly* what you think of the missionaries. I saw your sketch pad the other night. That was quite a portrait of . . . Sister Kent, wasn't it?"

The chair legs thudded to the floor. Scott clamped his lips together in a hard line as wide streaks of crimson coursed up both sides of his neck. "Hey, I—I don't know what you're—"

"Oh, yes, you do. Just spare me the innocent act, okay? At least TJ's motives are somewhere besides in the gutter." Paula mentally flinched at the harshness of her own words, but she let them hang in the air without further comment.

"Yeah, right," Scott mumbled through clenched teeth after a few moments of dark silence, broken only by the faint sound of Millie clearing her throat. "I've got things to do."

"I'm sure you do," Paula said coldly as her son shoved his chair back and stalked from the room. *Give my regards to the Crawlers.* A muscle in her cheek twitched as she crumpled her napkin and tossed it on the table. *So much for catching up.*

A movement to one side caught her eye. Millie was standing close beside her, and she reached out to touch Paula's shoulder. "Was that really necessary, dear?" she asked mildly.

Paula looked up into Millie's troubled eyes, then averted her gaze and stared out the window, where two dozen rosebushes in full bloom framed the backyard. "Was *what* really necessary?" she asked, her voice edged with irritation.

"The arguing. I just hoped . . ." Millie hesitated, then began again. "I hoped you'd be more understanding about TJ's joining the Church, that's all." When Paula pressed two fingers to her temple and squeezed her eyes shut, Millie continued quickly. "It's not like he'd be alone in the Church . . . he's made some good friends in the ward, he knows the missionaries, and I could look out for him, too. He knows it's true, without a doubt . . . we both know. I don't see any harm—"

Paula pushed back her chair and rose to face the older woman. "My dear Millie," she said stiffly in cool, measured tones, "I don't need anyone to *look out* for my son, or to tell me what he knows or doesn't know. Your joining the Mormons, for whatever reason, is your business; *his* joining the Mormons is *my* business, and I'll take care of it. Do we understand each other?"

"Yes, Paula, I believe we do." Millie's voice was controlled, but her gray-blue eyes flashed briefly in a rare display of indignation. "I'll just clear up the breakfast things." She brushed past Paula and moved briskly to pick up a half-empty pitcher of juice from the table.

"Fine. I have to get to the office. I'll be home late." Paula grabbed her purse and strode toward the garage.

"Fine." Millie slammed the refrigerator door.

CHAPTER 20

TJ wasn't making any baskets. He'd been practicing for over an hour, but his dribble was sluggish and his shooting was off—way off. He should have gone over to the church to work out with the team earlier, but his confrontation with his mother had sapped him of any desire to see the guys. How could he possibly face them now, knowing they were expecting the announcement of his upcoming baptism? He'd been so sure of himself at Thursday's practice—telling them he knew it was true, he knew he wanted to join the Church, he *knew* his mom would go along with it. Well, she didn't . . . and now where was he? Caught in a no-man's land between the baptismal font and a stubborn, hard-hearted mother who wouldn't give the Church a chance. For the first time since he'd begun to read the Book of Mormon and meet with the elders, TJ felt despair cloaking his heart.

He tossed off a few more unsuccessful shots, then pitched the ball into a corner of the yard. Flinging himself on his back in the warm grass, he stared unseeing at the gray, overcast sky. When Millie called him for lunch, he ignored her until she stacked two sandwiches on a plate, shuffled down the front steps, and sat carefully beside him on the lawn. "Care to join me?" she asked, adjusting her arthritic hip to a more comfortable position. "I've got your favorite . . . peanut butter and tuna. Just plain tuna for myself," she smiled.

"Naw," he sighed. "Not hungry. But thanks." He continued to stare upward, his hands clasped behind his neck.

After a few minutes of silence, Millie began to speak in soft tones. "TJ," she began slowly, "I know how disappointed you must be . . . probably angry, too." She recalled her own flash of resentment at

Paula's obstinance. "It's awfully upsetting to know the truth and not be able to share it with someone we love."

"Because they won't listen—*she* won't listen," TJ mumbled.

"I know," Millie said quietly.

"At least you get to be baptized. I don't think she'll ever let me." TJ's voice was spiritless.

"She was pretty tough," Millie admitted. "But with faith and patience, I'm sure it'll all work out in the end." She rested her hand lightly on TJ's leg.

"How?" he questioned forlornly. "How can anything work out? I can't get baptized. I can't get the Holy Ghost. I can't get the priesthood. All the promises the elders told me about . . . I can't get 'em. Which leaves me exactly nowhere." TJ pounded his heel into the grass in frustration.

Millie shook her head slowly and patted his leg. "It's hard to understand, that's for sure," she said. "But I suppose God has a plan for what'll happen next. I can't imagine he'd lead you to the gospel, then just let it slip out of your reach, like a helium balloon with a string that's too short."

"Well, maybe not," TJ said gruffly, "but that's sure the way it feels." He flung one arm across his eyes, and Millie saw the muscles in his jaw tightening. "I even wanted to go on a mission, y'know?" he sobbed. "I'd go on one today, if I could."

"I know, dear. I know," Millie said, swallowing the knot of grief in her own throat. "Just give it a little time, okay? Your mom might come around—maybe sooner than you think. I wouldn't be surprised," she added with less than total confidence.

"Yeah? Well, *I* would. You heard what she said in there."

"I'm afraid I did," Millie admitted, grateful that TJ hadn't heard the rest of their heated conversation. "But I can't help thinking—"

"Not now, Millie, okay? I mean, I appreciate the sandwich and everything, but I'd just as soon hang out by myself for a while, all right?" His voice sounded distant, uncertain. Lost.

"Sure, sweetie. I understand," she said kindly, leaning over to kiss his warm cheek and tenderly brush away the tears pooling at his hairline. "I'll be here whenever you want to talk about it." She swung her bad hip into position and got to her feet with a small groan. "Are you going to be okay?"

"Yeah," he answered listlessly, his arm still covering his eyes. "I'll get back to practicing in a minute."

"All right, then. I'll be in the kitchen or my room if you need me." She turned and shuffled slowly toward the house, favoring her aching hip. As she opened the door, Rudy brushed past her, bounded down the front steps, and trotted toward TJ, who still lay sprawled on the lawn. He playfully nuzzled the boy's neck, shoulder, and side, then gently lowered one giant paw to the middle of TJ's chest, all with no response. Finally, the old dog sank heavily to the grass and pressed the full length of his body firmly against TJ's, resting his shaggy head on his young friend's midsection.

Without moving his arm from his eyes, TJ reached out with his other arm, circling Rudy's neck and curling his fingers tightly in the thick, golden fur. The boy's shoulders heaved with involuntary sobs.

* * * * *

Paula wasn't making any progress. Her desk was strewn with correspondence, proposals, contracts, projects—all leftovers from a week of relentless demands on her time. She'd come to the office today to clear away the clutter, to make room for another week. So far, it had taken her just over three hours to turn on her computer, pour herself a cup of coffee, adjust the vertical Levelors on her window, sharpen a dozen pencils, pour herself another cup of coffee, and scan a single page of Ted's latest advertising copy. It was useless; no matter what task she started, her mind flipped back like a rubber band to one thing: breakfast.

You've done it now, Donroe. In a single stupid conversation, you've managed to alienate the three people who mean the most to you. TJ hates you because you won't let him take up with the Mormons. Scott hates you for finding his precious sketch pad, then embarrassing him about it. And even Millie—gentle, sweet Millie, who doesn't have a vindictive bone in her body, could've taken you over her knee and given you a few good whacks for shooting your mouth off. If Ted had been there, you would have found a way to raise his hackles, too. A real landmark morning.

She slumped in her leather chair and felt a cold chill snake up her arms. *What is it about those blasted Mormons, anyway? Haven't they got enough recruits without stealing my son, too? I can't let him do this . . . not yet. He's just a kid; he needs more time to grow up and decide what he really wants.* A sharp nod of her head confirmed the decision. *There's plenty of time.* She inhaled deeply to clear her mind, but her heart felt like a thirty-pound lump of coal in her chest.

Two hours later, with nothing accomplished but the re-shuffling of papers on her desk, Paula gave it up. She'd go home and apologize. No . . . she'd go home and act like nothing had happened. No . . . she'd go home and sulk in her room until Monday. No . . . she'd go . . . somewhere else. Just for a few hours; just to put things back into perspective. Just to let them know she wasn't going to come crawling back or change her mind about anything.

Leaving her car in the parking garage, she pushed through the front doors of her office building. There was a small, exclusive shopping mall a few blocks down the street, tucked so snugly in among the skyscrapers that a casual passerby could easily miss its entrance. Paula, however, was a regular visitor to the mall's dozen or so upscale shops, where she could always count on finding something to satisfy her expensive tastes. *Just what the doctor ordered,* she thought as she flung her purse strap over her shoulder and strode purposefully down the sidewalk. *When the going gets tough, the tough go shopping.* It felt good to stretch her legs, and the sultry mid-afternoon air was freshened by a steady breeze from the ocean. By the time she reached the mall, she was feeling better.

Her elevated mood was short-lived. For the next hour, as she strolled the cool Italian marble corridor connecting the shops, stopping to study their elegant merchandise displays, her eyes were invariably drawn to subtle reminders of exactly what she was running from—the little family of three who loved her. Or who *had* loved her until the crisis at hand had raised its ugly head. Or who might love her still, if given a chance; she didn't know. All she knew was that a peculiar pain tugged at her heart when she saw a display of glistening brooches rather like the one Millie had given her for her birthday; a collection of fine leather key cases similar to Scott's gift; and a rather stunning set of matched jewel boxes that had no resemblance whatsoever to the lopsided wooden chest so lovingly crafted by TJ for her special day. October tenth. Three weeks—no, three lifetimes ago.

Paula sank down on a wooden bench and pressed her fingertips to her temples. *Stop it! Get a grip, Donroe. This is obviously not a shopper's paradise for you today. What next? Something to get your mind going in a different direction, even for a little while. Something—*

"Well, yes. Of course," she said aloud. "Pure escape—that's what I need." Coming to her feet, she exited the building, walked half a block, and made a sharp right turn into a cluster of Cineplex movie theaters. She glanced up at the marquee and quickly planned a two-feature marathon. Or maybe three. Then she bought popcorn. Reality would just have to wait.

* * * * *

"Bummer. You been here all day?" Scott leaned against the door frame of his brother's room, where TJ lay stretched out on his bed.

"Naw," the younger boy said. "I played ball for a while . . . couldn't even hit the rim. Me an' Rudy have just been hangin'. What's goin' on?" His voice was flat.

"I went drivin' . . . it was cool." He stared into the murky silence of TJ's room. "Hey, you still croakin' over what Mom said at breakfast? Y'know, the church thing?"

"Yeah, I guess," TJ answered dully. "It just doesn't seem fair, that's all."

Scott snickered grimly. "So, who said anything about parents being fair? Besides, she did a number on me, too. After you left."

"Yeah?"

"Yeah . . . she was on one this morning, all right." He saw a small spider scurry into the hall and reached out to crush it with the toe of his Reebok.

"Well, I don't know why she won't let me join the Church." TJ stared at the ceiling.

"I don't know either. Geez, I don't know why you'd even *want* to join and do all that religious stuff . . . but, hey, it oughta be your choice, not hers."

"That's what I think." TJ folded his arms across his chest. "But there's nuthin' I can do."

Scott nodded solemnly. "Yeah, it's the curse of bein' a kid. Just give us a few years . . . we'll get even, eh?"

"I s'pose." TJ sighed deeply and continued to gaze upward.

After a long silence, Scott shifted from one foot to the other. "Criminy, little brother, I've never seen you like this—all dopey 'n stuff. What's happenin'?"

"Nuthin'. Just let it go, okay?" TJ turned on his side to face the wall.

Scott rubbed the back of his neck for a few seconds, then marched resolutely into the room and plopped down beside TJ on the bed. "Y'know," he said softly, "we could forget about all this crap and go have some fun." He nudged his brother's shoulder.

TJ shrugged off Scott's hand. "Maybe later."

"Aw, c'mon, my man," Scott insisted. "No need to troll around here when there's some really good stuff goin' on downtown. I can show ya where it's all happening."

"Downtown?"

"Yeah. I'm a *Crawler*, man. We know it *all*." Scott's eyes shone in the dim light from the doorway.

TJ turned onto his back and regarded his brother skeptically. "What's that s'posed to mean?"

"It means," Scott grinned, "that we know where the *action* is—the cool parties, the girls, the fast cars, the best hangouts—you name it. Whadya say?"

"I dunno. I don't think—"

"Aw, shoot. Thinkin' only gets ya into more trouble. Tell you what. You know we've been workin' real hard to get the C-House fixed up, right?"

"Yeah, you and the guys are always there," TJ agreed.

"Well, it's pretty much finished now, and it's *awesome*. I was gonna wait till next weekend to show you around—y'know, give you the grand tour and all—'cause we still need a little furniture, and Sam's dad thinks he can help us get some used couches on Wednesday. But what the heck? My little brother"—he punched TJ lightly on the shoulder—"who will one day follow in my hard-to-fill footsteps, deserves to see the place before anyone messes it up. You'll be the first, kid . . . and once you've been inside the C-House and know the code, club rules say you can go there anytime you want, listen to cool music, play video games, eat pizza, watch yourself grow a beard, whatever. It's just sittin' there waitin' for you, buddy. How 'bout it?"

"They got video games?" TJ's voice suggested a spark of interest.

"Hundreds. Maybe thousands. Wanna go?"

TJ's brows knit together in thought. "How do we get there?"

Scott snorted. "Since when has your big brother had any trouble getting where he wants to go? Not a problem . . . in fact, I was planning a little trip downtown in an hour or so; the guys are comin' for me. There's always room in that big Chevy clunker for another body—especially a little squirt like you," he said, playfully elbowing TJ in the ribs. "But we don't have all day . . . so what's it gonna be—lie here and go blind starin' at the stupid ceiling, or grab a piece of the action?"

TJ took in a deep breath and exhaled slowly. His big brother, one of the coolest guys on the planet, who usually ignored him, had just invited him—*begged* him—to tour the Crawlers' coveted sanctuary. What's more, he'd be *one* of them—almost. If he couldn't join the Mormons, why not hang with the Crawlers for a while? Why not? There were worse things than being a Crawler—like being a mama's boy, for instance. And his mama was definitely *not* one of his favorite people at the moment. He set his lips in a thin, determined line, sat up on the bed, and nodded crisply. "Okay, sure. Let's go."

"All right!" Scott exclaimed, clapping his kid brother on the back. "This is excellent! You just get yourself together and meet me out front in about an hour, and we'll scream outa here. It's gonna be awesome—you'll see!" He stood abruptly, then reached down to rumple TJ's sandy hair. "Good choice, bro!" He grinned broadly, then turned and strode from the room.

"Yeah . . . good choice," TJ muttered as he swung his legs over the side of the bed. "No big deal." But as he showered and changed into clean khaki Dockers—the same ones he'd worn to church the previous Sunday—and a blue plaid shirt, he started feeling better about his decision. Scotty was a *terrific* brother. He knew all the cool people, all the best places, all the right moves . . . and now, miraculously, he seemed willing to share the wealth with a pesky little kid who hardly knew anything at all. For sure, this would be a night to remember.

The old Chevy was just lurching up to the curb as TJ bounded down the steps to join Scott on the lawn. "You look good," Scott said, eyeing him up and down. "C'mon, let's go . . . we don't wanna keep the Crawlers waiting."

"No way," TJ grinned, jogging toward the car.

Ben Salter reached across the wide bench seat to open the Chevy's front door as the boys approached. "Hiya, Benny," Scott called. "Are ya up for another passenger? TJ here says he'd like to cruise with us for a while, then check out the C-House."

"Cool," Ben responded with a wave to TJ. "Why don't you guys sit up here with me? We've still gotta pick up Sam, Justin, Leo, and Twinkie."

"Twinkie?" TJ questioned as he slid into the car next to Ben. Scott climbed in and slammed the door.

"Yeah, Twinkie," Ben laughed. "He's kind of a nerd, but real good at high-tech stuff . . . he set up our stereo system at the C-House. And you'll never guess what his all-time favorite junk food is."

"Oh, right," TJ chuckled as he rested his feet on the carpeted hump in the floor. He felt good—just like one of the guys.

"Anyway," Ben continued, "we'll collect 'em all, then see what's happening downtown. I heard there's an awesome party goin' down across the Boulevard. Starts in a couple of hours."

"Isn't that the Sharks' territory?" Scott asked in a casual tone. The Sharks and the Crawlers were long-time rivals. Enemies.

"Sure," Ben confirmed, "but they're busy heating up for a row with the Angels. Those guys are so dense that they can only think of one war at a time. They won't even notice we're in the neighborhood."

"Okay, so let's party!" Scott rolled down the window and stuck his elbow out into the dusky air.

Their pickup rounds took them to the north and west sides of town, and more than an hour had passed by the time the Chevy pulled up in front of Twinkie's home in a tree-lined, middle-class neighborhood. The boy had been waiting at his front window, and now his tall, lean frame loped toward the car on spindly legs. He wore a blue baseball cap, a white Microsoft T-shirt, and cutoff jeans.

"Gol, I thought he'd be a lard bucket with a name like Twinkie," TJ whispered loudly as the gangly youth approached.

"Are you kidding?" Justin laughed from behind him. "He may be a nerd, but he's no couch potato. He's on the track team, and he works out a couple of hours every day in his basement. They've got a whole gym set up down there. He might even run in next year's L.A. Marathon."

"Cool," TJ breathed as Twinkie folded himself into the backseat with the other three boys.

"Hey," the new passenger said in a deep voice, reaching forward to give Scott a playful jab on the shoulder. "How's our star driving student?" Twinkie was also taking the driver's training course. "That was an awesome save you made this morning."

TJ's eyebrows shot up. "Save? What's he talkin' about, Scotty?"

Scott slid down in his seat, but there was a self-satisfied grin on his face. "Oh, nuthin'. I was just—"

"It *wasn't* nuthin'," Twinkie interjected. "We were on the north end of the Boulevard. Traffic was pretty light for a Saturday morning, but there was this one crazy guy weavin' from lane to lane, doin' about sixty—way too fast. He skidded or somethin', and came shooting right at us. Old man Swope just froze, and I thought we were dead. But ol' cool-head Scotty here happened to be driving, an' he just floored it, y'know? Beamed us right outa that goon's path. The guy managed to get back on the road, but he nearly creamed two or three other cars before he straightened out. It could've been *real* bad for us . . . but Donroe saved the day. He deserves a medal or somethin'."

"Wow," TJ said. He looked at his brother with wide-eyed adoration as the other boys murmured their approval.

"Well, I got somethin' even better than a medal," Ben said importantly. He leaned forward and looked at Scott. "Why don't you take the wheel and show us what you can do, buddy? I'm a licensed driver, after all, so you're entitled." He nodded at Scott, then opened the driver's side door.

Scott hesitated for a nanosecond, then his face erupted into a huge grin. "Wal, ah thought y'all would never ask," he drawled. "Piece 'o cake." He jumped out of the car, slammed the door, and sauntered around to the driver's side.

"Move over, shrimp," Ben ordered as he nudged TJ to the right. "I'll be the middle man, and it looks like you've got yourself a window seat."

"All right!" TJ hooted. He leaned against the passenger door and stuck his elbow boldly out the open window, imitating Scott's earlier posture. "Let's do it!" A round of cheers accompanied the Chevy's hulking departure from the curb, and within minutes they were barreling down the Boulevard, all four windows down, the wind whipping the words out of their mouths as they sang in concert with a loud heavy-metal radio station. Scott drove like he'd been behind the wheel for a decade. In a few minutes, they'd be in the heart of L.A.

The crimson sun was low in the sky and daylight was beginning to fade, giving the streets and inner-city neighborhoods a rosy, surrealistic quality as the car made its way through a maze of congested intersections crowded with irritable drivers and careless pedestrians. "Idiots," Ben mumbled under his breath as a trio of huge dark men wearing nose rings and sweaty T-shirts slouched into the street and crossed against the light. Scott slammed on the brakes and leaned on the horn. "Welcome to downtown, little brother," he smirked.

"Where we goin'?" TJ asked, leaning out the window to stare at a gruesome-looking life-size poster in one of the store windows. Somebody was stabbing somebody, and there was a lot of blood.

"Wanna do El Camino for a while?" Scott called out. His friends bellowed their approval, and he turned left at the next intersection. "It's the place where everything's happening," he explained to TJ. "Best place to drag in town. Rad women—hookers, some of 'em— and big cars, lotsa noise and stuff goin' on. You just gotta make sure you stay in the car and have plenty of gas t'get out if there's trouble. Like if there's some gangers lookin' for heads to crack."

"Heads to . . . crack?" TJ gulped, then smiled thinly. "Uh, sure . . . let's go." He drew his arm inside the car and leaned back in his seat.

"Relax, kid," Scott laughed. "Nuthin's gonna happen; it's pretty lame this time of day, before dark when the cops can see everything. The crummy stuff happens after midnight, when you'll be safe at home in your bed. Just think of this little ride as a 'preview of coming attractions'—something to look forward to when you're an adult, like me. We'll be spendin' most of our time at the C-House tonight . . . and trust me, the video games are *awesome*."

TJ relaxed. "Cool," he said, letting out the deep breath he'd been holding for a block or two. A chorus of titters came from the backseat, but the sound died instantly when Scott shot a withering glance over his shoulder. The boys rode in silence for a few miles.

El Camino, a broad avenue running nearly the length of California, had once been a popular thoroughfare used by travelers going north or south. But for the past several decades, outstripped by the interstate, the road had been used mostly by slower local traffic, and businesses of all types had sprung up along its perimeters. The downtown L.A. stretch was littered with pawnshops, adult bookstores, thrift shops, and seedy movie theaters. Police continually patrolled the area, where vagrant gangs were known to deal drugs and lurk in silent fury among the shadowed side streets, waiting to catch rival gang members alone and unprotected. For some reason, this part of town was also a magnet for middle- and upper-class teenagers who borrowed or stole their parents' cars and cruised the street at all hours, looking for a little excitement. If they were smart, they never got out of their vehicles. If they were not so smart, there was often a price to pay.

The Chevy lurched around a corner and into the main traffic, traveling slowly in the outside lane. TJ stared wide-eyed out his window at the odd convergence of humanity streaming along the side-walk—the homeless, the hapless, the hopeless, walking shoulder to shoulder with slick-suited hustlers, an occasional misdirected tourist, even a few stressed-out businessmen hurrying to catch taxis. At night, a more sinister element erupted from the shadows and took over.

A small group of cheaply clad women with big hair and bigger chests stood near an intersection. They smiled and waved as the boys drove by and made a few tentative catcalls. "Hookers," Scott explained with a grin when TJ looked at him questioningly. "They're out early; some of 'em work all day."

"Oh," TJ said. "Have you ever—"

"Are you kiddin'?" Scott's voice revealed a trace of scorn. "It's not worth it—too much could go wrong, if ya know what I mean. Besides, just lookin' over the merchandise is a whole lot cheaper—and it's, uh, *stimulating* entertainment," he observed lecherously. His five friends whistled their agreement while TJ squirmed in his seat.

The Chevy cruised El Camino for about half an hour, until a few streetlights flickered on and cast long shadows across the road. "Hey, this is pretty lame. Nuthin's happening," Justin complained from the back-seat. "Let's get pizza and head to the C-House. The party starts in about an hour." His suggestion met with a unanimous holler of approval.

"Good idea," Scott agreed. "I'm starvin'." He checked the rearview mirror and moved the car into position to make a U-turn at the next intersection. When the light turned green, he jerked the wheel sharply to the left, aiming for the inside lane. The Chevy responded sluggishly and wouldn't make such a tight turn, so he had to settle for the outside lane near the sidewalk. So much for the rules of the road.

As the car straightened out, there was a sudden movement behind the darkened window of a storefront just ahead and to the right, followed by the crashing sound of splintering glass. "What's that?" TJ shouted as the car drew up parallel to the building. He raised his arm to point at a figure crouching behind the broken window. "I think he's—"

There was an earsplitting crash and a blue-white puff of smoke from the window.

"What in the—we gotta get outa here!" Scott yelled as he pressed his foot to the gas pedal. TJ sat up rigidly, frozen with terror, and stared straight ahead. His lips moved wordlessly. The force of the car's sudden acceleration forced him back against the seat. He closed his eyes and leaned forward slightly, as if to put himself out of harm's way.

A few seconds later, Ben breathed a sigh of relief. "Whew," he said, "that could've been dangerous." He put his hand on TJ's knee. "But we're okay. You can open your eyes now, kid; the coast is clear." He squeezed the boy's knee playfully, but TJ didn't move.

"Oh, no," a voice whimpered from the backseat. "There's something on his neck."

"Don't play stupid games," Scott snarled over his shoulder. Then he spoke to TJ. "Pretty scary, huh, little brother? Bet you never thought you'd get to see something like—"

"Scotty," Ben interrupted, "TJ's not . . . awake."

Steeling himself to stay in control, Scott pulled the Chevy to the curb and shifted into park. Then he reached across Ben's back and firmly shook TJ's shoulder. "C'mon, buddy. Time to get on over to the C-House, okay? It'll be awesome." The boy didn't respond, so Scott shook him again. "TJ? Quit playin' around, okay? Okay?" Silence hung in the car like a shroud.

Moving his hand around TJ's neck, Scott felt something warm and pulled away. His fingers were covered with blood. "TJ!" he cried as the color drained from his face. "*TJ!*"

CHAPTER 21

Paula hummed softly to herself as the Jaguar pulled smoothly off the freeway and approached Woodland Hills. She smiled as she tried to recall when she'd last done something like this—spent an entire afternoon holed up in a half-empty movie theater, munching butter-soaked popcorn and losing herself in the drama, pathos, and romance of not one, but *two* first-run feature films. Ordinarily, she frowned on such activities as an utter waste of time; but today, she couldn't deny that this type of escape was exactly what she'd needed—and she had the wadded-up Kleenex in her pocket to prove it. Shedding all those tears on behalf of Harrison Ford and Julia Roberts had actually made her feel better—refreshed and relaxed, in a strange sort of way. Now she could go home, pick up the pieces of the day's fractured beginning, and make amends. She certainly wasn't angry anymore, and by now Millie and the boys would've had a chance to cool down. Maybe they could still do something fun tomorrow . . . forget this silly religion thing. What was the big deal, anyhow? Her heart felt light and optimistic as she turned onto Valley View Drive.

The sight of two police cars in her driveway sucked the air out of her lungs.

Paula couldn't get past the shiny blue and white vehicles to get into the garage, so she parked at the curb and slowly opened the door of her car. Its metal felt icy against her hand as she gripped the door frame tightly, swinging her legs sideways and planting her feet on the road. She slammed the door and walked quickly up the gently sloping driveway, taking in great gulps of the mild evening air. It seemed to scorch her throat as her mind raced. *No one has the police in their*

driveway unless there's been a crime . . . or an accident. She took the
front steps two at a time.

Pushing the door open, Paula found herself face to face with three
uniformed officers. Millie was standing with them in the entryway,
twisting a damp handkerchief in her hands. Tears welled in her eyes as
Paula looked at her with a dozen unspoken questions.

"Oh, my dear girl!" Millie exclaimed. She rushed to wrap her arms
around Paula, then pulled back. "Where in the world have you been?
We've been calling your office, then your cell phone for over an hour."

"I had some . . . things to do after work, and I guess my cellular
was turned off." Paula's gaze moved from Millie to the officers and
back again, and her voice was deep and intense when she asked the
question. "What's going on?"

"Uh, ma'am," one of the policemen began in a burly voice,
"there's been an . . . incident."

Paula looked at him sharply. "An incident? What are you saying,
officer?" The man shifted from one foot to the other and gazed at the
floor. "Well?" Paula pressed.

"Mrs. Donroe," a second deep voice said behind her, "Your two
sons were driving with some of their friends on El Camino a couple
of hours ago. There was somebody in one of the abandoned store-
fronts, and he . . . shot at the car."

Paula's eyes bored into the officer's. "What, a . . . drive-by
shooting?" she rasped.

"Well, technically we call it a random shooting, ma'am," he clarified. "That's because the one who fired wasn't driving by. Not that it
matters . . ." His voice trailed off into a heavy silence.

"I see." Suddenly unsteady on her feet, Paula moved a few paces
backward and leaned against the wall. Her throat was knotted with
dread, but she had to know. "Was anyone . . . hurt?"

He nodded again. "I'm afraid so. Your son—" he glanced down at
a small black notebook in his hand, "—TJ—was in the front
passenger seat. He was hit in the neck."

Paula stared, unseeing, unbelieving, at the uniformed man who
had spoken these words. *Who could do such a thing? Who could put a
bullet in my son—my sweet, funny, basketball-loving, wonderful son? It's
not possible.* She pressed one hand tightly over her mouth, squeezed

her eyes shut, and shook her head fiercely.

Millie's plump arm encircled her shoulders. "He's alive, dear," she whispered. "You need to be with him."

Paula's hand trembled as she moved it from her mouth. "How bad is it?" she croaked.

"He was still unconscious when the ambulance came," the officer said quietly. "I called the hospital a few minutes ago, and there's been no change. They're taking him to Intensive Care when he's stabilized. That's all I know. Would you like a ride to the hospital, ma'am?"

Paula sighed heavily. "Yes, please. Millie, will you come?"

"Of course," the older woman said. "Scotty's already there. They said he wouldn't leave TJ's side for a minute."

"Then let's go," Paula said blankly. "TJ needs us."

The lumbering silhouette of Los Angeles County General Hospital rose above the skyline as the patrol car, its red and blue lights flashing, approached the ungainly building. As the two women stepped from the car near the emergency entrance and walked through its automatic sliding doors, Paula noticed the mood of hushed urgency that animated the movements of hospital personnel. She wondered if it was always this quiet. *Probably not. I'll bet it's a madhouse most of the time, what with all those gangs and hoodlums shooting each other up . . .* A small gasp escaped her lips as the stark reality hit. *They've shot* my son *up.* She leaned against the reception desk.

"Excuse me, may I help you?"

Paula glanced down to see a thin, youngish woman smiling up at her through silver wire-rimmed glasses. She wore a crisp white uniform, and a soft turquoise blue sweater was thrown casually about her shoulders. The room's fluorescent lighting made her shoulder-length blonde hair glow like a halo around her head.

"Uh, yes, please," Paula replied, shocked at the hollowness of her own voice. "My son was brought in a couple of hours ago . . . TJ Donroe. His brother was with him. Somebody . . . shot him. Shot TJ, that is." *Am I making any sense?*

"Yes, Mrs. Donroe," the receptionist said kindly. "I was here when they brought him in. Let me see what I can find out." She stood abruptly and disappeared into a small room behind her. A few moments later, she was back. "He was here in Emergency for about an hour—until they got him stabilized," she explained. "He's been moved to Intensive Care now; his brother went with him."

"I see," Paula said flatly. "Can you tell me anything about his condition?"

"Not really," the woman replied. "He hadn't regained consciousness when he was transferred, but with a trauma like his, he may not come around for a day or two. They can tell you more upstairs." She pointed down one of the long corridors. "The elevators are that way. Fifth floor is the one you want." Paula nodded her thanks and walked briskly in the direction of the elevators. Millie followed close behind.

The elevator door opened noiselessly on the fifth floor, and the two women stepped into a blue-carpeted maze of several short hallways. Each hall was lined by a few glass-enclosed cubicles, feeding into a large circular area where several nurses sat at small desks, staring at monitors or hunched over paperwork. Off to one side was the Intensive Care waiting room, where half a dozen people sat or dozed or visited quietly or paced the floor, their faces etched with varying degrees of anxiety. No one seemed to notice when Paula and Millie entered the room.

"Where's Scotty?" Millie whispered. "They said he'd be here."

"I don't know . . . maybe he's with TJ," Paula said in a hushed tone. "Let's check at the desk. I'm sure he's—"

"Mom?" A gravelly voice behind Paula caused her to turn abruptly. Scott stood just outside the waiting room, his hands shoved deep into the front pockets of his jeans, his shoulders slumping forward, giving him the appearance of a much older man. Tiny rivulets of moisture trickled down his dark hairline, and his forehead and cheeks were damp as if he had dowsed his face with water and toweled it haphazardly. His hazel eyes met Paula's, and she could think of only one word to describe them. Tortured.

"I was . . . in the rest room," he explained. "You been here long? They said they were trying to find you. I . . . I don't know how it happened, Mom. We were just cruising El Camino, watchin' everyone on the street, and all of a sudden . . ." His voice cracked, and his gaze dropped to the floor.

"I know, Scotty," Paula said, wrapping her arms around him. "The officers told me." She ran her fingers quickly through the damp, dark curls at the nape of her son's neck, then pulled back to look at him. "You've been with him since it happened." Scott nodded. "What's going on? How is he?"

"I wish I knew," Scott answered forlornly. "They haven't told me anything—just made me sit and wait. It's driving me crazy."

Paula smiled grimly. "I'll bet it is. You've never been the patient type." She squeezed his arm. "You have a seat over there with Millie, and I'll go see what I can find out, okay?"

"Okay," he agreed bleakly. Millie put her arm around his waist and guided him gently toward a cluster of unoccupied chairs in one corner of the waiting room.

Paula's ten steps to the nurses' station seemed like ten thousand; her mind quivered with raw emotion as she willed her leaden feet to carry her toward whatever news awaited her. *He's alive . . . he's got to be alive, or they would've told Scotty. Or were they just being kind—waiting to tell me first? Dear God, let him be alive. That's all I ask. Please . . . is that too much to ask?* Paula stared blankly at the plump, silver-haired nurse who rose as she approached the desk.

"You must be Mrs. Donroe," the nurse said in a deep, melodious voice. "I saw you with the boy over there." She glanced toward the waiting room. Paula nodded, her throat too tight to speak.

"Just a moment, please," the nurse said, and turned to study several monitors intently before continuing. Finally, she let out a deep sigh. "Your son is stable," she said with a smile that revealed large, well-shaped teeth that were stained and slightly yellowish. *Too much coffee or tobacco. Or both,* Paula surmised, briefly taken aback by her own attention to such details at a time like this. She forced herself to listen to what the nurse was saying. "That's all I can tell you at this point. But let me see if I can find the doctor who's handling TJ's case. I saw her in the lounge a few minutes ago; she's probably still in the building. Just stay right here, will you?" Without waiting for Paula to answer, she quickly maneuvered her ample body sideways through a narrow gated opening at the side of the round reception desk.

"Thank you, I'll do that," Paula breathed as the nurse disappeared into a room across the hall. *Where else would I go?* She rested her arms on the desk and stared idly at the two nurses remaining in the enclosed area. *It's like a command post—machines keeping track of people breathing, sleeping, hurting, living, dying . . . dying.* She pushed the thought firmly to the back of her mind. *Living . . . that's it . . . living. That's all I ask.* She pressed a hand over her eyes and pictured TJ shooting baskets—making every one of them—until she felt someone standing beside her.

"Mrs. Donroe, I'm Dr. Cabrini." The voice was feminine, warm, and full-throated. Inclining her head in the direction of the sound, Paula opened her eyes and found herself looking into the face of a middle-aged woman who could have been her sister: large, dark eyes, a fair complexion, a small, thin nose, and artfully chiseled facial features. The hair was different—dark, but not as wavy as Paula's. This woman's glossy brunette hair hung lightly against her cheeks, circling her face like a pair of caressing hands. The genuine warmth in her eyes put Paula at ease, and the two women shook hands.

"Yes, doctor," Paula said. "Thank you for seeing me. My son—"

"TJ," the doctor interjected. "I've spent a good deal of time with him since he arrived." Her eyes never left Paula's face as she spoke.

"Then you know . . . how he is," Paula said, her eyes asking the questions she couldn't vocalize.

A shadow passed briefly across the doctor's face as she organized her thoughts. "What I have to tell you isn't easy, Mrs. Donroe," she began. "TJ is alive, but he's in extremely critical condition."

Paula willed herself to be calm; hysteria would not play well in this drama. "What are the extent of his injuries?" she asked, gripping the edge of the reception desk.

"He was shot once in the neck."

"Yes, the police explained that," Paula replied. "What kind of damage did it do?"

"Quite a bit, I'm afraid," the doctor explained. "More than we originally thought. The x-rays showed that the bullet apparently nicked TJ's aorta, ricocheted off one of the vertebrae near the top of the spine, then lodged near the brain stem. We've got to leave it there for the time being, until the swelling goes down and it's feasible to operate. In the meantime, it could move and cause more damage . . . even . . . ." Her voice trailed off, then came back. "The next twenty-four hours will be critical."

Paula had to say it, though she didn't have to believe it. "He could die." The doctor's solemn nod confirmed her statement.

Paula felt the hope draining from her heart, from her body. "Is he conscious? Can I see him?"

"He's not awake," Dr. Cabrini explained, "but I've always felt, in cases like these, that patients could very well be aware of a loved one's presence. Of course you can see him—but only for a few minutes at a time—about five minutes every hour. If he remains stable, we can let other family members see him tomorrow."

"Then just give me a minute," Paula said, "and I'll send Scott and Millie home. I'll stay here with him."

"That would probably be best," the doctor said.

Millie and Scott, who had been sitting together in a corner of the waiting room, rose expectantly when Paula turned toward them and forced her mouth into a tiny smile. She covered the distance between them in a few steps, and her voice was carefully measured as she spoke. "He's stable," she reported, "and it'll be a while before we know any more. The doctor says it would be best if I stayed, but the two of you should go home, and—"

"No way," Scott said emphatically, and Millie nodded in agreement. "We're staying. I *have* to be here, Mom."

Paula rested her hand on Scott's arm. "I know how you feel, honey, but there's absolutely nothing you—either of you—can do here. They'll only let me see him for five minutes every hour, at least until he comes around. No one else is allowed in his room."

"But Mom . . ." Paula had never heard such a plaintive tone in her son's voice.

"You need someone here . . . to be with you," Millie said softly.

Paula shook her head. "I'll be fine. Look at it this way: if all three of us stay, we'll be totally exhausted by morning, and we won't be doing each other any good. Go home, get some rest; then you can spell me off in the morning, when I really need it. I'll call the second I have any news, even if it's the middle of the night. Please, let's not argue about it, okay? I need you to do this for me. For TJ. Please." Her voice was pleading but insistent—a tone they could not ignore.

"You *promise* you'll call?" Scott's eyes were riveted to hers. Millie clung to his arm.

"Promise . . . cross my heart," Paula vowed. She rummaged in her purse, found her billfold, and pressed it into Millie's hand. "Take a cab," she said, putting an arm around her friend's slightly stooped shoulders. "You can drive back in the morning, so we'll have some transportation."

"All right, dear," Millie murmured. "Are you sure you don't want us to—"

"I'm sure," Paula said firmly. "Everything will work out . . . you'll see." She deftly guided them toward the elevator and pushed the button. As the doors opened, Millie turned to face her, and for a few seconds the two women communicated without words—friend to friend, mother to mother. *It's not good, is it?* Millie asked with her eyes. Paula answered with an almost imperceptible shake of her head, then raised her hand in a silent farewell as the elevator doors closed. She wiped at her eyes quickly before retracing her steps to the reception desk and Dr. Cabrini. "I'm ready to see my son now," she said.

They moved down one of the short hallways, past a succession of glassed-in cubicles where patients lay quiet and unmoving, their pale faces drawn with pain or heavy-lidded with sedation, their bodies fettered to tubes and monitors and respirators. Paula fought the tide of nausea rising in her throat as they paused outside one of the curtained cubicles. *This is no place for a twelve-year-old kid. He belongs at home in the driveway, shooting baskets.* She followed docilely when Dr. Cabrini pushed the door open and moved into the room. "Welcome to the best accommodations in the house," she whispered as Paula glanced toward the bed. "You have five minutes. We'll let you know when it's time. Just talk to him." She touched Paula's shoulder lightly, then turned and left the room.

Paula's feet felt like large cement blocks as she shuffled to the bed and looked down at her son. TJ lay quietly on his back, hands at his sides—an unnatural position, she thought. *When I wake him up for school, he's usually sprawled on his stomach, each arm and leg going a different direction, half on and half off the bed. But now he's not . . . asleep. Not just asleep.* At least he wasn't hooked up to a dozen machines—just an IV and a few lines to a computer monitor, which beeped relentlessly. A two-inch-square bandage was taped to one side of his neck, midway between his jawline and his collarbone. There was no other evidence of injury. *But the bullet is still there . . . inside.*

She reached out to brush a stray lock of sandy hair from his fore-head. His skin felt clammy as she smoothed his unruly brows with her fingertips and laid her palm against his cheek. *Talk to him,* she reminded herself. *You've only got five minutes.*

"Hey, big guy," she said in a half whisper, leaning close to his upturned face. "Isn't this the craziest thing? I mean, who would've thought this morning that we'd be here, like this . . ." She choked, mentally replaying their unhappy conversation, picturing his dark eyes brimming with frustration. "Anyway," she went on, "I'm with you now. The doctor says you could wake up any time, and we're all counting on that." She smiled thinly, remembering one of his favorite jokes. "Okay, okay . . . who do we think you are—an abacus? But you're just such a *cute* abacus." *Keep talking. He might hear you.*

Taking his hand in both of hers, she squeezed and caressed it tenderly. "You know what? This'll all be just a bad dream in a few days. When you've had enough beauty sleep and decide to get out of here, let's plan a little family vacation, okay? You and Scotty can play hooky from school for a few days, I'll give myself a leave of absence, and we'll go somewhere fun . . . you name the place. Disneyland, Yosemite, Hawaii—I'm up for anything within reason. What do you think?" She could feel the youthful flesh of his hand resting heavily against her palms, and long moments passed as she studied his face for any sign of a response. There was none.

She pressed her lips to his hand's cool, still surface. "Come on, TJ," she urged, "you can do this. You can come back. You've still got a lot of basketball to play. Besides, I *won't* let you go—do you hear me?" Her tears splashed onto TJ's hand as she brought his palm to her cheek. "Dear God," she breathed, "please bring him back."

"Mrs. Donroe," a voice said behind her, "it's time to go now."

Paula stared down at her son. "Did you hear that, kiddo? I have to leave for a while, but I'll be back the second they'll let me. In the meantime, you be good, and mind your manners—don't go giving these nice nurses any trouble now, okay?" She leaned over the bed's side railing and kissed his forehead. "I love you, TJ," she whispered close to his ear, "and I'll be right here when you wake up." She care-fully smoothed the light blue blanket under his chin, then quickly left the room.

Dr. Cabrini was studying a patient's chart at the nurses' station. She looked up when Paula tapped her on the shoulder. "How did it go?" she asked.

Paula smiled wryly. "Well, it was pretty much a one-sided conversation," she said. "If he heard me, he wasn't letting on." Her voice was even, but her face threatened to crumble.

"I know," the doctor responded simply. "Just give it a little time."

Paula looked at the other woman with an expression somewhere between defiance and desperation. "Time, my dear doctor, is all I have. And all TJ has. At the moment, I suppose it will have to do. Please have someone tell me when I can see him again, or if there's a change in his condition."

"You'll be the first to know."

"Thanks," Paula said. "I'll be in the waiting room." The doctor nodded and went back to reading her chart.

An hour passed. Aside from thumbing through stacks of dog-eared, outdated magazines, there was little to do but watch the clock. Paula chatted briefly with an anxious middle-aged couple seated across from her; the woman's mother had suffered a stroke, and her future was uncertain. *It's not the same,* Paula thought to herself. *Everybody knows their parents will die; it's expected. A parent, on the other hand, never expects to outlive her child. It's unnatural . . . against all reason . . . unthinkable. But will it happen to me—to TJ? Will I outlive my own son?* She blinked rapidly against the sudden stab of pain behind her eyes.

Right on schedule, a nurse escorted her to TJ's bedside for the second time. He lay as before, unmoving, unseeing, unfeeling. Un-anything. *Like a patient etherized upon a table,* Paula thought, recalling a line from one of T.S. Eliot's poems. She pulled up a chair, cradled his hand in hers, and chattered meaninglessly for her allotted five minutes. What she really wanted to do was climb onto that bed, lie down beside him, and squeeze him until his eyes popped open and he yelled, "Cut it out, Mom! You're stranglin' me!" She settled for a firm, hopeful pinch to his cheek. It brought no response. She finally kissed the end of his nose, whispered a few final words of endearment into his ear, and shuffled back to the waiting room.

By the time this five-minute ritual had repeated itself twice more, Paula's sanity was ready to take a leave of absence. Dr. Cabrini had left for the evening, and the uniformed clones at the nurses' station could offer no new information on TJ's condition. "We'll know more in a few hours," they said. Paula shook her head. *A few more hours? So much for compassionate health care professionals. They have no idea how long "a few hours" can be.* Back in the waiting room, she noticed that the middle-aged couple had left. *Did her mother die? I liked them; we should have talked more. I didn't even get their names.*

Her gaze moved inevitably to the clock; it was a few minutes past ten. Scott and Millie would be going to bed soon . . . she should call and update them. But why? There was nothing to report. It could wait. She slumped onto one of the brown fabric-covered couches, leaned her head back, and closed her scorched, aching eyes. *Another hour . . . maybe he'll be awake next time, and we can get out of this stupid place.* Her thoughts began to blur as weariness washed over her.

CHAPTER 22

The sound of someone softly clearing his throat filtered into Paula's ears, interrupting her slippery-slide descent into welcome oblivion. Vaguely irritated, she shifted in her seat and raised one eyelid a fraction of an inch. Something long and dark seemed to be blocking her field of vision. She screwed her eye open a bit further and determined the object to be a man's pant leg. She clamped her eye shut and turned to one side. *Let him find his own couch. This one's taken.*

"Uh . . . Mrs. Donroe?"

The deep voice had an engaging, familiar lilt to it, like an old friend who was calling, just for the heck of it, after ten years or so. She'd have to at least give it the time of day. "Mmm?" she murmured, her eyes still unopened.

"We came right away . . . when we heard."

Her brow knit in puzzlement as her thoughts raced. *Who could possibly have heard about the shooting? Unless Millie . . .* She grudgingly opened her eyes. "Oh, it's you." Paula groaned inwardly as the two Mormon elders came into view. "How did you know—?"

Elder Richland was the first to speak. "We stopped by your home earlier. Millie and Scott were just back from the hospital, so we got the whole story. We would've come sooner, but we had a couple of appointments . . . we got here as fast as we could."

"Well, that's very nice of you," Paula said dryly, "but it wasn't necessary. There's nothing to do, really, but wait." She glanced up at the two missionaries, who looked awkward standing in front of her, each with a black nylon backpack dangling from his arm. "Please, sit. You can't see him, you know."

"Yeah, we know," Elder Stucki said as they lowered their back-packs to the floor and arranged themselves on a couch across from her. "But we thought maybe you could use a little moral support. How's he doing?"

Paula shrugged. "No change. He was unconscious when they brought him in, he's still unconscious. I guess a bullet can do that." There was a hard edge of bitterness in her voice.

Elder Richland shook his head like a confused puppy. "It's unbeliev-able, you know? I've heard of drive-by and random shootings, but when it happens to someone you know, that's a whole different ball game."

"Tell me about it," Paula said tersely, pulling at a stray ball of fuzz on the leg of her sweat pants.

After a few seconds Elder Stucki elbowed his companion nervously, as though he had just remembered something, and glanced at one of the backpacks. "Oh, yeah, I almost forgot," Elder Richland whispered loudly. He turned to Paula. "Millie thought you could use a refueling break, so she made you up a little care package. We stopped by after our last appointment and picked it up, along with strict orders from Millie that we're to sit right here and annoy you until you've eaten every bite. So here goes . . . ta-*dah!*" He grabbed his backpack and tossed it easily across to Paula's couch.

She smiled in spite of herself, and at the thought of food, a sudden pang of hunger reminded her that many hours—more like a lifetime—had passed since she'd munched her last morsel of butter-soaked popcorn in a darkened movie theater. Now, as she cautiously opened the pack, out tumbled more than she could ever consume at a single sitting: two thick roast beef sandwiches, a plastic container of potato salad, several assorted pieces of fresh fruit, two cans of soda, and half a dozen small squares of Rice Krispies treats. "Good grief," she chuckled, grinning crookedly at the young men. "She sent enough to feed a small army." Suddenly, the thought of Millie's kind hands carefully, lovingly assembling this portable feast was too much, and Paula felt tears springing to her eyes. Quickly lowering her head, she fumbled with the plastic wrap on one of the sandwiches.

"Just enjoy," Elder Richland said amiably. "No one's in any hurry." She found an inexplicable comfort in the gentle way he encouraged her to relax.

"I guess you've got that one right," she smiled. "Seems like all you ever do in a hospital is wait." She picked at a piece of beef hanging from one end of the sandwich.

"I know exactly what you mean," Elder Richland agreed. "When my dad had his heart attack, it was round-the-clock waiting for three days until we knew anything."

Paula lifted her head and gazed at him intently. His statement penetrated her mind like a laser, and all at once she understood a newly revealed truth. *This kid is a real person. He actually has parents, probably a brother and sister or two, a place he calls home, favorite foods, maybe even a girlfriend. Certainly a girlfriend; he's cute enough. Amazing that I didn't even think of it before . . . the sum total of his parts has got to equal more than just a squeaky-clean Mormon missionary . . . and odds are that Elder Stucki has a life beyond the suit and tie, too. I should ask; it's the sociable thing to do.* She felt her brain, mouth, and tongue actually engaging to form a question, which she then directed toward Elder Richland. "Your father . . . did he . . . make it?" *That was crass.*

The elder's large, dark eyes glittered; he was obviously pleased that Paula was interested. "Yes, ma'am," he replied. "Pop pulled through just fine. It took a while for him to come back, but he's good as new now. Except for a few lifestyle changes here and there . . . my mom won't let him near the pork chops and gravy anymore, for one thing. Her famous knock-'em-dead cheesecake is definitely off limits, too—she says it really *would* knock him dead." He chuckled good-naturedly, and Paula smiled at his easy humor.

"I'm glad he's all right," she said, popping open a can of soda. She was raising the thick, succulent beef sandwich to her lips when another idea crossed her mind. She acted on it immediately, feeling a shade of embarrassment for not having thought of it before. "Hey, guys, there's plenty of food here, and I'm sure it's been a while since you had dinner. You're welcome to as much of this as you like." Gesturing toward the pile of food lying beside her on the couch, she looked at them expectantly. *They've gone out of their way for me . . . it's the least I can do.*

Seeing their hesitation, she decided to appeal to their sense of social decorum. "What do you say? This may not be the Waldorf, but I'd still prefer not to dine alone. Don't be shy, now." She picked up a large red delicious apple and held it out toward Elder Richland, but he shook his head. She then offered it to Elder Stucki, but his response was the same. Paula was mystified. *I don't understand . . . these guys are always hungry. Maybe Mormons don't eat fruit.* She leaned back against the couch and studied them curiously.

Elder Richland glanced quickly over at his companion, then looked directly at Paula and spoke in quiet, reassuring tones. "We thank you so much for your generosity," he began, "and the food looks great. But we've come here tonight to try to be of assistance to you and TJ. One of the best ways we know to do this is by fasting and prayer. We started our fast a few hours ago, and of course you've both been in our prayers continually. Scott and Millie, too."

"I see," Paula said slowly. She was still perplexed. "So you're fasting . . . I assume that means going without food."

Elder Richland nodded. "Or water," Elder Stucki added.

"Okay, so you're not eating or drinking," Paula repeated. Her next question seemed only natural. "But why?"

Elder Richland leaned forward and rested his forearms on his knees. "Well, it's like this, Mrs. Don—"

"Please, call me Paula," she interrupted with a wave of her hand. *No use getting bogged down in formalities at a time like this.*

"Okay, thanks . . . Paula." He said her name warmly, and she found herself drawn to this earnest young man. "Anyway," he continued, "God has told us in the scriptures that fasting and prayer, working together, can bring about miracles in our lives. For myself, I like to think of it as a little stockpile of spiritual ammunition. When we pray and ask Heavenly Father to help us, he always listens; he's right there, ready to answer. But some problems are tougher than others, and we need to show him we're willing to go the extra mile—maybe do without nourishment for a time—so he knows we're really serious about getting the help we need. Fasting makes us more receptive to the Spirit, too, so we can hear God's voice more clearly and get direction more easily. The way I see it, when we fast and pray, we're creating the greatest possible opportunity for him to bless and help us. We figured TJ needs all the help he can get right now; he's a great kid, and Heavenly Father wants to bless him. So fasting, along with a lot of prayer, just seemed to be the logical thing to do. Am I making any sense?"

"Yes, I think so," Paula said dubiously. "But are you, like, going to pass out on me or something? I mean, this fasting thing could be dangerous to your health, couldn't it?"

"I think we can manage for twenty-four hours or so," Elder Richland smiled. "Actually, we consider it a privilege to do this for TJ." Elder Stucki nodded his assent.

A large knot of emotion suddenly formed in Paula's throat as she struggled to respond. "This is so . . . nice of you," she murmured. "I'm sure TJ would be incredibly touched to know what you're doing . . . for him."

"He'd do the same for us," Elder Richland replied. "Your son is quite a remarkable young man, Mrs.—uh, Paula. He has a good, caring heart, an inquisitive mind, and he seems to feel spiritual things deeply—right here." He placed his hand over the left side of his chest. His eyes sparkled as he added, "Not to mention the fact that he's a darn good basketball player."

"Yes, well," Paula sighed, "I'll just be glad when he's back on the court."

"That makes three of us," Elder Stucki observed. He hesitated briefly, then glanced at his senior companion. Elder Richland inclined his head slightly as if encouraging him, and the younger missionary continued. "You know, there is something else we could do for TJ."

"I can't imagine what," she protested. "You've already done so much . . ."

"But we really meant it when we said that Heavenly Father wants to bless him," Elder Richland said fervently. He had Paula's attention. "Using God's authority, which we call the priesthood, we could give him a—"

"Excuse me, Mrs. Donroe." The chilly, efficient tones of a nurse's voice cut through the calm intensity of the moment. "You may see your son now."

Paula's attention was instantly riveted on the nurse. "Does that mean there's been a change?" she pressed, moving forward to the edge of the couch. "Is he awake?"

"No change," the nurse said flatly. "Dr. Cabrini just asked me to tell you when you could see him, that's all."

Paula's shoulders drooped. "Well, I guess that'll have to do for now," she said wearily, coming to her feet. She turned apologetically to the elders. "I'll only be a few minutes, but don't feel like you have to wait."

"We'll be here," Elder Richland said. Paula nodded and disappeared down a hallway.

The missionaries were talking softly when she returned, looking pale and distracted, less than ten minutes later. "They've added a few more wires and tubes," she reported, settling herself on the couch. "Other than that, he seems to be holding his own." She didn't believe it, and neither did they.

This unlikely trio sat in silence for a minute or two, unable or unwilling to put words to an unthinkable possibility—that they might lose this fresh young life before its time. Finally, Elder Richland moved quietly to sit beside Paula. He interlaced his fingers in front of him and began to speak slowly, carefully. "Paula, just before you went in to see TJ, we were talking about how we might help."

"What? Oh . . . yes." Paula's thoughts were clearly elsewhere as her eyes remained focused on the hallway where her son's room was located. "You were saying something about, uh . . . what was it?"

"If I could just explain . . ." Elder Richland began. Paula nodded absently, so he took a deep breath and continued. "Elder Stucki and I hold the priesthood, which means that we've been given authority to act in the name of God."

Paula snickered a little under her breath. "Wow," she said with a touch of sarcasm, "acting in the name of God . . . that must be quite a power trip."

"Not really," he replied, the trace of a smile playing across his lips. "It's more like a tremendous responsibility and privilege. God expects us to use it for righteous purposes—to take care of business in his church, and to bless his children. We don't use it lightly."

"That's nice," Paula said, leaning back against the couch. Her head was throbbing. "But I don't see what that has to do with me. I'm not a Mormon, in case you hadn't noticed. And neither is TJ."

"We know," the missionary said quietly. "The thing is, Heavenly Father loves all his children, whether or not they're members of the Church. He'd want us to use his authority to make a difference wherever we could. In TJ's case, it seems like he could use a little help right about now."

"So, what did you have in mind?" Paula asked warily.

"We could give him a blessing."

Paula blinked her eyes and stared at him curiously. "A blessing?"

"Yes, ma'am," Elder Stucki said from the other couch. "Using our priesthood authority, we could give TJ a blessing for the healing of the sick. If it's the Lord's will, he'll get better."

Paula's gaze bored piercingly into the elder's eyes. "And if it *isn't* the Lord's will?"

The young man's face suddenly burned crimson, and he stared at the floor. The air was thick with silence until Elder Richland spoke. "Paula," he said simply, "Heavenly Father knows each one of us intimately—you, and me, and Elder Stucki, and TJ—because he's the father of our spirits. He has a plan for each of our lives, and sometimes we just need to have faith that he knows what's best. There's no doubt that faith can work miracles . . . I've seen it too often. It brought my father back from almost certain death, and I've seen its effects dozens of times during my mission. The power and authority of God are real, Paula, and we can use them to help TJ. Will you let us do it?"

The earnestness in his voice made her trust him—almost. "Well, I don't know," she said uncertainly. "This 'blessing' . . . how is it done?"

"We—Elder Stucki and I—would put our hands on TJ's head, and each of us would say a special prayer, asking God to bless and heal your son. We do this by the power of our priesthood, and the Spirit will often tell us just what to say in the blessing. It's pretty simple, really . . . nothing spectacular, but the results can be miraculous." He looked at her expectantly.

Paula closed her eyes and let out a long, slow breath. "I need some time," she said. "This is all quite . . . unusual."

"I'm sure it seems that way," Elder Richland agreed. "I can tell you, though, that we were able to teach TJ about the priesthood last week, and he was pretty excited about having this authority himself one day." The elder's voice wavered slightly as he continued. "Just a couple of days ago, he told us he'd use it to help Scotty find his way . . . and to help you find happiness. He loves you both a lot."

Paula used a napkin to wipe at the corner of her eye. "I know," she said, struggling to keep her voice steady. "He's such a little softie." She looked at Elder Richland, her eyes swimming with emotion. "This blessing thing . . . it sounds pretty good. But give me a little while to think about it, will you? I'm just not sure. I want it to be . . . right."

"We understand," he said. He reached into his inside jacket pocket and pulled out a small white card. "This is where we live," he said, handing the card to her. "Right now," he added with an apologetic smile, "we're way past curfew—mission rules, you know—so we'll be heading home. But if there's an emergency, there are always exceptions to the rules; so please call us anytime, and we'll drop everything to be here. In the meantime, is there anything—anything at all we can do for you before we go?" There was a gentleness in his deep voice that somehow calmed her.

"I don't think so," she replied, pushing back the gloom that shrouded her heart. "Really, you've done more than enough . . . the food, the fasting, the prayers. Thank you so much."

"No problem," Elder Stucki said as they stood and extended their hands. Paula shook them warmly. Elder Richland gazed down at her with a crooked, dimpled smile, and she resisted an impulse to hug him tightly. *No wonder TJ likes these guys so much. They've got heart.* The thought buoyed her as she watched them disappear into the elevator.

Alone in the empty waiting room, she paced until it was time to see TJ again. When the nurse finally led her into his small, sterile room, Paula could detect no change in his condition or level of consciousness. Still, she hoped that her presence, her caring, her maternal love would somehow count for something.

She sat beside the bed and stroked his cool cheek with her fingers. "Hey, kiddo, you'll never guess who dropped by," she said in the most cheerful voice she could manage. "Your missionary friends, the elders. They miss their basketball buddy." She smoothed a tuft of sandy hair away from his forehead. "You know, I hate to admit it, but they're pretty nice guys . . . bet you never thought you'd hear me say that, huh?" She smiled ruefully. "Well, I've gotta hand it to them; they really seem to care. They explained to me about fasting and prayer— they're doing it for you, you know. And they told me about this priesthood thing . . . but then I guess you already know about that, don't you? Anyway, they said they could give you a blessing—said they could heal you by the power of God. I dunno . . . it seems like a pretty tall order. But then we *are* talking about God here, aren't we? I mean, if anyone could make you well, he could, right? Assuming, of course, there *is* a God." She chuckled nervously. "And if there is, I guess that was a pretty uncool thing to say, wasn't it?" *And if there is, I hope he won't hold it against me.* "I told the elders I'd think about the blessing . . . but in the meantime, I need you to be as strong as you can, kiddo. I need you to come back to me, okay?"

She squeezed his hand and stared intently at his still features, willing him to open his eyes and ask for a peanut butter and tuna sandwich. Nothing. "Okay," she whispered, "so your appetite isn't quite what it used to be. We can work on that later. For now, just concentrate on waking up. I'll see you again in an hour. 'Bye, kiddo . . . love you." She pressed kisses to his closed eyelids and slipped quietly from the room.

Hours passed. Between her brief visits to TJ's bedside, Paula nibbled at the food Millie had sent, questioned the floor nurses incessantly, leafed through a pile of old magazines, dozed a little, wandered up and down the silent corridors. On one of her excursions, she found the chapel and stepped inside. Its dozen or so pews were empty and dark; there was an altar of some sort at the front of the room, and an inverted "v" of lighted candles glowed eerily beneath a simulated stained-glass window on a side wall. She felt uncomfortable, disoriented—like an intruder. *I haven't been inside a church for a dozen years . . . God probably sees me as a hypocrite in progress. But then I've got nothing to lose, have I? Except . . . perhaps . . . my son. Should I pray? Whine? Beg? Make promises I can't keep?* Finally, unable to reconcile herself to petitioning a God who was probably too busy to listen anyhow, she left the chapel and retraced her steps to the waiting room, where she kicked off her shoes, curled her legs beneath her on one of the couches, and rested her head in her hands. In a few minutes, it would be time to see TJ again. *If you're listening, God, I could use a wake-up call for my boy right about now.*

Moments before her scheduled five-minute visit, a flurry of activity at the nurses' station alerted Paula that something was out of the ordinary. She felt her body go rigid as a nurse studied one of the patient monitors and spoke curtly into the phone: "The boy's vitals aren't holding. Tell Cabrini to get here *stat*. We'll do what we can." She slammed down the receiver and nodded brusquely toward a pair of nurses a few feet to her side. Paula watched, riddled with alarm, as the three women filed quickly through the station's narrow exit and moved efficiently toward the hallway where TJ's room was located.

It took her two seconds to catch up with the nurses as they bustled toward a cubicle at the end of the hall. It *was* TJ's room. When they didn't appear to notice her, she grabbed a white-clad arm and pressed her fingers firmly into the soft flesh. "Excuse me . . . that's my son's room. What's going on?"

"We're not sure, Mrs. Donroe," the nurse answered flatly, pulling her arm away from Paula's viselike grip. "Please wait here. The doctor will be along shortly." Her severe tone dismissed any further inquiries, and Paula leaned heavily against the wall as TJ's door closed with a solid click. There was nothing to do but wait.

Less than a minute later, Dr. Cabrini rounded the corner at a dead run, nearly losing her balance as one of her white Nike sneakers scuffed against the wall. As she righted herself, she glanced at Paula. The doctor's jaw was set in a grim line, but she managed a thin smile as she sprinted in the direction of TJ's room.

Paula stepped squarely in front of her. "TJ's in trouble, isn't he?" Her question sounded hollow and seemed to bounce off the walls of the brightly lit corridor.

The doctor paused in mid-stride. "I'm afraid so," she admitted. "But I won't know what the problem is until I evaluate him, so if you'll excuse me . . ." She moved to circumvent Paula, who would not let her pass. "I can see you're upset," Dr. Cabrini said crisply, "but I need to get to TJ. *Now.*"

The two women stood facing each other, at an impasse, until Paula's face crumbled and her shoulders sagged. "He's losing the fight," she moaned, running trembling fingers through her dark hair.

"We don't know that," the doctor replied in clipped tones. Her voice softened as she added, "It's not over, Mrs. Donroe. I can promise you that. But I do need to *be* there if I'm going to help him pull out of this. Do you understand?" Paula nodded forlornly and stepped aside. "Thanks. Now, try to relax for a little bit. I'll let you know." She gave Paula's elbow a light squeeze and hurried into TJ's room.

"Yeah, right . . . relax," Paula mumbled as she headed back toward the waiting room. "Like an antelope relaxes when there's a hungry lion in the bushes." *I could use a good stiff drink right about now.* She sank down on her favorite couch, now littered with sandwich wrappings, empty plastic containers, and wadded napkins. For an hour she stared straight ahead, seeing nothing, until the squeak of rubber on vinyl flooring roused her senses. She looked up into Dr. Cabrini's deep chestnut eyes.

"He's still with us," the doctor said in a subdued tone. She shoved one hand into the pocket of her blue lab coat. "But I'll have to be honest with you . . . it doesn't look very good. The swelling in his brain stem is increasing, and if we can't stabilize him enough to do surgery within the next few hours . . ." Her voice drifted into an awkward silence, and Paula didn't have the heart to ask for an explanation. She nodded silently.

The doctor glanced at her watch. "It's four o'clock; I think I'll head down to the cafeteria and see if I can dredge up a stale pastrami sandwich or something. Maybe a piece of yesterday's pie. But I swear to you I won't leave the hospital. I'll be here if TJ needs me. Okay?"

Her intense stare seemed to penetrate Paula's forehead and settle behind her burning eyes. "Okay," she said faintly. "I'm not going anywhere, either."

"That's good," the doctor breathed. "TJ needs you now . . . more than ever. You can see him again in an hour. Meanwhile, the nurses know where to find me. I'll be back." She pulled the black stethoscope from around her neck and stuffed it in her pocket, then turned and walked briskly toward the elevators.

Paula wrapped her arms around her middle and leaned forward on the couch, groaning softly. Her worry for TJ was almost a physical pain, and she rocked back and forth to ease its insistent throbbing. Squeezing her eyes tightly shut, she felt legions of despair gathering inside her chest, filling her exhausted body with darkness, extinguishing the sliver of light, of hope, to which she had been dutifully clinging for the past ten hours. She knew, now, how this would end; yet, even knowing, she could not accept it. How does—how can— one accept the loss of a child? *If only God would answer . . .*

She pressed her lips together to subdue the scream rising in her throat, and her fingers gripped the edges of the couch in white-knuckled desperation. The feel of heavy paper crinkling under one palm temporarily distracted her from careening over the cliff of hysteria. Opening her eyes to glance down at her left hand, she discovered a small white card crumpled beneath it. She picked the card up, smoothed it on her knee, and turned it over. *They left their card. The Mormon elders. "Any time," they said. "Whatever we can do to help." What was it they offered? A blessing . . . by divine authority. Could it help? Is there any other option?*

Paula's eyes shot to the number on the card, then to her watch. Four-thirty in the morning. *Do I dare?* "Why not?" she said to herself in a rough whisper. "They said they'd come, and this is certainly an emergency." She felt her legs move numbly, mechanically as she rose and shuffled toward the pay phone a few feet away. Her fingers felt like tightly packed sausages as she reached into a pocket for some loose coins. *Change from the popcorn at the movies. Was that only yesterday—or last year?*

Nickel, dime, dime. Paula punched in the number, then drummed her fingernails against the phone until a slightly groggy male voice answered.

"Hello, this is Elder Richland."

Her throat went dry. *This is crazy. What am I doing?* She spoke warily into the phone. "Elder? I'm sorry, this is—"

"Paula." His voice was warm with recognition. "Are you at the hospital?"

"Yes," she said breathlessly. "It's TJ . . . there's been a crisis, and I . . . thought you'd want to know. The doctor says he's very critical, and I . . ."

She could almost feel him jumping to his feet as he listened. "Just hang on," he said. "We're on our way."

At his words, a strange mixture of relief and anxiety flooded through her. "I will hang on," she murmured, then thought of her son, fighting for his life. "*We* will."

"Good," Elder Richland said. "And saying a little prayer wouldn't hurt, either."

Paula crushed the phone against her ear and nodded. "All right," she said. "I'll try." She slowly placed the receiver in its cradle and made her way back to the brown couch, where she sank down and buried her face in her hands. *A prayer . . . okay . . . a prayer. I can do this. I can do anything if it'll help TJ . . . I just called the Mormon elders, didn't I?* The thought caused a weak smile to form at the corners of her mouth. When she turned her attention to the petition at hand, the words shaped themselves silently in the deep recesses of her heart.

Dear God . . . this isn't easy, but please hear me out. My son's in a coma, nearer death than life . . . but then, if you're really there, like the young missionaries say, you probably already know that. And if you know me—even a little—you know I'm not used to asking other people for help. She paused to rock her head slowly from side to side. *But somehow, this seems bigger than that—beyond asking. Begging would be a good word. I'm begging you, God . . . save him. Spare him an early death, because he's so bright and warm and good. Because he loves me, and because there's no one I love more than my darling boy. My darling TJ. He makes me laugh, makes me glad to be his mother, makes me alive. Don't take him, God. Please . . . please.*

Paula pressed her hands tighter against her face as the tears came. *What more can I say? I'd take his place if I could, you know. I'd have taken the bullet . . . willingly. But I can't . . . the most I can do now is promise to do everything within my power to raise him to be a good man. Let me try . . . give us both another chance. Please.* Her shoulders heaved as sobs wracked her willowy frame. When they finally subsided, she sat quietly and stared at the blinking monitor lights across the gray-white counter of the nurses' station.

The clock had barely registered five a.m. when the elevator doors slid open, momentarily suspending the Mormon elders in a frame of dim light before they stepped into the reception area. Paula's eyes focused on them at once, drawing them to her with a soulful expression as she gripped the edges of the couch and pushed herself to a standing position. She swayed unsteadily as the two young men approached, and Elder Richland moved quickly to her side. She leaned heavily against his arm. "Are you okay?" he asked, looking down at her with concern.

Paula smiled weakly. "Hanging on . . . but I must admit I'm glad to see you."

Elder Stucki stifled a yawn with the back of his hand, then looked earnestly at Paula. "We're glad to do whatever we can . . . to help." He glanced at his companion.

"Paula," Elder Richland began as he grasped her elbow and guided her toward the couch, "we both care a lot about TJ—and about you. How can we help?" His voice was husky.

She stopped abruptly and turned her face upward toward his. She stared intently into the young man's luminous brown eyes, searching for faith, reassurance, anything. Something in his expression gave her hope. "You mentioned a . . . blessing," she said softly, her gaze never leaving his face.

He nodded solemnly. "Yes . . . a blessing. The priesthood gives us authority to bless the sick. Would you like us to give TJ a blessing?"

Paula closed her eyes and sighed deeply. "Yes . . . please," she whispered.

"All *right!*" Elder Stucki beamed. "Let's do it! Uh, I mean," he corrected, catching his companion's stern glance, "we'd be pleased to give TJ a blessing." His expression sobered, but his eyes still danced. "It'll help . . . I know it."

"I'll need to check with the nurse," Paula said. "I'm due to see him in a few minutes, but I don't know if they'll let you—"

"No problem. We're clergy, so they'll let us in long enough to give TJ his blessing. We've done this before." Elder Richland smiled down at her, and the warmth of his gaze seemed to disarm the icy shafts of fear embedded in her heart. "I'll just check at the desk." He squeezed her arm lightly, then turned and strode toward the nurses' station, with Elder Stucki following close behind. After a few seconds of subdued conversation with one of the nurses, he motioned for Paula to join them at the desk. "It's all set," he whispered. "We can do it right away." Paula glanced toward the nurse for confirmation, and the portly woman nodded her assent. Without further comment, she led the trio down the hall to TJ's room.

It seemed to Paula that nothing had changed in the past hour, except perhaps that TJ seemed smaller, colder, more pale and shrunken on the white-sheeted bed. She bent to press her lips against his pasty forehead and whispered, "Hey, kiddo, I brought you some company. The Mormon elders—remember them? They said they could help—said they'd give you a blessing. You probably know more about what that means than I do, but I'm willing to give it a try, okay?" As expected, TJ did not respond, and she continued. "I'm going to let them do their thing now, but I'll be right here . . . right beside you." She pulled a chair close to the bed and reached through the railing to cradle her son's hand in hers. Then she looked up and nodded slightly toward Elder Richland.

As Paula watched in silence, the two young men positioned themselves on opposite sides of the bed, near where TJ's head rested on a thin pillow. Elder Stucki reached into a pocket of his suit jacket and drew out a small vial of amber-colored liquid. "Consecrated oil," he whispered as Paula looked at him questioningly. "For the first part of the blessing." She nodded, and he poured a few drops of the oil on the top of TJ's head, then placed his hands firmly on the boy's head and bowed his own head. Paula also tucked her chin down toward her chest, closed her eyes, and listened intently as the elder spoke a few words about "anointing" and "healing of the sick." There was a pause after his "amen," then Elder Richland's sonorous voice gently filled the room with its reverent petition.

Again Paula listened carefully, but a sudden deluge of feeling overshadowed her ability to discern the words clearly. An outpouring of inexpressible comfort seemed to begin near the top of her head, flowing downward, flooding her body with light and warmth. It was like being completely wrapped in the softest, most luxuriant blanket ever fashioned by human hands.

Her heart beat faster, but not with fear. What was it, then? She knew without thinking: it was love. From some incredible font of divine compassion, it had calmed her troubled mind, bathed her aching heart in solace. And now it was going to heal her son. She knew it. A few snatches of the blessing—"The Lord knows and loves you," "your life is an inspiration to many," "relief from suffering or infirmity," "by faith the sick are made whole"—penetrated her brain, bolstering her feelings of peace and optimism. Her mouth moved soundlessly to form the words *thank you* at the same moment Elder Richland said, "In the name of Jesus Christ, amen." She kept her eyes closed tightly for a few seconds, drinking in the benevolent spirit filling the room.

She looked up in time to see the elders slowly withdrawing their hands from TJ's head. The boy lay still as before, but Paula thought he looked more peaceful—more ready to wake up and flash her one of his toothy grins before cracking a joke or two. She could hardly wait.

Still clinging to her son's hand, Paula lifted her gaze to Elder Richland's moist brown eyes. "I could feel it," she murmured. "I could feel your power."

"It was God's power," he corrected gently. "We felt it, too. TJ's life is in his hands now."

"I know." Her voice was barely more than a whisper. "And as soon as he wakes up, I'm going to tell him it's all right if he joins your church. It could only do him good, and I was a fool not to give him permission right away." She chuckled. "Remind me to apologize to my son, will you?"

"And you, Paula?" Elder Stucki asked from the other side of the bed.

She turned toward him with a puzzled expression. "Me? What about me?"

"Well, you felt the Spirit during TJ's blessing; it was evidence of the Lord's love for you. I'm sure he'd be pleased if you looked into his church, too."

"Me? Oh, I—I don't think so," she sputtered. "I'm not really the religious type, you know—not like TJ, who seems to have a sense of it."

"But you felt the Spirit." Elder Stucki's voice was kind but persistent.

"Oh, I felt something, all right," Paula admitted, "and I won't forget it. It's just that I'll never be the kind of person who settles for only one way of doing something, you know?" Her reasoning sounded hollow and pathetic, even to her own ears. *But one doesn't become a Mormon overnight, just because of a few minutes of warm, fuzzy feelings.*

Elder Richland looked at her solemnly. "As my mother always says, 'Never say never.'"

Paula started, vaguely recalling the glint of sunlight on a long, narrow trumpet. *Never say never. Where have I heard that before?* She stared at his black and white name tag. "Well, let's wait and see how it goes when TJ's better, okay? I'm not promising anything, you understand . . . let's just wait."

The missionaries exchanged glances across the bed. "We'll be here," Elder Richland said.

"It's been nearly ten minutes, Mrs. Donroe," a nurse's voice reminded her. Paula squeezed TJ's hand tightly, then stood and leaned over to rest her cheek against his. Her lips brushed lightly against his ear as she whispered, "I'll see you later, kiddo. Don't be too slow about waking up, okay? Now that you've had a good, long nap, we've got a lot of catching up to do." She straightened up and smiled down at him.

The elders accompanied Paula to the waiting room, where they sat for a few moments in comfortable silence before she spoke. "You know," she said, "I thought I'd lost him . . . but everything's different now. That incredible feeling I had during the blessing . . . I just *know* it'll be all right. TJ will be all right. And I have you to thank for that." Her dark eyes glowed as she tried to express her gratitude. "How can I repay you for this miracle?"

"It was our privilege to serve in this way," Elder Richland replied. "And of course we'll keep praying for TJ. I believe the Lord has some very special things in mind for him."

"That's nice," Paula said agreeably. "And, well, I guess sharing him with your church is the least I can do in return for . . . for his life." Her expression became pensive for a moment, as though she couldn't quite believe what she'd just said. Her face shone with quiet intensity as she added, "I just want him to have a good life."

"That's what Heavenly Father wants for each of us," Elder Stucki observed.

She smiled at him. "Well, I'm his mother, and I intend to see that he gets it. Now," she continued, turning to Elder Richland, "why don't you boys go home and get some sleep? Goodness knows you deserve it, seeing as how I dragged you out of bed in the middle of the night. I think I could probably use a little nap myself at this point." She leaned back against the couch and yawned, feeling more relaxed than she had in many hours.

"Are you sure?" the elder asked. "We could stay for a while longer . . ."

"No need, really. Dr. Cabrini should be here in an hour or so; as soon as I've spoken with her, I'll call Millie. I'm sure the news will be good. Now go . . . you need your beauty sleep." She laughed good-naturedly.

"Well, all right," Elder Richland said. "I suppose we could get in a little more shut-eye before our first meeting this morning. But if you need us again—for any reason at all—you have our number."

"That I do," Paula said as they stood and shook her hand. "But you've already gone way beyond the extra mile, and I appreciate it. TJ appreciates it, too. With any luck at all, he'll be able to tell you that himself very soon."

"That'd be terrific. Really great," the tall elder said, and Elder Stucki nodded his agreement. "We'll check in with you later today. And we'll keep TJ in our prayers."

"I'd be grateful for that," she said softly. "And thanks again."

"You bet," Elder Richland said, lifting his arm in a half-wave of farewell. "We'll be in touch."

Paula watched the pair disappear into an elevator, then glanced at the clock. Five forty-five. *Half an hour, and they'll let me see TJ again. There's just time for a little power nap.* Kicking off her shoes, she drew her knees up toward her chin, arranged herself comfortably on the couch, and rested her head against a small cushion. Her eyelids slowly drooped, and she began to feel deliciously relaxed as her body sagged against the brown upholstery.

Drifting rapidly toward sleep, she allowed her mind to range like a wide, sweet river of imagination over the fertile soil of her subconscious. A curious procession of random thoughts and questions gently deluged her brain as she moved along the slow-motion track to cozy oblivion. *Will TJ be awake when I see him? How long until he can play basketball again? Where does one buy consecrated oil? Do the elders sleep in their suits? That guy with the horn who says "Never say never" . . . he might be on to something. I'll never ask God for another thing in my life, so help me. Must call home . . . tell them I've seen a miracle . . . life is good. And Ted—what about him? Ted is friendly . . . even . . . under . . . fire.* The last notion coaxed her lips into a gentle smile as she rolled out to sea on a wave of contentment.

She slept deeply for the better part of two hours, secure in her sense of divine protection for her son. When she finally opened her eyes, Dr. Cabrini was staring down at her with a wide, thoughtful gaze.

Paula stretched her arms out in front of her and smiled up at the dark-haired woman. "Good morning, doctor," she said, then focused on the clock. "Good grief! I've slept way past my time with TJ!" She sat up and slid to the edge of the couch, smoothing her tousled hair with one hand, then grinned again at the doctor. "I know, I know . . . you've come to tell me how well he's doing. Pretty great, huh? Any idea when he'll be released? If you could just let me know, I'll call Millie. She'll want to fix some of his favorite meals, and—"

"Mrs. Donroe." The doctor sat down beside her. "I have news, but it's not—"

"Oh, I understand," Paula interrupted. "Of course you can't tell me *exactly* when he'll be up to going home . . . but a ballpark figure will do. Just let me know anytime today." She quickly slipped her feet into her shoes and began to rise. "Now, if you'll excuse me, I need to check on him before—"

Dr. Cabrini's firm hand on her arm pulled her back to the couch. "Mrs. Donroe, please." Something in her tone caught Paula's attention.

"Oh, I'm sorry," Paula said sweetly. "Guess I got a little carried away. Was there something you wanted to say? TJ's waited this long; I guess he can wait a minute more." She focused her eyes cheerfully on the doctor's face.

Long moments passed in silence before Dr. Cabrini spoke in a low, reluctant voice. "I'm afraid there's nothing more to be done," she said. "TJ died twenty minutes ago."

CHAPTER 23

Paula stared vacantly at the doctor. "No," she said in a dry whisper. "It's not possible."

"I know how hard this must be," the doctor said in a soothing tone. "Almost an hour ago, TJ had a slight convulsion—nothing serious by itself, but apparently it tore some of his damaged blood vessels. His aorta ruptured; we tried everything, but the bleeding couldn't be stopped fast enough. I can't tell you how sorry I—"

Paula shook her head and raised a trembling hand. "I was so sure he'd be all right . . . I *knew* it." She slumped back against the couch and clapped her hand over her mouth, closing her eyes tightly.

"These things happen. They're hard to explain. Is there anything I can do?" Dr. Cabrini's voice vibrated with emotion.

"No . . . yes." Paula opened her eyes, still too dazed to grasp the reality. "Can I see him?"

"Of course. He's still . . . in his room." The two women stood, and the doctor put an arm around Paula's shoulders and guided her down the dimly lit hallway. Pausing in front of a closed door, the doctor asked softly, "Would you like me to go in with you?"

"No . . . thank you," Paula responded hollowly. "I just want to . . . be with him."

"I understand. I'll be here when you're finished." Dr. Cabrini gave Paula's shoulders a gentle squeeze and pushed the door open. Looking straight ahead, Paula shuffled into the darkened room. A solitary light above the headboard illuminated the sheeted figure on the bed.

A few hesitant steps brought her to TJ's side. He lay still and silent, much as he had for the past twelve hours. But now . . . now there was no breath, no warmth, no flutter of an eyelid, no color. No life.

She touched his forehead, his cheek, his shoulder, lifted his hand to her lips. *This wasn't supposed to happen . . . and now I have to say goodbye.* She began to speak in a dull, halting monotone. "Well, kiddo, I guess this is it. Who would've thought . . . I can't believe . . . just . . . can't . . . believe . . . you're . . ." A sharp intake of breath constricted her throat. "Gone." Still clinging to his hand, she slumped into a chair beside the bed. "Dear God, you were so young, so happy, so . . . *alive*. How can this be?" She shook her head firmly and reached out to curl a stray lock of sandy hair behind his ear.

A sense of someone standing nearby caused Paula to turn in her chair and stare into the empty darkness behind her. *I could have sworn . . . no, it's nothing. Just my imagination. Or was it?* She returned her gaze to TJ's face and spoke to him again. "I keep thinking you'll wake up any second now, end the nightmare, come home with me." She chuckled grimly. "Pretty silly, huh? By now, you're probably off on some great cosmic adventure, having the time of your . . . life." The word caught in her throat, and a sob replaced it. "Well, wherever you are, don't forget me, will you, kiddo? Don't you *ever* forget . . . because I won't. I promise." Draping one arm across TJ's unmoving chest, she laid her head carefully on the white sheet beside his shoulder and closed her eyes, feeling warm tears course over the bridge and sides of her nose. In gentle, barely audible tones, she whispered words of love and longing into his ear. Then silence swathed mother and son in a final, somber embrace.

Half an hour later, Paula emerged, pale and hollow-eyed, from TJ's room and walked unsteadily toward the nurses' station. Dr. Cabrini met her halfway, grasping her elbow and guiding her toward the waiting room. "We've made arrangements," the doctor said evenly. "I've spoken with your housekeeper; she's sending someone to bring you home. And we'll see that your son is taken to whatever funeral home you wish." Paula nodded silently, staring straight ahead. "Is there anything else I can—"

"No. Thank you," Paula said hoarsely as she sank down on the brown couch. "I'll be . . . all right." She looked up at the doctor with brimming eyes. *All right? I'll never be all right again in my life. My son has just died.* "I'll just wait here . . . for my ride."

"Very well," Dr. Cabrini said quietly, reaching down to squeeze Paula's hand. "Again, I'm terribly sorry."

"I know you tried," Paula breathed. "Thanks for that." She leaned back against the couch and lowered her burning eyelids as the doctor excused herself and walked slowly down the hall, her shoulders drooping. *How can she do this, day after day?* Paula wondered. *People so sick . . . dying . . . kids . . . parents wild with grief. I could never handle it.* She pressed a quivering hand over her eyes.

She had no idea how much time had passed when she heard the sound of footsteps coming toward her from the elevator. She pressed her hand tighter against her eyes, hoping whoever it was would ignore her.

"Paula?"

She recognized the voice instantly, but for a moment couldn't connect it to a face. Finally, she screwed her aching eyes open and looked up. Elder Richland was gazing at her sympathetically, his own eyes shining with barely controlled emotion. "Millie called with the news. We came right over. We're *so* sorry. What can we do?" He sat on the couch beside Paula, and Elder Stucki lowered himself into a chair across from them.

Paula stared blankly at the young man next to her for endless moments, feeling nothing. Then, as the reality seeped into her mind, a hard knot of rage gradually began working its way up from her stomach to settle in her eyes with burning intensity. A short, mocking laugh forced its way between her clenched teeth. "Oh, I think you've done quite enough already, *Elder*," she hissed. "Such a *wonderful* blessing you gave him . . . fool that I was, you almost had me thinking it was something special. And now this . . . my son dead . . . and you couldn't do a stinking thing about it, could you? So much for divine intervention, huh? Is this how your Mormon God helps all his little boys? Well, pardon me, but I'm *not* impressed." Her voice seethed with resentment.

Elder Richland shook his head mournfully. "I—I don't know what to say . . . except that Heavenly Father knows what's best. He must have had some reason for—"

"For killing TJ?" Paula's eyes flashed. "I can't imagine what that might be, can you? To get even with me for my many sins? To make himself feel important? For *fun?* Yeah, that must be it . . . your God gets a kick out of punishing innocent children—for nothing. Nice guy." She folded her arms tightly across her chest and stared straight ahead.

Both elders looked stricken. "Paula," Elder Richland said, "we can't tell you why this happened, because only God knows . . ."

"And obviously, he's not talking," Paula interjected, the words dripping like acid from her tongue.

"He *will* talk to us, if we just listen," the missionary continued intently. "He'll tell you that TJ may not be here anymore, but he's well and happy in another place, learning and—"

"That's *not* what I'd want to hear, even if I felt like asking," Paula snarled. "Frankly, I don't *care* if he's somewhere else. What I *want* is for him to be *here* . . . with *me*, where he's *supposed* to be. Nothing else matters—or doesn't your God *care* that families are ripped apart by senseless violence?" She glared at Elder Richland, whose face had paled to a sickly gray color.

"Of course he cares," Elder Stucki said fervently. "It's just that in the eternal scheme of things, this mortal life isn't the only—"

"Oh, save it for Sunday School," Paula cut in sharply. "I just need to get home. Thanks for coming, but if you boys will excuse me . . ." She stood abruptly.

A brief shadow of confusion passed over Elder Richland's ashen face, then he stood to face her. "Actually, Millie sent us to give you a ride home."

Paula regarded him coldly for a few seconds before her lips curled into a sardonic half-grin. "I don't think so," she rasped. "I'll call a taxi." She reached into her pocket for some loose change.

"But, really," Elder Stucki insisted, "We'd be more than happy to take you home."

A flicker of hesitation rose in her eyes, but was quickly squelched by a rush of hard-edged determination. "Thank you, no. I'll find my own way." Her tone was bitter. She turned curtly away from them and strode into an open elevator, where she punched the "Lobby" button and stared defiantly at the missionaries until the heavy doors slid closed. Alone in the softly vibrating cubicle, she leaned heavily against the steel wall and tried to collect her thoughts. *If I never see those guys again, it'll be too soon.*

Sometime later, without knowing or thinking or feeling, Paula found herself being led from a taxi into her own home, Millie's arm tightly circling her waist. The older woman guided her gently to a sofa in the living room, then sat beside her and took her hand. "You're home now, dear," she said soothingly. "What do you need?"

Paula turned to look at Millie's tear-stained face. *What do you think I need? I need my son. I need TJ.* "A drink," she said aloud. "A big one."

Millie shook her head sadly. "Oh, I don't think that would be such a good idea."

"I'm not asking you to think," Paula replied sharply. "I'm asking you to get me a *drink.*" Seeing the pain in Millie's eyes, she softened her approach. "I'm sorry, Millie. I didn't mean to snap at you. I just need something . . . to help, that's all. Maybe just a little one . . . please?"

Millie nodded and shuffled toward the den, returning a few moments later with a small shot glass half-filled with amber liquid. Seeing it, Paula managed a weak smile. "I did say a little one, didn't I?" She took it gratefully from Millie's hand and swallowed the scotch in a single gulp. Then she kicked off her shoes and drew her legs up beneath her on the sofa. "He's gone, Millie. I can't believe it." Her words hung gloomily in the still air. "TJ's gone."

"I know," Millie said. "It's like the worst nightmare you could possibly imagine." She sat close to Paula on the sofa and wiped at her eyes with a wad of tissue. "It *is* the worst nightmare." The two women sat quietly for several minutes, each consumed by her own thoughts and memories. The mournful silence of the moment was broken only by a small gray bird twittering cheerfully near the open kitchen window.

Finally, Millie spoke reluctantly. "We need to talk about the . . . arrangements."

"I know," Paula sighed. "The funeral. And I need to make some calls." *To tell people my son is dead.* The thought made her stomach churn.

"I can do that for you, dear. You should rest. Just give me a list, and I'll take care of it."

"Thanks," Paula said absently. She ran her fingers through her dark hair. "As far as the rest goes, I don't know where to start. I've never put together a funeral before." *A cocktail party, a weekend retreat, a catered dinner for three hundred, an international conference . . . but never a funeral. Never a funeral for my child.* "Something simple, I suppose . . ."

"Could I make a suggestion?" Millie asked.

"Of course." *She's done two funerals . . . her daughter's and her husband's.* "I'd be grateful for any . . . advice."

"Well, you know TJ cared a lot about the Church."

Paula's muscles tensed. *The Mormons.* "Yes, I know that."

"He only attended church a few times, but he had a lot of friends in the ward . . . the basketball team, his Sunday School class, things like that . . ." Millie paused.

"And?"

"Well, I've spoken with the bishop, and they're all grieving over this tragedy. He said he'd be perfectly willing to take care of all the arrangements—the church, the service, the burial. Everything. Said it would be an honor to remember TJ for the fine young man he was."

"I see." Paula couldn't speak further, couldn't even think. She rested her head against the back of the sofa.

Millie continued. "You know, dear, TJ and I have learned a lot about the purposes of life over the past few weeks, and I believe he understood the big picture—including what happens after we leave this earth. The Church would have been a big part of his life, and it seems right that it should be a part of his death, as well. I think he would want this."

Paula closed her eyes and let out a long, slow breath. *Now the Mormons want to bury my son. How could this be happening?* With every shred of her waning strength, she wanted to reject this ludicrous proposal, to scream at the top of her lungs that she had no use for some do-gooder religion, to rage at the brash young men who had made such shining promises and then left her to deal with the tarnished reality of TJ's death. She wanted to say all that and more, but she couldn't. Her tongue lay like a rock in the bottom of her mouth.

"I think he'd want it too, Mom."

She opened her eyes to see Scott standing near the sofa. His face was haggard, and he stared at her with red-rimmed eyes. His hands were stuffed into the pockets of his jeans, and she could see that the front of his rumpled blue T-shirt was covered with small, damp spots. When she held out her arms, he knelt in front of the sofa and laid his head in her lap, much as he'd done when he was a toddler. She smoothed his dark hair, and Millie reached over to rub his shoulder.

A few moments passed, and Scott raised his head to look steadfastly into his mother's moist eyes. "I meant it, y' know," he declared. "TJ cared about the Church . . . and even if we don't believe the same way, I think we owe it to him . . . to do this." Fresh tears welled in his eyes. "Shouldn't we do it his way, Mom?"

"You really think Mormonism meant that much to him?" she asked after a long silence, glancing from Scott to Millie and back to the boy again.

"We know it," Millie whispered, reaching out to touch Paula's arm.

She nodded slightly. "Well, then . . . let's do it his way." Her shoulders sagged. "Millie, will you call the bishop?"

"Right away." Millie glanced at her watch. "He should be between meetings now." She leaned over to kiss the younger woman's cheek. "Thank you, Paula. This is a good thing you've done . . . you'll see."

"I don't know," Paula murmured as she watched Millie hurry toward the kitchen.

"She's right, Mom," Scott said. "I mean, I don't care one way or another about the Church, but we *need* to do this. For TJ."

"I guess," she agreed. "For TJ." She hugged Scott, then stood and walked slowly into her den, where she poured herself another drink. A big one.

By mid-afternoon, a steady stream of visitors—friendly strangers, mostly women and young teenagers—began to appear at Paula's door. "From the ward" was their usual introduction. They brought food, flowers, words of comfort and encouragement. The Relief Society president, Sister Martin, came to ask a few questions and assure Paula that she and her family would be well taken care of. She was a large, elegantly dressed woman in her mid-fifties whose deep green eyes, it seemed to Paula, were like rivers of compassion that overflowed into her open-hearted smile. "We'll get through this," she whispered as she wrapped her arms around Paula at the end of her visit. Paula almost believed her.

It was past eight o'clock by the time Bishop Peters appeared at her door. A short, wiry man whose Adam's apple protruded over the collar of his white button-down shirt, he seemed slightly ill at ease as he introduced himself and shook her hand. "I'd hoped we would meet under more favorable circumstances," he said. "Perhaps at TJ's baptism."

Paula bristled a bit, but responded calmly. "Yes, well, here we are. I appreciate your stopping by."

She called Millie, and the three sat together on the living room sofa, conversing in subdued tones. Within an hour, plans had been made for a viewing and brief funeral service the following Wednesday. To Paula's relief, Bishop Peters seemed willing and able to coordinate the many details involved; when she commented on his organizational abilities, he looked at her through warm, caring eyes. "I've done this before," he confided. "More times than I'd care to remember." He paused and cleared his throat. "The hardest ones are for the children; I've helped with two since I've been bishop. Adults who have lived long, fruitful lives are one thing. But the youngsters . . . there are never any easy answers." He shook his head. "TJ was a fine young man."

"Thank you," Paula said in a slightly uneven voice. "Is there anything else we need to talk about?"

"I think that's about it," the bishop replied, then appeared to change his mind. "Except for . . . the pallbearers. Is there anyone in your family who'd be willing to serve in this way?"

"I'm not sure," Paula responded. "My father died some time ago, and my former husband—TJ's father—well, frankly, I'm not even sure where he is at the moment. And even if I could find him, it's likely he won't come for the services. Maybe a friend or two from my office . . . and I think Scotty will do it, but I'll need to ask him. How many do you need?"

"The usual number is six," Bishop Peters said. "A couple of his friends in the ward—boys on the basketball team—have already volunteered, and of course the elders would like to—"

"*No.*" Paula's voice was suddenly sharp and glacial, her gaze fixed severely on the bishop's face. "I will *not* have the elders participate in any way, and I prefer that they not attend the services."

The bishop returned her stare with a puzzled expression. "I—I don't understand. They were teaching TJ the gospel. Why . . . ?"

"My reasons are personal," Paula said curtly. *They made promises to both of us, then they betrayed me and let my son die.* "In any case, I will *not* have them anywhere near the funeral, and I'd like you to inform them of my wishes. If you can't do that, I'll find another church and another minister. Is that understood?"

He stared at her for a moment longer, his mouth open slightly, then nodded slowly. "Of course. If that's what you really want."

His statement struck her as impertinent, but she willed herself to remain in control. "That's exactly what I want," she said coolly. "No elders." Out of the corner of her eye, she saw Millie's dumbfounded expression. She would explain later. "Are we agreed?"

"Yes . . . yes. I'll see to it." His mild voice held no rancor, but Paula couldn't miss the disappointment in his eyes as he stood and offered his hand. "I'll be in touch very soon," he added. "In the meantime, is there anything you need—anything at all we can do?"

This man's genuine kindness, even in the wake of her barbed demands, disarmed Paula's arsenal of bitter recriminations. She gripped his hand tightly. "I—I think I'm all right for now. Thank you," was all she could say, her voice pinched with emotion.

"Let me know," he said warmly, squeezing her hand in both of his. "You have my numbers at home and work." She nodded, glancing at the small card he had laid on the coffee table. "Any time, day or night. I'll be here." She knew he meant it, and she smiled her thanks. She closed the door behind him and leaned against it, breathing deeply. *Maybe I can get through this, after all.*

Millie's voice penetrated her silent thoughts. "Come and eat something, dear. It's been a long time, and you need to keep your strength up. I've made chicken with plum sauce—or there are about a dozen casseroles in the fridge."

"Bless you, Millie," Paula smiled, remembering the food she'd sent to the hospital. "The chicken sounds wonderful." She followed her friend into the kitchen and dutifully sat down at the table. Half a dozen bites satisfied her flagging appetite, but she lingered over her plate, feeling a certain comfort in the room's cozy, familiar surroundings. A gentle pressure against her leg reminded her that Rudy, too, had lost a friend. She reached down to stroke the dog's wide, golden head. "How are you, buddy?" she whispered. He answered with a solemn thump of his tail on the floor as he rested his chin on her foot. His flanks heaved in a massive sigh. "I know, Rudy," she murmured. "I know." The two commiserated in silence.

Millie's voice came from the other side of the kitchen, where she was filling the dishwasher. "You know," she said meekly, "I couldn't help hearing what you said to Bishop Peters . . . about the elders. Do you want to talk about it? I mean, I can't imagine why you'd say something like that." She closed the dishwasher, shuffled over to the table, and sat down across from Paula. "Elder Richland called me from the hospital. He could hardly get the words out . . . said you were angry and wouldn't let them bring you home. That's all I know."

"Well, that's about all there is to know," Paula said, suddenly feeling bone-weary. "Did he tell you they gave TJ one of their Mormon blessings?"

"Yes, but he didn't go into any details—just said he'd thought it would turn out differently, but we still needed to have faith that the Lord had his reasons for letting TJ . . . pass on."

Paula snorted softly. "Yes, that's pretty much what he told me, too. But I don't buy it. Their little prayer over TJ just didn't work, that's all. It sounded good enough, even made me feel nice, got my hopes up. And then, just like that, it was over. Nothing could've saved him—and they never should have promised what they couldn't deliver. I let myself hope too much . . . let myself trust them too much. And now . . ." Her jaw tightened and tears filled her eyes. "I just don't want to see them again."

Millie's eyes brimmed with sympathy and her own grief. "Those boys loved TJ . . . I could see it on their faces every time they came to visit or shoot baskets with him. Surely you can't think they did this on purpose."

Paula shook her head. "I really don't know what to think, Millie. All I know is they let me down . . . and they let TJ down. They let him *die*, Millie—and I'll never be able to forgive that. So let's just leave it alone, okay?" She wiped a tear from the corner of one eye and gave the older woman a firm glance that closed the discussion.

"Okay," Millie agreed. "But thanks . . . for letting the ward do the services. TJ would have wanted it."

"I hope so." Paula pushed her chair back from the table. "Where's Scotty, anyway?"

"In his room," Millie reported. "I took some dinner up to him earlier."

"Thanks, Millie. You take good care of us," Paula said gratefully. "I guess we should all try to get some rest now. The next few days won't be easy."

"You're right about that," Millie said, rising slowly from her chair. "I'll say good night now." She wrapped her arms around Paula, and the two women held each other for a long moment. "We'll manage, with the Lord's help," Millie whispered. Paula said nothing. "I'll call everyone on your list first thing in the morning."

"That'll be fine," Paula said, moving toward the entryway. "Good night, Millie." As she slowly climbed the stairs, Rudy followed her. He paused in front of TJ's closed door and lifted a front paw. "Not tonight, pal," she murmured. *Not any night. Not ever again.* She raised a hand to touch the knob, but couldn't find the strength to turn it. *Later . . . I'll go through his things later. After it's all over.* Rudy slumped to the floor like a deflated balloon, and Paula moved noiselessly down the hall to her own room.

Exhausted, she sank into the rocking chair by her bed and massaged her throbbing temples, trying to decide what to do. *How long since I actually laid my head on a pillow . . . scissor-kicked my legs between the cool sheets . . . took a long, hot shower?* The last thought triggered in her an inscrutable longing for the intense, rhythmic beat of a million drops of water on her back, her face, her body. Could they magically soothe away the knots of pain in every muscle? Drown out the pulsing cadence of bitterness thumping in her chest? Masquerade the torrents of grief cascading down her cheeks? *It's worth a try. At the very least, I'll be clean.*

An hour later, Paula was still huddled, waif-like, sobbing, in a steamy corner of her marble-walled shower, her tears mingling with all the other drops of water on her face, her neck, her body. She was clean, but it didn't matter.

CHAPTER 24

"Your mother said she'd come."

Paula's pancake-laden fork stopped halfway to her mouth, dripping heavy maple syrup onto her plate as she tried to make sense of Millie's words. She stared incredulously at her housekeeper. "You *called* her?" The comfortable numbness of early-morning unreality had suddenly evaporated, along with her appetite.

"I did," Millie admitted. "She wasn't on your list, but I thought she should know. She's the boy's grandmother, after all."

"*Absentee* grandmother," Paula corrected, lowering her fork to the plate. "She never even came to TJ's christening." Memories of their twenty-two-year estrangement—and her recent fruitless visit to Marjorie Enfield's Connecticut estate—assaulted her already raw nerves.

"I know," Millie said. "That's why I was so surprised when she said she'd come."

"When?"

"Tuesday night. She'll leave right after the services on Wednesday. Said she won't bother us; she'll stay in a motel."

"Fine with me. I just wish you hadn't—"

"I think she was crying, Paula. She hung up real fast."

"Well, it's done; we'll manage. Have you called the others?"

"Everyone. The folks at your office . . . all devastated. Carmine says to call if there's anything they can do. They'll keep things under control until you feel up to getting back to it. I expect they'll be over to visit . . . and of course they'll be at the services."

"That's nice," Paula said absently. "Anything else I should know?"

"I couldn't find Richard," Millie reported, speaking the name of

Paula's former husband as though it was a disease. "His girlfriend thought he was in Europe; she said she'd give him the message if he calls."

Paula stood and carried her half-empty plate to the sink. "I won't hold my breath," she joked grimly, stopping to wipe a drop of syrup off her blue sweat pants. "TJ never had much use for Richard anyway."

"You were that boy's whole life," Millie said softly.

"After basketball," Paula added with a sad smile.

The doorbell rang, and both women started. "Who in the world . . . ? It's pretty early for visitors," Paula observed, glancing at the clock. It was barely past nine. "I'll get it," she said, smoothing her unruly hair as she walked toward the entryway. "It's probably just . . ." Her voice trailed off as she opened the door.

Ted stood awkwardly on the porch, his face chalky, his lips pressed together in a thin line. The moment he saw Paula, his searing blue eyes burned into hers with the shock of new grief. He bounded through the half-open door and gathered her into his arms. "Carmine told us," he breathed raggedly against her hair. "I had to come. Dear Lord, Paula, I'm *so sorry.*" He crushed her body against his, and she returned his fierce embrace. Words were useless, but the way she and Ted held each other spoke volumes. Paula sobbed against his shoulder, and his own warm tears made small, damp patches in her dark hair.

When they finally eased apart, Paula wiped at her cheeks and smiled up at him. "You have no idea, Mr. Barstow," she said, "how good it was to see you on my porch. Thanks for coming . . . can you stay for a little while?" She reached for his arm and guided him toward the living room. He followed docilely.

They sat together on the sofa, and he took her hand in his. "Can you tell me about it?" he asked softly. And she did—about the shooting, her long hospital vigil, the sudden crisis . . . and the end. When she stopped talking and rested her head back against the sofa, he squeezed his eyes closed like a man in pain. "How unbelievably horrible for you," he groaned. She nodded in silent agreement. "What about the . . ." He hesitated.

"The funeral?" Paula said, finishing the question for him. "It's all been taken care of. The Mormons are doing it." She watched him closely, expecting an angry eruption. There was nothing—only a slightly surprised look in his eyes.

"I thought you had no use for the Church," he said evenly, though there was a puzzled expression on his face.

"I didn't—I don't," she replied. "But TJ got to know the missionaries—a couple of elders played basketball with him and taught him and Millie about their religion. He wanted to join, but I . . ." She wavered, then began again. "Anyway, it seemed like the right thing to do, you know? Give him what he wanted, even if it's . . . too late." Paula stared at the floor.

Ted nodded. "It's the right thing to do."

Now it was Paula's turn to be surprised. "Hey, I thought *you* had no use for the Church," she said, recalling his bitter comments of a few days earlier. "Didn't I once hear you say something about 'pushy, self-righteous hypocrites'?"

He chuckled dryly. "Yeah, that was me. But it didn't have all that much to do with the Church—only with certain *people* in the Church."

"Excuse me?" Paula was baffled and intrigued.

"It's a long story," he sighed, "and some of it ain't so pretty."

"I'm listening," she said.

"Okay." Ted took a breath and exhaled slowly. Then, still holding her hand, he spilled out his story, pausing now and again to collect his thoughts before continuing.

His first ten years had been spent in the quiet suburb of West Jordan, Utah, where his family—mother, father, two brothers and a sister—had been no different from most other members of the Church in their neighborhood. Ted had Mormon friends, Mormon cousins, Mormon teachers, Mormon doctors, Mormon everything. He'd been baptized, along with fourteen of his closest friends, when he was eight, and he'd had no thoughts of being anything else but a faithful member for the rest of his life.

But over the next two years, Ted's secure Mormon world had been shaken to its roots. His father, an upstanding member of the bishopric, had somehow gotten tangled up in a relationship with another ward member—a woman who knew better but couldn't help herself. Jeffery Barstow's dalliance had split the family apart; he was excommunicated and later married the other woman, leaving Ted's mother to fend for herself with four young children. The entire family had slipped into sullen inactivity, leaving a particularly sour taste in Ted's mouth. Bitter and resentful, he'd left home at eighteen and never looked back.

"So, that's it," he said, leaning back against the sofa cushions. "Ted Barstow becomes a non-Mormon by default. End of story."

Paula regarded him curiously. "But you still think it's the right thing to do—the Mormon funeral, I mean."

"Yeah, I suppose so," he said in a wistful tone. "I remember the early years, when I never doubted. Too much water under the bridge now, I guess. But you know, there's still something about the Church—some basic truth that I've never been able to dislodge . . . from here." He tapped his chest with a finger. "It's buried pretty deep, but at times like this . . . well, it gives me something to think about."

"Are you saying," Paula pressed, "that you're a believer? That Mormonism is still part of your life?"

"Not really," he said. "I haven't been in Mormonland for a long time, and I'm not about to go back now. I'm just saying I think this funeral is the right thing—for TJ, because he would've wanted it. As for me, I'm beyond shaping myself to fit any religion. Life goes on; I'm over it."

Paula peered intently into his eyes. "I'm not sure I believe you," she said quietly. "But aside from that, would you come to the services? I'd really appreciate it, and the bishop says they could use another pallbearer."

"Consider me there," he said, squeezing her hand. "Anything else I can do?"

"I don't think so," she said. "You've been an enormous help already." She leaned over and kissed him softly on the cheek. "Tell the others I'm okay, will you?"

"Yes, but they'll know better," he replied. "We'll all be there on Wednesday."

"I'm glad. I don't see how I can get back to the office until—"

"Not to worry, Paula," he said firmly. "Take as long as you need; we'll keep everything under control. It's the least we can do." He released her hand and they both stood up. At the door, he took her into his arms again and pressed his lips to her forehead. "I'm here for you, any time of the day or night," he whispered. "You know that."

"I do." She looked up at him with brimming eyes. "Thank you." She watched from the open door until his Cherokee disappeared around the corner.

"Who was that, Mom?" Paula turned around to see Scott standing on the bottom stair. He looked terrible. She found herself wishing he was two years old again so she could scoop him up into her arms, carry him to her rocking chair, and kiss away all his pain as she held him snugly to her breast and rocked him to sleep. Instead, she just smiled timidly at him and reached up to put an arm around his shoulders. He shrugged her away.

"That was Ted Barstow," she said, moving a step back. "He just wanted to see how we were doing." Scott nodded absently and moved sluggishly toward the kitchen, the ends of his slumping shoulder bones forming miniature tents in the corners of his ragged blue T-shirt. His gray sweat pants hung loosely on his lean frame as his bare feet thudded against the floor tiles. *Sixteen going on ninety-two*, Paula mused. She left him to Millie's care and slipped into the den, where she sat alone for a few minutes before making her way to the liquor cabinet. *TJ should be at school, suffering through math and English,* she told herself. *Not languishing somewhere in a mortuary, waiting to be laid out. Not my son.*

Two days passed in a blur of necessary activity, quietly supervised by Bishop Peters and Sister Martin. By Tuesday evening, all was ready for the viewing, funeral service, burial, and a family meal afterward. Paula answered questions and made simple decisions when required, but for the most part remained a passive, mournful observer. Even her mother's arrival late Tuesday failed to evoke much of a response. "Let her get settled in at the motel," she directed when Millie asked. "I'll see her tomorrow."

Wednesday was sunny and cool. *A perfect day for shooting hoops,* Paula thought as Bishop Peters escorted her, Millie, and Scott to his car and introduced them to his wife, Georgia. It was a short drive to the chapel, where TJ's open casket had been placed at one end of the Relief Society room. Dozens of vivid floral arrangements surrounded it.

They were half an hour early, so Paula spent the time gazing down at her young son, lying so uncharacteristically still and quiet in this oak-and-brass-and-satin box, dressed in a too-formal dark suit. Scott and Millie joined her, but there were no words to express their feelings, only deep sighs and the occasional movement of a hand to brush away a tear. *Strange*, Paula thought. *He's there, lying in front of us, yet it's almost as if he's . . . not there. As if he's . . . closer. Beside me. Wearing the faded brown cords he loved.* Overtaken by a sudden rush of emotion, she couldn't resist an impulse to glance sideways. Seeing no one, she shook her head. *Get a grip, Donroe.* But the intimate feeling lingered with her, even brought a tiny smile to her lips.

"They did a good job. He looks natural."

Paula knew the voice instantly. She pivoted on one heel to face a tall, porcelain-skinned woman dressed in black. "Mother."

"Hello, Paula." Marjorie Enfield stood unmoving, regal, statue-like beneath her halo of white hair.

Seconds passed. Paula's arms hung limply at her sides, as if she didn't know quite what to do with them. Finally, she reached out tentatively and took her mother's gloved hand. "It was good of you to come," she said.

Marjorie withdrew her hand from her daughter's with a slow, dignified movement. "He is—was—my grandson, after all. I should be here." Her voice was flat and toneless.

"Yes . . . of course," Paula responded. *And he had to die before you'd even . . .* She pursed her lips. *Stop it, Donroe; this is no time for recriminations. Just be gracious.* She willed herself to smile. "I appreciate your coming, Mother. I really do."

Marjorie nodded curtly. "As I said, they did a good job. He looks"—she glanced toward the casket—"natural."

"I suppose so," Paula replied. *What's "natural" about a twelve-year-old lying in a coffin?* "The viewing should start in a couple of minutes, and the services begin at eleven. Would you like to have a seat, or—"

"Yes, I believe I will." Without further comment, Marjorie turned her back to Paula and moved sedately toward a single row of chairs at one side of the room. She lowered herself to one of them, centered her small black handbag in the middle of her lap, and proceeded to stare straight ahead. Paula watched her curiously for a few moments, then was drawn back to the solemn reality of the occasion as Bishop Peters gently informed her that it was time to begin.

For the next hour, a steady stream of mourners filed past Paula and her fallen son—her friends, dozens of TJ's classmates and church friends, ward members, Scott's buddies who had been part of the tragedy. The lady missionaries hugged her and wept. "He was a fine young man," Sister Tibbetts said, her voice quavering. "I'm sure the Lord has something wonderful for him to do on the other side." Paula nodded wordlessly and thanked them for coming.

A few minutes before eleven, Bishop Peters quietly ushered all but a few close friends and family members from the room. "It's time to say goodbye now," he whispered close to Paula's ear. "Would you like me to say a prayer before we close the casket?"

"Yes . . . please," she answered mechanically, her eyes fixed on TJ's face. When the small group had gathered in a semicircle, the bishop bowed his head reverently and asked for the blessings of heaven to attend and comfort this grieving mother and those close to her. Standing with her eyes closed tightly and one arm encircling Scott's waist, Paula imagined once again that her youngest son stood on her other side, this time with his arm about her shoulders. The feeling was too intense, too delicious to spoil by opening her eyes, so she concentrated on simply relishing his nearness. At the sound of Bishop Peters' "amen," she reluctantly raised her eyelids to find only Millie standing beside her. *He was here. I know it.* She glanced at the bishop, whose eyes glittered as he nodded almost imperceptibly. *He knows.* She smiled sadly.

"We're ready now," the bishop said. This was Paula's cue to say her farewells. She did so gracefully, bending slowly over the casket's oak side to cup TJ's chin in her palm and brush her lips one last time across his forehead. A tear fell on his cheek, and she tenderly wiped it away. *Be happy, wherever you are,* she said to him from the silent depths of her aching heart. *I love you, kiddo . . . always.* With a final kiss to his sandy brow, she straightened up and turned away from the casket. Her tear-streaked face was a mask of grief as she waited for the others to follow her lead. Finally the lid was closed, and Paula leaned heavily on Ted's arm as the mournful little entourage made its way slowly to the chapel.

The funeral service was brief, simple, and oddly comforting, even to someone of Paula's skeptical nature. A cluster of twenty or thirty well-scrubbed children filled the choir seats, and she wondered what they could possibly contribute to this occasion. Then they began to sing:

I am a child of God,
And he has sent me here,

Has given me an earthly home
With parents kind and dear.

Lead me, guide me, walk beside me,
Help me find the way.
Teach me all that I must do
To live with him someday.

Their shining faces reflected the promises in each verse of the song. *They really believe this,* she mused, wiping at her streaming eyes. *Is that where TJ has gone now—to live with God?*

Bishop Peters spoke for a few minutes, his kind eyes rarely leaving Paula's face. He talked about the bonds of affection between parents and children, about the hope—no, the certainty—of life after death, about a loving Heavenly Father who is mindful of his children and yearns to bless and comfort them. *This would be easy to believe,* Paula thought, *if God hadn't willfully taken my son away. What do I do now, with a big hole in my heart where TJ used to be?* She lowered her eyes and stared at the floor, unwilling to meet the bishop's steady gaze.

The service concluded with a double trio of TJ's Sunday School classmates; the boys had played basketball with him, the girls had befriended him. Before they sang, one of them—a delicate blonde girl with azure eyes and full, tremulous lips, said, "This is for TJ; it was his favorite hymn. We know this is how he felt . . . and we know he's with Heavenly Father now." The lilting melody and lyrics cut into Paula's heart:

O my Father, thou that dwellest
In the high and glorious place,
When shall I regain thy presence
And again behold thy face?

In thy holy habitation,
Did my spirit once reside?
In my first primeval childhood,
Was I nurtured near thy side?

Paula studied the faces of these bright youngsters, so full of faith and hope even as grief welled in their eyes. *They knew you in a way I didn't. I should have seen how much it meant to you. Forgive me, TJ. Forgive me . . . please.* A fresh deluge of tears slid down her cheeks as she bowed her head for the benediction.

The early afternoon sun was warm on Paula's back as she sat a few feet from the deep, narrow hole that would soon close over her son's earthly remains forever. She firmly pushed the image from her mind, concentrating instead on the rather large group of people who had gathered at the cemetery. Ted and Carmine sat on her right side in a short row of metal chairs; Millie, Scott, and Marjorie Enfield were seated on her left. A few dozen other mourners—some were Paula's business associates, but most were young people and their parents from the ward—stood around the grave, visiting quietly amongst themselves.

"It's very peaceful here," Millie whispered, squeezing Paula's hand.

"Yes, it is," Paula agreed, her eyes ranging over the lush, impeccably landscaped grounds. A small sparrow had perched itself on a nearby headstone, and was chirping at the top of its tiny lungs. Paula couldn't help smiling. *He must enjoy singing for a crowd.*

Bishop Peters approached Paula's chair and leaned toward her, gently taking one of her hands in his. "Are you all right?" he asked, his voice barely above a murmur. When she nodded, he said, "Then we'll begin." As he took his place at one end of the casket, the youthful double trio arranged itself at the other end and began to sing in quiet, graceful harmony.

Abide with me; 'tis eventide.
The day is past and gone;
The shadows of the evening fall;
The night is coming on.

Within my heart a welcome guest,
Within my home abide.
O Savior, stay this night with me;
Behold, 'tis eventide.

This is nice, she thought as a slight breeze rippled the still, warm air. *TJ would have liked this.*

When the hymn's final verse had been sung, the bishop explained that it was customary for a priesthood holder to "dedicate" the grave. Paula was perplexed but not offended, and nodded for him to continue. He bowed his head and offered a brief prayer, committing TJ's body to the earth and declaring the burial site "sanctified and secure until the resurrection, when the bodies and the spirits of the dead will be reunited." Paula's heart pounded at the possibility that such an event could—might—one day take place. *A nice thing to hope for.* It occurred to her that she ought to look into purchasing a burial plot for herself nearby—just in case.

With the bishop's "amen" the brief service was concluded, and it was time to leave. He shook Paula's hand warmly and reminded her that a meal had been prepared for the family; it was now waiting for them at Paula's home. Millie had given Sister Martin a key to the house before the funeral, and the Relief Society had taken it from there. Paula thanked the bishop and tried to press a small envelope into his hand. "For all your trouble," she explained.

"How gracious of you," Bishop Peters said gently as he handed back the unopened envelope. "But this service is freely given, and we feel privileged to do it in the name of the Lord. Please accept it in a spirit of love—for you, and for your son."

Paula hesitated, then seemed to understand. "Thank you," she said simply. Ted offered his arm, and they moved slowly away from the casket behind Millie, Scott, and Marjorie.

As they set foot on the tree-lined walk to their vehicles, Paula glanced back for a final look at TJ's grave. A gasp caught in her throat when she saw two young men in dark suits standing a few yards to one side of the burial plot, their heads bowed. As if he could feel her eyes on him, Elder Richland lifted his head and met her gaze. Even from a distance, she could see the agony etched on his features. His red-rimmed, watery eyes and the dusky shadows beneath them gave his sallow face a ghostly appearance, and his cheeks looked sunken and withered. He stared at her sorrowfully, pleading silently for something, she didn't know what. Understanding? Tolerance? Forgiveness? A sudden thought penetrated her mind. *I should go to him.* Instead, she grasped Ted's arm more tightly and turned away. *They weren't invited,* she reminded herself.

Their car pulled away from the cemetery, and Paula looked back one more time. The missionaries were still standing by the grave, lost in thought. Elder Richland's hands were stuffed into his suit pockets, and his shoulders drooped dejectedly.

It was nearing three o'clock by the time Bishop Peters turned his late-model Buick into Paula's driveway. "I'm sure Sister Martin and her helpers have set out quite a spread by now," he joked as he opened one of the back doors for Paula, Millie, and Scott. Marjorie Enfield pulled up behind them in her rental car.

Paula had warmed to this quiet, self-effacing man over the past few days, and now she was at a loss to express her deep gratitude for his many hours of service in her behalf. "We'd love it if you and your wife would join us," was all she could say.

He smiled genially as he helped her out of the car. "Thanks so much," he said, "but I've got several things to take care of at my office before closing time, and my bride here"—he glanced lovingly at Georgia Peters, who smiled back at him from the front seat—"has a date with a couple of our grandchildren this afternoon. So, if you don't mind, I think we'll leave you in Sister Martin's capable hands." His expression sobered, and he looked at her intently. "But you have my number, Paula, and if there's anything at all you need, I hope you'll call. I mean it."

"I know you do." She gave his hand a firm squeeze. "And I'll keep that in mind."

"Good." He shook hands with Millie and Scott, waved toward Marjorie's car, and climbed back into the Buick. A few other cars were pulling up to the curb as he backed out of the driveway.

Ted took the steps two at a time and caught up with Paula just as she opened the front door. He inhaled deeply as they moved into the entryway. "Wow—I can tell the Relief Society has been up to something," he said. "They're famous for their post-funeral dinners, you know." Paula smiled tightly but said nothing.

He followed her into the kitchen, where Sister Martin had things well under control. Several other women of assorted ages and sizes were bustling about at her direction, adding the final touches to a buffet that would have rivaled the quality of any fine restaurant. Turkey, ham, roast beef, mashed and scalloped potatoes, salads of every description—the breakfast bar and kitchen table were completely covered with the tasty handiwork of these and other women from the ward. *People I don't even know,* Paula mused as she stopped near the table to collect her emotions. It was not an easy task. Ted put his arm around her shoulders for support, and she leaned against him. "I told you they'd knock themselves out," he whispered. "It happens every time."

"Yes, well, I can see how they'd want to do something like this for someone they already knew and cared about," she whispered back, "but they don't know me from Adam, and they only knew TJ for a couple of weeks. It's . . . incredible. I don't know how . . ." She wiped hurriedly at a tear slipping down one cheek.

"Just enjoy, Paula," Ted advised. "They love doing it. It's in the Mormon genes or something." He smiled down at her.

"Hello, dear," Eloise Martin said as she moved quickly across the room to enfold Paula in a motherly embrace. "I hope you don't mind our taking over your kitchen like this. Millie told us about the larger room downstairs, so we've set up some chairs and small tables down there. I think it'll be less crowded than if you all try to fit into the kitchen."

"I suppose so," Paula said. Suddenly, her mind was reeling with memories. *October tenth . . . was it only three weeks ago that we cele-brated my birthday in that room? And three weeks since I sat alone upstairs, mourning the loss of my first son. Now it's one gone, one dead, but I've still lost both of them. I don't think the mourning will ever end.* She closed her eyes tightly for a moment and bit down firmly on her trembling bottom lip.

A slight pressure against her leg caused her to glance down. Rudy's deep brown eyes were staring up at her, his feathered tail swaying gently. Paula reached down to pat his wide, golden head. "Hi, there, buddy," she said, genuinely happy to see her faithful pet. The dog woofed softly in greeting. "I hope you haven't given these ladies too much grief," she teased.

"Oh, he's been a perfect gentleman," Sister Martin beamed. "Seemed to know we were here to help; he's spent most of the time just lying in the entryway, watching. The girls and I have enjoyed his company." She reached down to scratch the short hair behind Rudy's ears. He sighed contentedly. "I wish children were so easy to please," she laughed.

One by one, the dozen or so family members and business associates filled their heavy-duty paper plates with food and carefully made their way downstairs. They sat solemnly at four round card tables and ate slowly, like dutiful children under a watchful parent's eye. Ted made some small talk with Paula as she moved a piece of meat around her plate with a fork. "Are you going to eat that ham," he finally asked, "or just scoot it to death?" She smiled wearily and lifted a small chunk of ham to her mouth. "That's better," he said.

Within an hour, the cooks and the guests had departed with hugs and a few final words of sympathy. Ted was the last to leave. As he stood with his arms around Paula at the front door, he spoke softly. "Don't worry about the office, chief. You just take it easy and come back when you're ready. We'll try not to mess things up too badly." He stepped back, keeping his hands on her shoulders, and looked intently into her eyes. "And if there's *anything* . . . well, you know where to find me." She nodded, and he hugged her to his chest again. "The bishop was right, you know," he murmured against her hair.

"About what?" she asked, her head still resting against his blue and white striped shirt.

"TJ's spirit is alive. He's *alive*—and that's not just my Mormon background talking. It's my heart. That's where I feel it. You've got to believe that, too, Paula."

"I don't know," she said. "I want to, but I just don't know, Ted. Right now, I—" Her voice cracked.

"Well, maybe we can talk about it sometime. I mean, I'm a pretty poor excuse for a religious person, but . . . I dunno . . . today has *done* something to me, you know? I can't explain, but it's more than I've felt for a long, long time. Anyway, we'll talk later, okay?"

"Okay." Paula's voice was low and paper-dry. She drew away from him and peered into the depths of his blue eyes. "Thanks for coming, Ted. For everything." She reached up and brushed her hand across his cheek, bringing it to rest alongside his mouth. "I'll see you soon."

"You can bet on it," he replied, turning his head to kiss her palm lightly. With the hint of a smile, he quickly disappeared through the front door, closing it behind him. Paula pressed her freshly kissed palm to her own cheek for a moment, then walked slowly to the kitchen.

Millie was arranging neatly-labeled Tupperware containers in precise rows on the refrigerator shelves. Turning to face Paula, she shook her head in bewilderment. "I've never seen the likes of this," she said. "We'll have enough to eat until the cows come home."

"Now that, in suburban L.A., would be a rather long time," Paula chuckled. She looked around at the kitchen, left gleaming by the Relief Society women. "Where is everybody, anyway?" Millie knew what she meant.

"Scotty's in his room. I think he needs to be alone for a bit." She scratched her gray head. "I don't know about your mother—seems like I saw her go upstairs while we were eating, but I haven't seen her since. Maybe she went to my room for a nap; I told her she was welcome. She's due to leave for the airport in an hour or so. I could go wake her—"

"Let her rest," Paula said quickly. "I'm exhausted. I think I'll go upstairs for a little nap myself."

"Fine, dear. I'll just finish up here," she said, turning back to her labeling.

Paula's feet and legs felt like blocks of stone as she lifted them laboriously to climb the stairs, and her gait was little more than a shuffle as she trudged down the hall. She looked straight ahead as she approached TJ's room, but a peculiar noise caused her to stop and turn toward his door. It was slightly ajar, and a muffled sound was coming from inside the room. She placed her hand silently on the door and pushed. The sound was louder now. Someone was sobbing.

She stepped into the room and waited for a few seconds while her eyes adjusted to the darkness. Then she followed the sobs to the bed, where a figure sat hunched over, rocking slowly from side to side. A mane of white hair glowed softly in the dim light from the hall.

"Mother?"

The sobs and rocking stopped instantly, and Marjorie Enfield looked up at her daughter. "Paula. I—I thought you'd still be . . . with the others." Her gloved hands wiped frantically at her eyes.

"They've all gone." Paula sat down beside her mother on the bed. "I thought you were resting in Millie's room."

Marjorie sighed and stared at the floor. "I was looking for a rest room, but somehow ended up here—in TJ's room. I turned on the light, and saw him everywhere . . ." Her voice choked, and she continued with difficulty. "His posters . . . his clothes . . . his things . . . I couldn't bear it, so I've been here in the dark . . ." She lifted her head fiercely and met Paula's eyes, tears streaming down her cheeks. "Good Lord, Paula, I've missed his *life*. My own grandson's life, and I wasn't here for a minute of it. I only came for his death. What kind of a person would . . . what kind of a person am I?" She bent forward, her hands covering her face, and began to cry again. Her thin body shuddered with great, wracking sobs.

Paula put her arm around her mother's shoulders. Five, ten minutes passed before Marjorie spoke again in a small, fragile voice.

"It's been more than twenty years since . . . since that first child, and I've nursed a grudge against you all this time. Why? Because I thought you'd taken something away from me—you'd given away my grandson, done something wrong, somehow betrayed me." She lifted her head and studied Paula's face in the dim light. "But it was I who betrayed you, wasn't it? It was stupid, foolish pride; Howard and I were both to blame. While we sat there in Connecticut nursing our wounds, you were making a life for yourself. And we missed it—all of it. No excuses; it was just stupid. Whatever can I do to . . ." Her voice lost all its strength, and she collapsed against Paula's shoulder, moaning weakly.

"Shhh," Paula whispered, cradling her mother gently against her breast. "It's all right, Mother. It's all right." Her own tears dropped silently onto Marjorie's white hair as she stroked the older woman's narrow back.

A few minutes later, Marjorie spoke in muffled tones. "I was there, you know. I saw you."

Paula wasn't sure she'd heard clearly. "Excuse me?" she said.

"At the estate—week before last. I was at the upstairs window, and I saw you come to the door."

"But you didn't answer." Paula's voice was barely audible as she continued to stroke her mother's back and shoulders.

"No. You can't know how much I wanted to rush downstairs, throw the door open, and just . . . hold you. But I couldn't . . . I was afraid."

Her words caused Paula to smile to herself. *I don't recall Mother being afraid of anything in her life.* She had to ask. "Why?"

Marjorie sighed. "It had been so long; I'd hurt you so much over the years. I guess I just expected you to be . . . angry with me. You had a right, after all."

Paula held her mother closer, and her lips moved against the older woman's temple. "I just wanted to see you, talk to you—I thought maybe we could mend some fences. There wasn't any anger . . . but I was afraid, too. Afraid *you'd* still be angry with *me.*"

"Oh, my dear," Marjorie said, chuckling wryly, "I really should have let you in." Her tone became subdued. "And now it's taken this awful tragedy for us to find each other again, hasn't it? I hope this foolish old woman still has a place in your life." A tiny sob escaped her lips.

Paula sniffed and wiped at her eyes. "I've been waiting twenty-two years to hear you say that. Welcome to my life, Mother."

An impression swept into Paula's heart like a revelation. *I'm actually sitting here, holding my mother in my arms, comforting her. Forgiving her. Loving her. This is . . . a miracle.* She laid her cheek carefully against Marjorie's head and savored her nearness. *A miracle.*

Friday morning, Paula was awakened early by sunlight streaming through her bedroom window. As usual, her first conscious thought was of TJ, followed immediately by a wave of profound sadness. But today, her burden of grief felt slightly more bearable as she lay still, listening to the twitter of a bird or two in her garden, and contemplated recent events.

Marjorie had canceled her flight on Wednesday and stayed over for another day. Mother and daughter, meekly exploring their fresh new kinship, had walked and talked, wept and talked, laughed and talked, remembered and talked. The day had been a balm for their shared pain, a new beginning for their lives, a place to start over. And as Paula kissed her mother's softly powdered cheek and watched her board a plane for Connecticut late that evening, she knew she would never really be alone again.

Now, she just had to find a way to go on living without TJ.

CHAPTER 25

After Marjorie left, the weekend drifted by in a haze of wordless melancholy. Scott spent most of his time closeted in his room, while Millie silently kept the house dust-free and the meals on schedule. No one bothered to make conversation. One afternoon, sitting outside on the cool, quiet patio, Paula couldn't help reflecting that odd little Emily Dickinson, isolated though her physical life had been, had certainly put her poetic finger on the pulse of grief when she wrote, "After great pain, a formal feeling comes, the Nerves sit ceremonious, like Tombs, the stiff Heart questions." *I'm like that inside,* she thought. *Like a living tomb. But there's a difference; my heart is altogether too stiff just now to do any questioning. Well, maybe just one question: Why?*

On Sunday evening, she considered going back to work. But when her clock radio came to life at six a.m. the next morning, she couldn't talk herself into getting up. *Maybe tomorrow,* she reasoned. *I'll be doing better then.* She switched off the radio and drifted back to sleep. Three hours later, she coaxed her lethargic body out of bed and into the shower. As the steaming water pulsed against her skin, she pondered her options for the day. There was really only one thing she wanted to do. One thing she *had* to do.

"I think I'll drive out to the cemetery for a little while," she announced as Millie set a small plate of scrambled eggs before her. She paused as the older woman looked at her expectantly. *I should invite Millie to go along. But no . . . not today. Not this first time.*

"That would be nice, dear," Millie said after a few moments. "I should go myself this week—perhaps tomorrow. I'll take Scotty in the afternoon."

Paula nodded, relieved. "Sounds good." She took a long, slow drink of orange juice. "I guess he went back to school today."

"Yes, he said he was bored just lying around in his room. The boy's hurting a lot, but he doesn't seem to want to open up just yet. He's hardly said a word since . . . well, he's been real quiet."

"Give him time," Paula said. "We're all a little tight-lipped these days."

"I suppose." Millie shuffled around the bar and began to load the dishwasher. "A lot of folks asked about you at church yesterday."

Paula looked up in surprise. "Oh? I didn't know you'd gone."

"Didn't feel much like going without TJ," Millie admitted, "but it was the right thing to do. Just because he's gone doesn't mean the gospel is any less true."

Paula grimaced slightly but let the comment pass.

"Bishop Peters asked if we needed anything. I told him we had enough food in the house to keep a small army fat and happy for the next two months." She smiled. "He's a good man, you know. He really cares."

"I know," Paula agreed. "Please tell him thanks again the next time you see him. The same goes for Eloise Martin. She's a jewel."

"No doubt about that." Millie closed the dishwasher and pushed the start button. "Will you be leaving soon?"

Paula pushed her chair back and stood up. "I'm on my way," she said, turning back the cuffs of her blue chambray shirt. "Don't know when I'll be home." She grabbed a light sweater from the hall closet and walked purposefully toward the garage. A minute later, the red Jaguar glided noiselessly down the driveway's gradual slope. At the bottom, she glanced up at the basketball net, then over at the empty passenger seat beside her. This was the first time she'd driven the Jag since the day of the shooting. *TJ never even got to ride in my new car. I should have taken him for a spin.* A large lump of grief and regret formed in her throat as she backed into the street.

She stopped to buy red and white roses before turning onto the interstate for the half-hour drive to her destination. It was after eleven o'clock when she pulled onto the immaculate grounds of the Rolling Hills Cemetery. Not a blade in the wide expanse of emerald grass was out of place, and the entrance drive was flanked by long, perfect beds of multi-hued flowers. When a stray thought occurred to her, Paula couldn't help smiling. *I'll bet a lawn Mormon works here. Maybe a whole bunch of them.*

Her smile quickly faded as she pulled up across the drive from TJ's grave. A stranger, dressed in jeans and a dark blue sweatshirt, was kneeling near the freshly broken earth.

Paula let the Jag idle and watched the figure for a minute or two. His back was toward her, but he seemed to be smoothing a bit of stray grass at one end of the new sod covering her son's resting place. Then he moved slightly to one side, and she saw a small cluster of flowers where his hand had been. *One of his school friends or basketball buddies,* she surmised. *A sweet thing to do.* She caught herself. *But wait a minute . . . this is a school day. All his friends would be—*

She gasped audibly when the tall, lean figure stood and turned in her direction. His gaze was riveted on the ground in front of him, but there was no mistaking his identity. *Elder Richland.*

At that moment, the young missionary raised his eyes and met her questioning stare. "Hello, Paula." He spoke quietly, but his voice carried clearly across the dozen yards between them.

"Elder." She slowly reached down to turn off the motor while her mind raced to think of what to say next. "I . . . uh . . . I didn't recognize you at first in your . . . civilian clothes." She quickly pulled the key from the ignition and swung open the door. By this time, Elder Richland had crossed the drive and was standing near the hood of her car, his hands in his back pockets. Paula thought his face had a haunted look, as though he hadn't slept or eaten for days. His dark eyes appeared sunken and unfocused.

"This is our P-day . . . our day off," he explained.

"I see." Paula leaned awkwardly against the Jag. "Where's your partner? I thought you two were joined at the hip."

"Somewhere over there," he said, gesturing broadly toward another part of the cemetery. "He likes to look at old headstones—thinks he might even have a relative or two here."

"Uh-huh. So," she looked pointedly at her son's grave, "I guess that makes two of us." She reached into the car to gather the roses in her arms, then moved to cross the narrow drive. "Now, if you're finished here, I'd like to be alone with—"

"No, Paula, I'm not finished." His expression was calm, but she couldn't miss the urgency in his voice or the sudden pleading in his eyes. "This will never be finished. Not until . . . until we've had a chance to talk."

She stopped and regarded him coolly. "What could we possibly have to talk about? What's done is done."

"Maybe," he said, taking a step toward her, "but I've been thinking and fasting and praying almost nonstop since TJ's death—wondering, asking why it all turned out the way it did. Why he couldn't have been spared. Why you asked us to stay away from the funeral. I've been questioning my own ability to hear the voice of the Spirit. Begging for understanding."

"And?" Paula was vaguely interested in the conclusions he'd reached.

The young man's jaw began to work furiously. He folded his muscular arms across his chest for a few seconds, then unfolded them and curled his thumbs through the front belt loops of his jeans. When he looked at her, his eyes were brimming. He took a deep breath and exhaled slowly.

"And . . . I still don't have many answers. But, looking back, I think we all might have mistaken a beautiful blessing for a promise of healing; mixed up a feeling of peace and comfort with our own hopes for TJ's recovery. I wanted *so much* for him to live . . . but maybe we just weren't listening carefully enough, and only heard what we wanted to. So when TJ died, I was surprised . . . and you felt betrayed by God. And betrayed by two missionaries who told you they could heal your son."

Paula was listening intently now. "But you did say that, didn't you?"

"Well, not exactly." He wiped a streak of dust off the shiny red surface of Paula's car. "We said the priesthood gave us power to heal the sick—*if* it was the Lord's will. See, the scriptures say that a person can be healed if he isn't 'appointed unto death.' And believe me, this was one time I really *wanted* that healing—*wanted* it to be the Lord's will. I think deep down, when the actual words of healing didn't come in the blessing, I tried to believe he'd be all right anyway. I really liked that kid, Paula . . . he was something great." His voice broke, and he paused.

"I know," Paula said quietly.

"He reminded me so much of my own little brother . . . and I couldn't—didn't want to let him go. Obviously, the Lord had other plans." Shaking his head as if he still couldn't believe it, he rubbed the back of his neck with one hand. "Anyway," he continued, "I think the peaceful feeling you had was a gift from the Lord to comfort you—not to tell you TJ would live. I should have explained that right away, instead of letting you think . . . it's just that we all wanted it so much that we weren't listening to the real message." He looked at her through desolate eyes. "Am I making any sense here?"

"I suppose so," she said warily. "Not that it does me any good now. TJ is still gone." Her gaze dropped toward the ground, and she focused on one of his scuffed sneakers.

"Yes, but . . ." He impulsively reached out a hand to lightly touch her shoulder. "I need to say something."

The searing earnestness in his voice cut through her like a hot blade, and an unexpected but vaguely familiar longing caught her off guard. She raised her eyes to meet his intense stare. "I'm listening," she said.

He cleared his throat and began to speak in low, fervent tones. "If there is anything—anything at all I've learned on my mission, it's that God—Heavenly Father—and his son, Jesus Christ, the Savior of the world, know every person who ever lived on this earth. They don't just know us, they *love* us—in the truest, purest sense of the word, person-ally, unconditionally, and forever. I know that because I've felt their love, and I've seen it flowing into the lives of hundreds of people over the last two years. It doesn't matter who they are, or what they've done, or if they even believe . . . they are loved. *You* are loved, Paula. Your Heavenly Father and your Savior know you and love you more than anything. They love TJ, too; he's with them at this very moment. He's never stopped living, never stopped loving you; he's just in another time and place right now, waiting until he can be with you again. I know you're desperately sad that he's left so soon, and I can't remember when I've felt so awful myself. But . . ." He quickly brushed a thin stream of tears from his cheek. "But *there is a plan*, Paula—a plan that answers the questions about life and death and eternity. I know it. I *know* it. TJ was just beginning to understand it when . . . this happened. He under-stands a lot more now, but you and I . . . we're left here to walk by faith. I know it seems so very, very hard, and it is. I feel like I've really messed up on this one. But if I could only help you understand, show you there's hope, teach you . . ." His sentence ended in a deep, muffled sob.

Paula's face had lost all its color, and now she covered her eyes with one hand and slumped heavily against the car, clutching the flowers to her chest. Seconds, then minutes passed in deep silence; she seemed oblivious to her surroundings while Elder Richland struggled to bring his emotions under control. Finally, he gazed forlornly at her hunched figure for a final, agonized moment before turning away. His shoulders bowing under some invisible, unbearable weight, he moved haltingly in the direction of his small white car.

"Then teach me."

He froze with one foot slightly off the ground. Paula could see the muscles in his back tense and quiver. Lowering his sneaker to the pavement, he pivoted slowly to face her. "Excuse me?"

"I said, then *teach* me." Paula was staring at him almost fiercely, her eyes bright with unshed tears. A few spilled onto her cheeks as she said, "I want to know. I *have* to know." She raised her hand to ward off the question in his wide, dark eyes. "Don't ask me why . . . there was something in what you said . . . how you said it . . . I just need to know."

"Okay," he breathed meekly. "That's what I'm—what we're here for." His face was still a mask of stunned disbelief. "When would you like to, uh, get together?"

Paula relaxed and allowed a delicate smile to play at the corners of her mouth. "Well, I don't suppose you boys would be interested in having dinner with us tonight, it being your day off and all," she teased.

"Are you kidding?" he grinned. "We've tasted Millie's cooking, and it beats the heck out of whatever grungy stuff is lurking in our refrigerator."

"Good, then I'll ask her to put together something mold-free. Can you be there about six? That'll give us some time to . . . talk afterward."

"You bet," he agreed quickly, reaching out to grasp her hand and pump it vigorously. Then his grip loosened and lingered. "And thank you, Paula. Thank you . . . so much." His eyes glistened.

She laughed lightly. "Let's just see how it goes tonight." She glanced down at the roses nestled in the crook of her elbow. "Now, I think I'll take these over to my son and spend a few minutes with him."

"Absolutely," the elder said as he stepped to one side. He looked over his shoulder at a figure in the distance. "I can see Elder Stucki heading for the car, too . . . so I guess we'll see you later, okay?"

"I'll count on it," she said, smiling a little as she thought of TJ's abacus joke. Then she turned and crossed the drive to his grave.

Paula knelt where the headstone would be and gently laid her roses next to Elder Richland's small bouquet of carnations and daisies. "There you go, kiddo," she whispered. "A gift of beauty and fragrance for your . . . sweet dreams." She closed her eyes to absorb the tranquility of her surroundings, the warmth of the ripe autumn sun on her back. In a moment, her thoughts turned to her conversation with Elder Richland. *I hope I'm doing the right thing*, she mused.

Just then, she heard a car door opening and slamming. Glancing over her shoulder, she saw that Elder Stucki had rejoined his companion, and the two seemed deep in conversation. A few seconds later, Elder Stucki's voice, booming through the open car window, sliced the still air. "All *right!*"

"No need to guess where that came from," Paula chuckled. *The Mormon elders ride again.* The thought seemed to whisper peace to her heart as she smoothed the fresh earth around TJ's grave.

"So, tell me what you believe." Paula leaned back against the couch and folded her arms. The elders, now wearing their customary dark suits, sat in two large, upholstered chairs to her right. Millie was perched expectantly on a small loveseat at Paula's left, and Scott had sullenly dragged in a small folding chair from the den. He slouched against its metal back, looking bored and resentful. "You owe it to your brother," Paula had explained beforehand.

"Why? *You* were the one who wouldn't let him join," Scott had retaliated, glaring at her. She'd winced at his words, knowing the truth of them, but had insisted that he sit through this first meeting. "All right," he'd growled, "but just this one time."

"Fair enough," she'd agreed.

Now here they were, none of them knowing quite what to expect, ready for—well, for the worst. *Maybe I acted too impulsively this morning*, Paula thought as the elders pulled out their bulky books of scripture. *This could be a disaster. Just cool it and let them talk, Donroe. You can take anything for an hour . . . sixty tiny minutes, and it'll be over.*

The disaster never happened. As Elder Stucki began with a brief prayer, a feeling of quiet anticipation seeped into Paula's mind. When she opened her eyes, she was ready to hear what the missionaries had to say. An hour later, she was not ready to stop listening. Instead, she pressed them for more information. Their eyes gleamed as they answered each of her questions calmly, precisely, with a subdued energy that seemed to breathe life into her calloused soul.

At the end, they asked her to pray. "Oh, I couldn't," she said. "I don't know how."

"You've learned a lot about Heavenly Father tonight," Elder Richland prompted gently. Paula nodded, her mind swirling with images of an all-knowing, all-loving Being. "Just talk to him. Thank him for what you're grateful for, ask him for what you need, close in the name of Jesus Christ. You'll do fine."

"Well, all right," she finally agreed with a little smile. "But I hope he won't hold a grudge if I make a fool of myself."

"No problem," the elder grinned.

Paula bowed her head. "Dear God . . . dear Heavenly Father," she began, then lapsed into silence for several moments. When she spoke again, her voice was choked with emotion and barely audible. "Thank you for this night . . . for helping me understand a few things. Especially about life . . . after death. Please watch over TJ, Father, and take good care of him until . . . please, just watch over him. It's so hard not having him with us . . . help us to understand. Please, just help us. In the name of Jesus Christ, amen." A muffled sob escaped her throat.

She raised her head just in time to see Scott wipe quickly at one eye. He hadn't spoken all evening, but he seemed less belligerent than before. "'Scuse me," he said gruffly, nodding toward the elders. "I've got homework." He stood and walked abruptly from the room.

"See ya, Scott," Elder Stucki called after him.

Later, when the house was quiet except for a gentle autumn rain tapping at the windows, Paula found Millie in the kitchen, arranging a colorful Thanksgiving centerpiece on the table. She smiled kindly when she saw Paula leaning against the door frame.

"You didn't have much to say this evening," Paula observed. Millie continued her work, humming softly to herself. "So, what do you think?" Paula pressed.

Millie stopped what she was doing and met Paula's gaze directly. "I think," she said, her eyes dancing, "that after tonight, I believe in miracles."

Paula took a few steps forward and bent over slightly to kiss her friend on the cheek. "I know what you mean, Millie," she said. "Now, if you'll excuse me, I think I have a little reading to do." She grinned. "Something about this cool guy named Nephi . . . and an angel."

Upstairs, she retrieved the "hornblower edition," as she called it, of the book from a dresser drawer and settled into her rocker. She had not opened it since returning from Connecticut, but now she studied the Polaroid photo of the young family intently and read their message with new purpose. *These kids are all grown up and out of the nest by now,* she reflected. *I wonder if they're still so sure of this book, so fired up about their church.* Paula recalled her own childhood, her marriages, her lost sons. *Does anything really last that long?* Her thoughts were pensive as she turned to the book's introductory pages. An hour later, having carefully read, re-read, and digested the background and origins of the book, she closed her eyes and leaned back against the rocker. Her mind quickly called up the memory of a certain gilded trumpeter who had delivered his three-word message with such understated authority, then traipsed off to rehearse for the Second Coming. A comfortable smile tugged at the corners of her mouth. "So *that,*" she whispered, "is who Moroni is. An angel." *But I don't believe in angels—do I?*

Early the next morning, Paula called her office and left a message on Carmine's voice mail. "I won't be in this week," she said. "I have some . . . things to take care of, and I need a little time. Call if you need me, but I trust you to take care of whatever comes up. See you next week."

She spent the next few days reading, plying the elders with questions, visiting TJ's grave, strolling a stretch of private beach where she could ponder undisturbed and allow the pristine beauty of the sea to clear her mind and temper her grief. When the burdens of her past and the reality of her losses overpowered her, she would fall to her knees in the warm, damp sand, tears coursing down her cheeks, and plead for solace and understanding. Occasionally she raged at some unknown, uncaring God who seemed to have withdrawn to a far corner of the universe and could neither feel nor ease her pain. Shouting into the wind, she demanded answers, but heard nothing. In these moments of desolation, she wondered if her search for truth had come to a dead end.

On Sunday, Paula accompanied Millie and the elders to church, where she was greeted warmly by Bishop Peters and many others who had helped with TJ's funeral. She sat quietly during sacrament meeting, interested but unmoved until the final speaker, a balding, middle-aged man, took his place at the pulpit. He seemed ill at ease and spoke hesitantly at first, but as he warmed to his subject Paula recognized an unmistakable conviction in his words. "I'd like to talk to you," he said, "about having a change of heart."

His text was from the Book of Mormon, and he immediately had Paula's attention. She'd finished reading the book, but had she somehow failed to find what she was looking for? Could he point her in the right direction? Could her prayers ever amount to anything more than hollow repetition?

He took an intriguing approach. "The prophet Alma had something to say about . . . well," he chuckled, "Alma had something to say about almost everything." A wave of gentle laughter rippled through the audience. "Anyway," he continued, "this great prophet asked some pretty tough questions. For example, he asked the people: 'Could ye say, if ye were called to die at this time, within yourselves, that ye have been sufficiently humble? . . . Behold, are ye stripped of pride? I say unto you, if ye are not ye are not prepared to meet God.'"

Sufficiently humble . . . stripped of pride. The words penetrated Paula's brain like liquid fire. *Have I ever had a humble day in my life?* Every terse, sarcastic, unkind word or thought she had directed at the missionaries—even at God himself—suddenly flooded her memory, and she felt her cheeks burning. *I could do better,* she thought.

Another verse of scripture caught her attention. "'Behold,'" the speaker read in comforting tones, "'he sendeth an invitation unto all men, for the arms of mercy are extended towards them, and he saith: Repent, and I will receive you.'"

The arms of mercy . . . I will receive you. Paula inhaled deeply and felt a rush of hope as she pictured a loving Father with welcoming arms outstretched. *Maybe I can do this.* She nudged Elder Stucki, who was sitting next to her. "Where are these scriptures?" she whispered.

"Alma, chapter five." He quickly found the passages and laid his large book of scripture in her hands, pointing to a few verses highlighted in red. Although she had read them previously, the words now seemed to draw her into realms of spiritual inquiry that she'd not considered before. *Have ye spiritually been born of God? . . . Have ye experienced this mighty change in your hearts? . . . I say unto you, can ye look up to God at that day with a pure heart and clean hands . . . having the image of God engraven upon your countenances?*

Paula was transfixed by the penetrating issues addressed by this ancient prophet. Had she truly felt this "mighty change"? She didn't think so—not yet, anyway. Exactly what did it take to have "a pure heart and clean hands"? The elders had taught her a little about repentance, but she wasn't sure. And how could anyone presume to know what "the image of God" looked like, much less have it somehow "engraven" upon one's countenance? What did it all mean? Her brain whirled with insistent, unanswered questions for the next two hours.

"Is something the matter, dear?" Millie's voice cut through Paula's reverie as they sat in the backseat of the elders' car on the way home. "You seem very distracted."

"Oh, just wondering about some things, I suppose," Paula answered vaguely. "This church thing is still awfully new to me, and it's a little overwhelming. Along with everything else."

"I know what you mean," Millie sighed. "Sometimes life just sort of . . . piles up on you."

"Why, Millie Hampton," Paula laughed, "I've never even seen the *laundry* pile up on you. You're not having second thoughts about the Church, are you?"

"Oh, goodness no," the older woman answered firmly. "It's just that we've all been through so much lately, and it's bound to have some effect. That's where having faith comes in, I guess."

Paula nodded, then lapsed into silence as her mind resumed its flurry of activity. *Is that it? Is faith the answer? Or is it only one of the questions?*

Millie had invited the elders for dinner, and they wasted no time in doing serious damage to her meatloaf with mushroom sauce, fresh steamed vegetables, and tossed green salad. Their conversation was light and amiable, but Paula's mood was more reserved than usual. She had something to say, but she couldn't quite find the words. Finally, over a dessert of pineapple sherbet and thin, wafer-like cookies, she took advantage of a brief silence and plunged in.

"You know," she said in subdued tones as three pairs of eyes turned toward her, "I've been thinking a lot about what one of the speakers—the last one—said in sacrament meeting today, and I—"

"That would be Brother Tolman," Elder Stucki interjected. "He's on the high council. A real nice guy . . . he's a social worker or something."

"Yes . . . Brother Tolman," Paula repeated. "Anyway, he talked about being humble, stripped of pride, things like that. It started me thinking that maybe I should set a few things right . . . maybe I haven't exactly been Ms. Humble as far as the Church goes—as far as *anything* goes, for that matter." She saw hints of smiles on three faces, and held up a hand. "All right, I've been nowhere *near* humble." Her expression sobered and intensified. "In fact, I've been rude, ornery, sarcastic, arrogant, and utterly inconsiderate toward all of you—the sisters, you elders, and even you, Millie—just about every time you've tried to talk to me about the Church. It's a miracle any of you are still speaking to me." She paused, shaking her head. "I guess what I need to say is . . ." She swallowed hard. "I—I'm sorry. I was wrong. I hope you can forgive me. I'll try to do better."

"That's all any of us can do," Elder Richland said quietly. "Try to do better."

"Besides, it hasn't been all that bad . . . lately," Elder Stucki grinned.

"And we love you for saying it," Millie added, reaching out to squeeze her hand.

Paula nodded gratefully. "Thanks. That means a lot to me." Then a shadow darkened her eyes as a more painful thought pressed itself into her mind. "I just wish I could take back some of the awful things I said to TJ. If only I hadn't been so cynical and stubborn, he might still be . . ." Tears sprang to her eyes, and she choked on the knot of grief and remorse in her throat.

"He understands, Paula," Elder Richland said. "You've got to believe that. He's already forgiven you."

"I hope so," she sniffed. "Oh, I hope so."

Late that evening, Paula knelt beside her bed. Cool air from an open window gently circulated in the room as she began to speak in low, hesitant tones. "Heavenly Father," she whispered reverently, "I've come this far, and now I need to know. Please . . . help me to know."

An hour later, as she slipped between the smooth cotton sheets and lowered her head to the pillow, she had her answer. And she knew exactly who would be the first to know.

A lazy pink dawn was just brushing the sky as Paula, dressed in a loose-fitting navy sweat suit, knelt beside her son's grave. "Good morning, my precious boy," she said, patting the fresh green sod that was now beginning to mingle with the older grass around it. Her hand rested gently where the granite stone would soon be placed. "I know it's early, but I couldn't wait. The most extraordinary thing has happened . . ." She smiled as a small bird chirped nearby, then hopped off to look for breakfast.

"You told me it was true," she continued, "but I didn't believe you. In fact, I made life pretty miserable for you, didn't I?" She paused, closing her eyes against the painful memory of their last conversation. "I'm *so sorry*, TJ. You deserved a lot better, and I know that now. I just wish I could have known sooner, before . . ." Her voice trailed off as she wiped at her eyes. "Anyway, I'm sorry. Please forgive me. If you can. I hope you can."

She sat down and drew her knees up beneath her chin. "The thing is, I wanted to tell you about last night. Do you remember in the Book of Mormon, where Alma talks about having a 'mighty change of heart'? About having God's image 'engraven upon your countenance'? Well, for the first time ever, I really *wanted* that change—wanted it so much that I spent a long time on my knees, pleading for it. I cried, I begged . . . I even apologized for all the rotten things I'd done and thought and said in my whole life. Then I made a special apology for my feelings about the Church—which, as you know, have not exactly been all sweetness and light."

She imagined the amused gleam in TJ's eye as he nodded and chimed in, "That's fer sure."

"So there I was," she continued, "trying to make sense of it, figuring maybe I didn't really deserve that kind of absolution after all, feeling myself sink into total despair. Then, gradually, things changed. It was like something—somebody—was *there*, you know? Like a divine Being was wrapping his arms around me, warming me from the inside out, assuring me without words that my prayer had been answered, that truth was within my grasp. I actually *felt* it, TJ—the change. My heart was different somehow, and I knew I'd never be quite the same person again. It was an incredible, indescribable feeling." She breathed deeply and wiped the arm of her sweatshirt across both eyes before going on.

"Well, I'd been crying so hard that by the time I thanked the Lord and closed my prayer, my face, neck, and the front of my nightshirt were sopping wet, so I headed to the bathroom for some Kleenex. I flipped on the light switch, and at that moment I saw my own reflection in the mirror. I swear to you, TJ, the person I saw wasn't me . . . well, it was me, but it was a *different* me—a purer, more refined version of myself, almost transparent and glowing with some kind of inner light. It was like I could see clear through myself to the eternal part of me—to a being who was absolutely radiant with love and perfect intelligence. I was speechless and moved beyond belief as I looked into the eyes of this wonderful person who returned my gaze with complete acceptance and affection.

"A fraction of a second later, I felt the sensation of a gentle hand resting ever so lightly on my head. At the same instant, a few quiet words flowed into my mind: 'His image in your countenance.' I knew beyond doubt that I had seen his Spirit resting on me—on *me!* Can you believe it, TJ? He was there; I know it. As I watched the brightness gradually fade and finally disappear from my reflection, I knew I'd been blessed with a remarkable experience. Could I have been so filled with the Spirit toward the end of my prayer that it stayed with me for a little while afterward? I think we both know the answer to that one, don't we? It seemed the right thing to tell you first, kiddo. Your old mom has actually seen the light—literally! And it's beginning to look like she just might become one of those Mormons—if they'll have her." She chuckled wryly. "But then, you knew that all along, didn't you?"

Paula stretched her legs out in front of her, then slowly rolled onto her side and laid her cheek against the fragrant grass blanketing TJ's grave. She would spend a few peaceful, contemplative moments here before going home to a new day . . . a new beginning.

* * * * *

Paula's fingers drummed rapidly against the soft black leather of her purse as she waited with the elders outside Bishop Peters' office. "I feel like I did before my master's oral exam," she whispered loudly. "My heart was in my stomach, and my stomach was in my throat— not exactly a picnic in the park. I mean, it's only been two weeks, and I still don't know very much about—"

"Not to worry," Elder Richland smiled. "This is just a visit with the bishop, not an interrogation. Besides, it's not what you know . . . it's what you *feel.*"

"Yes, well," she replied nervously, "right about now I *feel* like I could use a good stiff . . . oh." She pressed her lips together as a streak of crimson colored her cheeks. "Uh, I guess a drink would be out of the question at this point, wouldn't it?"

"Hey, I have this friend who makes a mean ginger ale chaser," Elder Stucki quipped. Paula groaned good-naturedly.

"You'll be fine, Paula," Elder Richland said. "Just tell him what's in your heart."

"Yes, I suppose that's the thing to do." She looked fondly at the earnest, straightforward young men who had guided her gently, surely, toward the truth over these past two weeks of intense study, prayer, and soul-searching. Elder Stucki had been wonderful; his eager, buoyant faith and unquenchable humor had often cheered and encouraged her as she struggled with a gospel concept here and there. But it was his tall, intro- spective, deeply-rooted companion who had finally broken through her wall of reserve and grief, urging her to build a fortress of faith in its place, rejoicing with her when the quiet, unmistakable assurance had come at the end of a heart-wrenching prayer. *If TJ had lived,* she thought, *he would have been like Elder Richland. He would have served an honorable mission.* The thought comforted her. How could she ever thank these young men? *How does one express gratitude for the gift of a new life?*

The bishop's voice sliced through her reverie. "Hello, Paula," he said warmly, reaching out to shake her hand. "Please come in." He motioned toward his office, and she soon found herself smiling cautiously at him across a large, glass-topped desk.

"So," Bishop Peters said, placing both hands palm down on the desk in front of him, "I understand you've expressed a desire to become a member of the Church."

"That's correct," she answered calmly as her thoughts raced. *To my own surprise, and everyone else's.* She recalled Millie's gratitude for "the good Lord's power of persuasion"; Marjorie Enfield's resigned declaration that "you always did keep your own counsel"; Ted's open-mouthed gaze of disbelief, followed by his quick hug and guarded observation that "if anyone can make it stick, you can, boss." And then there was Scotty, who had simply rolled his eyes and disappeared into his room when he'd heard the news.

"The elders have said some wonderful things about your conversion," the bishop continued. "Apparently, once you understood the basics of the gospel and read the Book of Mormon, there was no stopping you." His eyes twinkled. "I must say, you've given those young men a run for their money. Two weeks ago, none of us thought this would be happening."

"Neither did I," she responded. "But here I am."

"I can see that," he chuckled.

Paula nodded, and they spent the next few minutes reviewing basic gospel principles and requirements for baptism. He gently probed her mind and heart to satisfy himself that her belief was genuine, her testimony firm enough to warrant committing herself to baptism. And he listened compassionately to her hopes and dreams for a future reunion with the son she'd so recently buried. "The gospel tells me he'll be mine again," she said meekly, "and I must believe that. I *do* believe it."

"And have you now done everything in your power to make your life right before the Lord, so your baptism can make you clean and pure in his sight?" the bishop asked.

She quickly lowered her eyes, momentarily shaken by his penetrating question. *I knew this was coming—the part about repentance. I've done everything I can, everything I know . . . but will it be enough? I've got to tell him; otherwise, I can't go through with it. God knows my secret, after all; he's the one who'll be doing the judging. I owe it to him to come clean.* She spoke without looking up. "Well, there is one thing that I, uh, I think I ought to tell you, and . . . well, it's never come up before . . . and I, uh . . . don't know if . . ." Her tongue felt like a lump of cold mashed potatoes.

"It's all right, Paula. Just take your time." She could feel his kind eyes searching her face.

She inhaled deeply, willing herself to remain calm. "Sorry," she breathed. "It's just that I've never said this to anyone before, and it's . . . not easy."

"I understand."

Paula heard only patience and acceptance in the bishop's voice. *Will he be so tolerant when he hears what I've done?* She slowly straightened in her chair and raised her eyes to meet his.

"The thing is," she began carefully, "a long time ago, when I was very young, . . . I had a child."

He gently encouraged her to continue. "Was there anything . . . unusual about this birth?"

Paula shook her head. "I was—had been—married . . . to a wonderful man. But he died before we even knew I was pregnant. My parents had pretty much disowned me for marrying him, and I couldn't go home to have the baby. So I had to . . . to make a terrible decision." She sighed heavily.

"But you didn't have an abortion," the bishop prompted.

"Oh, no, I couldn't have done that. This child was a part of me . . . a part of the man I loved. But I knew I couldn't give him the kind of life Greg and I had dreamed of; I was poor and uneducated, barely one paycheck away from welfare. I wanted something better for my—our son. So I did what I thought was best at the time. I . . . I . . . ." Her throat felt paralyzed, but she forced the words out between quivering lips. "I gave him away. I gave my child away." She covered her face with her hands and rested her elbows on the glass-topped desk.

Bishop Peters waited a few seconds before asking, "Are you saying you gave the baby up for adoption?"

"Yes," Paula squeaked, lowering her hands to reveal a tear-streaked face. "And even though I did it for the right reasons—at least I thought they were right at the time—I've never been free from guilt over it. When my parents found out, they couldn't forgive me for giving up their grandchild . . . so how could I forgive myself? I mean, he was *my child*, and I *gave him away*. Could God ever forgive me for that? Would he even want me in his church?" Her anguished eyes locked onto the bishop's. "I have to know, Bishop: will this twenty-two-year-old sin keep me from baptism?"

Without hesitating, Bishop Peters reached across the desk and squeezed her hand. "My dear," he said gently, "what you did was not a sin. It was an unselfish act of love—the greatest gift you could have given your child under such difficult circumstances." He smiled tenderly. "And I daresay it was also a wonderful and cherished gift to some young couple who couldn't have a child of their own. There's no need for repentance or forgiveness here, Paula; as a servant of the Lord, I can assure you of that. Heavenly Father knows your heart and wants you to be happy. And he will most certainly welcome you into his church with open arms."

Paula closed her eyes and savored the warm feelings washing over her. "You can't know how sweet those words sound to me," she said at last. "Thank you, Bishop."

"No, thank *you*," he replied. "For sharing this with me. I know it wasn't easy."

"You're right about that," she said with a shy smile. Then her expression became more serious. "I only hope . . . I hope my son has had a good life."

The bishop leaned back in his chair and flashed her an almost boyish grin. "With your genes, I'd say he's had a major head start on success."

They sat together for a few minutes longer, quietly discussing plans for Paula's and Millie's baptisms the following Saturday. Then, after a final handshake, Paula returned to the small waiting area.

Both elders stood when they saw the bishop's office door opening. "Well, you took long enough," Elder Richland teased. "Did you pass?"

"Oh, I guess you could say that," she said demurely. Her eyes were glowing. "We're on for Saturday."

"All *right!*" Elder Stucki exulted. "Break out the white duds!"

"We will, Elder," Paula smiled. "We surely will."

CHAPTER 26

Before leaving for the church on Saturday morning, Paula knocked softly on Scott's door No answer. "Scotty, honey, can I come in?" she called, her lips almost touching the polished oak.

"It's open," a low voice droned from the other side. Paula turned the knob and slowly pushed the door open.

Scott was sitting cross-legged on his bed, a sketch pad balanced across his knees. He looked up when his mother entered the room.

"Hey, guy," she said warmly, glancing at the pad and then at her son. "Just thought I'd let you know . . . there's still time to make it to the service. We'll even wait a few minutes more, if you'd like to—"

"Thanks, Mom, but . . . no." His voice was gruff, but his eyes pleaded for understanding. "I know you and Millie are gonna do this baptism thing, whether I come or not. But I just can't; not when I don't believe. Maybe sometime I'll get some kinda religion; I've got my whole life to decide. I know TJ wanted it, but that doesn't mean I . . . just give me a little space here, okay?" His eyes glittered in the dim light of a lamp near his bed.

"Well, okay." Paula reached down to rumple his dark hair. "But just remember that sometimes life is . . . way too short. What are your plans for the day?"

"Thought I'd go down to the clubhouse for a little while; the guys are pickin' me up later. I haven't been there since TJ . . ." His voice trailed off. "We need to do a little painting."

Paula swallowed hard and nodded. "Just be careful, okay?"

"I will, Mom," he answered as she leaned over to kiss his cheek. His voice turned mischievous as he added, "And you be careful, too. I mean, don't go getting drowned or anything."

"I promise," she laughed. Just then, her eyes came to rest on his sketch pad. The drawing was upside down from where she stood, but something about it seemed familiar. "Mind if I have a look?" she asked, gesturing toward the pad.

He hesitated, partially covering the pad with his arm. "Well, it's not quite done, and I wanted to wait until . . ." He grinned slyly up at her. "I mean, it's not a naked missionary or anything, but it's not exactly . . ."

She knelt in front of him and stared deeply into his hazel eyes. "Please, Scotty?"

". . . finished." He turned the pad around and carefully slid it into her waiting hands.

"Dear Lord." Paula clapped a hand over her mouth as tears leapt to her eyes.

Scott was alarmed. "Mom? What's wrong, Mom? I know it's not very good, but I was gonna work on it some more—"

She shook her head fiercely, unable to speak for several moments. Finally a few words came. "No . . . oh, no. It's *beautiful*, Scotty. The most beautiful thing I've ever seen."

The boy sighed with relief. "Then I'll finish it, and we'll have it framed."

She carefully touched her fingertips to one corner of the rich charcoal portrait of TJ. "Absolutely. A magnificent frame."

"So get out of here and let me finish it," Scott growled playfully. "It'll be your Christmas present."

"You've got a deal," Paula sniffed, handing the pad back to him. "My son, the incredibly gifted artist."

Scott smirked self-consciously and rolled his eyes. "Geez, just go get yourself dunked already, will ya? I got things to do."

"I'm on my way." She rose and smoothed the skirt of her tailored navy blue suit. "I'm sorry you won't be there, but I understand. We'll talk later, okay?"

"Okay," he said absently, already re-absorbed in his drawing.

Paula walked quickly down the hall to her room and spent a minute or two retouching her eye makeup. *Like this is really necessary,* she joked to herself. *I'll look like a drowned rat in less than an hour, anyway.* Then her thoughts sobered. *But I'll be clean—really clean. From the inside out.* Smiling with anticipation, she hurried from her room and down the stairs.

Millie was waiting in the entryway. "You look lovely, dear," she said. Her gaily flowered dress seemed to light up the entryway, and Paula thought her round face beamed more brightly than the autumn sunshine flooding through the kitchen windows.

"Thanks, my friend—and so do you. This is a pretty big day, huh?"

"More than that . . . it's the beginning of a brand-new life," Millie said with a broad, expectant smile. "I can hardly wait."

"Then let's do it," Paula urged, linking her arm through Millie's. Side by side, the two women moved eagerly toward the garage.

Sister Tibbetts played a soft medley of hymns on the small portable organ as a steady stream of ward members filed into the Relief Society room. Paula and Millie, clad in simple white cotton dresses, sat on the front row of chairs beside the elders, facing the blue-tiled baptismal font. To Paula's right, Elder Richland seemed at ease in his meticulously ironed, French-cuffed white shirt, white silk tie, sharply creased white trousers, and spotless white socks. On her left sat Elder Stucki, his one-piece white polyester jumpsuit bulging slightly where his rounded midsection strained the zipper. *Cute,* Paula thought wryly, glancing at his matching white polyester tie. *There must be a Mormon fashion statement in all of this.* Instantly repenting of her droll observation, she cleared her mind by turning around to survey the small crowd filling three or four rows of chairs behind her.

Within seconds, her gaze was drawn like a heat-seeking missile to a pair of intense blue eyes two rows back. *Ted. What in the world is he doing here?*

Ted's mouth crinkled in a comical little grin, then widened into a dazzling smile when he saw her look of utter surprise. He said nothing, but winked and gave her a thumbs-up signal. Paula felt her heart pump a sudden rush of blood to her face. She flashed him a timorous smile, then quickly turned back toward the baptismal font.

After a hymn and prayer, Bishop Peters spoke briefly, followed by Sister Kent and Elder Richland. Paula smiled and nodded at their remarks, but later couldn't have told anyone what they said. Instead, her attention was riveted on the reason she was here in the first place: the six-by-ten-foot pool of warm, still water in front of her. It beckoned her like a mother's arms, promising peace and safety and a replenishment of love. Would she be able to feel all those things once she slipped beneath its glistening blue-green surface? Or would her new life come a little at a time, like a rich leather glove being carefully smoothed over her waiting fingers until the fit was perfect? *The sooner the better,* she thought.

Millie was first. Elder Stucki escorted her into the font and performed the ordinance, reciting the brief prayer without a hitch, then deftly submerging her plump body and guiding it upward again in a single smooth motion. Millie was beaming when she broke the surface, and she clung tightly to Elder Stucki's arm as he helped her up the half dozen steps leading to the women's dressing room. Eloise Martin met her with a hug at the top of the steps.

Now it was Paula's turn. Poised gracefully on the top step, she saw Elder Richland enter the font from the opposite side and move slowly through the water until he was directly below her at the bottom of the steps. She grasped the brass side rail and moved down two steps until his hand was within reach. As he guided her into the center of the font, the comfortably warm water swirled around her legs and waist like a million tender caresses.

Elder Richland rested his hand gently against her back and looked down at her. "Ready?" he whispered.

Paula took a deep breath. "As I'll ever be," she murmured.

He raised his right arm to the square, bowed his head, and spoke the words in deep, reverent tones. A split second after his "amen," she felt herself being lowered backward into the water. At the same instant, all movement seemed to slow to a tiny fraction of its normal speed, and Paula found herself observing several people standing near the font. One was unusual . . . a young, sandy-haired boy, dressed all in white, his freckled face split by the biggest grin she had ever—

TJ.

Paula studied the boy's features carefully, just to make sure—his dark, luminous eyes set beneath unruly brows; the small dimple at one side of his mouth, noticeable only when he smiled; a smooth white scar just in front of his left ear, the result of a Christmas morning accident with his new woodburning set; the ruddy, freckled complexion that made him seem younger than his years. If she believed her own eyes, there could be no mistake.

His lips didn't move, but she heard the words as clearly as if he had shouted them. *"Way to go, Mom! I knew you'd do it. You're the best!"* His eyes, riveted on hers, brimmed with inexpressible love. *"Geez, this is the best thing you've ever done . . . well, next to having me, of course."* His shoulders shook with silent mirth, as they had so often in life.

Paula's heart raced with joy as time recaptured its momentum and her body slipped beneath the cleansing water. As soon as Elder Richland's strong arms brought her back to the surface, she quickly sought out TJ's loving gaze, but her son was gone. Ted stood near the font, looking down at her tenderly. Did she see a tear in his eye, or was it just a stray drop of water in hers?

He was the first to greet her after she and Millie had been confirmed. "You look mahvelous," he said, putting his arms around her and pressing his lips against her damp hair. "And very happy, too. Being a Mormon seems to agree with you."

She stepped back and focused on his clear blue eyes. "Am I to assume, then, Mr. Barstow, that you actually approve of my taking the plunge?" Her tone was half-teasing.

Ted chose his words carefully. "I'm saying that if you're happy, I can't very well argue with your decision. In fact, if I had it all to do over again myself, I think I'd . . . well, I think maybe I'd make some different choices. But after so many years on the wrong side of the Church, I could never—"

"Whoa," Paula interjected, holding up her hand as the image of a trumpet-playing figure in white flashed through her mind. "One should never say never . . . and I have that on good authority."

Ted grinned. "Okay; I'll take it on advisement. Meanwhile, I think the Relief Society has set up some refreshments in the cultural hall. Care to join me?"

"With pleasure," Paula replied, taking his arm. "But we'll talk about this again soon."

"You're the boss," he said affably.

"I know," she said, raising one eyebrow comically. "So we'll talk."

When the crowd thinned, Paula and Millie made their way to the door, where the elders were waiting. Paula looked at them expectantly. "So, what now?" she asked.

Elder Richland laughed good-naturedly. "Now you find out what life as a Latter-day Saint is all about. Knowing you and Millie, you'll jump in with both feet, and it'll be quite a ride." He paused, and his smile dimmed slightly. "I sure wish I could be here for it, but Elder Stucki will—"

"Excuse me?" Paula interrupted. "I thought you were a regular fixture in this ward."

"Only for a couple more weeks. I'm afraid these are my last days as a missionary, Paula. I'll be home in Idaho before Christmas." He scuffed one shoe against the blue carpet.

"I see," Paula said quietly, a lump of disappointment forming in her throat. *What did you expect, Donroe?* she chided herself. *He has a life, after all, and he's not going to use it up shepherding you into Mormonism. Besides, you can do it on your own—no need for a young kid to teach you the ropes.*

"Oh, my!" Millie exclaimed. "We're certainly going to miss you, young man."

"Thanks, Millie," the elder smiled. "It's going to be tough leaving the mission field, but it'll be good to be home, too. Elder Stucki will get a great new companion; you can bet on that."

Paula squared her shoulders and forced a smile in Elder Richland's direction. "So, you're looking forward to getting back to civilian life, are you?"

"I guess so," he hedged. "It'll be an adjustment, that's for sure. And to leave all the friends I've made here . . . it won't be easy." He looked directly at Paula.

Play along, Donroe. "Well, the way I see it," she said lightly, glancing at Millie, "we still have a few days left to continue our tradition of missionary-feeding before the good elder here departs for the frozen northland." She turned back to Elder Richland. "Thanksgiving's next week . . . would you gentlemen honor us with your presence? You haven't been to heaven, you know, if you haven't experienced Millie's slow-roasted turkey with sage dressing." She closed her eyes briefly and ran her tongue over her lips, savoring the memory of last year's feast.

Millie nodded enthusiastically. "We'd love it if you'd come. I'll even make my special apple-cinnamon pie, and a carrot cake, and—"

"Oooh, twist my arm," Elder Stucki groaned. He turned to his companion. "Whadya say, Elder?"

"I say," Elder Richland replied, pulling a small black book from his breast pocket, "this is one appointment we'll have no trouble keeping." Grinning, he opened the book and made a quick notation.

"Good. We'll see you about two in the afternoon," Paula said. "Come hungry."

"No problem," Elder Stucki vowed. "This'll be my first Thanksgiving away from home, and . . . well, I can't think of anywhere I'd rather spend it."

"Yeah," Elder Richland added with a wistful smile. "This'll be my *last* Thanksgiving away from home, and I was just thinking the same thing. We'll see you on Thursday, then."

"And tomorrow, too—at church," his companion quickly added.

"Tomorrow it is," Paula repeated, shaking their hands. "And thank you both—for everything. It's been a memorable day." Then, smoothing her still-damp curls away from her forehead, she followed Millie through the church door into the mild autumn afternoon.

Paula spent Thanksgiving morning cleaning out her liquor cabinet. One by one, she picked up several heavy crystal decanters, fingering their gleaming prismed surfaces, remembering the smooth, comfortable burn of the amber liquid as it slid gently down her throat. *Is it a sin to wish this small indulgence wasn't a sin?* she wondered. "I'll miss you, old friends," she whispered to an array of bottles standing at attention on the cabinet shelves. "By the way," she added, smiling wickedly at an unopened flask of vodka, "how much do *you* know about the Mormon Church?" She waited for a few seconds as though listening for a reply, then shook her head in mock resignation. "I know, I know," she sighed. "The Mormons are bad for business. But I'm sure you guys'll get along just fine without them . . . without us . . . without me." She solemnly poured the contents of each decanter down the bathroom sink, rinsed them, then returned the empty crystal containers to the cabinet. Next, she filled a heavy-duty plastic trash bag with full and partly-full liquor bottles, then lugged it out to the garage. "Cheers," she murmured softly as she hefted the bag into a large trash bin.

At precisely two p.m., the doorbell rang. Paula, dressed in a royal blue silk pantsuit, ushered the elders into the breakfast nook, which overnight Millie had somehow transformed into an elegant dining area. An extra leaf and a crisp white linen cloth had been added to the table, where five place settings of gold-rimmed china and crystal glistened in the flickering light of three sculpted centerpiece candles.

"This is fantastic," Elder Stucki said reverently. "Like a five-star restaurant."

"Only better," Elder Richland added. "Better food, better company, better—"

"Prices," Paula teased. "Have a seat, gentlemen." She motioned toward two chairs on one side of the table. "I'll get Scotty."

"It's about time. I'm starvin'," Scott called out when his mother knocked. He yanked open the door.

"Well," Paula laughed, "I think I could safely say there are a couple of hollow-legged young men downstairs who share your sentiments. Let's not keep them waiting, shall we?" She noticed he was wearing a pair of dark brown cords and a green plaid shirt—something of a departure from his usual tattered jeans and faded T-shirt. His dark, curly hair had been hastily combed back from his forehead. "You look nice," she said. He grunted as he headed toward the stairs.

Millie's face glowed as she sat at one end of the table and watched the others settle into their chairs. "My, my," she bubbled, "it looks like we've got some hungry folks here." Four heads nodded in unison. "Well, that's my specialty—feeding the famished." She glanced over her shoulder toward the breakfast bar, now laden with a fragrant cornucopia of traditional Thanksgiving fare. "It's all ready . . . now let's thank the good Lord, shall we?" The missionaries obediently folded their arms, while Scott groaned audibly from across the table.

Stifling a giggle, Paula looked over at the two dark-suited young men. "Elder Richland, would you do the honors?"

"My pleasure," he replied, bowing his head. The blessing was brief but heartfelt—an expression of gratitude for the bounties of life, the care of a benevolent Father in Heaven, the assurance of life everlasting.

He closed with a soft "amen," and there was a moment of subdued silence before Scott bolted for the bar and began to load his plate.

"I guess that's your cue," Millie chortled. "Eat up, everyone. There's plenty to go around, and then some."

Paula gracefully lifted her plate from the table and moved toward the bar. The elders followed close behind, while Millie carefully filled five long-stemmed crystal goblets with iced sparkling grape juice. In the meantime, Rudy, his wide black nostrils quivering with anticipation, had optimistically positioned his golden body near Paula's end of the table. He was ready to beg without shame.

A few minutes passed in comfortable silence, broken here and there by a contented sigh, the musical tinkle of silver against china, or Rudy's appreciative gulp as Paula slipped him a sliver of turkey. *Definitely Norman Rockwell,* she mused. *This could be a magazine cover.* She smiled at the thought.

Elder Richland's mouth was just making contact with a forkful of mashed potatoes and gravy when Elder Stucki nudged his arm and pointed to the cranberries. "Elder, could you please pass—"

The unexpected jostle propelled a large dollop of gravied potato sideways onto Elder Richland's suit lapel. It clung to the dark fabric for a moment, then began sliding downward, leaving a slick brown trail in its wake. The elder quickly wiped at his suit with his linen napkin, but groaned when he surveyed the damage. He rubbed harder.

"You'll never get rid of a gravy stain that way," Millie observed. "But if you'd be willing to part with your jacket for a little while, I think I can clean it up for you. My husband used to spill things all the time, and I've got a few tricks that might work."

"I'd sure appreciate that," the elder said sheepishly. "Seems like Mormon missionaries keep the dry cleaners in business around here." He stood and shrugged his jacket off one shoulder, then the other. "We have an appointment later this afternoon, and I really need to be presentable. I hope this won't be too much trouble." His face shone with relief and gratitude as he handed the jacket to Millie.

"Not to worry," Paula said, having watched the episode with quiet amusement. "I remember when TJ spilled half a bottle of brown shoe polish on one of my best white blouses." She took in a quick breath, expecting a wave of grief to wash over her at the mention of his name, but there was only a small tug in the vicinity of her heart. She continued. "He was so scared that he hid the blouse in the bottom of a clothes hamper, and no one found it for a week. I thought for sure it was a goner. Then Millie worked her stain-removing magic, and voilá! My blouse was back, whiter than ever. Her touch is awesome, I tell you."

Paula noticed that Elder Richland was sitting with his arms beneath the table, his shoulders slightly hunched, the muscles in his jaw twitching a little. *He probably feels naked without his uniform,* she reflected. *I'll just get his mind back on this scrumptious food.* "Elder," she said sweetly, reaching for one of Millie's flaky dinner rolls, "would you please pass the butter?"

"Oh, yes . . . of course." He looked at her gratefully, then brought his right arm from beneath the table and extended it toward the small crystal butter dish in front of him. As he moved, the short sleeve of his white shirt slid upward.

Paula froze. There was a small purple birthmark on the smooth inside of his arm, just below his elbow. It had the unmistakable shape of a bumble bee in flight.

CHAPTER 27

The roll in Paula's hand dropped to the table with a soft thud. Time stopped as she focused on the elder's arm—on the wine-colored silhouette that had embedded itself in her memory more than two decades earlier. Or was she just imagining it, deluding herself into believing the unbelievable? *Impossible. There's not a chance it could be . . . or could it?* She suddenly felt trapped, lightheaded, barely on the edge of consciousness. Her trembling hand curled around the side of the table like a vise. *No, it can't be. Get a grip, Donroe.* She forced her gaze away from the elder's arm, closed her eyes, and took in a great gulp of air.

"Paula, are you all right?" Millie's voice seemed to be coming from far away . . . from across an ocean, perhaps. "You're so pale all of a sudden, and fluttery. What's the matter, dear?"

Don't do this, Donroe. Don't lose control. There's a logical explanation; you've just got to find it. Hysteria will get you exactly nowhere. Don't make a fool of yourself.

Gathering every particle of her mental strength, Paula willed herself to open her eyes and smile up at Millie, who had rushed to her side. "Oh, I'm fine," she lied. "It's just . . . you know, all the memories . . . TJ and everything. It just sort of got to me for a minute." Millie and the elders nodded sympathetically, while Scott stared uncomfortably at his plate. For the moment, Paula felt relief. *No one noticed what I was looking at . . . no one knows. Knows what?* Another wave of confusion assaulted her. *Gotta think about this, figure it out.* She gazed evenly at one elder, then the other. "Would you excuse me for a moment? I think I just need to, uh . . . freshen up a bit."

"Sure thing," Elder Stucki said. "Take your time. You know where to find us."

"Thanks. I'll be right back." She pushed her chair back and rose slowly, then turned and walked deliberately to the guest bathroom off the entryway.

Once inside the small, tidy room, Paula slumped against the closed door and pressed the knuckles of one hand fiercely between her perfect front teeth. *Don't scream. They'll know something's going on.* Her eyes were squeezed tightly shut, but tears coursed down the sides of her face as she struggled to contain the eruption of pure emotion welling in her chest and stomach. Was it fear? Uncertainty? Guilt? Apprehension? Joy? *All of the above, and then some.* Every nerve in her body felt unsheathed.

Finally, driven by the realization that she had nowhere else to go, Paula fell to her knees on the thickly carpeted floor. She clasped her hands tightly against her chest, inclined her head forward, and began to whisper in low, breathless tones. "Dear Lord . . . dear, dear Lord . . . am I dreaming, or can this actually be happening? Is it in any way possible that Elder Richland, this extraordinary young man, could really be—" She could barely bring herself to utter the words "—*my son?*" A sharp gasp caught in her throat and quickly turned to a plaintive sob. "How can I be sure, Heavenly Father? How can I know?" Her desire felt like a white-hot piece of steel flaming from the center of her being. "Because if I thought for one minute this was just a cruel joke of some kind, or a horrible mistake . . ." Her shoulders sagged as she covered her face with both hands. "Please . . . I need some help here."

Endless moments passed as she waited, her body trembling uncontrollably. Finally she sank to the floor, exhausted. *I don't have the strength for this,* she thought. *How can I figure it all out?* She lay on her back, listening to her own ragged breathing.

Within seconds, starting at the top of her head, a comfortable stillness began to settle over Paula's body, calming her distress and wrapping her in a golden swath of light and warmth. She felt peaceful, though curious at this sudden transformation in her mental state. *What now?* she wondered idly. Strangely, she felt no inclination to move—or even think—for several minutes. But gradually her faculties and energy returned, along with a sense of quiet anticipation.

By the time she had splashed her face with cool water and was ready to rejoin her guests, she had a plan.

Elder Richland had been telling basketball stories, and even Scott was convulsed with laughter by the time Paula slipped quietly into her chair. Avoiding the elder's curious gaze, she calmly smoothed a napkin across her lap.

"Feeling better, dear?" Millie asked.

"Much, thanks," Paula responded with a light smile. "Sounds like I've missed some good entertainment."

"Yeah," Scott said, swirling his half-eaten roll in a pool of gravy on his plate. "Did you know Elder Richland actually met Michael Jordan?" He glanced at the elder with a look of awe.

"Really?" Paula said. "Do I get to hear the details?" *Bide your time, Donroe. Ease into this gradually.*

"No big deal," the elder replied. Scott rolled his eyes. "It was at a basketball camp after my junior year in high school. I'd done pretty well on the team, and my folks knew how much I loved to play, so they sent me to Chicago for a couple of weeks that summer. Michael was great, and he's even bigger than he looks. At the time, I thought he was at least nine feet tall."

"Awesome," Scott murmured between forkfuls of dressing.

"Sounds like your parents gave you some good opportunities," Paula observed. *Forget the "gradually" part. There's no time like the present.* "Didn't you tell me you're the oldest of several children?"

"Five," Elder Richland said.

"Which," Elder Stucki interjected, "isn't all that big a family in Mormon terms." He grinned proudly. "I, for example, have five brothers and four sisters."

Scott made a choking sound. "Whoa," he gasped, "that's like a whole *neighborhood* living in one house."

"Yeah," the elder laughed, "and since I was the youngest, I felt like I had a whole neighborhood on my back sometimes. But you know what? It was great growing up with that many kids. Most of them are married and have families of their own now. I miss 'em all . . . a lot." A wistful shadow crossed his face for a moment.

Paula, who had been listening politely, focused again on Elder Richland. "So, does your basketball talent come naturally? I mean, which side of the family did you inherit your height and coordination from—your mom's or your dad's?"

"That's hard to say," he said evenly. "I guess I've just always been athletic."

"Uh-huh." Paula felt momentarily derailed, but she quickly tried another approach. "Your family must be very proud of you. Who's the next to serve a mission?"

"My brother Alex is already in the field, serving in Germany. In fact, we had our missionary farewell together." He smiled. "Two for the price of one, you might say."

"Okay," Paula said slowly, a quizzical expression rising in her eyes. *Am I missing something here?* She swallowed a quick flash of disappointment. "So you're . . . twins?"

"Good guess," he laughed, his cheeks dimpling. "Actually, Alex and I are ten months apart—one of those weird things that happens sometimes."

Paula looked at him intently. "More surprising than weird, I'd say. Your mother must've had her hands full."

Elder Richland laid his fork across his plate and leaned back in his chair. "Oh, no," he said in a firm voice. "My mom and dad had waited almost ten years to have children, and they'd just about given up. When they finally found me, it was a miracle; and then to have a second—"

"*Found* you?" Paula's voice cracked, and she coughed to cover it.

"Yeah . . . I was adopted," he said matter-of-factly.

"I see," Paula said mechanically. Her heart felt like it was poised at the top of her rib cage, ready to leap out of her chest. "And your brother?"

The elder rose and sauntered over to the bar to refill his plate. He explained as he speared several large pieces of turkey with a fork. "That's where the weird part comes in. Alex came the usual way, born naturally to my parents." He ladled gravy over his turkey, dressing, and potatoes. "Boy, was *that* ever a surprise . . . followed closely by three more surprises, my little brother and sisters. They called us their 'miracle children' . . . always said I started it and brought them good luck." He looked over at Paula, who felt her face grow hot. "But you know what?"

"What?" she squeaked.

"I think *I* was the lucky one," he said.

"How do you figure that?" she asked, raising her glass for a sip of juice. Her eyes never left his face.

"Well, I've had a great life—not measured in material things, but there was always more than enough love to go around. I never doubted that I was wanted and cared for. And on top of that, I had the gospel. What more could anyone ask? I can't imagine growing up in any other family. They're all mine—forever." He flashed her a satisfied smile.

"Hey, wait a minute," Elder Stucki broke in. "Your brother—Alex—had to be at least nineteen when he left on his mission, right?"

Elder Richland nodded.

"So if Alex was nineteen, and you had a joint farewell, then you must've been—"

"Twenty . . . just turned twenty. See, when my dad had his heart attack, things got put on hold for a while; Alex and I had to pretty much take over working the farm for a year or so. We kind of decided that if Dad was okay by the time Alex turned nineteen, we'd both leave on our missions at the same time. As it turned out, that's exactly what happened."

"So that explains it," Elder Stucki observed with a smirk.

"Explains what?" his companion asked.

"Explains why you're always acting so much *older* than the rest of us. It's because you *are*. You're an *old man!*"

"Thanks a lot, *little* brother," Elder Richland teased. He glanced downward. "Hey, isn't that an empty spot I see on your plate?"

"Yeah, it is. And if you'll excuse me for a minute, I think I'll just go take care of it." He pushed his chair back and lumbered a few steps to the bar.

Paula gingerly picked up where Elder Stucki had left off. "You must be what, then? Twenty-two?"

"Twenty-two last month."

Paula's heart stopped in mid-beat, then started to bang against her ribs in double time. *Twenty-two in October.*

"I still feel pretty young, though," he grinned.

She smiled weakly. "You've got your whole life ahead of you."

Scott had been listening carefully to their conversation, and now looked at Elder Richland with new interest. "Adopted," he repeated. "Cool. Do you feel, like, *different* or anything?"

"Scotty!" Paula scolded. "That's not a very polite—"

"No problem," Elder Richland said. "It's a good question—one I'd probably ask if I knew someone was adopted. I guess some adopted children do feel different, but I'm just as much a member of my family as any of the other kids. After the adoption was final, I was sealed to my parents in the temple, making us a family unit forever. You can't have much more togetherness than that. And it's part of why I'm so grateful for the gospel."

"Yeah, but . . ." Scott bit his lip and continued. "Don't you ever feel like you were, y'know, *abandoned* in the first place? I mean, it seems pretty cruel for a mom to want to get rid of her baby."

Paula cast her son a curious glance. *I don't know where you're coming up with these impertinent questions,* she thought. *Just . . . don't stop now. We're so close.*

Elder Richland leaned back in his chair as Millie collected his empty plate. "It does seem cruel, I admit it." He paused, his gaze moving toward the window then back to Scott. "And I suppose some mothers really do want to get rid of their babies; they see them as mistakes. With me, it was just the opposite."

Paula couldn't resist posing the next question. "And how is that?" she asked, her voice a study in nonchalance. Her throat felt as tight as a new rubber band.

"My birth mother wrote me a letter the day I was born," he said. "Mom gave it to me as soon as I could read." He took a long drink of juice, then slowly lowered his goblet to the table and began to run his fingers up and down its long, narrow stem. A minute passed, the silence broken only by the clatter of dishes as Millie deposited them in the sink.

Tension hung inside Paula's brain like a steel cobweb, and she couldn't speak. Finally, Scott pushed his empty plate aside and rested his arms on the table. "And?" he pressed.

"And," the elder continued, "It gave me all the answers I needed." He lapsed into silence again.

"Like?" Scott wouldn't be put off.

Thank you, Paula said silently. She smiled absently when Millie placed a large slice of pumpkin pie in front of her, then gave Scott an oversized piece of carrot cake.

"Ready for my special apple-cinnamon pie, gentlemen?" Millie asked. Both elders nodded gratefully. "With ice cream?" Elder Richland grinned, and she thought Elder Stucki was going to kiss her hand.

"*Like?*" Scott was drumming his fingers on the table.

Paula cheered inwardly. *Good boy.*

"Oh, yeah," Elder Richland sighed. "She was real young when I was born, and my father had been killed a few months earlier."

"An accident?" Paula heard herself ask.

"Motorcycle. He never even knew she was pregnant."

Paula calmly rested an elbow on the table and cupped her chin in the palm of her hand. "How sad," she said. She felt dizzy, barely able to collect her thoughts.

"Yeah. Anyway, she wanted the best for her child, but she knew she couldn't provide that for him on her tiny salary as a waitress, and she wanted to get an education for herself, too. So she made the decision to give him—me—up for adoption. I could tell it was the hardest thing she'd ever done in her life."

Paula's mouth was dust-dry, her tongue nearly paralyzed, but she had to ask. "Then you don't . . . blame her for what she did?"

"Blame her?" Elder Richland's warm, dark eyes flashed as they bored into hers. "No. I love her for it."

She tore her gaze from his and stared at the table, struggling to control the tears gathering at the corners of her eyes. *He loves her.* "That's . . . very nice," she murmured, wiping at her lips with her napkin.

"Awesome," Scott added, his eyes wide. "D'ya think you'll ever find out who she is?"

"I've thought about that," the elder said. "Someday, if it works out, I'd like to thank her personally for giving me life. And I'd like to give her a gift of my own . . . the best one I could possibly give."

"What would you give her?" Paula asked, her voice barely above a whisper.

"I'd teach her the gospel."

Paula nodded. "Who knows?" she said with a tiny smile. "It could happen."

"Bet she'd rather have a BMW," Scott grumbled.

Elder Richland laughed and reached up to run the fingers of his right hand through his dark hair, once again causing his shirt sleeve to fall back and reveal the small purple birthmark. Paula studied it circumspectly while her guests moved on to other topics of conversation. By the time dessert was finished, there was little doubt in her mind about the identity of the young man sitting at her Thanksgiving table. But she had to know one more thing—just to be sure.

At four-thirty, the elders were ready to leave for their late-afternoon appointment. Paula stood with them for a few moments inside the entryway, waiting for Millie to bring Elder Richland's suit jacket. Scott had gone downstairs to watch TV.

Paula decided to ask about the birthmark. "That's an interesting-looking critter," she said, pointing to his arm. "I've seen bumble bees that look less like the real thing than he does."

"Yeah, I reckon," he replied, pushing up his sleeve so the mark was in full view. "I named him Fat Albert . . . pretty original, huh? But I was marked for life as far as all the other kids were concerned. I grew up being called Buzz . . . kinda liked it." He laughed and rubbed the spot affectionately.

"Well, Elder *Buzz,*" she quipped, "it seems to fit." They were both relaxed and smiling. *Ask him. Ask him now.* She willed her voice to be calm, dispassionate. "By the way, I've been thinking about what you told us—you know, about being adopted."

"I hope I didn't bore you to death," he said sheepishly.

"Not at all. But I was curious about one thing, and wondered if I could ask you . . ." She hesitated, not quite sure how to proceed.

"Shoot," he said genially. "I'm not keeping any secrets."

She nodded. *That makes one of us.* "Being a mother myself, I can't help wondering just how a young woman could even begin to explain to her child why she was giving him away. What in the world made you believe her?" Paula held her breath expectantly.

"I could *feel* her love—in here," he said, tapping his chest as he looked at her steadily. "And I could hear it echoing through the words of her letter. I've read it so many times that I have it memorized." He closed his eyes, seeming to look inward for a moment, then began to recite softly. "'When it was time, I held you close for one last moment, closing my eyes and inhaling the sweet scent of you until I thought my lungs would burst. The nurse came, and through my tears I watched her disappear down the hallway, carrying my baby. I haven't stopped crying since.'" His eyes brimmed. "I have the feeling she's still crying, twenty-two years later."

"Perhaps," Paula said gently, now knowing. "But *you* know she did a good thing . . . and one day she'll understand that, too."

"I hope so," he sighed. "Thanks for believing that."

She shrugged. "So, when do you make the big leap back into civilian life?"

"Next Thursday . . . a week from today."

Paula nodded and folded her arms across her chest. "Well, I'll see you on Sunday, then."

He smiled warmly. "I'll look forward to it."

Millie trundled in from the laundry room. She held out Elder Richland's jacket, beaming triumphantly. "Good as new," she reported. "Clean as a whistle."

"It sure is," he said, examining the lapel. "Thanks a bunch, Millie. I owe you one."

"And thanks for a fantastic Thanksgiving," Elder Stucki added. "Can't remember when I've had such an awesome meal." He grinned and patted his round stomach.

"Any time," Millie clucked. They all shook hands, and the missionaries ambled to their car. Paula stood watching until the small white vehicle disappeared around a corner.

"That was nice," Millie said as Paula slowly closed the door.

"It was more than nice," Paula replied, her mind replaying the afternoon's wondrous revelations. "You really outdid yourself this time, Millie. Let me help you with the cleanup."

"Goodness, no," the older woman said cheerfully. "I like putting things back in order almost as much as I enjoy getting up a good meal in the first place."

Paula sighed and shook her head good-naturedly. "I know—and I'll never understand why. You and I are cut from different fabric, Millie."

"I know," Millie smiled. "That's why one of us runs a business, and the other one runs a household." She gave Paula a quick hug. "Now, you just go relax, and I'll have everything tidied up in no time." She turned and bustled toward the kitchen.

Paula spent the evening in her room, sorting through the little box of memories that was not only a poignant link with the past, but had now become, in the space of less than three hours, a tantalizing bridge to the future. She studied and re-studied the picture of her young husband, Greg, noting each minute detail of his features, then calling up her mind's-eye view of Elder Richland for comparison. The resemblance was striking; why hadn't she noticed it earlier? *Because I wasn't looking for it,* she concluded. *I never would've thought a Mormon missionary, of all people . . .* She smiled. *I guess that angel had it figured out all along, didn't he? Never say never. Thank you, Mr. Moroni. I owe you one.*

Only one agonizing decision remained. *How should I tell him? When?* The answer eluded her as life seemed to ooze forward in slow motion over the next two days. Her mind was simultaneously numb with joy, supercharged with anticipation, harrowed by fear. Was there *ever* a right time or place for such a life-changing disclosure?

On Sunday, she and Millie sat two rows behind and a little to one side of the elders during sacrament meeting. Off and on, Paula studied Elder Richland's profile intently—just to be sure. *He's got Greg's ears,* she decided. *A stroke of good luck; mine are too squinchy.* She smiled to herself. *What's "squinchy," anyway?* She watched as his head inclined and his shoulders moved slightly; she knew he was thumbing through his scriptures.

During the sacrament, Paula opened her mind and asked for guidance. *How? When?* She looked again at Elder Richland's clean, handsome profile. His head was bowed, his eyes closed; he was obviously deep in concentration. *Just as I would have expected—faithful and determined, right up to his last few days of missionary service. He'll be teaching people the gospel, bearing his testimony until they rip the name tag off his suit—and that probably won't even slow him down. But I could . . . I could stop him in his tracks if I told him. Told him his mother was sitting two rows behind him in church.*

She bowed her head as the realization came. *No. We've got a lifetime to know each other; a few days will hardly make a difference. Let him stay focused on the work; he's got enough on his mind. I'll call him . . . write to him . . . visit him. But it should be later—after he's had time to get to know his family again. (Would thirty seconds be pushing it?) I'll figure something out. But for now, knowing is enough.* She leaned back against the pew. *As a kid, I loved to keep secrets. I just hope I can hold on to this one. Don't blow it, Donroe.*

After church, she saw the elders heading for the foyer and hurried to intercept them. "I hoped I'd run into you," she said, feigning nonchalance.

Elder Stucki grinned. "Well, we're still moving pretty slow after that incredible meal," he drawled. "Our Thursday appointment offered us some pie, but there wasn't anywhere to put it." He puffed out his ruddy cheeks and crossed his eyes. *He could have a good future with the circus,* Paula mused.

Elder Richland shook her hand vigorously, and she grasped his big hand a little longer than necessary, noticing its gentle strength in a new way. *Hard to believe he once weighed less than seven pounds . . . and fit so easily into the crook of my elbow.* She forced her thoughts in another direction. "I guess this is your last Sunday in L.A.," she said.

He nodded, and a faraway look washed briefly over his face. "Yeah . . . I can hardly believe I'll be home for church next week."

"Wearing an overcoat and galoshes, no doubt," Paula said.

"I'm sure of it," he smiled. "The last weather report from home said it was snowing, with temperatures in the teens. Pretty normal for Idaho this time of year."

She shivered involuntarily, then looked up into his chocolate-brown eyes. "I don't suppose I could, uh, see you off . . . on Thursday."

He smiled, and she saw Greg's dimples at the corners of his mouth. "I'd like that," he said. "My flight leaves at nine-fifteen on Thursday morning. Delta, to Salt Lake City."

"I'll be there." Her heart was thudding in her chest. "Now, go convert a few more people in the meantime, okay?"

He saluted sharply. "Okay. We've got an appointment right now, in fact. With any luck, we'll have a baptism—maybe two—on Wednesday night."

"That's wonderful, Elder," she said. "I'll see you on Thursday, then."

"You bet." He lifted a hand in farewell as his companion pushed open the glass door. Paula stood transfixed, watching the two elders stride briskly down the walk. Her eyes seemed riveted to their backs.

"Paula?" Millie's voice cut through her reverie. "Sunday School starts in a minute."

Jolted back to the present, Paula stammered a response. "What? Oh, yes, I'm with you." She absently linked arms with her friend.

Millie cast her a concerned glance. "You know, dear," she whispered loudly, patting Paula's hand, "you've seemed awfully preoccupied these past few days. Is something wrong?"

Paula took her time before answering, then met Millie's gaze evenly. "Actually," she said, "I'm fine. In fact, I've never been better." Her eyes glistened. *If only she knew . . . but this secret will have to keep.*

"Well, that's a relief," Millie sighed. "I know things have been stressful since . . . you know, with TJ's leaving and all, and your missing so much time at the office. Not to mention such an important decision as joining the Church—the *right* decision, mind you, but a big one nevertheless. It all adds up, I guess. I'm glad everything's okay."

"A-okay," Paula smiled as they walked down the hall to Sunday School.

Monday, Tuesday, Wednesday spun in a free-fall toward Thursday. Paula worked from early morning until late evening, rarely emerging from her office cocoon. Since TJ's death, the staff had respected her new aloofness, figuring that one day she'd regain her equilibrium. Even Ted was keeping to himself; since her baptism they'd spoken infrequently, and only about business. At the moment, Paula was glad for the distance between them. One ardent stare from those deep blue eyes, and she just might spill everything. It was a strangely vulnerable feeling, and she rather enjoyed it.

Thursday morning was damp and foggy; a slight chill hung in the air as Paula steered her Jaguar into an airport parking stall. She was early by at least half an hour, so she took a moment to collect her thoughts before leaving the car. Adjusting the rearview mirror, she looked herself squarely in the eye and began a brief monologue. "Yes, yes," she murmured, "I know it'd be *so easy* to just tell him—tell him everything, all at once, right now. But think about it, Donroe; you've got to respect the life he's already built for himself. You can't just suddenly drop a bomb like this; can't just say, 'Oh, by the way, Elder Richland, I'm your mama. Have a nice flight back to Idaho.' There has to be some kind of *decorum* in a situation like this . . . a right time and place. Just offhand, I'd say the airport isn't it." She bit her lip nervously, then bowed her head. "Dear Father," she breathed, "please help me to know when and how to do this. And to keep my mouth shut." Reaching her hand into the pocket of her light overcoat, she fingered a small, blue bootie. *Patience, Lord. That's what I need.*

They met at the gate, twenty minutes before departure. Elder Richland broke into an engaging grin when he saw Paula. "I wondered if you'd make it," he said.

"Hey, they can live without me at the office for a couple of hours," she returned lightly. "I just wanted to say thanks, and to . . . wish you well."

"You're terrific, Paula," he said, then chuckled softly. "You know, of all the people I've taught in the past two years, I never would have pegged you for such a fast and thorough conversion."

"So," she laughed, "you thought I was a pretty tough cookie, huh?"

His dark eyes twinkled. "Let's just say the Lord works in mysterious ways."

Elder Stucki interrupted. "Paula, there's someone I'd like you to meet," he said. "Elder Straub, meet Sister Donroe. She's one of our newest members."

A very short, very thin, very blond young man stepped up to Paula and extended his hand. "P-pleased to meet you, Sister Donroe," he stammered. His hand was cold and clammy.

"Elder Straub just arrived from the MTC," Elder Stucki explained. "He's a real greenie, and now I'm the new, uh, senior companion." He made a loud gulping sound. "Wish me luck."

"I do, and you'll be just fine," Paula said warmly.

The quartet perched on a long row of empty seats to wait for the boarding call. Soon Elder Stucki began an animated conversation with his new companion, and Paula turned sideways in her seat to face Elder Richland. She glanced at his suit lapel. "You're still wearing your missionary name tag," she observed. *If I asked, would he give it to me? I'd keep it under my pillow until . . .*

He stretched his long, muscular legs in front of him. "Yeah . . . that's because I'm not quite finished being a missionary yet. Not until my stake president releases me—probably in a couple of days."

"I see. And when does Alex get home?"

"Next Wednesday." His eyes flashed with boyish excitement. "In less than a week, the family will all be back together again. I can hardly wait."

"I'm sure it'll be wonderful . . . an occasion to celebrate," Paula said. *We could celebrate right here, right now. I could tell him.* She squeezed her eyes shut and resisted the urge.

"Something the matter?" Elder Richland asked.

Paula forced herself to smile benignly. "No . . . nothing," she said. "It's just that, well, we've been through quite a bit together, and . . . did I ever tell you that you have the most incredible eyes?" *Just like your father's.* She blushed at her own brashness. "I mean, someday a beautiful young woman will lose herself in those eyes. Or maybe there's someone already waiting at home?"

Now it was the elder's turn to blush. "Not really," he said, "although there are a couple of girls in the ward who like to think they've been waiting. We'll see what happens. I'm not ready for anything serious just yet."

"Ladies and gentlemen, Flight 5641, with service to Salt Lake City, Utah, will begin boarding in ten minutes."

Elder Richland shook hands with the two elders, then turned back to Paula. "I guess this is it," he said, his eyes burning with intensity. "Stay close to the Lord, close to the Church, Paula. And if there's ever anything I can do for you . . . anything at all . . ." He pulled a small white card from his pocket and handed it to her. "My home address. I'd love to hear how you're doing."

"You will, Elder," she said, tears welling in her eyes. "You will."

"Call me Mark," he said, grinning through a thin sheen of moisture in his own eyes.

"Mark." *A good name. I could tell him now, make the connection, let him know who he's leaving behind, swear how much I've missed him all these years . . . No. It can wait. It has to wait.* "Mark. I'll remember that."

"I certainly hope so," he said, standing abruptly.

She rose with him, and they stood close together. "Elder . . . Mark," Paula said slowly, "I want you to know how very much I appreciate everything you've done—for befriending TJ, for caring so much when I lost him, for helping me clear out the cobwebs and finally see the wisdom of God's ways. And for teaching me the gospel. You've given me a priceless gift."

She stared wordlessly up at him until he inclined his shoulders slightly, wrapped his long arms around her, and drew her to him in a firm embrace. *Goodbye for now, my darling son,* she moaned silently as her lips brushed his cheek. Any moment, her heart would break.

His whispered words were barely audible against her ear. "Goodbye for now, my . . . darling . . . mother."

Paula's back tensed and arched as if a thousand volts of electricity had surged through her bones. "Excuse me?" She pulled away from him slightly, but clung to his arms to keep herself upright on legs that had suddenly turned to water. "Could it be possible that you just said . . ." Her voice trailed off.

He studied her upturned face for an infinity of moments. "It's true, isn't it?" he finally asked, a deep gentleness flowing through his words.

Paula nodded weakly, then sank heavily against him. Putting his arm around her shoulders, he carefully guided her to the nearest chair and sat down beside her.

"Ladies and gentlemen, Flight 5641, with service to Salt Lake City, Utah, will begin boarding in five minutes."

Paula stared at Mark Richland as if seeing him for the first time. When she found her voice, the words rushed out breathlessly. "But how did you know . . . when did you . . . how long have you . . . ?" Unable to form whole sentences, she simply looked at him wide-eyed and shook her head.

"Not until now—I didn't know for sure," he admitted. "And what I'm about to say may not make any sense at all . . . but I'd like to give it a try, okay?"

Paula nodded.

"During my whole mission," he continued, "I prayed that somehow, some way, my service would make it possible for my birth mother—whoever and wherever she was—to hear the gospel. I didn't really expect to find her myself, but I prayed for her every day, every night—prayed she'd be guided to the truth. That hope, that urgency was always in the back of my mind. Until . . ." His voice broke.

"I'm with you," Paula whispered.

"Until I baptized you. After that, the urgency seemed to mellow out to a more relaxed feeling. I honestly didn't think much about it at the time, didn't really connect it to you. I just figured my mission was winding down. But then, on Thanksgiving, when I saw your reaction to Fat Albert here," he rubbed the inside of his arm, "something clicked in my mind. I told myself it just couldn't be true—but then you started asking questions about the adoption, and I couldn't help wondering. Finally, when I quoted that part of my birth mother's letter, I saw something in your eyes that—well, that prompted me to risk saying what I did just now."

Paula filled her lungs with air and blew out a long, slow breath. "I'd say it was a risk worth taking." She timidly stroked his cheek with her hand. "I can't believe it."

"Yeah, me neither," he echoed. "It's awesome. Incredible."

"All of the above. And you know what the best part is?" she asked.

"I can think of about three million best parts at this moment," he replied.

"Well, the best for me is knowing that you don't resent her—me—for making the decision to give you up." Her eyes glinted in the dim airport light. "You did mean that when you said it on Thanksgiving, didn't you?"

"With all my heart," he said firmly. "Besides, we're even now."

She looked at him with a puzzled expression.

"The way I see it," he said eagerly, "we've been able to give each other the most precious gifts available to Heavenly Father's children. Years ago, you gave me the gift of mortal life. Then, a few weeks ago, I was privileged to share with you the great plan of *eternal* life. Seems like a fair exchange, don't you think?"

"More than fair," she agreed. "In less than two months, I've lost one son and found another." Her delicate mouth curved into a tremulous smile. "But then, I haven't really lost TJ, have I?" The thought sent tears coursing down her cheeks. "And by the way," she added, "I think I have something that belongs to you." Plunging a hand into her coat pocket, she drew out the blue bootie and pressed it into his hand. "I'll keep the other one—for old times' sake." He smiled tenderly and closed his fingers tightly around the little shoe.

"Ladies and gentlemen, Flight 5641 is now boarding."

Paula wiped at her eyes and shared a final embrace with her son. "Call . . . write . . . whatever," she whispered close to his ear. "Whenever you're ready. I'll be waiting."

"I will," he promised. "Take care." Squeezing her hand one last time, he turned and walked quickly through the gate.

A voice startled her. "So, what was that all about?" Elder Stucki questioned. "I heard a lot of pretty intense whispering between you and Elder Richland."

"Oh," Paula said, "he was just telling me about his . . . family. It seems that we might have some relatives in common." She smiled mysteriously.

"That's great. Small world, huh?" the elder said. "Well, we'd better be going . . . lotsa places to go, people to see. See ya later." He shook her hand and hurried off with his new companion.

Paula stood at the window until Mark's plane had circled out of sight. Then she walked through the airport's sliding glass doors into a clear, golden morning. The fog had lifted, and she could hear a bird chirping in a small shrub along the curb. "It's going to be a fine day, Donroe," she said aloud as she slid behind the Jag's wheel. "The finest day ever." She turned the key and blew a kiss skyward as the car's engine roared joyously to life.

ABOUT THE AUTHOR

JoAnn Jolley, a graduate of Brigham Young University, has enjoyed a successful career as a writer and editor. She has worked as a publications manager for two international corporations, as an editor at the *Ensign*, and has published dozens of feature articles and personal essays in national and regional markets. *Secrets of the Heart* is her first novel.

Among JoAnn's favorite pastimes are music, animals, spending time with friends and family, basketball, reading, writing, and ironing. She currently works as an editor and lives in Orem, Utah, where she teaches Relief Society in her ward. She also serves on a general Church writing committee.

JoAnn welcomes readers' comments. You can write to her in care of Covenant Communications, P.O. Box 416, American Fork, Utah 84003-0416.